Dear Olivia and Bernie

Thank you so
much for your support.

Helen Wayne

The
Big
Heart

by
Helen Weyand

authorHOUSE™

1663 LIBERTY DRIVE, SUITE 200
BLOOMINGTON, INDIANA 47403
(800) 839-8640
WWW.AUTHORHOUSE.COM

First published by AuthorHouse 06/03/05

ISBN: 1-4208-3966-7 (sc)
ISBN: 1-4208-3965-9 (dj)

Printed in the United States of America
Bloomington, Indiana

This book is printed on acid-free paper.

SYNOPSIS

This fiction is about a man born in the late nineteenth century in one of the flourishing ports of South East Asia. His exciting career as a young and upcoming actor was disrupted by a fatal mistake. With the help of his parents, he recovered, and went abroad to study. He came back with a degree and became a successful business man. With much ado, he finally married the girl of his dreams. The longing for a son weakened his resolve to stay forever faithful to his barren wife. He fell in love with another woman, and took her in as his second wife. Even though she fulfilled his desires and gave him sons, he became vulnerable to beautiful women and after that, married two more times. At that time it was not uncommon for a rich man to have more than one wife, but each wife had a home of her own. This man lived with all of his four wives and children under one roof. The four women loved him through wealth, poverty, sickness and death.

While his love for his four wives were unbiased, it was not so with his children. He had a special bond with one of his daughters, who played a great part in the last days of his life. After he died, she faced the consequences of his biased love in the form of abuses that stemmed from subdued jealousies over the years. However, her special relationship with a nun helped her through the difficult times. When this nun died, another emerged to take her place. That confirmed her belief that her father had kept his promise when he said, he would always be there for her no matter where he was. Then in the midst of a horrific situation which would have taken her life that conviction saved her.

CHAPTER 1

Marlene looked at the clock in the library and saw that she still had plenty of time to take the bus to Kuala Lumpur, the capital of Malaysia. Normally, she had sports practice in the afternoon, but the heavy downpour of rain in the morning had caused all outdoor activities to be cancelled. Her mother and two sisters expected her on Saturday, but since she was free that Friday afternoon, she decided to surprise them by showing up a day earlier. However, she had to let her guardian know of her plans. She sought the help of one of her classmates, who lived quite close by. The girl agreed to tell her guardian that Marlene was going to visit her mother. She also volunteered to take Marlene's school bag and sports satchel home for her. Marlene was grateful but was uneasy about imposing upon her friend with her heavy school bag. It would have been different if it was her half sister who took her bags home. Lily, Marlene's half sister had completed school last year and was now working as a cashier in a local bank. Her mother was Marlene's guardian. When Marlene's mother moved to work in Kuala Lumpur, she took her two younger daughters and only son with her. It was Marlene's wish to remain in Klang, in the State of Selangor, to finish her Secondary education in the Klang Convent. When asked, Cheng Mee, Lily's mother agreed to look after Marlene for the next few years. Cheng Mee loved Marlene as though she was her own daughter.

Marlene was of average height for her age. At fifteen, she was four feet ten inches tall and weighed eighty eight pounds. She was not a beauty, but her short hair gave her an impish look. Her slim and athletic figure made her an attractive teenager. Many boys her age had tried to gain her attention, but she had other important things on her mind to bother with them. She was ambitious in her study and in her sports career. She had excelled in athletics, field hockey and badminton. She was one of the youngest to be chosen to represent her district in the Junior Athletics Team. That required a lot of training and discipline. The district had appointed an official coach for the team, and every member had to be on the training ground in the hot afternoon sun for three hours, three times a week. There would be inter-district competitions every first and third weekends of the month. This was the weekend off, so Marlene was looking forward to a long weekend with her family.

It would only take her ten minutes to walk from the school to the bus terminal, but she always enjoyed the freshness of the air and clean smell of the grass and trees after the rain. So, even though she had another half an hour to take the bus to Kuala Lumpur, she decided to leave school early, with only a book in her hand and a wallet containing enough money for the bus and cab fare, in the pocket of her school uniform. She had clothes at her mother's place so that whenever she visited, she would not have to take extra luggage. Marlene was tempted to go through the playground which separated the bus terminal from the Convent grounds, but the grass was still very wet and her white canvas shoes would get muddy and wet, so she kept to the side of the main road. As she strolled towards the bus terminal, she breathed in the freshness of the air and savored the delicious smell of the grass. She was happy. She had found a wonderful friend in the new Reverend Mother. This new relationship eased the pain of the loss of another nun, who had changed her life and that of her whole family. She still thought fondly of Sister Renee, who was her class teacher when she was about nine years old. The memory of that special friendship was one of those that Marlene would always treasure. Thinking of Sister Renee also brought back painful memories of the loss of her beloved father four years ago. She would never get over the loss, but the promise he made before he died gave her the strength to live without his physical being. He had told her that no matter where he was, he would be watching over her. She felt that his spirit was always with her.

Lost in a world of her own, she was unaware of a car slowing down behind her. It drew alongside her and without warning, before she could react, the back door burst open and a pair of strong arms pulled her roughly into the still moving vehicle. Marlene was too shocked to even scream. She was pushed face down to the floor and as the car sped away, her head was held down by the pressure of a heavily booted foot. Her hands, one of them had still been holding on to her book, were pulled behind her and tied tightly together with a rope which cut into her wrists. Her book was still wedged under her chest. The full realization of her predicament suddenly dawned on her, and she began to struggle and scream until a hard kick to the head left her dizzy with pain. She felt a tug at her hair and her face was lifted up, but she was blindfolded before she could see her captors. In fear and desperation, Marlene began to whimper until a dirty piece of cloth was pushed into her mouth, almost choking her, and then covered with a gag. A pair of heavy feet on her back pinned her down. In agony and terror, the blindfold quickly became sodden with tears. She could only hear the drone of the engine as the car bumped and she knew that they were leaving the main road.

Marlene must have fainted more than once, for she lost track of time, but she became aware that the car was stopping and, for the first time since her abduction, she heard a voice saying in Malay, "Take her out now. Do not remove the blindfold or the gag. I shall come back later this evening." She knew then that one of her captors was a Malay man and the one who had kept her pinned to the floor was also a man because of the weight of his feet on her body. She also realized the presence of a third person as the door of the passenger seat in front opened and closed. She was jerked up from behind by her tied hands. Marlene was small and light and it was easy for her captor to pull her up with one hand. When she was out of the car, he dragged her aching body a short distance. It was then that she heard the voice of the third person. He, too, spoke in Malay and his words sent a chill running through her body. He said, "Let the lessons begin." She heard a heavy door being opened and once inside, she was thrown to the floor. Her face hit the hard concrete and her right cheek began to burn. The contact had scraped her tender skin. She was still lying face down on the floor when her hands were untied. She felt some relief as the rope loosened but her relief was short-lived as two pairs of rough hands began to strip off her uniform. She tried to struggle and scream through the gag, but a smack at the back of her head stopped her. When they removed her panties, she heard them swear and curse. It was then that she could identify the man in the back seat as being Malay. They were furious that she had her period. She had heard that the period was a curse, but at this point it was a blessing in disguise.

Marlene was completely naked except for the white socks and canvas shoes on her feet, when they pulled her up. She could hardly stand, but the first thing her hands did was to cover as much of her nudity as possible, before they pulled her hands and tied them together in front of her. Then, she was half dragged and half carried to another spot. Breathing was getting more and more difficult for her and they must have noticed it. One of them removed the gag and the cloth from her mouth, with this warning, "If you say or make any noise, we will beat you and put the gag back. Nod if you understand." She nodded eagerly for it was such a relief to be able to breathe normally again. In a way, she was quite glad that they did not remove her blindfold. She could not bear to see their eyes on her naked body. A tin cup was then placed into her tied hands. She drank thirstily from it and began to spit out when she realized how stagnant the water was. All they did was laugh at her as she threw the cup away. Then she felt a pair of hands lifting her tied hands over her head. An agonizing pain shot through her shoulders as she was lifted from the ground. It was as if her arms were being ripped off from her shoulders. Her naked body swayed in mid-air and she begged for mercy. She felt a slap on her stomach as one of them said, "Do you want us to shut you up again?" Marlene was quiet, but it was more because the pain was so unbearable that she was beginning to lose consciousness than the fear of being gagged again.

Her bliss of unconsciousness was rudely interrupted by a splash of water on her face. She woke up to agonizing pain. She was still naked and hanging in mid-air. Her period which was at its light days began to drip heavily. She did not know how long she had been unconscious, but the sound of the driver's voice told her that it was late evening or night. He asked, "How long has she been hanging?" Another voice said, "Since we brought her in." The driver muttered inaudibly and she felt a tug. Then as her feet touched the ground, her knees gave way. She could not fall because her hands were still attached to something over her head. She felt a rough hand forcing her mouth open and water was poured into it. She gulped down the liquid so fast that she almost choked. The driver spoke to her. He was obviously the leader, and he asked in Malay, "Do you know why you are being punished?" She could only whimper, "No." "Well, you are so young, but you already know how to be a temptress. If we do not teach you a lesson now, you would continue in your wicked ways. The normal punishment for someone who has an affair with a married man is death by stoning or being staked through the anus." At first, Marlene was confused and unable to understand what he was trying to tell her. Then as he went on accusing her of being an adulteress, the words sank in. But she could not imagine why she was being accused of those horrible things. She had never had a relationship with any boy or man. She had not even gone out on a date. She opened her mouth to protest, but was slapped so hard that she could taste the blood on her lips. His next words jolted her memory. "You seduced a man who was kind to you, and jeopardized his marriage," the driver continued.

A few weeks ago, her classmate had warned her of rumors about her and the coach. The friend said that the coach's wife had been making enquires about her. Marlene had taken her warning lightly, because there was nothing between them except friendship. Malik, who was also a Muslim man, like all the Malays in Malaysia, had been very kind to her. He had offered her transportation to and from the sports field. He had been her confidante in many of her problems. He was old enough to be her father and she did look up to him as a father figure. He was married and had two teenage daughters almost as old as she. There was never any physical

4

contact between them or exchange of affectionate words. She could not comprehend how the rumors about them could have started. Now, she was at the mercy of these three men who believed the lies. They would not allow her to plead her innocence. She shivered with the thoughts that she was going to die a horrible death. But the leader's next words gave her some hope, "We are not going to kill you. We will let you go tomorrow after we have punished you for your sins." Death would have been a better alternative to what they were about to do to her.

Her tied hands were pulled tautly above her head, but her feet were still on the ground. She heard cigarettes being lighted and could smell the smoke as they gathered round her. Then they started torturing her with the lighted butts. They touched her stomach, thighs, and her buttocks with them. She could only squirm and scream in pain. They were merciless and continued scorching her body. Her screams began to fade as her throat became dry. They were relentless and just as she thought that they had stopped, she felt heat close to her nipple, but before it could touch her nipple, the leader said, "Leave those parts alone." Obviously, the culprit was not fully satisfied, for he began to grab her nipples with his fingers and squeeze them hard. The scorching pain on her body and attack on her breast were so unbearable that she fainted.

Marlene was unconscious for a few hours. When she recovered, the first thing she felt was as if her flesh was still burning. It took her a few minutes to realize that she was lying on her side on the hard cement floor. She also realized that she was still naked as her flesh felt the coldness of the floor. There was no more feeling in her hands and feet. Her hands were now bound at her back and her feet were tied together. She lay quietly for sometime and when she could not hear anything, she thought that she was alone. Everything was quiet, except for the sounds of the night creatures. Marlene could hear the owls hooting and crickets calling to each other. She knew then that she was either in the middle of a jungle or close to it. She wondered if they had left her alone, knowing that she was too weak and powerless to escape. She had to find out, so she tried calling out, but she could not even hear herself. Her throat was dry and painful. She was also hungry and thirsty. She felt wet and dirty and smelt the stench of her period and her own urine on her and around her. She tried to move, but could hardly push herself anywhere. She was very weak. She tried bending and straightening her legs at the knees. Eventually she began to move. With hope and renewed energy she began to move a little at a time. She was still blindfolded so she had no idea of direction, but as long as she could move she knew she was going somewhere, until her legs hit something which fell with a thud. It sounded like a wooden stool. In the stillness of the night, the sound was so loud that she froze. She heard the door of her prison opening and the voice of one of the other two captors growling, "What are you up to? Looks like you are asking for more punishment." Then he kicked her hard in her stomach, which caused her to cry out in pain. "Okay, you asked for it." It was obvious that he was smoking for the next moment, Marlene felt the lighted butt of the cigarette on her thigh. She had not recovered from the first attack on her stomach, so the second pain almost knocked her out again. Then she was left alone groaning in agony. She heard him cursing and a door shutting. Since there were no other voices she presumed that he was the only one left to guard her. He must have been outside smoking or in another room. She could not tell. She was not even sure what her prison was.

Marlene slept on and off from pain and exhaustion. She woke up to the sound of voices. It must be day, for she could feel the heat of the sun through the roof. As the men talked, she knew that the leader was not with them. When they noticed that she was awake, one of them said, "Well, since we have to put up with her for a few more hours, we may as well have some fun with her." Marlene found her voice again and said, "Please don't hurt me anymore." "Who said we are going to hurt you," one of them replied, "We are going to have some fun together." It was obvious that torture was their idea of fun. They pulled her up on to her feet and the other one said jeeringly, "My, aren't we smelly and dirty." Then she felt a couple of splashes of cold water on her body especially from the waist downwards. Her hands were untied again to be retied in the front. "Oh no," she cried, "Don't hang me up again." She was slapped in the face by one of the tormentors, while the other finished tying her up and stretching her hands above her head. Again she felt a jerk, only this time, her feet were still touching the ground. Then one of them said, "She is too small. We will have to pull her up higher." Then she felt the repeated experience of her arms being ripped off her shoulders as they pulled her up.

For a moment she thought that they were going to start scorching her body again with their cigarette butts. But when she felt a pair of arms parting her legs, she knew what they were about to do. As they took turns in sodomizing her, she cried in pain. She wished that death would end the agony that she was going through. Every thrust of their penis was like a knife cutting its way into her body. Each had their fun more than once. When they stopped, she was still hoping for death. Then one of them said, "One last punishment for the adulteress." Marlene felt a sharp object being forced into her already torn anus. The pain was so excruciating that she felt her wish for death had come true. Then for the first time since her captivity, she thought of her father. He had promised to be always with her in spirit; he would always be there to love and protect her. Just before she faded into nothingness she called out to him, "Papa, help me."

Marlene found herself walking aimlessly in complete darkness. She did not know where she was. She could not even see the sky. She was walking, but it was like she was treading on air. She kept on going in different directions trying to find her bearings when she saw a light in the distance. She went towards it and it got brighter. Then she saw her father in his white suit stretching his arms out to her. She was overjoyed and ran towards him. He too was running to her. They ran and ran, but somehow they did not cover the distance between them. Nevertheless, they kept running towards each other and finally, they were close to each other. But before she could be in his arms he disappeared. She yelled and cried for him to come back. She wanted to continue running, but felt strong arms holding her back. Suddenly her dark world was bright and she saw a familiar face looking at her. It was Reverend Mother, the headmistress of the Convent School that Marlene was attending. She was trying to hold Marlene down. She said, "Hush my love, you are safe now." Marlene shuddered in her arms as she felt great pain from her waist downwards. The nun, known to all the Convent school girls as Reverend Mother Irene gently pushed Marlene's head to rest on soft pillows and before she fell into unconsciousness again, she heard the nun whisper, "God has given you back to us."

Reverend Mother Irene was again the first person Marlene saw when she woke up the second time. She was by the bed saying the rosary with her eyes closed. This time Marlene was more conscious of her whereabouts. She knew that she was in a hospital for she could see the furnishings of the room she was in. There was another empty bed in the same room. She tried to sit up, but winced in pain. That was when Reverend Mother Irene noticed that she was awake. She got out of the chair that she was sitting on and sat on Marlene's bed. "Don't talk, my dear. Just listen to me. You have been here for three days now. You had a very severe operation and part of your intestine had to be removed. We did not know how you got to the Convent gate. It was around two on Sunday morning that the guard heard the dogs barking continuously. You were holding on to the gate half sitting and half squatting, but you were unconscious. When he called us, we found you drenched in blood and the first thing we did was to rush you to our hospital without informing anyone. We have brought you to our Catholic hospital where you would get the best care possible. I know that something very bad had happened to you. The doctor was about to call the police, but I managed to stop him. I wanted to hear from you first." Marlene looked at her with gratitude and could only whisper, "Thank you."

Reverend Mother Irene held Marlene's hand when she asked, "Are you strong enough to tell me everything?" Marlene shook her head and tears began to swell in her eyes. Reverend Mother Irene took out a handkerchief from the pocket of her habit and gently dabbed Marlene's tears away. "Your mother was here while you were sleeping. She had not slept for two days so I sent her back to rest." Then when she noticed that Marlene had stopped crying, she said, "I have to inform the doctor that you are awake." She kissed Marlene on the forehead and left, promising to return after the doctor had seen her.

Left alone, Marlene knew that she could trust the revered nun to do what was best for her. She would never be able to describe the horrors of those two days without reliving the agonies. But if she never told the godly nun the story, how could the nun help her. Then she thought of Malik, her coach. She could not implicate him. He had been very kind to her, and if his wife was behind the kidnapping and abuse, she would be punished as severely as the kidnappers. That would destroy his whole family. No matter how much Marlene wished for justice, she could not destroy the lives of Malik and his two daughters. Sister Irene had to help her keep the police out of this. Just as she felt her pain returning, the doctor and another nun came in. The doctor was an Indian and the nun was Chinese. The kindly doctor asked, "How are you dear? I am Dr. Pratap and this is Sister Theresa. I was the attending physician when you came in, and later the surgeon who operated on you will drop by to check your wounds." Sister Theresa smiled at Marlene and said, "Well dear, the doctor would like to check on the burns on your body, so I will have to undress you and turn you around. It may hurt a little, but I promise to be gentle." Marlene thought to herself, "After what I have gone through, I am thankful for such small pains."

It was quite painful to move, but when the hospital garment was removed from her body, Marlene saw that her stomach and thighs were bandaged. She winced as she remembered the scorching pains. She closed her eyes as the bandages were removed. The nun had gently turned her on her stomach so that the doctor could treat her back wounds again. She could not help but count the numbers of dabs the doctor administered. Each dab of some medication meant a burn. There were about twenty two of them. Then a clean bandage was put on top, and Sister Theresa turned her over again as gently as she could. Marlene opened her eyes again, and looked at Sister Theresa noticing that her eyes were wet. The doctor tried to maintain an emotionless face, but she could also detect some sadness. Her heart went out to both of them for they felt for her. This time she did not count as Dr. Pratap dabbed the same medicine with a cotton bud on the burns. She closed her eyes again and wondered if those wounds would leave permanent marks that would be a continuous reminder of her captivity. When all her wounds were treated, Sister Theresa wrapped her up with the bandages again and the doctor gave her an antibiotic injection and some painkiller pills to swallow. Before they left, the doctor said, "Marlene, you must be brave and tell Reverend Mother everything. We want to help you and we can only do so if we know everything." Marlene nodded; he said, "Goodnight" and left. Sister Theresa lingered a little longer to tuck her in. Then she made the sign of the cross with her finger on Marlene's forehead and kissed her cheek. She said, "Goodnight and God be with you." She too left.

When Marlene fainted, the two men thought she had died, and they quickly withdrew the stake. They did not mean to kill her. They just wanted to let her know the pain of dying when a stake was pushed into a body. They quickly untied her and tried to get rid of the blood that flowed out of her body onto the floor. They were afraid of the wrath of their leader. They could not get rid of the blood because Marlene was bleeding profusely. She only stopped bleeding when she was flat on the floor. It was then that the leader and driver arrived. There was a heated argument. The driver shouted at them, that they had agreed to frighten her with some burns and she was not to be brutally harmed. He was never told that she was also sodomized. Marlene stirred and they were relieved that she was still alive. But almost immediately, she fainted again. The leader checked her pulse. It was weak but there was still life in her. He ordered the other two to clothe her again. They did, but to prevent more blood from dripping they stuffed, the gags and blindfold they used on her into her panties. Then the leader forced some water through her dry lips, but Marlene remained unconscious. They had to wait for a few hours for midnight to take her somewhere. They were supposed to drop her off in a field and let her find her way back. But due to the situation she was in, they decided to drop

9

her off at her school. They waited until about one o'clock in the morning. They carried the lifeless Marlene into the car and drove to the Convent gates. When they were sure that no one saw them, they left her at the gate, half sitting, and rang the bell. Then they drove off into the night.

Marlene could not explain to Reverend Mother Irene how she got to the Convent. She told her trusted friend everything that happened and the conversations that took place to indicate that her coach Malik was implicated. When she finished her story, she looked at Reverend Mother Irene with pleading eyes and said, "If the police got involved and this became public, I would never be able to lead a normal life again, and all I wanted was to grow up like a normal person." Reverend Mother was almost in tears herself when she said, "But without the police these criminals will never be brought to justice. For almost killing you they need to be punished severely." "I know," Marlene said, "But not only will I suffer the humiliation of what has been done to me, Malik's family will be destroyed and his two innocent daughters will suffer." The surgeon came in at this point and told Reverend Mother Irene that it was time for her to leave. Marlene could also feel the drugs working. When Reverend Mother Irene got up to go, she held on to her hand with pleading eyes. The nun kissed her on the forehead and whispered in her ear, "You are very precious and your happiness is what matters most. I promise you that everything will be alright. Go to sleep in God's care."

The surgeon was also Indian. He did not examine Marlene but explained the whole surgery to her. He began by saying, "God was with you. You could have bled to death. I had to remove about six inches of your intestine and made twenty stitches in your rectum. The tube inserted in your vagina is attached to your bladder. It automatically drains your urine. Your bowel has been emptied and you will be on a liquid diet for a few days until the wounds in your body heal. The drip that is going into the vein in your hand is glucose. This will keep the hunger at bay and also help you to regain your strength. You must never leave your bed without the help of a nurse. If you should feel an urge to empty your bowel, which I hope will not happen, call the nurse and let her know. She will help you." Then he became more personal and smiled when he said, "You are very brave and strong. You will recover sooner than you think." Marlene was feeling very tired and sleepy. He noticed that and said, "I will come back tomorrow morning and examine your external wound. Is there anything you need before I leave? If not, Good Night and God be with you". Marlene felt safe and slept soundly without any dreams or nightmares.

She woke the next morning to the bustling of footsteps and the bright sunshine from the window of her room. Sister Theresa was in her room ready to clean her up. When she saw that Marlene was awake, she said, "Good Morning my love. How do you feel today? We have to get you cleaned for the good doctor. Remember Dr. Rama said he will examine you this morning." Marlene smiled at her and asked, "Is Reverend Mother Irene here?" "Oh yes, in fact you have quite a number of visitors waiting to see you this morning. But they will all have to wait until after your examination." Then she handed Marlene a toothbrush and toothpaste while she held a jug of water and an empty bowl. "I am sure you would like to brush your own teeth." Marlene did and when she was done, the nun removed the garment and began wiping her face and exposed parts of her body with a damp cloth. Marlene noticed that she avoided looking at the bandaged parts of her body. Then the nun helped her put on a clean garment. Just as Sister Theresa was brushing her short hair, Dr. Rama walked in. He too asked how she was and Marlene answered, "Great, and thanks for saving my life." "Oh no, God must have great plans for you. It was him who kept you alive." Sister Theresa raised her garment and after some gentle probing, the doctor said, "I am satisfied. The bleeding has stopped, but we will have to leave the bandage on in case it starts again. I shall remove the stitches in a few days." Then he put some pressure on her lower abdomen and asked if it hurt. Marlene winced a little for it felt very sensitive. "That will take more time to heal, but it is getting better. Don't forget what I told you last night about going to the bathroom." Marlene nodded. The doctor smiled and took his leave after giving Sister Theresa some instructions. She dabbed some medication on Marlene's rectum and put on new bandages. Then she told Marlene that she could have her visitors. Marlene held her hand and said, "Can I see Reverend Mother Irene alone first?" She nodded and left the room.

Reverend Mother Irene came directly to Marlene's bed and hugged her saying, "I am so glad to see that some color has returned to your face. The doctor said that you are recovering faster than expected." Then she sat on Marlene's bed and answered her un-asked questions, "We, your mother, the doctors and I have decided to leave the police out if that is your greatest wish. It would have been different if you were not going to make it or if you are permanently handicapped. You are out of danger and your well-being is more important than anything else." Marlene was so grateful that she began to sob, which hurt her stomach. Reverend Mother Irene dried her eyes again and said, "Your mothers, brother and sisters are waiting impatiently to see you. Put on a smile for them." Marlene managed a smile and the nun went out and came back with Marlene's mother Keng Yi, her third mother, Cheng Mee, her half sister Lily, her two younger sisters Anna and Mona, and her brother, Michael. Each took their turn in hugging her. Keng Yi was tearful as she explained that both she and Cheng Mee thought that Marlene was with the other person during those two days. When Marlene did not show up on Saturday in Kuala Lumpur, Keng Yi concluded that there was a competition that weekend. They were both shocked when Reverend Mother Irene sent messengers to inform them that Marlene was in the hospital. Marlene was glad that after the emotional explanation, the rest of the conversation was light and easy. None of them touched the subject of her abduction. After an hour, they all left except Reverend Mother Irene. She had more to say to Marlene.

She drew a chair and sat by the bed, taking Marlene's hand in hers and started to talk, "The doctor informed me that if your recovery continues at the same speed, you should be out of the hospital in two weeks. Under normal circumstances, you would have to see a psychologist because of your traumatic experience. But I know your inner strength and I do not think that would be necessary. I have spoken to your mother and she agreed to what I am going to suggest to you. I hope you will agree too. When you leave the hospital, I would like to send you to our novitiate in Cheras, which is outside Kuala Lumpur. It is a place for young women who would like to serve God, the way I do. You will convalesce there until you are strong enough to attend school. One of the novices will help you with your studies so that you can keep up with the rest of your classmates when you are well enough to come back to school. It is a peaceful place and you will find love among the residents there. You will feel safe and will be able to put this horrible experience behind you when you come back to school." She looked at Marlene hopefully. As she listened, Marlene could not believe how much this nun cared for her. She could not hope for a better place to forget the horrors of her experience. Her eyes were wet when she said, "Oh Reverend Mother, what have I done to deserve such kindness. I will go to wherever you send me." Reverend Mother Irene kissed her hand and continued, "Then when you return you will be my first boarder. You are going to stay in the Convent until you have finished your final Examinations." Marlene believed that her father had kept his promise. He had saved her and put her into the hands of this kind servant of God.

CHAPTER 2

Marlene's father was born in the year of 1896 in Malacca. During its days as a more than thriving port, Malacca was truly cosmopolitan, considered the place to be if one was pursuing wealth, culture and knowledge. Malay, the local language of this region, was the lingua franca, used by all. Many of the traders, including the colonists stayed on and married local women, giving birth to two unique cultures, the Malayan-Portuguese and the Babas and Nyonyas. Of the two hybrid cultures, the latter, the Babas and Nyonyas were more prominent. The Chinese left their homeland in droves, some to escape the Manchu rule, to begin a new life elsewhere, while others were lured by the prospects of earning a better living. When they married the local Malay women, their male offspring came to be known as Baba, while the ladies were known as Nyonyas. Marlene's grandfather and grandmother were a Baba and a Nyonya. Their ancestors left China to sail into the Port of Malacca during the sixteenth century, when the harbor was bristling with the sails and masts of Chinese junks, and spice-laden vessels from all over the hemisphere. The city was so coveted by the European powers that a writer wrote: "Whoever is Lord in Malacca has his hand on the throat of Venice." Sloping rooftops of traditional Malay houses hung over the water. It was the river side of the city that defied the Portuguese, who captured the city in 1511 and occupied it for over a century. However, Chinese influence was still predominant on the streets of the city. As they had done for hundreds of years, Chinese merchants advertised the wares inside their shop houses with bright red characters.

Thus Marlene's father was born in a typical Baba-Nyonya household. He was the third and last child of the Shih family. Unlike most Chinese babies, he had sharp features and very dark skin, which was not uncommon for this unique society. But, since he was much darker than his parents and his older brothers, they nick-named him Malam (the Malay word for night), and that was the name he was known by his family and friends all his life. His official Chinese name of Shih Tai Sun was only used for documents such as birth certificates and other important government papers. After having two sons, the Shihs longed for a daughter, but their disappointment was short-lived, when Malam showed signs of intelligence at a very early age. He was also very handsome. His parents doted on him, and were happy that his elder brothers, who were four and five years older than him, loved their little brother just as much. Since the British had been dominant in Malaya for a long time now, most of the families of this society were bi-lingual or tri-lingual. They could speak English and Malay fluently, and in most cases, Hokkien, a southern Chinese dialect. Although they claimed to be of pure Chinese heritage, Chinese was not spoken in the Shih's household.

Malam's father, Mr. Shih, like his father before him was a merchant. He was quite a wealthy man and was able to send all his sons to good English schools. However, when it was time for Malam to go to school, Mr. Shih felt that his third son was special and decided to send him to a school for very bright children. The children that were admitted into this school would have to pass an intelligence test. Even when the parents could afford the high school fees their children had to be intelligent enough to become students of this special school. It was run by the British and all teachers of that school were trained in England. Mr. Shih was confident that his son would make it, and true enough, Malam passed the test.

Malam grew up to be a very good-looking teenager. Not only was he good at studies, he also excelled in Sports. He began to represent his school in track and field events. His young body developed well, and by the time he was sixteen, he was five foot eleven inches tall. That was over average height for an Asian, maybe because he had some Portuguese blood in him. He was beginning to attract the local girls, and he seemed to enjoy the attention. Mr. Shih noticed that, but as long as Malam brought back good grades, it was alright. He had great plans for his son. Malam had another year to finish his Secondary education, and after that he was going to send him abroad to England for further education, to major in business and administration. The British had a very strong influence on Mr. Shih. He made sure that his family spoke only English at home.

One day, just before Malam entered his last year of school, he came home and told his father, "Papa, I am going to be an actor." Mr. Shih was thrown off balance. "What about university?" he stormed. Malam said, "If I am good, I could earn good money. I don't have to study to be an actor." His father was outraged. He could not believe the sudden change in his son. Malam had been so studious, and there was no sign or warning that he was not going for further studies. Malam tried to reason with his father, "Well, I could still go to university a little later. I found out that I could act and sing, and there is a talent scout looking for young actors for road shows. He was at our rehearsal for the annual concert. He came to me afterwards and offered me a part in his new show." Mr. Shih was speechless, but he knew that if his son made up his mind to do something, nothing he said would make a difference. "Papa," Malam continued, "I won't neglect my studies. I promise you that I will pass the final Examinations with flying colors. I do want to try my luck in acting." Mr. Shih gave in, but he was still very disappointed. It would have been different if his son showed interest in Sports instead, for he was quite talented in that field too.

At seventeen, Malam was almost six foot tall. His athletic body, sharp features and dark complexion enhanced his good looks, and the village girls competed for his attention. He joined a company that performed road shows during the weekends. Malam was glad that the performances took place within a hundred miles radius. He did not want to displease his father too much. He had to give up his sports activities completely to have time for his studies and rehearsals. Within months, he was given the major roles, either as a villain or a hero, but mostly as the latter. The majority of the audiences were young girls who would give anything to win Malam's attention. Knowing this, Malam flirted outrageously with them. His manager also encouraged him, saying that it would help him in his career of acting. However, fathers of those girls that Malam dated were not happy, and very often showed their disapproval. Malam was smart enough not to get intimate with any of them. But one girl managed to weaken his resolve. She was exceptionally pretty and was a member of his acting company. She was petite, and Malam had a soft spot for small girls. She was Muslim, and Malam, a Buddhist, knew that there could never be a future between them. However, he did fall in love with her, and they shared some intimate moments together.

True to his word, Malam passed his final Examinations with distinction, which qualified him to study in a university in England. But he was so obsessed with acting, and earning quite a lot of money for someone his age that Mr. Shih, his father, did not push him to go abroad. With his studies over, Malam became more involved in acting and started auditioning for the film industry. He was accepted to co-star in a Malay movie, and would have taken that part if not for Aminah, the girl he had been intimate with for sometime. He came home from rehearsal one day and saw his father deep in conversation with a Malay man. Malam did not want to disturb them, so he tried to sneak into the kitchen, when he heard a shout in Malay, "There is the low-down son of yours!" Malam stopped in his tracks and faced the man who said those words. He recognized Aminah's father. He was taken by surprise when the man pounced on him, and clutched his throat with both hands. Choking for air, Malam heard him say, "You are going to marry my daughter or die." Mr. Shih rushed to help his son, but the man was so angry that his strength was abnormal. He pushed Mr. Shih with one hand, the other still on Malam's throat. Seeing his father on the floor gave Malam the strength to fight back. A hard punch on the man's ribs freed Malam's throat. He was still choking and rubbing his throat when Aminah's father got on his feet. Mr. Shih too was standing up. Before another onslaught of the angry man on his son, Mr. Shih stood between them and said as calmly as he could, "Let us sit down as gentlemen and resolve this matter." That seemed to pacify the other man and he grunted, "I hope so or else."

All three men sat down at the dining table, and Malam's mother, who had been in the kitchen during the turmoil, came out with a pot of Chinese tea and some cups. She poured the tea in the cup, looked at her son sadly and went back into the kitchen. "Well son," Mr. Shih said in Malay, which was unusual, for he always spoke to his son in English. But, as Aminah's father did not speak English, it was polite to use the nation's language. As he continued, he sipped the hot tea, indicating that the other two should do the same, "Mr. Osman has accused you of making his daughter pregnant. Has he a reason for it?" Mr. Osman looked hard at Malam as Malam answered, "I have been dating Aminah because I love her." "You made love to her!" Mr. Osman shouted. Malam looked ashamed and said timidly, "Yes, we did have some intimacies, but she told me that she was taking precautions." Mr. Osman stood up angrily and said, "What precautions do you young people know. She is pregnant and the doctor has confirmed that she is now in her third month. You have been with each other for at least five months. Am I not right?" Malam nodded and was about to say something when his father intervened, "Sit down, Mr. Osman." When he saw that the other man sat down and was calm again, he continued, "If Malam is the father, we can work a way out, but marriage is out of the question. Our religions will not permit it." Mr. Osman was strangely quieter when he said, "Malam can embrace our religion." "Oh no, my son is born a Buddhist and there is no way I will permit him to embrace another religion. This pregnancy can be terminated. I shall pay for everything and more to help Aminah in the future." Mr. Osman lost his temper again and was about to say something, when Malam said, "No father, we have to let Aminah decide what she wants to do with the baby. I will embrace the religion and marry her, if that is what she wants. I love her and I am ready to take responsibility for my actions." Malam's words must have affected Mr. Osman positively, for he kept quiet and looked at Malam with respect in his eyes. All three men were quiet for sometime. Then Mr. Osman said, "Malam, I appreciate your concern for my daughter's feelings. But you have both done something wrong. She is to be blamed as much as you. Will you leave your father and me alone to discuss what is best for both of you? You are both still underage and even though you have both made a mistake, it is our responsibility to make the final decision." Malam began to protest, but his mother came in and gently nudged him to follow her.

Mrs. Shih was a very quiet woman. Like her husband, she was tri-lingual, but as her husband wished, she also spoke to her three sons only in English. Even though they had two servants, she did a lot of cooking and housework herself. She was the ideal mother and wife. She was obedient to her husband and agreed to whatever decisions or steps that he made. She also left the discipline of her children to her husband. She was brought up in the old fashioned way and that was to please her husband. But there were times when she knew that her sons needed her support, and she would always be there for them. At this time, she felt that Malam needed her. She went into Malam's room with him and as they sat on his bed, she put her arms round him and said, "Trust your father. He has never let you down. You are too young to marry, and so is Aminah. You have both made a mistake, but that should not destroy your futures." Malam broke down and cried, "I am so sorry and ashamed. I really thought that she was taking precautions." Mrs. Shih held him tightly to her chest. She wished with all her heart that he was the young innocent little boy again.

After an hour later, Mr. Shih came into his son's room. His wife planted an encouraging kiss on Malam's forehead and left. Both father and son sat on the bed quietly for sometime. Then Mr. Shih said, "You know that you have committed a very wrong deed, and I am sure you are sorry for it. But still there is a price to pay. I helped you this time, and I sincerely hope there will be no next time. Mr. Osman and I have settled on an agreement. Aminah will move out of town and have the baby. She may come back or she may not. We will always be responsible for her and the child financially. You are never to see her again or to lay any claim to the child. I have also given her father money for damages to his family name." Malam was quiet. He knew there was nothing he could do. He and Aminah were not yet eighteen years old and there was no way they could marry without their parents' permission. It hurt him to think that he would never know anything of his child, or to see Aminah again. Then a thought came to him. He would come of age in a few months time. He earned enough money to be able to support a family. When that time comes, he would find her and they could marry. Right now, he had to pretend to agree to his father's decision. After sometime, he looked at his father and said, "I am sorry. This will not happen again and thank you for your help."

Meanwhile, Mr. Osman went home not too happy, but satisfied. Mr. Shih was a generous man. He had given him enough money to give his three younger children a better education. Aminah would not be in financial difficulty, and no one in their village would know of her pregnancy if she left for another town. She could stay on and continue with her acting career in that town. Maybe, she would be wise enough to give up the bastard child for adoption. What he did not expect was that Aminah was truly in love with Malam. She was happy to bear his child, and she was sure that he loved her just as much, to embrace her religion and marry her. When her father told her of what transpired between him and Mr. Shih, Aminah cried out, "No, you both have no right to destroy our love. Malam loves me and he will marry me. Let me go to him." "Stay here!" her father commanded. "You have brought me enough shame. You will only make yourself cheaper and worthless, by running after a man who does not want you." With tears in her eyes, Aminah looked at her father and asked, "What do you mean by that?" Mr. Osman felt a lie would help Aminah so he said, "Malam agreed to our suggestion. He loves you, but he will not allow you or the baby to destroy his career. He has planned to go abroad for further studies in the near future." Aminah could not believe her ears, but she was brought up to believe everything her father said. So instead of running out of the door, she ran into her room, locked herself in and cried. After a few hours alone, the faint hope that Malam would come to tell her that everything was alright, and that they would marry, disappeared. She was completely heartbroken. Then she made a rash decision. If he did not love her, she would not bear his child.

She had to find a long and sharp object. She looked around in her room, and her eyes fell on the dress that she wore when she and Malam went on their first date. It was hanging on a wire hanger. She saw the irony of it, and was determined to use that instrument to end the product of what she thought was love. First she took off the dress from the hanger and ripped it up. Then furiously, she began to untwine the wire, until she got a piece long enough to do the work. She took off her panties and lay on the bed with her legs spread out. Closing her eyes and biting her lips, she placed the sharp object through the cervix and into the uterus. Even as the object entered her body, she felt pain, and the pain increased as it went into her uterus. The agony was unbearable as she began poking and probing, but she kept on biting her lips and continued. Tears were developing in her eyes and she could taste the blood on her bitten lips. Then she felt intense pain as blood began to flow out of her vagina like the flow of water coming from the tap. She could not go on. She could not pull out the object. Her groans of pain and anguish became so loud, that her parents heard her.

It was late evening, and her mother was in the kitchen preparing their evening meal. She was not happy with her husband's decision. She felt that it was Malam's responsibility to marry Aminah and father his child. She argued with him about that, but finally agreed that they could make use of the money that Mr. Shih had generously given them. They had two younger daughters and a son. She would make sure that they would not make the same mistake as their sister. She wanted to go into Aminah's room to comfort her, but her husband insisted that Aminah should cry her shame away. When she heard the first groan, she thought it was a sob. Then, it became louder and eerier. She looked at her husband, who was sitting at the dining table and enjoying a pipe, and noticed that he too heard the sound. Without an exchange of word, they ran into Aminah's room. Their house was made of cheap quality wood and it was easy to break down a locked door. When they called Aminah to open the door, the reply they got was a shrill cry of pain. Mr. Osman wasted no time in breaking down the door. They found their daughter's body twisted and covered with blood. Then they saw the object of their daughter's anguish sticking out from under her. Aminah's mother was hysterical and began shouting at her husband. He was calm, and called out to one of his children who were playing outside. "Go and get the 'bomoh'!" He commanded his son. 'Bomoh' is the Malay term for a miracle worker who uses prayers and herbs to supposedly cure pain and diseases. Then the wife shouted, "No, we have to take her to the hospital or else she will bleed to death." Aminah had stopped groaning or making any sounds at all. She had fainted. Mr. Osman did not heed his wife's request. He could not face the shame of his unmarried daughter being pregnant. Thus, the son ran as fast as he could to get the miracle worker.

When the 'bomoh' arrived, Aminah was still unconscious and bleeding profusely. The 'bomoh' tried to remove the object gently, but it would not come out. Then he chanted some prayers and used a little more effort, and began to twist and turn. As he did so, more blood poured out. When he managed to pull it out completely, Aminah opened her eyes and closed them almost immediately. She was beyond help. The 'bomoh' examined her and shook his head sadly. He proclaimed her dead. The mother lost her mind and began pounding her husband with her fists, blaming him and his greed for money. "You sold our daughter's life! You and the Shihs killed her! You will all suffer for this!" Friends and neighbors heard the commotion and came pouring in, some to help, and some out of curiosity. There was no one to stop them from entering the dead girl's room. The three young children ranging from ages six to eleven were trying to pull their mother away from their father. The 'bomoh' was still chanting some prayers for the spirit of the dead girl.

Some got sick when they saw the blood on the bed and the twisted body of Aminah. A few had the common sense to help pull the three children away from the raving mother, and some took in the scene, with the realization that a tragedy had occurred. When Mr. Osman was freed of his wife's onslaught, he put up his hand to gain some control in the room. With a sad voice he said, "Please leave the room. Let my daughter go in peace. Wait in the living room and I will tell you what happened." Everyone, except for the 'bomoh' left. When they were alone, the 'bomoh' said, "I had to remove the wire from her body. I am sure you don't want anyone else to know how she died." Mr. Osman nodded and said, "Thank you." Then they both left the room to join the others. His wife was sitting down quietly, but was staring into space. Mr. Osman explained that his daughter committed suicide, because he forbade her to have anything more to do with Malam. She felt she could not live without him. He then begged them to leave the house and allow his family to grieve their loss. Everyone respected his wish, and when they all left, including the 'bomoh' he broke down and cried. He went to his wife and fell on his knees, begging for forgiveness, but she just stared ahead. His three children were weeping quietly, and he gently told them to wash up and go to bed. Dinner was forgotten. He could not get through to his wife, so he left her alone and went into his daughter's room. With a heavy heart, he carried her lifeless body, and laid it gently on the floor. She had stopped bleeding. He removed the bloody sheets, tried to dry the mattress with some towels and laid new sheets on the bed. Then, he cleaned his daughter's body as much as he could, and dressed her up with some clean clothes. A professional lady will come in the next day to wash her, and dress her properly for viewing before the funeral. His eyes were brimming with tears as he carried her corpse and laid it on the clean sheets. His wife was right. His greed had cost his daughter her life. He hated Malam for it, but he hated himself more for not telling his daughter the truth. The important thing now was to maintain her good name. No one else must know of her pregnancy.

It was almost midnight of that fatal day when Hamid, Malam's best friend, showed up at the Shih's residence. He knocked urgently at the door and woke up the Shihs. When Mr. Shih opened the door, he knew that something was very wrong. Hamid looked very sad but did not tell the older man anything. He insisted on speaking to Malam, who was leaving his room to see who was at the door. Seeing Hamid's face sent a chill up his spine, but he managed to greet his friend, "What's up?" Hamid simply said, "Can we go to your room?" Both the boys left an exasperated Mr. Shih at the door and went into Malam's room. Hamid closed the door behind him and said, "Aminah killed herself today." Malam looked at him unbelievingly and sat slowly on his bed. Then when the words sank in, he became hysterical and sobbed like a baby. His father heard the commotion and banged at the door, demanding to come in. Hamid let him in and said, "Sorry, but I had to let Malam know what happened." Mr. Shih looked at his sobbing son and asked, "What did you tell him?" It was Malam who screamed at his father, "You killed her because of your ideas about love and religion." Then he got up and would have attacked his father if not for Hamid and his mother who just came in. When they managed to control Malam, the mother said, "Will you two please leave the room?" Without a word, Hamid led Mr. Shih out of the room. Malam's mother locked the door after them and went to her weeping son. She cradled his head and felt his body shaking with pain and emotion. All she could say was, "It is not your fault. You wanted to do the right thing. I overheard Hamid telling you that Aminah committed suicide." Malam just continued crying in his mother's arms, until total exhaustion overcame him. His body stopped shaking, but his eyes were still wet, when his mother gently laid his head on his pillow to sleep.

Malam slept restlessly for about three hours. He got up in the dark hours of the morning, feeling groggy and sick. He hoped that he had a bad nightmare, but as his mind became clearer, the tragedy of the night before became realistic and he was about to give in to his grief when he made up his mind to go to Aminah's house. It was four o'clock in the morning when Malam sneaked out of his house. His father was one of the few who owned a car, but Malam was still too young to have a driving license. However, his father had taught him some driving and Aminah's house was only three miles away. Malam was too weak to walk that distance, so he decided to drive. Mr. Shih heard the engine of the car and knew where his son was heading. He did not stop him, but knew that he had to find a way to follow his son. Aminah's house was lighted, when Malam arrived. He knocked at the door and was greeted coldly by Aminah's eleven year old brother. Malam heard Mr. Osman's voice asking who it was. The son simply said, "It's him." Mr. Osman's eyes were swollen from crying when he came to the door. He was not angry when he said, "Go home. You are not welcomed here. Don't cause us any more grief." Malam's tears began to roll down as he begged, "Please let me see her. I loved her and if I could give up my life for her, I would do it." Aminah's mother, who was still sitting on the same chair, came to life. She rushed at Malam cursing and swearing at him. Most of what she said was inaudible, but Malam heard a few sentences that would affect him in the future. "You killed my child. The same fate will befall your children. I lost one; you will lose two or more." Then before she could attack him, her husband held on to her, telling Malam to go away. But Malam went on his knees, bent his head and begged for forgiveness. He was pulled up by his father, who managed to get one of his business associates to drive him to where his son went. He begged Malam to go back with him saying, "You have paid dearly for your mistake. You have begged for their forgiveness. There is nothing more you can do. Mourn for Aminah in your own way. Let them mourn for her their way." Malam was too distraught and weak to resist his father's strong arms, as he was led to the waiting car of his father's friend. Malam was in a daze as he was driven home. Mr. Shih drove his own car back.

Aminah's funeral took place that same day. Mr. Shih had ordered his family doctor to drug Malam so that he slept all that day. If he was awake, it would be hard to restrain him from attending the funeral. The bereaved family wanted the reason for the death of their child to be hidden, and Malam's presence would jeopardize their wishes. Besides, Aminah's mother was losing her mind and she would react very violently towards Malam. When all this was over, he would beg his son's forgiveness. After all, whatever he did, he did it for Malam. It was wrong not to consider the girl's feelings, but like all mistakes, some could be undone and some could only be a lesson for the future. Mr. Shih felt that he had to be strong and help his son, for he knew that his son would take a long time to recover from this tragedy.

CHAPTER 3

Malam was never the same again. For three months he lived like a hermit, leaving his room only to eat, and that too was like once a day. He did not join his family for meals. He would go into the kitchen when no one was about and make a simple meal for himself. He lost weight and allowed his hair and beard to grow. His mother was heartbroken whenever she caught sight of him. Even she could not get through to him. His married brothers would come with their children to visit, but Malam would not talk or see anyone. He never went for anymore rehearsals, thus ending his acting career. His parents could hear him in his room playing melancholy songs on his record player. They did not know how long he slept or whether he slept at all. His room was always locked, and whenever someone knocked at his door, all they heard was "Leave me alone." Mr. Shih was getting very worried. He felt that his son was becoming suicidal, and that he had to do something before it was too late. He had always believed that sometimes kindness came in the form of cruelty. Since gentle persuasions could not bring Malam out of his traumatic state, he had to enforce some threats.

Mr. Shih knocked on Malam's room door and said, "Malam, open the door or I shall break it. I find your behavior pathetic and I shall not condone it any longer." Malam grunted, "What do you want?" "Either you talk to me or you talk to someone professional. It is up to you," his father replied. Malam was quiet for sometime, then his father heard him unlocking the door. Mr. Shih was speechless when he saw how his once handsome son had changed. Not only was the hair long, it was unkempt and falling all over his face. His beard too was growing wildly. His room reeked of cigarettes and his clothes were all over the floor. The young man looked and smelled like he had never washed himself for months. From the circles around his eyes, Mr. Shih knew that Malam must have cried himself to sleep every night; either that or he hardly had slept. Mr. Shih was more determined to carry out his decisions. He pushed Malam towards his messed up bed and made his son sit down. Malam gave no resistance, and when Mr. Shih managed to clear the chair in his room of records, he sat down. He looked hard at his son who was avoiding his eyes, and said, "You are going to shower, and we will both go to the barber to have your hair trimmed and your beard shaved. Then we are going to pay a visit to the doctor. If you disagree, I will have to get the police to help me. You know that I have my way of securing their help." Malam looked up, and for the first time after the tragedy did he speak directly to his father. His voice was quite shaky when he said, "I wish you will let me rot. I don't deserve to live." He could not say more for he started sobbing. His father's heart went out to him and he went to his son and hugged him saying, "No son, it is not your fault. It is ours. We thought we were doing the right thing, but we were wrong. It is too late to ask forgiveness from the dead, but you are still living and I beg you to forgive me." He allowed Malam to continue crying, and when he stopped, he offered the young man his handkerchief, and said, "Her spirit knows the truth. You were ready to take the responsibility. It was us, her father and I who were blind and stupid. Come, go and clean yourself up."

Mr. Shih took his son to the barber and was glad to have his handsome son back, even though he must have lost about twenty pounds. As they drove towards the family doctor, Malam placed a hand on his father's and said, "I am all right now. We don't have to see the doctor. Just give me some time to be alone. I won't grieve, but I need time to think." Mr. Shih did not argue, instead he smiled at his son and they both drove home. That night, for the first time for three months, Malam sat down and had dinner with his parents. His mother had cooked his favorite dish, pork ribs in soy bean sauce. She looked at her husband gratefully as their youngest son ate heartily. While the men were at the barber's, she and the maid cleared and cleaned Malam's room. All the records were put back into their covers and stacked away. His dirty clothes were removed, and she even had time to shop for some new ones for him. She did her best to wipe off any trace of his mourning and grief for the last three months. When Malam retired for the night, they did not hear any music from his room. His father passed by and stood by the door. He heard the rustle of the blanket and the soft movement of the mattress. He knew that everything was going to be all right. That was the first night after the tragedy, that Mr. and Mrs. Shih were able to sleep peacefully and contentedly.

Although Malam was recovering from his traumatic loss, he still kept away from friends and relatives. He would stay in his room when his brothers and their family visited his parents. They respected his wishes and knew that he needed more time. Malam would get up very early and take a long hike in the rubber plantation close by. His father was a share-holder of that property. He enjoyed watching the rubber tappers at work. Most of them were immigrants from India and they did not speak Malay or English. Since Malam was not in a communicative mood, it was good to just smile at them and they would return his smile, showing their glistening white teeth. He would walk and sometimes jog to keep fit.

Then he would come back and have breakfast with his parents, and go into their courtyard with a book. That was his routine for the two weeks after his father entered his room.

One day, while they were at breakfast, Malam surprised his parents by starting the conversation. Normally, he would be quiet and only answer questions. But this particular morning, he said, "Papa, Mama, I have decided that it is time for me to continue with my life. I appreciate and love you both for what you have gone through for me." Then he looked at his father directly and asked, "Will you send me abroad to study?" Mr. Shih couldn't believe his ears. His eyes welled with happy tears as he said, "Malam, nothing will make me happier. I have always wished for the day when you will continue further education. I am not getting any younger, and both your brothers have their own interest and business. My business is doing well, and I need someone to help me run it." "Yes father, I would like to go to England to study business administration. I did some research, and I could study in Cambridge for four years to get a Bachelor's degree. When I come back, I will be happy to help you." Malam's mother went over to her son and hugged him. She said, "I will miss you, but you have my blessings. You have made us so happy. But first of all, we will celebrate your birthday which is in two weeks time. That is if you are ready." Malam returned her hug and said, "It will take more than a month to apply for admittance into the university and to get a study visa. Sure, I would like to have a birthday party. I owe it to my friends to say goodbye to them properly."

Malam became more himself, but he still kept away from his friends, except for Hamid. Hamid was Malay and he and Malam spoke only Malay to each other. Hamid too was a part-time actor, but never had the leading parts like Malam. Nevertheless, he had always admired Malam's maturity and intelligence. He was two years older than Malam and had a valid driving license. Mr. Shih allowed Hamid to use his car to drive Malam to the capital city of Malaya, Kuala Lumpur. The British Consulate and all other government offices were in the capital. It was there that Malam had to apply for a legal passport, admittance into England, and other important documents for the big move. Kuala Lumpur was about five hours drive from Malacca. Sometimes, the young men would spend a night in the hotel and explore the excitement of what the big city could offer. They always had a good time, but Malam shied away from the girls. Hamid too was quite good-looking, so it was common to find the bold city girls eying them hungrily.

Meanwhile, Mr. and Mrs. Shih were preparing a big birthday party for their youngest son who would turn eighteen on October 22, 1914. All Malam's friends and relatives were invited, including Mr. Shih's business associates. With the use of the courtyard, the house was big enough to entertain a hundred guests quite easily. Food catering services were used. The banquet would consist of Chinese, Malay and Indian cuisines. Many friends had volunteered to get the house ready for that event. Amidst the preparations, Mr. Shih was worried about his other two sons. He hoped that they would not be jealous of Malam, since he had never celebrated any of their birthdays on such a big scale. But his eldest son assured him that there were good reasons to celebrate. They almost lost Malam and he came back to them. Besides that, he was going to fulfill his father's dream that one of his sons would take over the business that had belonged to them for a few generations. Mr. Shih was happy to know that Malam's brothers loved him as dearly as their parents.

Just before his birthday, Malam received all his documents for traveling to Great Britain. He was also accepted into one of the oldest and most prominent colleges in Cambridge, King's College. Although his semester would only start in January of 1915, he had to leave in November, as the only way to get to Great Britain was by steam ship. It would take more than a month, because there were so many ports of call before they arrived in London. His father had booked a passage for him with the British India Steam Navigation company. Many of these ships carried only a few passengers, because they were mostly cargo ships. With his good influence, Mr. Shih had secured a classy accommodation for his son. The fare at that time was only about fifty two British pounds. Malam would have to take a smaller ship from Singapore, an independent island on the southern tip of Peninsular Malaya to Calcutta. In Calcutta, India, he would board the bigger vessel to take him to London via Madras, Colombo, and Port Said.

On the day of Malam's eighteenth birthday, regardless of the war that was going on in Europe, guests poured in. Many had admired the Shih's residence, but very few had seen the inside of the big house. It was a double-storey brick building built at the edge of the historical Malacca River. A branching out of the stairs led to the heavy oak door which was painted in red. The door opened to a big space, filled with expensive antique furniture. At the end of the wall was a big Buddhist altar, where the Statue of Buddha sat. Joysticks and incense burned twenty four hours a day. Behind this wall were steps leading to the four bedrooms and a huge modern bathroom. Beyond this staircase, were the great dining room and an open kitchen. There was another big bathroom to the side of the kitchen. The kitchen door opened to the big courtyard which was surrounded by a high brick fence. The ground was completely cemented, but pots of blooming flowers grew along the wall of the brick fence. The door to the courtyard was opened to the guests that day. Tables and chairs now filled the courtyard. Malam had gained his normal weight back and the people who shook his hand to congratulate him, were not aware of what he had gone through or the deep pain he still kept in his heart. He wore a flowery shirt and a pair of white pants. He was as handsome as ever. He chatted with almost every guest, but kept away from the young girls who were competing with each other for his attentions. The party started at four in the afternoon and ended around mid-night. Most of the food was gone and a lot of alcohol was consumed. Malam drank very little. He was careful not to let his defenses down. It came as a shock to some of his close friends that he would be leaving for England soon, especially as there was a war going on. But, Malam assured them that his route would not take him into the path of war. If he were to wait for the war to be over, he may be too old to study.

For the next few days, Malam and his parents spent a lot of time in Kuala Lumpur, shopping for clothes for Malam and also spending some precious hours together. Mr. Shih was used to the quiet and simplicity of Malacca, so he had never liked to visit this bustling city. He only came once in a while for business. However, with his son and wife, he seemed to appreciate the British colonial buildings and the midnight lamps of the night markets. In the same way, like Malacca, Kuala Lumpur's commercial center was a grand meeting place for merchants and travelers from all over the world. Kuala Lumpur was situated midway along the west coast of Peninsular Malaya, now known as Malaysia at the confluence of the Klang and Gombak rivers. It was approximately thirty miles from the coast, and sat at the center of the Peninsula's extensive and modern transportation network. It was the largest city in the nation, possessing a population of people drawn from Malaya's ethnic group. Malam loved the city, but only as a visitor. He was sure that he would return to Malacca and live there for the rest of his life like his father and grandfathers before him.

It was time for Malam to leave for England. His brothers, their wives and children came to the Shihs' residence to say goodbye to him. His mother tried her best not to cry, but failed. Malam's father hugged his son tightly and wished him all the best, saying, "We will miss you, but we also know that you have a great destiny ahead of you. Four years is not forever. You will come home a young highly educated man and we will be very proud of you. Go with our blessings." Malam was very sad to leave his parents, but he held back his tears. Hamid was designated to drive Malam to Singapore. Malam was entering the car when he heard someone calling out to him. He turned round and was surprised to see Mr. Osman hurrying towards him. Mr. Shih tried to stop Mr. Osman from approaching Malam, but Malam insisted on talking to the man. To everybody's surprise, when they were close enough, both ran into each other's arms. Malam, who had held back his tears for such a long time, began to weep and ask for forgiveness, but Mr. Osman pulled away from him and gripped him by the shoulders, looked into his eyes and said, "It is I who should be asking for forgiveness. What is done cannot be undone, but my daughter is at peace and I want to send you off with peace in your heart too. Go and may God speed you." Then he turned away and walked off without a backward glance. Malam entered the car and Hamid drove him to Singapore where he would board a smaller vessel to take him to Calcutta, where a bigger ship would take him to London.

During the long drive, Malam was quiet and Hamid respected the silence. It was only when they were reaching the port of Singapore did Malam speak, "Hamid," he began, "Please buy a bouquet of flowers and place it on Aminah's grave. No one must know that it came from me." Hamid nodded. Malam had a lot of luggage, which Hamid helped him with. Once Malam was checked in, both the friends went to a nearby café for a drink. While they were drinking coffee, Malam said, "Hamid, you have been a wonderful friend, and I am very grateful for it. I shall write to you as often as I can. If by any chance you could visit me, I will welcome you with open arms." Hamid was holding back his tears as Malam continued, "Please keep an eye on my aging parents, and do not hesitate to tell me if anyone of them gets sick." Hamid could hardly talk for his heart was aching for his dear friend. He would miss Malam terribly. But just before Malam entered the departure gate to board the smaller vessel, Hamid hugged him and said, "Goodbye dear friend. I shall do everything you asked me. I know that it would be impossible to visit you, but I shall await your return patiently. Like your wise father said, four years is not forever. The time will fly faster than we think." Then Malam boarded the ship with tears in his eyes. He did not look back at his dear friend, who too turned away to walk back to the car.

It took Malam four days by ship to arrive in Calcutta. He had never been to this Indian city and would like to visit it, but the bigger vessel Hindu, built in 1894 was ready to make its voyage in a few hours, and Malam was afraid that he may get lost in the overpopulated city, so he went on board and viewed the city from the deck. He would explore the ship once they started sailing. He was sea-sick most of the time while he was in the smaller vessel. Besides, it was too small and too crowded, and the last thing he wanted to do was to be among people. The Hindu was different. It was large and there were only about fifty passengers and about another fifty crew members on board. Most of its space was filled with all kinds of merchandise from Asia. Most of the cargo was spices, raw rubber, rice and clothes. The scent of the spices was pleasing. It made up for the not so pleasant smell of the rubber. From the deck of the ship Malam took in the scene of the harbor beneath. He could detect the existence of great poverty. There were beggars everywhere, and hungry children crowding well-dressed inhabitants and foreigners for money. There were poor people too in his country, but not as pathetic as the people here in Calcutta. He felt sick watching the suffering, and went down to his cabin to check on his luggage, which was transferred from the other vessel to the Hindu by coolies.

Since the ship was not a passenger ship, there were not too many places that Malam could go to, so he spent a lot of his time on deck reading and enjoying the sea breeze. The ship kept as close to the mainland as it sailed along the Gulf of Bengal and arrived in Madras two days later. It was going to be a short stop, just enough time to load more spices and goods for the European market. Malam decided to stay on board, but managed to do some research about the city. It was the gateway to the south and was the largest city in South India, and the fourth largest in the country. It was located on the Coromandel Coast of the Bay of Bengal. The city's development started after 1639, when the British East India Company established a Fort, and a couple of Trading posts at the small fishing village called Chennai. Here too, Malam could see from his deck how poor the population was, so he was glad not to have to mingle with them. He wanted to avoid melancholy as much as he could.

The steam ship left Madras and sailed along the coast for twenty hours until it reached Colombo, now known as Sri Lanka. The stop was also for more loading, and that same evening it sailed away from the coast of India into the Arabian Sea. Malam felt alone and lost in the middle of the ocean. Because of the length of time out in the deep blue sea, the crew held some parties and the fifty passengers were invited to join them. The captain and his mates were English and there were some European engineers too, but most of the people who worked in the steam room and cargo departments were local Indians. They were not included in the celebrations above, but held their own parties in the lower deck. The passengers comprised mostly of Europeans, about six Egyptians, a few rich Indian business men and a handful of Malayans. There was an Egyptian dancer among them, and during the party nights she would perform belly-dancing. She was exotically beautifully with a well-shaped hip, flat stomach and voluptuous breasts. Her eyes were dark and seductive. All the men would have given anything to win her attentions, but as she danced, she never took her eyes off Malam. That very first evening after her performance, she came to his table which he shared with two other Malayan men and an Indian, and asked him if he would come to the bar to have a drink with her. The other men looked enviously at Malam, but encouraged him to accept her invitation. One of them said, "If you refuse the lady, you must either be gay or simply stupid." Malam was not impressed, but nevertheless he did not want the others to think that he was arrogant, so he stood up and followed the beautiful dancer to the bar.

Malam ordered himself a soft drink and she had a long drink with some whisky in it. Malam was quiet and she introduced herself in very good English, "My name is Ani and I think you are Mr. Shih. What do your friends call you?" Malam answered, "Malam. It is a nickname, and it means 'night' in the Malay language. Everyone who knows me has always called me by that name." She looked at him and said, "There is some kind of sadness in your eyes. You look too young to be carrying such a heavy burden." Malam shrugged and said, "I lost someone very dear." Seeing that he had no intention to continue this topic she changed the subject and the conversation became light and easy. They found out a lot about each other. She was working in a night-club in Singapore for the last two years. She decided to go back to Egypt to help her father with the carpet business. Malam told her of his study in Cambridge. As they talked, she ordered more of the long drinks and Malam, feeling relaxed in her company, began to start ordering the same alcoholic drinks. They were still at the bar when everyone had left to go to bed. When the barman told that it was time to close the bar, they decided to take a midnight stroll on the deck.

The sky was clear with scattered stars, but there was no moon. The sea was calm and the two young people were alone on the deck. The atmosphere was romantic enough for two lovers, and Ani was in a very seductive mood. Even though Malam was feeling a little light-headed, he avoided looking at her alluring lips and eyes. He brushed her hands aside when she tried touching him intimately. Nevertheless, he felt very attracted to his beautiful companion. She was insistent, and finally, he gave in and took her in his arms. They kissed each other hungrily and under the tropical sky, Ani began removing her attire. Malam was lost and unaware of where he was. Then she began to unbutton his pants. Unconsciously, they moved to a corner of the deck where no one could see them, and Ani guided him to lie down beside her on the moist deck. But as soon as Malam's almost naked body felt the coldness of the floor, he was shocked at how far he had gone. He got up shaking with fury at himself and quickly pulled up his pants again. Ani was half sitting on the floor and he pulled her up saying, "I am so sorry. It is not you, it is me. I am not ready for this. Please don't hate me. I have to go." He said goodnight and ran off to his room leaving Ani staring after him.

They had to sail for ten days in the Indian Ocean. Malam could not avoid seeing Ani, but somehow the girl knew that Malam had a very unhappy experience, and he needed more time, before he could love again. Whenever their paths crossed, she would give him a reassuring smile and then move away. She did not perform anymore for the rest of the trip. Malam still attended the parties, but would retire to his room once dinner was over. He was beginning to get seasick and wanted to touch solid ground again. Then on the tenth day, when he was on deck, he caught a glimpse of land. He knew that they will be sailing into the Red Sea soon. Still it would take another week before they arrived at the next port of call. Nevertheless, it was quite reassuring to know that the vessel would be sailing between Africa and Arabia. At least, he could see land on both sides; Africa on the left and Saudi Arabia on the right. The trip became exciting as the ship cruised into the Suez Channel. He could see Egypt quite easily and with the help of binoculars he could also see some pyramids. As they approached Port Said, Malam made enquiries of how long they were going to stay at the port. He would very much like to step on solid land and explore the exciting and historical country. He was told that they would dock for two days, for some passengers whose journey ended at Port Said and for new passengers to come aboard. They were also unloading some goods and reloading some Egyptian wares. Malam had spent twenty four days at sea and there would be no more stops until they arrived in London, which would take another three weeks.

Finally the ship made its last call at Port Said before sailing to its final destination. Like all the other passengers, Malam could not wait to get out. He was on deck as the vessel was docking. He was pleasantly surprised when Ani came and stood beside him, "Well," she said, "I am finally home. I wanted to say that whatever happened that night was a nice encounter." Malam looked at the beautiful girl and knew that under other circumstances, he would have fallen in love with her. He shrugged off that feeling and said, "Thank you for being so understanding. I wish you all the best." She was quite tall so it was easy to plant a kiss on his cheek, which she did. Then she went away throwing him a flying kiss, which he returned with a smile. Then she was lost in the crowd of passengers waiting to leave. He took his time, and then began to walk towards the gangway. He felt overwhelming relief as soon as his feet touched solid ground.

The origins of Port Said went as far back as 1859. It was a working camp founded by Said Pasha to house men working on the Suez Canal. There was a National Museum which housed artifacts from most periods of Egypt's past. It was located on the main street, and Malam strolled down the street, as curious as any visitors and entered the museum. He spent the whole afternoon admiring the relics of ancient Egypt. Then he explored the outdoor markets and heard sellers and buyers bargaining over goods in Egyptian and sometimes in English. He tried to keep away from the crowds, but the streets were crowded, and peasant children would crowd him begging for money. Malam had managed to change some British pounds for Egyptian coins. He gave out a few, which was a mistake. More children and even some adults kept following him. Then he was rescued by one of the ship's crew, a Norwegian, who knew Port Said from two sailings. He took Malam under his wing for the two days they were there. He knew the best places to eat and the best night entertainments. Malam saw a few more belly-dancers, but felt that Ani was still the most beautiful of them all. All too soon it was time to leave Port Said.

The ship left the Suez Canal and sailed into the Mediterranean Sea. There was some worry that the ship may be caught in the midst of the war, but nothing happened, and it was an easy and uneventful sailing. The temperate climate was ideal, but Malam was used to the hot tropical climate of Malaya. He always had a thick jacket on when he was on deck, even though the sun was shining. By now, he had made friends with most of the passengers. Nothing exciting happened. Nevertheless, Malam was not bored. He would attend the regular celebrations in the evening and enjoy playing cards with the crew and some other passengers. There was a library where he could borrow books since he had read all the books that he brought along. He also spent a lot of time writing letters after letters to his family and Hamid. He would mail them once he arrived in London. It would take over a month before his family received them, but it would reassure them that he had survived the long journey.

CHAPTER 4

Malam was excited as the ship cruised its way into the Thames. His journey of almost one and a half months had ended. There was an English couple who had grown fond of him. They lived in London, and invited Malam to spend the few days in London with them before proceeding on to Cambridge. Malam accepted the invitation, but told them that he could only spend two days in London, for he had to get to Cambridge before Christmas. He had to find lodgings before the semester started. Although he had prepared himself for the cold, and was warmly dressed, he was shivering. It worried him whether he would ever get used to the cold. His host assured him that he would be acclimatized sooner than he thought. London was exciting. There were more cars than he had ever seen in Malaya. The streets were narrow, and there were many foreigners like him in the English city. His friends lived in a small apartment outside of London. They had to take two cabs to get there because of the amount of luggage that Malam had. Malam would have loved to explore the city during his two days there, but he stayed in for he could not stand the cold. All he managed to do was find out the train schedule to Cambridge and purchase the ticket. It would take him four to six hours to get to Cambridge by train. He decided that once it became warmer, he would make a trip back to London and then explore the exciting and bustling city. Right now, war was in the air and London was quite affected by it.

As the train chugged from Victoria Station towards Cambridge, Malam looked out the window and saw the serenity of country life, compared to the busy city. He thought he would see snow and was disappointed that it was just cold, wet and cloudy. He hoped Cambridge would be different. He was also feeling very cold in the first class cabin that he shared with two other passengers. He kept his thick coat on and slept through the rest of the journey. He was so tired that he was unaware of the few stops the train made. He woke up once to show his ticket to the conductor and dozed off again. Malam was gently woken up by one of the passengers when the train arrived in Cambridge. He said, "I think this is where you get off. You looked like a foreign student who has traveled from afar to study in one of our universities." Malam rubbed his eyes and thanked the gentleman, who having just a small briefcase helped Malam with his two huge suitcases. Malam had been given an address by the British Consulate, of an agency that helped foreign students to find homes or apartments. With the help of the kind man, he found a porter to help him with the suitcases. The place where Malam was heading for was fifteen minutes walking distance, so Malam paid the porter a bit more to help him get there with his luggage.

As they left the station, Malam was in awe. The city of Cambridge was the most beautiful and romantic city he had ever seen. It was situated in the quiet east of England, amid the rural countryside of Cambridgeshire. The residents, mainly students of the many universities there, had the best of all worlds; the combination of the romantic medieval image and an up to date city. Cambridge was not big, but had all the amenities of a University City. Its unique setting on the banks of the River Cam, and the magnificent architecture of the universities, combined to make it the most unforgettable place, one which will linger long in Malam's memory. As they walked through the city, the porter explained a bit of its history to Malam. His knowledge of history surprised Malam, until he told Malam, that he was a history student in one of the other colleges, and that he was doing this extra job to earn some money for Christmas presents for his parents. When Malam saw King's college, he mentioned to his new-found friend that this was the college he would attend. They stopped at the gate and Rick, the historian gave Malam a brief history of the college. It was founded by Henry VI in 1441. Except for the original great court, much of the college buildings were from the eighteenth and nineteenth centuries. Rick pointed to the King's college Chapel and said, "They started building it during the reign of King Henry VI but it was only completed a hundred years later. Today, it is the jewel in the crown of the college and of Cambridge itself. It is a magnificent example of gothic architecture. When you go in, you will see the breathtaking interior with the combination of the delicately fan-vaulted roof, the lavish woodcarving and the sixteenth century stained glass." When they arrived at the destination, Malam thanked Rick and gave him a very generous tip, saying, "Hopefully, we will meet again." "Sure, Cambridge is not big. Thank you and have a Merry Christmas." Then Rick was off to earn more money at the railway station.

Malam was greeted very warmly by a lady at the desk of the office to help foreign students. She found Malam a room in one of the buildings that housed a lot of students. Each had their own room fully furnished with a bed, a wooden desk and a chair, and a huge cupboard for clothes. There were built in shelves along one side of the wall for books. It was a double storey building with a large kitchen and bathroom on each floor. The rent was minimal. The building only housed men. Women were not allowed to visit. Malam was satisfied when he saw his room and met some of the residents. They were mostly from other countries and their welcomed smiles made him feel at home. Most of the English students must have gone home for the holidays. The great common room was decorated with a Christmas tree and colorful trimmings. One of the residents who introduced himself as Helmut, a German, told Malam that they would have their own Christmas party on Christmas Eve, which was in two days time. Being a Buddhist, Christmas was not celebrated at his home, although he and his friends would visit some of their Christian friends on Christmas Day. Anyway, he was glad to be invited to join the party. The war did not seem to affect the people and students here.

Christmas came and went and there was another party on New Year's Eve. By then, Malam knew all the six foreign residents who lived there. Then just before the colleges and universities reopened the other four English students returned from their homes in different parts of England. Malam got to know them too, and he felt settled and at home. He had sent the letters he wrote on the ship back with the ship. He began writing more letters before he started his studies. He hoped to receive some replies soon. He knew that it would take a month or more for the letters to arrive, but it was important that he did not stop writing. He missed his parents very much, and hoped that they continued to be in good health. But once the semester began, Malam was kept so busy with lectures and studying for examinations, that he hardly had time to feel home-sick. His housemates and co-students made sure of that.

Malam got into the full swing of student life, partying over the weekends and studying hard during the weekdays. He was used to the English climate by then but still welcomed the spring. He decided to postpone his trip to London until his last year. He wanted to earn some money during his vacation in the summer. His father had been sending him money quite generously, but he wanted to have some independence. There were a lot of pubs that were hiring students to work during the tourist season, and Malam had no problem getting a job as a bar tender. His interest in the theater came back, and he joined the drama society in his college. They put on quite a few of Shakespearean plays and Malam was contented to get small parts. His studies came before all. He also started taking part in some Sports, like soccer and badminton, the latter of which was a popular game in England at that time. He excelled in both, but did not want to take part in any competitions.

As the first year came to an end, Malam was beginning to forget the painful past. He was quite popular and made many friends. He was quite relaxed in the company of girls, but avoided dating any of them. Many of his friends had girlfriends and they knew that there were a few girls who would like to go out on dates with Malam, so they began to wonder if there was something wrong with him. Malam was aware of their feelings, but his priority was to study and graduate as soon as possible. Girls at this point would distract him from his goal. As time went by, his friends stopped bothering him about the girls. They realized that Malam was ambitious, and wanted to do his best at whatever he decided. His talent at acting was recognized, but he refused major roles. When his college pressed him to compete against other colleges in Badminton, he stopped playing badminton completely. He continued working in the pub all through summer, and put the money aside for his planned trip to visit London.

It was the summer of his third year in Cambridge when something happened to transform this serious and determined young man. He was working late in the pub one Saturday night, when one of his friends came to him and said, "See that crowded table over there. I would like to buy that beauty a drink. Could you do me a favor and ask the waitress to give her the same long drink that she is now having, and tell her that it is from a secret admirer." Malam casually looked at the table and said, "Don't you think you have tough competition here? Look at all the men around her waiting to buy her drinks." Then he heard a familiar laughter and looked back at the same table where the laughter came from. At first he could not believe his eyes. Then he left the bar and moved closer to the table. There she was, his Egyptian temptress in person. She was too busy flirting with her companions that he quickly turned back to get behind the safety of the counter. He knew that she had come to Cambridge to see him. The world was not that small for this to be a coincidence. She came to this particular pub because she knew that he was working there. If those were the reasons, why was she flirting with the others? He was not sure of his feelings. He was either angry with himself or fuming with jealousy. His friend who was still sitting at the bar saw the emotions on Malam's face. He said, "Please don't tell me that I have to compete with you too." Malam went about his job taking orders for more drinks. Then he heard her call his name. She had walked up to the bar.

"Why don't you make me my favorite drink? You know what it is." She was teasing him, which made him angrier. "No, I don't know," he retorted, "What do you want?"

"Come on Malam, give an old friend a hug. I came all the way from Cairo to see you." Then she stretched over the counter, pulled his head towards her and planted a kiss on his lips. He blushed, but his anger subsided and he smiled. He made her the same drink that she had on board the Hindu. Then he said, "Will you wait for me until my work is over?" "That is what I wanted to hear. I shall be contented and sit here all night watching you," she said seductively. But her other companions came and joined her at the bar. She knew that Malam was jealous, so she told them that she would like to be alone. She had a way with the men. They were afraid to displease her, so they went back to their table. Malam's friend who had been witnessing the scene decided to leave too, but with these parting words, "Some people have all the luck in the world, but they don't know how to appreciate it." Malam looked at Ani, winked at her and said, "I do."

It was two o'clock in the morning when Malam was able to leave. As soon as they were out on the street in the comfortable coolness of the summer morning, Malam took Ani in his arms and kissed her for a long time. When she finally managed to push him away she said, "Wow, so the sad young man is now out of his shell." He simply pulled her back to him and planted another kiss. Then still holding her, he asked, "How did you get here? Egypt is a long way away and I am sure this is not just a visit." As she guided Malam towards her place, she told him everything. She had no idea of how to run her father's business, so he wanted to send her for some education in that field. She managed to persuade him that Cambridge would be a good place for learning. After all, the main importers of Egyptian rugs were the Europeans. It was understood why she chose Cambridge. She arrived two days ago by another merchant ship, and took the same train from London to Cambridge. It was easy to get information about Malam from the lady who helped her with her lodgings, because she was the same person who helped Malam to find his. It took a day to settle down and when she went to his place, one of the residents told her where he was working. She came to the pub and was confronted by a few men, all promising to buy her drinks. She saw Malam, but decided to keep away until he saw her. They held hands like two lovers as they walked the street towards Ani's apartment. She shared the apartment with four other girls. At the door, Ani said, "Men are not forbidden to visit and I have my own room. We have a lot of catching up to do."

Malam felt that he was reborn into another world of beauty and love as he lay naked beside the also naked beautiful woman. They had made love, and there were no thoughts of the past except the present. He did not even want to think of the future. He was simply contented to have her close to him and he knew that they would be together for as long as they both remained in Cambridge. It was the same for Ani. She was satisfied to belong to him for as long as possible. She knew that Malam was a man with great qualities and respected and admired him. She was also very attracted to his good looks and lean athletic body. It did not matter to her that Malam was two years younger than her. She was confident in her own beauty and youthfulness.

Word went round the campuses that Malam had finally fallen in love. The word 'love' was never mentioned between them but Malam and Ani enjoyed being with each other completely, and where they went, envious eyes followed. They were the best-looking couple and seemed so much in love with each other. Ani attended another college which offered two years' courses. She would not get a degree, but she would earn a certificate to qualify her to start a business. Both Ani and Malam knew that Malam had another year to complete before he returned to his country. Ani would have to stay on another year. Nevertheless, after being together for a week, they decided to find an apartment on their own and move in together. It was quite easy to get a fully furnished one-bedroom apartment in Cambridge, for students came and went. Malam never mentioned Ani in his letters to his family and friends. All he mentioned was that he had moved in with another friend.

Malam had given up acting and sports to spend his precious spare time with Ani. He even stopped working in the pubs over the weekends. He had earned enough money for his plan to visit London on the summer of his last year. In fact, he had enough for both of them to spend one month in London. Ani was all for it, and when the time came, they boarded the train together with a small suitcase each. They both knew that after the time in London, the time of parting would be closing in on them. But they did not allow those thoughts to dampen their happiness of just being together. Even in the train they talked happily to each other, never letting go of each other, and kissing each other whenever their eyes met. Other passengers took it for granted that they were on their honeymoon.

They checked into an inexpensive hotel in the centre of London. They walked for hours along the Thames, and took in all the exciting sights London had to offer. They saw Big Ben, heard its chimes, and went to the historical London Tower, where the crown jewels were kept. They visited the dungeons. Sometimes they would just go into one of the parks and lay down on the grass, savoring each other's company. They never went out at night, but stayed in their room and made beautiful love. Time passed so fast that they wished it would stop. Soon they were back on the train to Cambridge.

Malam's last semester began in the fall of 1918. The First World War had come to an end. Germany was defeated and there was great rejoicing among the students. But for Malam the union with Ani was also reaching its end. Both of them could not join in the rejoicing. Without talking about it, they knew the heaviness in each others' hearts. Malam had to study hard for his finals, but at the same time, he dedicated himself completely to Ani. Soon it was Graduation Day, and Ani represented his family, to witness him going up and getting his Bachelor's Degree with honors in Business Administration. She was so proud to have been a part of this man's life for a while. She knew that it was time to say goodbye, her heart was breaking, but she had to be strong, so that he could go back in peace to his country. They both knew that although their paths crossed, different destinies awaited them. They spent their last week alone, and as much as possible in their own apartment. The last evening, after they had made passionate love, Malam lay on his side and looked sadly at Ani. He said, "My dearest, no matter where I am or what I do, I will never forget you. The time with you will be treasured in my heart." Ani stroked his face and replied, "It is the same way for me. I am thankful for the happiness we shared. It is brief, but it will last us a lifetime." Then they made love again and slept with tearful eyes, holding on to each other until the next morning.

Malam was grateful that his friends offered to help him with his luggage at the railway station. He also appreciated their understanding when they said goodbye to him, and left the couple alone to savor their last few minutes together. Left alone, they held on to each other without a word. Then when the whistle blew to announce that all passengers should start boarding, they kissed each other hard on the mouths. When Malam got into the train, he stood at the door and said, "I will always love you." That was the first and last time he professed his love to Ani. Her eyes were filled with tears as she blew him a flying kiss and replied, "I too will always love you." Then the train began to move. That was the last time Malam ever saw Ani again. As the train pulled out of the station, Malam felt a deep sadness, but he was not broken hearted. Ani had brought back meaning into his life and taught him how to love again. They had exchanged addresses without making any promises to each other. He knew that his destiny awaited him in the country of his birth.

When Malam was in London with Ani that summer, he had purchased his passage for home. This time the ship belonged to the Peninsular & Oriental Steam Navigation Company. The fare for his return journey was about four times more expensive than what the merchant ship cost. It was a little smaller than the Hindu, but could hold more passengers. The Devanha built in 1906, had accommodations for one hundred and sixty first class and eighty second class passengers. It would only make a stop at Port Said, Calcutta and Singapore before sailing on to Australia. Malam had to pay much more for this passage but it saved him the problem of boarding another vessel to Singapore. Besides that, the Devanha would take less than a month to arrive in Singapore. Malam's father had sent him enough money to make sure that his son traveled first class. As Malam approached the docks of London, he was amazed to see how many big ships were in dock. Four years ago there were more merchant ships. Now there were about four or five cruise ships from other European countries. The Devanha was one of the smallest, but its exotic magnificence made Malam excited and eager to board. Being a first class passenger, he was one of the first allowed to board, and his three heavy suitcases were also taken by a crew member and deposited into his cabin.

As before, Malam went to the highest deck with his thick winter jacket on. It was freezing cold in December, but Malam had got used to the cold English weather. From the deck, he could see the great changes in London within the four years. There were hardly any horse carriages. There were more cars and cabs carrying passengers to the docks and taking them away. He wondered if his home town would also have these changes. He still had a lingering sadness about leaving Ani, but he was looking forward to seeing his family again. He witnessed the scene below him and realized that there was poverty all over the world. There were beggar children running around begging for pennies. He felt fortunate, and hoped that he would not live to see his children in this situation. The cold was biting him, so even before all the passengers were abroad, Malam decided to retire to his cabin and check on his luggage. There was no one to wave him goodbye, and he needed some time alone to get over his painful parting from Ani. His cabin was small with a porthole. It was well furnished with a comfortable bed, a small dressing table which could also be used as a writing table, and a chair. He had a bathroom with a shower. He unpacked one of his suitcases which contained his clothes and essentials that he would use on the ship. The other two would be unpacked only when he got home.

It was late in the afternoon when the ship began to sail out of the harbor. The sea was quite rough, and remembering his first experience when he left Singapore, he decided to lie on his bed and sleep for a while. There would be time enough for exploration. Malam was tired and slept longer than he expected. He was awakened by a knock on his door, announcing that dinner was being served in the dining room for the first class passengers. He had been informed that formal attire was required each time they entered the dining room. Thus Malam was looking his best when he joined a few other passengers at his table. They introduced themselves formerly to each other. But soon, they were beginning to chat like old friends. There were six to a table. There was an elderly Chinese couple from Singapore, an Englishman, who would be getting off in Calcutta, and an Australian couple who would end their journey in New Zealand. When dinner was over, the Englishman invited Malam for a drink, but he was in no mood to socialize that night, but politely told the gentleman who was in his thirties that he would take a rain check. Malam was curious to find out the difference between first and second class, so after dinner he found his way to the lower decks of the ship. He found out that the upper cabins were for the first class and the second class passengers were in the lower desks. They had bunks instead of beds. There were all double or quadruple occupancy. There were no portholes in any of those rooms. There was a common bathroom at the end of each hallway. They sat in long tables in the dining room, which was also in one of the lower decks. Once more Malam felt grateful for his family's financial status.

Malam celebrated Christmas and New Year on a large scale with all the first class passengers. There were a few young girls, but Malam showed no interest in getting to know them. He wished that the journey would end soon. He could not wait to be among his family and friends again. When the ship docked at Port Said for half a day, Malam could not bear to get out. That place reminded him of the love he left behind in Cambridge. Instead, he spent his time playing cards with some of the crew members, read a book, and enjoyed the warmth of the Egyptian sun. He did get off at Calcutta this time, but just to feel solid ground under his feet. But as soon as he was plagued by the begging children, he ran back to the ship and stayed there until the ship sailed again. It would be just another few more days before they arrived at the docks of Singapore. He wondered if his dear friend Hamid would be there to receive him, or one of his brothers. His father never liked to drive too far. The night before the island of Singapore could be seen, Malam was unable to sleep. He wanted to witness his first tropical sunrise after four years of being away. He came out of his cabin in the early hours of the morning and sat on one of the deck chairs. Not only did he see the sun rising, he also caught the first view of Singapore. He never thought he could be so happy to be back again. He had finally returned to where he truly belonged.

He had to get back to his cabin to change and pack up his suitcase, so that the porters could start loading his luggage on to a cart, where they would be brought on land and Malam could collect them at a designated site. He rushed through, for he wanted to be on deck when the ship docked. He was amazed to see so many changes. There were just as many big ships from all over the world as there were in London. There were fewer rickshaws and more trishaws on wheels. There were also more cars bringing and taking away passengers. He looked at the big crowd of people waiting for the arrival of their loved ones. He wondered if he could recognize whoever was waiting for him, and if he himself could be recognized. He was eighteen when he left, now he was a young man of twenty two. Suddenly to his delight and surprise, he saw his parents waving frantically in his direction. His father had aged a little, but his slim mother looked the same. Then he saw someone else beside them. At first, he could not recognize him, for he had put on some weight and had grown a moustache. But as the ship finally docked and he had a much clearer view, he knew that his good friend Hamid had also come to meet him. When the passengers were allowed to get off the ship, Malam was the first on land. The reunion with his parents and best friend was emotional with lots of happy tears. When Malam said, "It is good to be home," he meant it from the bottom of his heart, and the painful farewell from Ani seemed distant.

Mr. and Mrs. Shih had driven from Malacca in their new Ford model T car, the day before, and spent the night in the Raffles Hotel, a landmark of Singapore, opened in 1886, with the legend that a tiger was shot underneath the Bar and Billiard room. It was also at the bar that the first Singapore sling was mixed. Hamid drove their old car, the Benz Velo that day to help, with the luggage and to welcome his friend. Once Malam's suitcases were collected and stored in the boot of the old car, Malam sat beside his old friend, and both cars crossed the bridge to hit the mainland of Peninsula Malaya. They stopped at a restaurant in Johore Bahru, the first town after the bridge, to have a late lunch. The conversation was light and easy. The Shihs told their son about his brothers and their family. Malam in return furnished them with details of his studies and described Cambridge and London as he saw them. There was no mention of his love life. He also said that although he enjoyed the sea voyages, he would not plan on going abroad, again unless they came up with air travel, which at the moment was a much talked about topic. When Hamid told Malam that he had married one of their mutual friends, and had a two year old son, Malam was happy for his friend. Hamid had taken over his father's business in batik printing and was doing part-time acting.

It was only when they were driving towards Malacca, did Malam bring out the subject of the dreadful past. He wanted to know how the Osmans were doing. Hamid looked at his friend and said, "I hope you have got over it." Malam replied, "Well, I am not suffering or blaming myself any more, but I cannot forget. That memory will be with me for as long as I live." Then Hamid said, "Well, Aminah's mother never recovered from her loss. She died two years later and Osman left Malacca with his children and remarried in another town outside Malacca. No one knows where they are. Osman wanted to keep it that way." Malam was quiet. Ani had taught him to accept fate and go on with the future. He was sad that Aminah's mother died of a broken heart, but he had stopped blaming himself for a long time. He shrugged off the thoughts and changed the conversation to a lighter topic, about their friends and the stage shows. Hamid said, "Four years is a long time. You will find out for yourself."

CHAPTER 5

Except for more cars on the narrow streets of Malacca, the city had not changed much, and Malam was thankful for it. However a concert hall was erected in the city center. Unlike those days when Malam was taking part in a lot of stage shows, where temporary platforms were built in and around the city, all entertaining events were now held in the hall. Most of Malam's classmates and friends were married or moved to new developing cities to find their fortune. Only a handful of his acting friends were around and they also welcomed him with open arms. They asked him to join their troop, which now had a new manager, but Malam declined. He was going to work full time for his father, whose business was extending as far as the European market. His father was now in his early fifties and would like to retire soon and enjoy his good health, spending more time with his six grandchildren. He hinted to Malam that he would be happy to have more than six. Malam purposely ignored his hint. In Europe, men got married at a later age and right now, Malam had no intention of following his brothers' footsteps of marrying in their early twenties. If he became thirty and he was still single, then he would start worrying. Right now, he was going to put the years of expensive education he had into full use.

After a week of getting accustomed to the tropical climate, Malam started working for his father. He got a driving license and his father gave him the old Benz. He was so good at his job that the business which was involved only in spices, rice and Malayan wares before, expanded to the export of raw materials like tin, rubber and palm oil to South East Asia, America and Europe. After a few months, Mr. Shih was confident that his son could run the family business on his own. He changed the name of their merchant enterprise from Shih to Shih and Son. A year later, Mr. Shih retired and left Malam alone to make all the big decisions. Malam worked hard and long. He had no time to indulge in any other activities. He started to import European products like furniture and house-ware articles. At first it did not pay off because it was too expensive, but as his business brought in other businesses from Kuala Lumpur and the new developing cities like Penang and Johore Bahru, it became stable and Malam could finally relax. Then he managed to find time for his sporting hobbies of playing Badminton and occasionally soccer. There were times when he thought fondly of Ani, but never took out her address to write to her. She must have finished her studies in Cambridge by now. She might also be as busy as he trying to run her father's business. It was a coincidence that both their parents were merchants.

By age twenty five, Malam was the most eligible bachelor in town. He was rich, good-looking and educated. Many parents eyed him for a son-in-law. Malam did go out with a few girls, but was never intimate with any of them. He was casual in his relationships, and whenever he felt that one of his dates were getting serious, he would stop seeing her. His parents started to worry. They felt that he had never gotten over the tragedy that happened seven years ago. Mr. Shih decided to have a serious talk with his son, so one night, after dinner when father and son were enjoying their pipes, Mr. Shih said, "Malam, I am not getting any younger. I would love to have your son sit on my lap sometimes." Malam smiled at his father and replied, "Dad, don't worry. I have not met the right girl yet. If it happens, you will be the first to know." "But there are so many beautiful girls waiting for your attention. The best ones will be gone before you know it," his father persisted. "If there is a girl destined for me, she will eventually appear one day." Mr. Shih knew that his son was not interested in any further conversation about the topic, so for the rest of the evening they talked about their business.

One day, Hamid showed up at Malam's office with an urgent plea, "Malam," he began, "We are looking for a character in a new play that we are putting up. We have looked around, but could find no one suitable for that part. It finally dawned on us that you fitted that part very well. It is the second leading role. It is the part of the prince who sent his best friend, the hero to bring his future wife back to him. Please tell me that you will try for the part." Malam was tempted. He had been to the concert hall a few times and watched some shows. He had contemplated on joining his old group again, but on a part-time basis. Hamid was excited, when Malam requested more information about the prince. So Hamid explained that when the prince found out that his princess fell in love with his best friend, he was furious and challenged his best friend to a fight to the death. Both killed each other finally and the princess sailed back to her land and remained a spinster all her life. When Hamid finished talking, Malam said, "Well, give me the script and I shall see if I could make it. Hopefully, I won't have to spend too much time learning it." Hamid eagerly took out the script from his bag and handed it to Malam saying, "We will be meeting tomorrow night at Abdullah's house." He left as fast as he could so that Malam had no time to change his mind. Abdullah was the director, producer and manager of the group.

After work, instead of going for a game of badminton, Malam went directly home. In the privacy of his room, he started reading the script. There were three songs that he had to sing. The first one was when he saw his princess, the second one was about his hopes for the future when his friend sailed away, and the last was when he was betrayed. He liked the singing parts, but he did have to spend more time than he wanted on memorizing the dialogue. His Malay was getting a little rusty as most of his business exchanges were in English. Nevertheless, he decided to give it a try. That night, he stayed up late memorizing some of the dialogue, so that when he went to Abdullah's house the next evening he would be prepared. He was not sure whether he would be accepted. After all, it was a long time since he acted. The last time he did any acting was in Cambridge, and it was a Shakespearean play, which was totally different from the Malay dramas. He knew that he still had a good voice but again it might not be good enough for the stage. His father heard him and was quite pleased. They were wrong to worry; their son was as normal as could be.

Abdullah, who had replaced Malam's previous manager, was very impressed by Malam's good looks, and when Malam read part of the script, he was more convinced. Then Malam was given the lyric of one of the songs that he had to sing. When he sang the first love song, Abdullah knew that the part was made for him. It did not take much to convince Malam to sign the contract. Knowing that he could still act and sing returned his love for the stage. Nevertheless, he did not want to commit himself to a long term contract. He was prepared to do only this show which will have its first opening performance in three months time. That meant every evening of practices and rehearsals, and for Malam, that was already time consuming. But he was a hard worker and he was sure he would manage that for three months and still do well at his business. He was sure that his father would step in to help in the business if things got a bit out of hand. Keen to have Malam on the team, Abdullah agreed to the short-term contract. Since he had no more time for Sports, Malam kept his athletic body in shape by running one hour every morning before going to work. He would work from nine in the morning until seven in the evening with an hour for lunch. Then after a shower and dinner at home, he would go for rehearsal at nine in the evening. The only free day he had was Sunday, which he spent quietly at home. That was his routine until the day of the show's first opening in the Concert Hall.

Word had gone round that the most eligible man in town was one of the actors in the new show. Many of Malam's previous fans were excited and tickets were sold out long before the opening day. Mr. and Mrs. Shih had bought tickets for the front row for their sons and their family. When the day finally came, Malam was excited and nervous. He had worked hard for his part, and although he was only a co-star, he would be doing some solos. He had shied away from crowds for such a long time and now he would have to face them. Knowing that his old fans would be there and that it was a full house did not help his anxiety. The performance was scheduled for Saturday evening at seven o'clock. All actors and stage hands met at the back of the Concert Hall three hours before the start. Malam sat alone in the changing room which he shared with the star of the show, and concentrated on his part, while the other actor went on stage to familiarize himself with the lighting. Malam felt that was not necessary as they had had a few rehearsals on the same stage before. It was more important for him to rid himself of every other thought and concentrate on being the broken hearted prince that night. His parents and brothers were allowed to come to his changing room to wish him good-luck. Their presence told Malam that it was almost time for the show to begin.

The first scene started with the main character teaching a group of young men the Malay art of defense called 'bersilat'. Then it was Malam's turn to make his appearance. He sat on his throne and listened to the news that his beloved princess accepted his proposal of marriage. When his servants left him alone, he was happy and started to sing his first love song. As was customary, he would look at the audience and dedicate the song to the young girls in the crowd. His eyes roamed the audience so that no one felt left out. Suddenly, his gaze was fixed on a certain face. It was surprisingly familiar and he almost lost his concentration. But he managed to pull himself together and the rest of his song was dedicated to that special girl in the audience. At first he thought, she was Ani, but as his sight got used to the dim lights, he saw that she was another person, but as beautiful as the Egyptian girl he left behind in Cambridge. Her eyes were almond shape, her lips were full, but she was much smaller and less voluptuous than Ani. Even though she was attentive and seemed to enjoy his song, there was a kind of sadness around her and Malam found that very appealing. He could not wait for his scene to be over. He would have some time before his next appearance to look at her longer from the hidden curtains.

As soon as he was off stage, he sought his friend Hamid, who was helping with the stage equipment at this particular time. They went to the side of the stage where they could see the audience without being noticed. Malam pointed at the object of his pounding heart and asked, "Who is she?" Hamid looked at the direction of his friend's pointing finger and immediately knew who she was. It was not difficult to pick out the most beautiful girl in the crowded hall. "Oh, oh," said Hamid warningly, "She arrived here a year before you came back. She has been the cause of much heartache. She is untouchable and unapproachable. She is never alone. You can see that she is flanked by her father and mother. When any man tried to get near her, he would face the angry eyes of her father, or if she was with her mother, they would just walk away." "Tell me her name," Malam pleaded, and then it was his turn to get ready for the next scene. Hamid managed to whisper, "Paini," before Malam went back on stage. The rest of his act was dedicated to Paini and his last two love songs were for her ears only. When the actors took their final bow the audience gave them a standing ovation. Malam looked hard for Paini and when he saw her, he had a flicker of hope, for her sad eyes were also looking at him. He knew then, that after all these years he had fallen in love again.

Malam could not wait to get into the changing room and he was the first one out. He was rushing out in his ordinary attire to the exit door of the hall. He had to talk to Paini, regardless of his friend's warning. But Paini had left with her parents as soon as the curtain came down and was nowhere to be seen. His friend, Hamid came to Malam who was still standing in front of the empty hall and looking sad and lost. Hamid said, "Well, I told you that she was untouchable. But if you must see her again, my wife knows a girl who is quite friendly with her. I could find out more about her through this girl. For your sake, do not be too hopeful." Malam held his friend's hand and begged, "Please do find out where she lives. She is the girl I have been waiting for." Hamid was worried about Malam. He could not bear to see his dear friend hurt again. Malam was such an intense person. However, he promised to do his best. Malam thanked him and walked to his changing room where his family was waiting to congratulate him. As soon as Mr. Shih saw his son, he knew that something had happened. However, he kept quiet about it and said instead, "That was one of the best performances of your life. We are all so proud of you." His mother hugged him, followed by his brothers and their wives. Then his nephews and nieces made him promise to sing those songs to them when they came to visit. Malam thanked all of them, and told his father that he would go for a drink with the group to celebrate their success. "Don't wait up for me," he said, "I will be back quite late."

The next day was Sunday and it was supposed to be a relaxing day for Malam. He came back late the night before, but he hardly slept. He could not get rid of the beautiful and sad girl out of his mind. He tossed and turned but sleep would not come. So he decided to go for a long run in the early hours of the morning. Normally, he would just get out of his house and run along the river. But for some reason, he decided to drive towards the country and run through the rubber plantation that his father had a share in. It was a half hour's drive and when he got there it was six in the morning. There were no rubber tappers around because it was a day of rest for them too. He was glad for the solitude.

He parked his car outside the plantation and started jogging through the rows of rubber trees. He ran for about an hour, and by the time he got back to his car he was sweating and totally exhausted. He had not brought any drinks with him, so he looked around to see if he could see any small grocery shop. He saw some small scattered huts in the distance and hoped that one of them would be a grocery shop. He drove towards those huts and saw a public well. The water in the wells was normally clean and a drink from it would refresh him for a while. So he stopped in front of the well and pulled out a pail of water. He drank some of it and washed his sweaty face with the rest of it. He heard someone shouting in Malay, "Hey, what do you think you are doing?" It came from a man who looked familiar. He was leaving the hut and approaching the well. As he came closer, Malam's heart skipped a beat. He was the man sitting beside Paini. The man continued shouting and saying, "You rich city boys can afford to waste water. That well is our means of livelihood. It is alright for you to take a drink, but to wash your face is a waste." Then he recognized Malam and apologized. Malam smiled and said, "I am sorry, but I was hot and thirsty." The older man introduced himself as Patamavenu and said, "You are a very good actor. How come you are not resting after the big performance last night?" Malam wished he could tell him the reason, but he kept quiet and said that he had to get going.

Malam's heart was rejoicing as he drove home. Fate had helped him to find his loved one. He knew where she lived, and he would drive around that area to run every morning. He was sure that fate would give them an opportunity to meet. If it did not happen soon, he would find a way to get to her. He had found the girl that he would like to spend the rest of his life with. No one could stop him, not even her father. Malam was whistling a love tune while he was showering and his father heard him. He was happy to know that his son was happy. However, he would like to know the source of the happiness. While they were breakfasting together, Mr. Shih discreetly asked, "Did you have a good time last night?" Malam answered with a nod. Then his father got a bit impatient and asked again, "Where were you when we all came to the room?" Malam looked at him and said, "Oh to check on someone, I thought I knew. I was mistaken though." His father was not satisfied and said, "You came back late last night and went running early this morning. Weren't you tired?" Malam had to give his father an answer or his father would not leave him alone. "I could not sleep because of the excitement, so I thought a run would tire me out. I shall go back to bed after breakfast." Then to change the subject, Malam continued, "By the way, we are going to perform again for the next three Saturdays consecutively. And I may decide to get back into serious acting." Then he winked at his father and said, "Of course, I shall still work full time at the office. Most of the actors have a daytime job, so all our rehearsals and practices will only be in the evenings."

Every morning before he went to work, Malam would drive to the same place and run, then he would stop for a drink at the well. For a few days, he did not see Patamavenu or his daughter. Then he decided to gather more information from Hamid about Paini and her origins. He left his house early to pick up Hamid for rehearsal. He parked the car somewhere and asked his friend, "Well did you get any information about Paini?" Hamid replied, "Oh I thought you had forgotten about her. After Saturday night, you never talked about her again." Malam nudged him and said, "Come on tell me what you know." Then Hamid told him what he had found out about the mysterious girl who broke many hearts, and was about to break the heart of his best friend.

Paini and her parents migrated from Siam two years ago. When they arrived in Malacca, they bought a fishing boat and made that their home. They also used it for commercial fishing and would be out together for days at sea. It worked well until Paini became quite sickly. Six months later, they sold the boat and bought a small hut. The father gave up fishing to be with his family, and did odd jobs like mending roof tops, painting and gardening. They also reared chickens and ducks and sold the birds and eggs to the local people around. They had spent almost all the money they brought with them for the doctor's bills for Paini. They lived quite poorly and it was a big treat for them to be able to see the opening show.

Malam digested all that quietly, but he was more determined than ever to get to know the girl of his dreams. If by the weekend, he still could not see Paini, he would certainly call at their house and ask Patamavenu's permission to court his daughter.

CHAPTER 6

Paini was born 1902 in Pataya, a fishing village in the country of Siam, now known as Thailand. Situated on a bay south of the country, with a curving coastline; it was a favorite haunt for holiday makers from Thailand and Malaya. Her father was a fisherman, who would spend days at sea to bring back a good catch for the fishing industry in Bangkok. In those days, education was considered a waste of time for girls, because they would get married at the age of sixteen and become a mother. She was the only child, because her mother was not very fertile. However, Patamavenu was contented with his only child. She was intelligent and able to learn languages from the different tourists that came to Pattaya. By the age of seven, besides her mother tongue, which was Siamese, she could speak two dialects of Chinese, Cantonese and Hokkien, Tamil, which was the dialect of South India, and last but not least, Malay. Like all girls, she learnt how to cook and sew and helped her mother in the household chores. Sometimes, when there were a lot of tourists, she and her mother would erect a food stand on the beach and sell food and drinks, to earn extra money. Paini had always been a pretty child, but her beauty became more refined as she matured. By the time that she was twelve, she was considered one of the beauties on the beach and the young bachelors were eying her for their future wife. Her parents were confident that their daughter would one day find a rich husband.

Paini's home was about a mile from the beach, and Paini had a great love for the sunsets of Pattaya. Since she was seven and allowed to go to the beach on her own, she had never missed a sunset, unless the weather was bad. She would sit on a rock with her legs folded to her chest, and savor the sun as it sank into the horizon. She pictured it as the sun going to sleep in her lover's arms. Paini was romantic, and had always imagined that one day, a prince would ride by on the beach and fall in love with her. She would be a princess, and they would build a castle on this very beach and she would never miss her sunset. There were times when she would walk with her father to his fishing boat in the early morning, and then witness the sun rising. It was just as beautiful. But she was not allowed to leave that early on her own, so she was contented with her sunsets. She had a favorite hobby, and that was collecting sea-shells. Her bedroom was full or ornaments made from these shells. She would make necklaces and bracelets which she would sell for a very cheap price to the tourists. She also made curtains out of those shells for her window and door. She had a few large shells which she painted, and kept them as decoration pieces along the wooden wall of her room. Her life was simple but not too poor. Her father earned enough money with his fishing to provide his family a good life. Paini was happy and contented with her life and her dreams. But just before she became fourteen years old, something terrible happened to change her whole life.

That day, Patamavenu did not sail out to sea because of the forecast of bad weather. Clouds were thick and the skies were dark, but it began to clear a little in the late afternoon and Paini was optimistic that she would be able to see the sunset. Her parents were not too happy when she asked them if she could go out to the beach, but she had been cooped up the whole day in the house, so thinking that the weather may turn up to be good after all, her father said, "Go, if you must, but promise to come running back as soon as the first drop of rain touches your arms." With a gleeful shout, she ran towards the beach. It was almost empty except for one or two beachcombers. There was no sign of the sun, but the sky was quite clear except for some scattered clouds. Paini looked around for some shells then climbed on her favorite rock. After sometime, she realized that it was getting late and there would be no chance of seeing the sun setting. She got off the rock and saw that she was now alone on the beach. So she quickened her steps towards home. The shortest cut was through a wooded path. She was about to reach it when she heard someone calling her name. She looked around and saw one of the village boys. She knew him as they had played together when they were children. He was sixteen and was one of the boys who were always trying to catch her attention. Banteung, the boy, had a big sea shell in his hand and said, "Look what I found. I know that you collect shells and I kept this for you." Paini was excited when she saw that it was bigger than any that she owned. She went up to him and said, "Is it really for me?" He nodded and said, "If you let me walk you home, you can have it." Paini nodded eagerly and he gave her the shell. She was admiring it so much that she was not aware of his arms around her as they took the wooded path.

They hardly took a few steps when they heard a loud thunder, followed by a heavy downpour of rain. Both began to run, but Banteung said that he knew of a place where they could shelter until the rain became lighter. Paini knew that by the time she reached home she would be completely drenched, so when the boy pointed to an old tumbling shed, she nodded and they ran towards it. The roof was leaking, but there were dry spots, so they cuddled in a dry corner to keep warm. Paini was shivering because of the cold, and the boy took advantage of it and put his arms around her. She felt comfortable and did not resist. She was admiring the shell and thinking of what she could do with it, when she felt the hands of her companion traveling her body. She was upset and pushed him away standing up at the same time. Then he pulled her down roughly and pinned her flat on her back with his weight. She was wearing a blouse and a wrap-around long skirt. He ripped her blouse and was excited by her still developing nipples. He started kissing them, while holding her hands together with one. Paini struggled to get free, but she was small and he was big and powerful. She screamed and cried, but the sound of the heavy rain drowned her voice. Then with his free hand, he loosened her skirt and pulled her panties down. He then unbuttoned his shorts and heedless of her screams, he plunged his manhood into her. Paini felt a sharp pain and stopped screaming. She was now sobbing not because of the pain, but because of what he had taken from her. When he was finished, he was still on top of her but his grip of her relaxed. With all the strength she could muster, she pulled herself out from under him, and covered her naked body with her skirt. He quickly stood, hurriedly buttoned his shorts and ran out into the rain without a backward glance.

Paini sat in the same corner for sometime sobbing and feeling ashamed and dirty. Her dreams of the future crumbled as she thought, "Where is my prince? Why didn't he rescue me?" She wished that the lightning would strike her dead and she would not have to bring back the shame to her parents. She had lost the most precious thing – her virginity. Then she saw the shell. She picked it up and threw it on the floor smashing it to fragments. She was still weeping when she heard her father's desperate voice calling her. Quickly, she looked for her panties and her torn blouse. She was completely dressed up when her father came running into the shed. He had a rain coat on and carried another in his hands. The relief of finding his daughter was so great that he did not notice her torn blouse and tear-stained face. He simply helped her put on the rain jacket and hurried her home saying, "I told your mother that you will have the common sense to seek shelter. It was not your fault that the rain came so suddenly. We have to get home now so that she will stop worrying. The rain had lessened when they left the hut. As soon as they arrived home, Paini's mother, Suji, who had already boiled hot water, hurried Paini into her room where she had prepared a tub with the now lukewarm water for her daughter to soak in. As soon as Paini came in, Suji noticed that something was wrong, and her fears were confirmed when she helped Paini to undress and saw the torn blouse and blood-stained panties. All Paini could mutter was "I am sorry." Suji tried to control her trembling voice when she asked,

"What happened?" Paini just stepped into the tin tub and buried her face in her hands and began to sob. Suji too started crying which brought Patamavenu running into the room when he heard the weeping females. Paini did not attempt to hide her naked body from her father. She was no more a virgin, but he threw a towel on top of her and asked, "What's wrong?" Suji just continued to cry and Paini felt that she had to tell the truth of what happened.

Patamavenu was so beside himself with fury that he rushed out of the house to confront and beat the boy to death. But before he went further than a few steps, his senses returned and he realized that his daughter's reputation was at stake. The boy would deny that it was a rape. After all, Paini did go with him into the shelter. He returned to his house a broken man. All the hopes they had for Paini shattered. Paini was dressed in clean clothes and sitting at the table with her mother when he came back. The sight of his pathetic daughter brought tears to his eyes. He had to be strong for her sake, so he went to her, pulled her out of the chair and hugged her saying, "I will always love you and I shall protect you with my life." His wife did the same thing, and Paini felt that she was lucky to have such wonderful parents. She was not seen again alone on the beach. She missed her sunsets and stayed away from friends. She became a recluse and kept herself to the confinement of her house. Then when she did not have any periods for three months, she knew that she was pregnant. She tried to hide it from her parents, but when she started to nauseate and vomit, her mother knew that something was terribly wrong. She confronted Paini with it. "You have to tell me the truth. Have you been missing your periods?" She demanded. Paini nodded and began weeping and saying, "I don't want the baby. Please help me to get rid of it." Her mother held her child and said, "Let us wait until your father comes home from his fishing trip. He will know what to do. Meanwhile, don't do anything foolish. We are with you all the way." Paini stopped crying and said, "My stomach is starting to show and if anyone sees me, they will know." "Hush, it is only your imagination. Your father will be home in two days time. Then everything will be alright." For the next two days, Paini stayed indoors and cried on and off. Then finally her father came home. He was devastated with the news, but like his wife, he supported his daughter and agreed that they should find a way to get rid of the baby.

Patamavenu tried as much as possible to be discreet with his investigations of someone who did abortions. He found a lady, who was also a mid-wife and who had aborted some unwanted children before. She was a very private person, so he was sure that Paini's reputation would not be soiled. Her fee was reasonable and she would come to their house in the middle of the night. That evening while awaiting her arrival, Paini's mother put lots of clean sheets on the dining table where the operation would be performed. She had lots of clean towels ready and began boiling water in as many pots as she could find. The lady knocked on the door close to midnight and was glad that everything was prepared as she had instructed. Paini had wrapped herself up in a light colored sheet and stood nervously as the mid-wife examined her stomach. Then she said, "This will be more difficult than I thought. She is quite advanced in her pregnancy. If the embryo is about two months old, it is easy, but with a fetus that is over three months there may be complications. Before I do anything, I would like all three of you to think about it." Paini was desperate and said, "I don't care. I just want to end this pregnancy." Then Patamavenu asked the lady, "What kind of complications are you talking about?" "Well, your daughter may bleed to death or her womb may be destroyed forever." The answer shocked him and he was ready to dismiss the lady when his wife intervened and said, "You mentioned 'may be'. There is a chance that it may work out well." The lady simply said, "May be." Then Patamavenu told the lady to go into Paini's room while the three of them discuss the situation.

When all three of them were alone, Paini said, "I would rather die than carry the shame in my womb and to see it for the rest of my life." Her father tried to reason with her that they could never forgive themselves if they lost her. She looked at both her parents and said with determination, "If you do not allow me to have the abortion this way. I swear that I will find my own way to get rid of the unwanted being in my body." Their daughter was normally very obedient, and this outburst of rebellion left them speechless. Then Patamavenu regained control and said, "Well, you have always been very strong. You have never ever been ill except for minor colds and the normal childhood diseases like chicken pox and mumps. Let us pray that your strength will help you through this. But believe me if you die, we will die with you."

The lady was summoned and nothing more was said except that they were prepared to risk the complications. The lady instructed Suji to heat up one of the bigger pots of water and then they should both leave the room. Paini was told to lie on her back on the table with her buttock at the edge of the table. The steaming pot of hot water was placed on the chair beside the table. The mid-wife, unwrapped the bundle she brought with her. She took out a long shining instrument with a hooked end. She dipped that into the water and instructed Paini to bring her knees to her chest thus exposing her genitals completely. Then she rolled a small towel tightly and told Paini to bite into it. Then as she started pressing her stomach, she said, "It is going to be very painful and if you scream your parents would come running out and things would go out of hand. Besides, we don't want the neighbors or anyone outside this house to know what is going on. Do you understand?" Paini just nodded. Then she felt something warm entering her body and she would have screamed if her mouth was free. The pain was excruciating as she felt the lady moving the instrument inside her. She clenched her fists so hard that her fingernails pressed into her flesh and made her palms bleed. Then she was unconscious.

She woke up in her room the next morning and felt great pain inside her. Suji shouted for her husband when she saw her daughter opening her eyes. He came running in and hugged her. Both her parents had not slept a wink, even though the mid-wife told them that she was alright. The abortion went well, but Paini had lost a lot of blood and should lie in bed for a few days. She had given them some herbs to boil. The herbs should help with the pain. Even though she was suffering, Paini put on a brave front and smiled at her parents. Then her mother immediately brought in a cup of the herbal drink and said, "Drink this child. Everything is going to be fine again." Paini had difficulty to sit up, but she did not want her parents to see her pain so she drank the tea and went back to sleep almost immediately. Patamavenu and his wife never left the house for as long as their daughter was convalescing. It was on the fourth day after the abortion that Paini felt strong enough to get up and walk. She still felt some pain, but she kept it to herself.

Their lives became normal again. Patamavenu went out on his fishing boat and Paini and her mother did their normal chores. However, Paini was never anywhere alone. She was accompanied by her mother wherever she went. She had a few girlfriends who had not seen her for a long time and missed her. When they saw her at the market with her mother, they asked her, "What have you been doing all this time? We have not seen you on the beach for ages." Paini answered, "I was not feeling well, and besides, there are lots of things to do in the house." The tourist season was approaching and Paini had the excuse that she was making more beads to sell. That was a lie, for Paini had lost all interest in any form of shells. Anyway, Suji invited the girls to come over to their house anytime they wanted to see Paini. She wanted Paini to lead a normal life again. All went well until one day, when Paini and her mother went to the beach to await the return of Patamavenu, who had been away at sea for a longer time than normal. When Paini saw her father's boat pulling in, she ran to greet him. Just before she reached him, she felt a sharp pain in her stomach and suddenly blood began to drip through her underwear. She clutched her stomach in pain and started rolling on the sand. Her mother saw her daughter's agony, and reached her as her husband got off the boat and instructed his co-fishermen to finish anchoring the boat. He ran to his wife and daughter. He was shocked to see the amount of blood staining her skirt. That day, there were quite a few people on the beach. One of them had a push cart with him. When he saw what was happening, he brought his cart to the distraught family and said, "Use this and push her to the clinic." The clinic was about two miles away from the beach. Patamavenu thanked the man, carried his daughter and put her into the cart. Then telling his wife to go home, he ran as fast as he could, dragging the cart along the sand. Paini was groaning in agony and the bumps increased the flow of blood.

Paini was half sitting and half lying in her own pool of blood. The nurses at the clinic wasted no time in unburdening the exhausted man of his daughter. Paini was taken to the emergency room and was examined by the doctor. The doctor managed to stop the bleeding, but he had to send Paini to a hospital nearby for further treatment. An ambulance came and took the almost unconscious Paini and her father to the village hospital. Patamavenu waited outside the examination room, while a doctor examined his daughter. The doctor came out after about an hour and said, "Did your daughter have a recent abortion?" Sadly Patamavenu nodded. Then the doctor continued to say, "Well, I am afraid that we have to do an immediate surgery on her. Her womb is badly infected and it has to be removed or she will die. We cannot wait too long. I need your permission to go ahead right now." Patamavenu could only nod. He had no strength left in him to make any enquiries. He just wanted his daughter to live. The doctor then told him that the operation will take a few hours but his daughter's condition was now stable. They had stopped the bleeding completely, and that removal of the womb did not involve too much risk. But before he turned to go back to his patient, he asked Patamavenu, "You know what that means? Your daughter will never be able to conceive again."

Paini was in hospital for three weeks. Suji visited her everyday and her father came whenever he was not at sea. Somehow none of her girlfriends showed up. One day while Suji was shopping for some groceries, she met one of the girls and said, "Hi, why don't you go and visit Paini. She is feeling much better and would be happy to see you." The girl looked at the mother and said rudely, "I don't want to have anything to do with an immoral girl." She left Paini's mother in tears. The scene on the beach was witnessed by so many, that they came to the conclusion that Paini was bleeding because she had a miscarriage. They had tried to save her reputation, but now the rumors were worse than rape. Her daughter would never be able to lead a normal life again. It was not enough that she could never be a mother for as long as she lived, she would be shunned all her life. She wished that her husband would come back soon. She could not leave her house anymore except to visit her daughter in the hospital. At whatever cost, she must protect Paini from hearing the rumors. It will kill her.

Patamavenu came back a few days before Paini was dismissed from the hospital. When his wife told him what she heard, he was furious. He could not believe that his daughter's suffering did not end at the hospital. She was the innocent victim of a sixteen year old boy out for a good time, and now she was the victim of gossip. There was no future for her anymore. No man would marry a childless woman. His heart went to his daughter. He had vowed to protect her and he would. The night before Paini came home he told his wife, "We will leave this place and go far away where no one knows us. I have counted our savings, and we will have enough to cross the border to Malaya and start a new life there. We shall settle in Malacca and hopefully, I will be able to continue fishing. If not, I will take any job I can get. I will provide for you and Paini." His wife listened quietly. Her parents had died and she was the only child. This was the only family she had. She too wanted to protect her daughter. Her silence was enough for her husband to know that she agreed to his decision. They would leave as soon as Paini was strong enough.

When they told Paini of their plans, she too was agreeable. Although she was never told of the rumors, she knew that something was not right. Otherwise, her friends would have visited her. She was glad to get away from the beach and village of her birth, for they held too many painful memories. Paini was strong enough to make the journey after staying at home for a month. Patamavenu sold his fishing boat at a good price, but they lost some money on the sale of their house. They packed only what they needed, for they were traveling by train across the border. They would have to change trains quite often and also spend nights in some other villages or towns. It would take almost a week for them to get to Malacca. On the last evening before their tedious journey, Paini went to her father and said, "Father please come with me to the beach. I would like to see my beloved sunset for the last time." Not only did Patamvenu accompany her, her mother came along. They sat long on the beach until the sun went down into the horizon. It was the most beautiful sunset that Paini ever saw. In her heart she said, "Goodbye dear Prince. I am not worthy of you." As the three of them went back to their house for the last time, they were all crying in their hearts. But they willed themselves to leave the past and look forward to the future in another country.

CHAPTER 7

On the evening of the second performance, the concert hall was just as crowded. There were some who came again and there were many from out of town. They had heard of how good the show was. In fact, tickets were already sold out for the next two performances. It was another great repeat and amidst the applause, all Malam could think of, was his plan to meet Paini the next day. He had been at the well even on the morning of the show and had no opportunity to see her. So he had decided that he would not run on Sunday, but dress up in his best casual attire and visit her house. He hoped that his courage will not let him down. So after the show, he excused himself and went home immediately. He wanted to look his best and not tired and sleepy for the visit. He would go there after breakfast. That night, his sleep was filled with dreams of Paini in his arms and the beautiful love songs they sang to each other. He got up early that morning feeling optimistic. When he came down to breakfast fully dressed, his parents looked surprised. Malam had also decided to tell his father of his intentions.

"Father," he began as he sat down, "I have fallen in love with a girl. I only saw her once, but I know for sure that she is the one I have been waiting for." His mother was all ears and asked eagerly, "Who is she? Where did you meet her?" Mr. Shih looked thoughtful, and before Malam could answer his mother's questions, he said quietly, "It was the same girl that you ran to meet after the opening show. How could you be in love with someone you haven't even talked to?" "I don't know how, but she has captured my heart with her sad and attractive eyes. I have lost a lot of sleep because of her. I had tried to see her for the whole of last week by running close to her place. But she never came out of the house. So I have to make a definite move today. I am going to call on her and ask her father's permission to court her." Mr. Shih knew that his son would do what he intended no matter what he said, so he advised his son, "Just be prepared for a rejection. I have a strong suspicion of who she is, and if I am right, her father will not let you get near her." Mrs. Shih looked at her husband with questioning eyes and he told her, "I think our son, like all the other young men, has fallen blindly in love with the new beauty from Siam. I heard that she is only sixteen years old and her parents never allowed any man near her."

Malam had heard enough. He got up, hardly touching his breakfast, and drove to challenge fate. He stopped at a distance and looked at the shabby hut, which was Paini's home. He felt such great compassion that he was more determined than ever to complete his mission. He put on the gear and drove right in front of the hut. He got out of the car and the door opened before he could knock at it. It was the mother and behind her and in the shadows stood the object of his dreams. The mother asked in Malay, "What can I do for you?" Malam just looked behind her and whispered, "Paini." The mother banged the door shut immediately and told him to go away. Malam insisted, "I would like to speak to Mr. Patamavenu." On hearing her husband's name, the woman opened the door again and said, "Who are you? My husband is not in and will be back in a few hours. If you want to see him, come back later." This time Malam put his foot between the door and the doorway and said, "Can I have a word with Paini?" Paini moved into the light and stood beside her mother. When Malam saw her in the light, he could not believe that she was more beautiful than his Egyptian lover. Shyly, she said, "You are the prince." Malam was overjoyed to hear her voice and to know that she recognized him. He said, "Yes, I am the prince who has come to take his princess away." Paini felt that she was going to faint for the dream that she gave up long ago is back. The mother noticed that her daughter was in a state of shock. She pushed Malam away from the door and banged it shut, shouting, "Don't you ever come here again or you will face my husband's wrath!"

Malam kept banging on the door, but there was no sound from inside. Some neighbors came out of their house to check on the commotion. Malam felt hostile eyes on him. Rejected and broken-hearted he went back to his car. Tears were beginning to gather in his eyes as he drove off. Then his strength returned and he decided to wait in the distance for the return of the father. He must try once more. His happiness lay in Paini's hands. She was the most beautiful girl he had ever seen. He once thought that no one could be more beautiful than Ani, but he was wrong. Paini was small and petite, with straight black hair combed back and held together by a rubber band. Her skin was almost as dark as his. Her almond shaped eyes were well placed to flank a small impish nose. Her unpainted lips were well shaped and Malam was sure that they could produce the most wonderful smile, if she did not look so sad. For a moment, when she looked at him, he had seen her eyes shining with appreciation for him. He felt that given a chance, she would love him as much as he now loved her. It was hot in the car, but Malam waited patiently. After an hour's wait, he decided to drive around the area, but as he started the car he saw Patamavenu pulling a cart full of sacks toward his home. Malam waited until he entered the hut. Then he drove back to the hut and knocked on the door again. He did not want to give the wife time to tell the husband of his earlier visit. Patamavenu opened the door and looked wearily at Malam. Recognizing him, Patamavenu smiled and extended his hand. Before he could greet Malam, his wife pulled him inside and shut the door. Malam heard her talking to him in Siamese and after a few grunts Patamavenu opened the door again. This time he looked angry and said, "You were told to go away. Why did you come back?" He was going to shut the door, but Malam put out his hand and held the door. "I want to have a chance to get to know your daughter. My intentions are good," Malam pleaded. But Patamavenu shook his head and said, "My daughter does not want to see anyone. Goodbye and don't come back." He banged the door shut and the devastated Malam had no other choice but to return home.

Mr. Shih saw the first signs of another break-down when his son returned home and went into his room without saying a word. Then when it was time for lunch, Malam claimed that he was not hungry and remained in his room, his father got worried. He was not going to allow his son to get deeper into depression, so he went to Malam's room and knocked on the door. Malam answered the knock with, "Leave me alone." Mr. Shih was adamant and knocked harder saying, "You are a grown man now. Behave like one and let me in." Reluctantly, Malam opened the door and went under the blanket. Mr. Shih sat on the bed and pulled the blanket down. He said, "I know that you have been rejected. But I also know that if you want, you can accept the rejection like a man. You have come a long way and the future looks very bright for you. You have told me once that the right girl will come one day. Obviously, she is not the right girl." Malam sat up angrily and retorted, "She is the right girl. She was not even given a chance to talk to me. Why do parents always interfere and think that they know what is right or wrong for their child. Well like you said, I am a man now and I know what is right or wrong for me. I want Paini and I will find a way to get to her, even if I have to beat her father down. He had no right to keep her away from me." Mr. Shih saw his son's anguish and felt that this was the time to repay the wrong he had done many years ago. "I have heard from a very reliable source that something happened to them in Siam, and that is why they had to leave and find a new home here," he explained. Noticing that his son was paying attention to his words, he continued, "They tried to start a new life and maybe it is just too soon for them to get into any involvement. After all, she is only sixteen. Give them some more time to settle down." Seeing that he had pacified his son, he got up and left.

That day Malam never left his room. All day his parents could hear melancholy songs from his record player. When he did not come down for dinner his mother brought the food up to his room. He had not locked the door after his father left. So when he heard a knock he said, "Come in." Mrs. Shih too decided to talk to her son. So she set the food on the table and sat beside him on the bed and said, "Son, I know what love is. It is very painful when it is not reciprocated. But in this case, the girl is too young to make her own decisions. I am sure that if she has a chance, she will fall in love with you. Don't feel sad, just be patient. Now please eat your food before it gets cold." Then she left the room. Malam thought over what his parents said and decided that they were right. He shook off his melancholy and ate the food hungrily. He was not going to put his parents in the same dilemma as he did many years ago. He would be patient and if they were meant to be together, fate would find a way to bring them together.

Malam did not go for a run the next morning. His parents were glad to see him cheerfully eating his breakfast and then drove off to work. He was not going to let his heart control his mind, so he put a lot of effort into his work and the rehearsals for the next two shows. He had also decided that he would continue to be part of the acting crew for future plays. That would keep him busy, but that did not mean that he had given up on Paini. He was not getting any younger, but he would wait until she was ready to be courted. He still had fond memories of Ani and wondered how she was doing. She could be married by now. With that thought in mind, he looked for her address. He had kept it somewhere in his bedroom, and it took him a few days before he found it tugged snugly in his old wallet. He decided to send her a letter. He kept it simple and short. By that time, the postal services had improved, and his letter would take about two weeks to arrive in Egypt. He felt better after sending the letter off. He was sure that Ani would be a good listener and help him with his longing for Paini.

Malam's business expanded and his acting career was also at its peak. He was getting more and more lead roles, but whenever he was approached by the film industry, he declined. He was happy to be a business man like his father and forefathers. Two months passed by since Malam wrote to Ani, and he gave up on her thinking that she must be happily married, and that the past should remain the past as far as she was concerned. But one day, he received a letter from Egypt. He saw that it was not Ani's handwriting. With trembling fingers he tore open the envelope and read the contents.

It was written by a woman. The contents of the letter were as follows: Dear Malam, I made a promise to Ani to let you know about her only if you tried to contact her. Thus, I felt it my duty to read your letter to her and to let you know that Ani passed away a month after she returned from England. She had a terminal disease, and she knew that she had not more than two years to live before she went to Cambridge. She wanted me to let you know that you have made her the happiest woman during the last days of her life. She died on March 20th 1921. Yours sincerely, Naira.

Malam's eyes swelled with tears. He could not believe that he had been so blind. If only he had known, he would have stayed on with her until the end. He had loved her and still did in a very special way. Now, he knew why Ani never talked about the future and discreetly made sure that he too never brought it up. She was a brave girl and he felt that he did not deserve the short period of happiness she gave him. He could not explain to himself why he avoided writing to her earlier. Maybe he was afraid of being hurt himself. He knew that men were waiting in line for her favors, and without him around she might indulge them. He hated himself if jealousy was the cause of his silence. Then he reread the letter, and felt forgiven for Ani mentioned that he did make her happy for the short period. Fate did bring them together for a reason, he thought to himself. Ani had sought him to love, and he had loved her and made her happy. He would mourn for her quietly in his heart and she would be in his memory for as along as he lived. Life must go on. Ani expected that of him and he would not let her down. He went to the bathroom, washed his face, looked into the mirror and said, "Rest in peace my dearest lover and friend."

The relationship with Ani was Malam's secret. He mourned for her, but he did not show it. He went about his normal routine, work, acting and occasionally some Sports. He had stopped his morning jogging since the day he was rejected by Paini's parents. Neither Paini nor her parents ever showed up at the concert hall again, and Malam never saw her again, but he secretly pined for her and knew that he still loved her. He celebrated his twenty-sixth birthday quietly with his family. He enjoyed playing with his nephews and nieces and they all loved him. His brothers and their wives gently hinted that Malam would be a good father but Malam smiled and said, "Why, isn't being a good uncle enough?" Then he laughed and continued, "Don't worry, I will get married someday." Mr. Shih was getting worried about his son. He knew that Malam was still hoping to make Paini his wife. He was afraid that his youngest son would remain a bachelor. To everyone Malam seemed normal, but he detected sadness within his son. He felt that it was time for him to do something.

He made some investigations and found out that Patamavenu was having difficulty getting odd jobs. He was not a young man and his health was failing him. His wife and daughter helped him by cleaning houses cheaply. Mr. Shih had an idea, but he had to talk to his friend who owned the plantation, of which he was a share holder. So on a Sunday morning, he went to the owner's house and said, "Mr. Lee, you once mentioned to me that your superintendent was getting lazy and not doing a good job. Why don't you sack him and reinstate someone else?" Mr. Lee who had always liked and admired Mr. Shih replied, "If you have someone good in mind, I don't mind giving him a try." Mr. Shih nodded and said, "You will also be doing me a favor. I don't know him as a person, but I know he is hard working. He has suffered a lot in the past. I am sure that if you offer him this job, he will appreciate you and work hard." Mr. Lee asked, "Who is it and why will I be doing you a favor?" "Well," Mr. Shih replied, "It is personal, but one day you will understand. All I can do now is beg you to give him a chance. He and his family migrated from Siam three years ago. He was a fisherman then and tried to continue his profession here. But somehow that did not work out, and he had been doing a lot of odd jobs to keep his family going. I feel it is time for them all to have a better life." Mr. Lee was convinced and said that if Mr. Shih would send him to the estate the next day, he would talk to the man. Mr. Shih thanked his friend, and said that the man lived just outside the plantation and his name was Patamavenu.

That same day, while Malam was at work, Mr. Shih went to Hamid's small shop and told Hamid to take Patamavenu to see Mr. Lee at the office of the Lee Plantation. Hamid was told to say that Mr. Lee was looking for a worker and had heard that Patamavenu was looking for jobs. Hamid smiled and said, "I wished I had a father like you. But how would this help Malam get to his true love?" Mr. Shih winked and said, "This is the beginning of my strategy." Although Malam never talked to Hamid again about Paini, Hamid knew that his best friend was still pining away secretly. He too suspected that if Malam could not marry Paini, he would be a bachelor all his life. Early the next morning, Hamid took a rickshaw and went to the humble home of the Patamavenus. He felt sorry for the condition of the hut. It was the most broken-down in the neighborhood. He gently knocked on the door afraid that a harder one would break it. A tired-looking man opened the door and gruffly asked, "What do you want?" Hamid cleared his throat, and said, pointing in the direction of the plantation, "A friend of mine, who owned that plantation over there, would like you to work for him". Patamavenu's face looked happy for a moment and then he looked suspicious and asked warily, "Why me?" "Well, word went round that you were looking for jobs. And the people you worked with said that you are a good worker." "When does he want to see me?" Patamavenu asked eagerly. "Right now. Get changed and the rickshaw will take us both there. No more questions were asked. Patamavenu were ready in a few minutes. When he opened the door to come out, Hamid saw Paini in the shadows, and said to himself, "You are the luckiest girl alive, but you don't know it."

When Mr. Lee saw and talked to Patamavenu, he was impressed. From his physique, Mr. Lee could see that he had worked hard all his life. His answers to the questions Mr. Lee asked were short and honest. For a Siamese, his Malay was excellent and his knowledge of the Tamil language was a bonus. Most of the rubber tappers migrated from Southern India and could hardly speak Malay. Unlike the previous supervisor, Patamavenu would be able to give them clear and precise instructions in their own language, Mr. Lee could also detect the integrity and determination of the man. He had an unusual air of authority that would gain the respect of the laborers. Patamavenu could not believe that his job was to supervise the rubber tappers and to check on ailing trees. Then the pay that was mentioned was beyond his dream. Finally, he would be able to repair their crumbling hut, and his wife and daughter could stop cleaning other people's houses for so little money. He was so grateful that Mr. Lee was touched. Then, Mr. Lee said, "Well as supervisor, you will be staying in the house across this office." Mr. Lee pointed to a wooden and newly painted house with tiles on the roof. Patamavenu could not believe his good fortune. He vowed to work so hard that his new boss would not regret his kindness. Patamavenu was speechless, when Mr. Lee said he should start work the next day and by the weekend, he should start moving into the house. Hamid witnessed the whole interview, but he was sworn to secrecy. He was not to mention a word of this to Malam.

When the rickshaw pulled in front of the hut Patamavenu jumped off forgetting to thank Hamid, for he was so excited to break the good news to his family. Hamid was understanding, so he smiled to himself and told the rickshaw man to take him directly to his shop. He did not know what plans Mr. Shih had in mind, but he was glad for the poor family. If only he knew more about the family, and why they would not allow their daughter to talk to any man, he might be able to help his love-sick friend. Then, he thought to himself, "Well, Patamavenu now knows me. I will offer to help them move this weekend. I shall bring my wife along and that way, they will not think that I am another bachelor chasing after his daughter." That way, he and his wife would be their friends and in good time they would find out more about their past. He knew that Paini did associate with some girls, but as their financial situation got worse, she gave up their company to help her parents earn money. He wondered if Patamavenu and his wife had any friends at all. No one seemed to know much about them. Well, it was not only for Malam that Hamid decided to befriend the Patamavenus, it was also because he felt they needed friends.

Meanwhile, Patamavenu was hugging his wife and daughter saying, "All our troubles are over. A good man has just offered me a job with a salary that I had never ever earned before. Our ancestors have not forsaken us after all." There were tears in their eyes as he told them about the interview and about their new home. He also said, "I shall start work tomorrow morning, but I want you both to stay home and pack up everything, so that we can move into the cottage on Sunday. You need not go out to work anymore. We shall keep the house; because it is too run down to sell. It is also good to know that we have a house to return to in case something goes wrong." Paini was overjoyed. She realized that with the pay that her father will be getting, she can learn a new trade. Some of her girlfriends before had asked her to join them in the tailoring school. At that time, even though the fee was minimal, her parents could not afford it. Now she said with shining eyes, "Can I go to the sewing classes?" Her mother happily said, "Sure and if your father allows it, I may join you." Patamavenu laughed and said, "Of course, but please wait until I get my first pay. That night, they slaughtered one of their chickens and had a wonderful meal. Paini went to bed happily, but got up from a terrible dream. She dreamt of her prince on the beach, only this time the prince was in the form of Malam. He was coming to her, but a big black cloud carried him away and dirt started falling on her. Her happiness was short-lived. The dream was a reminder of her inability to be a mother and that she would never find the prince of her dreams again.

Patamavenu was at the office long before it was opened. Then Mr. Lee's assistant arrived and he walked with Patamavenu through the big rubber plantation, introducing him as the new supervisor to all the tappers that were already at work. Most of them were women in saris. The assistant also advised Patamavenu on how to check the trees to see if they were ready to produce latex, and to detect trees that were rotting. Patamavenu was a good listener and when he talked to the workers, it was obvious that they all liked and respected him. He spent twelve hours that day, watching the tappers at work and checking as many trees as he could. It was hard work, but he liked the responsibility. He went home that night tired but happy. For the next few days, he worked just as many hours and Mr. Lee's assistant had a good report for him when Mr. Lee showed up at the end of the week. Mr. Lee did not know what connection there was between Mr. Shih and his new supervisor, but he was thankful to his friend. Mr. Shih also turned up that Saturday at the office to find out how things were and to make a proposition. He was glad that Mr. Lee was satisfied with the new employee. He wanted to buy more shares in the estate and Mr. Lee was willing to comply. Both were good business men, and Mr. Lee had heard that Mr. Shih's youngest son was a very successful young man. He was more than willing to make Mr. Shih his partner, but the other man said, "Not right now, but maybe later."

It was Sunday and Patamavenu and his family had loaded a cartful of furniture to take the long walk to their new cottage, when Hamid showed up with his wife in an old borrowed car. He introduced his wife who was about twenty years old and was glad to see Paini talking happily to her. He knew that given the chance they could be good friends. He said, "We have come to help you move." Patamavenu, remembering that he had forgotten to thank Hamid said, "You have done enough for me. I am grateful and once we are settled, my wife, Suji and I, would like to invite you and your wife to a meal at our new home." Hamid insisted, "If you are grateful then don't refuse our help. We have borrowed this car for the sole purpose of helping you move into your new home." Patamavenu could not refuse the kind gesture and said, "Thank you." He also liked Hamid's friendly wife, Miriam. He felt that it was time for his daughter to have friends again. Using the car, the move was easy and by the evening, the Patamavenus were settled in. Hamid and his wife were invited to have dinner with them next Friday. After that, Miriam and Paini became good friends.

Paini was happy to have her own room. In their old hut, there was only one bedroom, a kitchen, and dining cum living room. Paini slept in a corner of that room. In this cottage, there were two bedrooms, a separate living room with a ceiling fan, and a kitchen large enough for a dining room. The compound was not fenced up, but there was a big clearing for them to start their own garden. It was surrounded by rubber trees and was a ten minute walk to the main office, where Patamavenu had to report every morning before his rounds, and every evening after his rounds. The only problem was to get to the town. They would have to walk about half an hour to the nearest village for their groceries, and then take a bus to the city for sewing lessons. Paini had always longed to own a bicycle, and she hoped that when her father got his first paycheck, he could buy her an old bicycle. But for the time being, Paini was more than contented with the great improvement in their living environment, and the security that her father's new job brought.

CHAPTER 8

Malam unaware of the happenings of his father's scheme and planning buried himself in his work and rehearsals. He was now a popular figure in the concert hall. Abdullah had produced a few more plays and Malam had the lead roles. The young girls were clamoring for his attentions, but Malam was not interested. He was still waiting for his loved one to show up for one of his performances. After sometime, he began to doubt if he would ever see her again. Then he became depressed which his father was quick to notice, when his son lost his appetite and became less energetic at work, and even missed some important rehearsals. The Shih family had attended every play that Malam performed and when Mr. Shih saw that Malam's heart was not in the last performance, he had to carry out his final plan. Since Patamavenu was employed, Mr. Shih had been frequenting the plantation. He introduced himself as the future partner of Mr. Lee to the supervisor, and never failed to have conversations with the man whenever he toured the plantation. By this time, they were on quite friendly terms. He decided to have a serious talk with the man about their children.

He contacted Mr. Lee and told him that if the offer was still open he would like to be his partner. When they met at the office to sign the contract, Mr. Lee jokingly said, "Your son is the most eligible bachelor in town. Why is he still single? He is good-looking and rich and he has a lot of girls to choose from." Malam's father looked at his new partner and sighed, "Well he fell in love with someone a year ago. She did not even know him, but he has made up his mind that it is either her or no one else." "I am beginning to get a clearer picture now," Mr. Lee said, "He is in love with the beautiful daughter of our supervisor. My, I can understand why. She is really something, but she does not seem to be interested in any man." Mr. Shih stood up and told his friend, "I am going to find out once and for all what the aloofness is all about." Mr. Lee wished him good luck, and Mr. Shih left the office and walked towards the rows of rubber trees.

He found Patamavenu talking to one of the laborers, and gently interrupted them, saying to the supervisor, "When you are finished, I would like to talk to you." Patamavenu quickly dismissed the laborer and followed Mr. Shih as he walked deeper into the plantation. "I hear you are doing a good job," he started to say as Patamvenu walked beside him. "But I am not here to talk about business. I hope that by now, you consider me your friend." Patamavenu nodded and said, "Yes, but I must not forget that you are one of my bosses too." "But today, I want you to forget that I am your boss. Let us talk as one man to another in friendship." Patamavenu looked puzzled but said, "Sure, what do you want to talk about?" Mr. Shih found a clearing and sat down, gesturing to the other man to do the same. They faced each other, and Mr. Shih decided to get to the point. "About a year ago, a young man came to your house to get your permission to court your daughter. Do you remember?" Patamavenu replied, "There were quite a few men who tried to see my daughter, but I remember one in particular. He was the actor. He was very insistent." "That actor is my son. He is not just any man. He had been in love with your daughter since then." Patamavenu stood up and said sadly, "I am sorry Mr. Shih, but if this is all about my daughter, I would like to end this conversation." He was ready to walk away when Mr. Shih said, "Wait, don't be angry. Just give me a reason, why you are so protective of your daughter. You will have to let her go one day." Patamavenu looked very sad and would have simply turned away, but he had to get a load off his chest, and it seemed quite easy to talk to this respected man.

He sat down again, drew a deep breath and said, "We left our home town to come here, because something terrible happened to my daughter. I don't want to go into details, but because of that, my child will never be able to conceive. She is destined to be an old maid, or if she is lucky, she may find a widower to marry who had enough children of his own. She cannot be the wife of a virile young man. She has lost that right for a normal life. I trust that this will be our secret." Mr. Shih listened and he was filled with compassion for the young girl and her parents. He stood up and shook Patamavenu's hand saying, "My lips are sealed. Thank you for telling me this." Then he walked back towards his car. His heart was heavy for his son. He too would not approve of his son's marriage to a girl who would never be able to bear his children. But how was he going to dissuade Malam from this pursuit, without telling Malam the truth.

Meanwhile, Paini had a bicycle and was already attending the tailoring school. Suji could not join her for she felt she was too old to be cycling. Paini left at eight every morning from Monday to Friday. She finished her classes at three in the afternoon, stopped for groceries, and was home by five in time to help her mother cook. She had also made a few friends with the women rubber tappers, because of her fluency in the Tamil language. She led quite a busy life and forgot all about her impairment. She seemed like a normal seventeen year old, except that her beauty was still the topic of conversation among the young men. One day, she came back happily unaware of the conversation between her father and Mr. Shih. Her father was still at work, but she had something on her mind, and she was too impatient to wait for her father. While helping her mother in the kitchen, she asked, "Mother, Miriam has invited me to see a drama this weekend. Hamid had managed to get an extra free ticket, so can I accept it?" Suji looked at her daughter's eager eyes and said, "Hopefully, your father will agree. But how are you going? It will be too late for you to cycle on your own." "Oh, Miriam said I could spend the night in their house." Paini had never spent a night without her parents, and for her to say that so easily and simply made her mother realize that she was no more a child. Suji thought to herself, "It is time that we let go. Paini must learn to survive on her own." Then she said aloud to Paini, "Don't say anything when your father comes home. Let me talk to him first." Paini smiled at her mother and continued to do her chores.

Patamavenu came back later than usual. After his conversation with Mr. Shih, he went about his duties, and then after he had reported the day's findings at the office, he went for a short stroll to think. He came to the conclusion that he should find a widower who would wed his daughter. He knew of a few, who had also shown great interest in the young girl, but they were old enough to be her father. Nevertheless, that would be a better alternative than for her to remain a spinster all her life. That would also stop the young men from pursuing her. Besides, she would be stepmother to her husband's children and would get some respect. He knew that he was getting old and she would have to fend for herself one day. He would speak to his wife about it. So after dinner, when Paini went out to visit some of her friends who lived close by, Patamavenu told his wife that they have to have a talk about Paini's future. Then Suji said, "But let me say what I have to say first." Her husband looked at her surprised. She continued, "Today Paini asked me if she could go to a play this weekend with her friends. One of them has invited her to spend the night at her place. She has also got a free ticket from a sick friend. I told her that I will discuss it with you." Her husband was about to say something, but she interrupted him. "I think we should let her go. She is now an adult, and we have to respect her show of independence. Now you can tell me what you have in mind." Patamavenu felt that not only had his daughter grown up, his wife was developing a mind of her own. He decided to keep his topic for later. Those words that came from his wife were heavy enough for the day. "Well tell her that she can go." Suji looked at him questionably, but he shrugged his shoulders and told her that he was quite tired, and would like to have an early night.

It was a happy Paini who cycled to her sewing class the next day, which was a Friday. Her friends were so glad for her. Although they had always been envious of her good looks and the attention that men paid her, they still liked her for her innocence and naivety. She was also very lively and a good talker and listener. Her multi-lingual talent was also an asset to her multi-racial friends. Paini herself wished that she had gone to a proper school and learnt some English, but it was now too late. Anyway, only a handful of the girls at the sewing school could speak English. Paini had been sewing a blouse for herself for the last few days. She worked hard that day to complete that blouse so that she could wear it for the concert on Saturday. The material was light blue with white flower prints. She had a pair of dark blue Chinese pants to go with it. Every one of her friends could see that Paini was excited, and they thought that it was because for the first time, that she was spending a night outside her home. Paini had kept a secret in her heart for a long time now. She had fallen in love with Malam the first time she saw him on stage as the prince. Then her heart was broken when he came to her house and was rudely rejected by her father. She knew that it was a hopeless love, but it would mean so much to her to be able to see him again, even if it was only from a distance.

Malam had decided that this Saturday's show would be his last performance. He told Abdullah about it, and Abdullah felt that it was a good decision. Malam had been going downhill, and Abdullah almost relieved him of the leading role, but it was too late to find a replacement. Malam also promised that he would give his best that night. When his family heard about it, they decided to come once more to the performance, although they had already seen the play on its first showing. Mr. Shih felt that it was time for his son to take a long vacation somewhere. He had promised not to talk about Paini's plight, and he was a man of his word. He knew that his son was still madly infatuated by her, and distance from Malacca might help him to recover. He would discuss the vacation with him after the show. The concert hall was not as crowded as before, but there was still some excitement among the audience, who were unaware that their favorite star would be performing for the last time. The play was a musical about a young man, who came back from the war to find his house burnt to the ground, killing his wife and two small children. He set out for revenge, and instead found love again. Malam played that young man. He had stopped looking at the audience for a long time now, but somehow, when he was singing the last song to his new love, his eyes seemed to rest on the audience, and to his joy and surprise, he saw his one true love among them. It took him a lot of self control to take the bows as calmly as he could, and when the curtain fell, he rushed out without changing his outfit. He was not going to lose her again.

He stood away from the opening doors, and partly hid behind a pillar so that no one could see him. He did not want to chance his fans pouncing on him. Then he saw Paini walking towards the bicycle stand with Miriam. He moved away from the crowd and carefully made his way to the stand without being noticed. When he was close enough, he quietly called her name, "Paini," he whispered. Miriam looked at him encouragingly, and moved away to join her husband, who was coming out to look for them. Paini was in a trance. She was face to face with her prince. Everybody disappeared in her mind. She was on her beach and her prince had come to take her away. Their eyes locked, and they moved towards each other unconsciously, but before they could touch each other, Paini woke up from her trance and tears filled her eyes. Malam said, "I love you." Paini said looking away, "Please go away. I can never be yours." Then she jumped on her bicycle and disappeared into the night. By that time, the crowd had noticed Malam, and if not for Hamid and his father, they would have been all over him. Malam, flanked by the two men who cared for him, was led back into the changing room. Her words kept on ringing in his ears. She said she could never be his. That meant that she was promised to someone else. It would have been easier for Malam if she had said that she did not love him. He did not remember getting changed and driving home. He was in the solitude of his room, and gave vent to his tears and anger. He was angry for being such a fool, for not realizing that a girl with such beauty, would have been betrothed a long time ago. But his sorrow was greater than his anger. Then, an inner strength in him seemed to surface, and he decided that he would not allow his sentiments to control his life. But he needed to get away for awhile.

The next day, it was Malam who brought up the subject of a long vacation. Mr. Shih listened to his son approvingly, as Malam said, "Father, mother, I would like to go away for a month or so, to spend some time with friends who are now living in Penang. I may tour some of the islands in that area. I heard that they are trying to make those islands into tourist resorts. I'd like to see them as they are now." His mother saw that her husband was very agreeable, so she said, "Son, all I ask of you is that you come back on your twenty-eighth birthday. We would like to celebrate that on a big scale." Mr. Shih looked at his wife and nodded, saying, "We have done that for your brothers in the past and we would like to do that for you. Go for your vacation and do not worry about the business. Chin has mentioned that he would like to get back into the family business, and I feel that this is the right time and opportunity for him." Chin was Malam's eldest brother. Malam was glad that his brother had decided to join them. He wished that Cheah the other brother would also do the same. After all, both their small businesses were not doing too well. Maybe, he would one day. Malam said, "Well, I shall brief Chin about what is going on before I leave. By the way, I hope you don't mind if I trade the old car for a faster and newer model." Mr. Shih laughed and said, "I had been wondering why you have not done that before. Ford has come out with a new Modal T. That would take you faster to Penang than this old car."

Three weeks later, Malam was ready, and packed to leave for Penang in his brand new car. He had promised his mother that he would be back before his birthday, which was in two months time. His father made sure that he had enough money to indulge in a wonderful vacation. Mr. Shih knew that his son had not got over Paini, but he had not shown signs of depression, which meant that his inborn level-headedness had taken over. He hoped that Malam would meet a nice normal girl on his vacation and bring her back to crown his birthday celebrations with an engagement. At that time, most men were married around the age of twenty five, unless they were deformed or mentally impaired. His son had everything nature could give, good looks, intelligence and much more. He was wasting his time chasing an impossible dream. As Mr. Shih said goodbye to his son, he added, "Leave the past behind, come back with a future." Malam hugged both his parents and drove off, leaving a cloud of dust behind him. His father was right. He would leave the past behind that veil of cloud and enjoy his vacation.

Malam arrived in Province Wellesley, the gateway to Penang. There he had to take a ferry across the strip of ocean to the island. It was a big ferry that also transported cars. Malam had never been to Penang before, but it reminded him so much of Malacca with big ships waiting in the harbor. Like Malacca, it was also a popular trading port in south East Asia, except here, there is much more British influence. Penang was originally named Prince of Wales and Georgetown, one of the first settlements to grow was named after King George III. Penang was also known as "Pearl of the Orient". Malam was warmly greeted by his host and friend, John Khoo, who also understood that Malam needed time to be alone. Thus Malam spent his vacation driving to the outstanding beaches and exotic sights. He also experienced some of Penang's deeper mysteries, like the Snake Temple and the Kek Lok Si Temple. According to local folklore, the Snake

Temple, dedicated to a Buddhist healer-priest, was inhabited by snakes that crawled out of the jungle on the night of the temple's completion. The snakes were still there, when Malam visited the temple. The other temple is reputed to be the most beautiful and largest temple complex in Southeast Asia. Its seven-story pagoda, over ninety feet high, was a harmonious blend of Chinese, Siamese, and Burmese architecture and craftsmanship. Malam also explored the delightful Bird Park, and Fort Cornvallis, the site of Francis Light's first landing in 1786. He knew about the romantic peak of Penang Hill, but avoided going there.

By that time, telecommunication had come a long way in Peninsular Malaya. Most offices and houses were installed with phone lines and phones. Distance did not cut contact from families and friends anymore. Thus Malam rang his parents once a week, and they were happy to know that he was well and enjoying himself on the big island of Penang. In one of the phone conversations, his father asked, "Besides all the sightseeing, are you also socializing?" From Malam's grunts he knew that his son had kept a lot to himself, so he continued to say, "Come on, do your friends and yourself a favor and go out with them." Malam did not take his father seriously, but John Khoo, who was married and had two children, had planned a party to entertain their visitor. It was the last evening before Malam would take another ferry to a small island close by. Like all his other friends, John was also puzzled that a man like Malam was still single. He felt that Malam must be very choosy, so he became quite careful in the choice of unmarried girls that he invited to the party. There was one in particular that he thought might draw Malam's interest. She had just returned from her studies in England, and was still looking around for an appropriate job. Her mother was English, and her father was a Penang-born Chinese. Physically, she had the best of both worlds. She had the sharp European features of her mother, and her father's dark hair and complexion. She was slim and tall and wore her hair shoulder length. She could be a model if she wanted to, but she had studied to be a lawyer, and that was what she would like to be. She was in her mid-twenties and still single, because at that time, men were wary of career-minded women.

Through another friend, Malam's host was able to get this girl, Gina Lee to attend the party. She was quite late, but when she arrived all eyes turned in her direction. She wore a red dress that clung to her beautiful body, and shoes to match that dress. She was the tallest girl in the room. Malam was talking to someone, and when his companion stopped talking, Malam followed his gaze and saw the object of everyone's attention. All he saw was a very attractive girl, who, aware of her beauty was flaunting it. He simply turned away as John's friend introduced her to the host and his wife. Meanwhile Malam tried to continue his conversation with his companion. But he did not get far as John came up to him with the girl and said, "Malam, there is someone I'd like you to meet. She just came back from England so I guess you both have something in common." Then he introduced them and left them alone, gesturing to Malam's companion to do the same. From a distance, she seemed to be quite artificial, but her smile was genuine and she was gorgeously beautiful. An easy flow of conversation started between them, and onlookers could see that they would make an ideal couple. Both were taller than everyone in the room, and both were elegantly good-looking.

As the lights dimmed for soft music and dancing, Malam led her to the floor, and they danced with ease and rhythm. They were still talking and laughing as they danced and Malam felt comfortable in her company. As the evening wore on, Malam had decided to skip the islands and spend the rest of his vacation in Penang. The more he got to know Gina, the more attractive he found her. Besides her beauty, she was also very intelligent. When the party was over, he and Gina went for a short stroll in the neighborhood, holding hands and finding out more about each other. Malam told her about his work and his acting career that he had ended. He avoided talking about his love life, and Gina was too intelligent to go into it. Gina told him that she studied law in Oxford University for four years, and was waiting to get into a law firm. It was not that easy because she was a woman. She would wait for a little while more, and if nothing happened, she would start her own business with the help of her parents. She too kept her love life out of the conversation. When it was time to leave, Malam walked her to her car. He opened the door for her, and before she stepped in, he planted a kiss on her lips and said, "It is already Sunday, so when do I see you again?" She put her arms around his neck and kissed him lingeringly. Then she pulled away and got into her car saying, "What about tonight?" She took out a piece of paper and pen out of the glove department of her car, and scribbled her address and phone number on it and handed it to Malam. Malam took it and smiled, "I will pick you up at seven then. Bye Gina, it was a great evening." Then she drove off in the early hours of the morning. Malam dated Gina every day after that for the next ten days, before he started for home. They had made love on many occasions, and Malam felt that he could fall in love with her. Gina was already very much in love with Malam, but for some reason, she knew that Malam was not ready for love. She would be patient, and when he invited her to come for his birthday in Malacca and spend a few days with him, she readily accepted. However, she did feel sad when he said goodbye to her on their last evening in Penang together. He would be driving home early the next morning. It was also hard for Malam to say goodbye, but knowing that they would meet again in Malacca in two weeks time, helped a little to ease the pain of parting. Maybe by then he could reciprocate her love. But first, he had to make sure that his heart was completely free of the past. He still thought of Paini occasionally, but with lesser pain.

When Paini left Malam that evening, she cycled all the way home, heedless of the dangers of the night. Her parents were shocked and were about to scold her, when her mother saw how distraught their daughter was. She sobbed and told them what happened. She finally confessed that she had loved Malam the first time she set eyes on him. Then Patamavenu intervened and said, "I think this is now the right time for us to discuss what has been in my mind for a long time." Paini looked at her father and asked tearfully, "Am I really doomed to be a spinster all my life? Is there no chance for me to live a normal life?" Suji, her mother, hugged her daughter and said, "Let us listen to what your father has to say." Patamavenu sat down wearily and begged his women to do the same. Then he said, "No, Paini, you don't have to be a spinster. But it is not fair to marry a man who is fruitful and ready to have children. You still have a chance to be a wife and mother of someone else's children. There is the shopkeeper, who I used to work for, that is looking for a wife. His wife died two years ago and left him with four children. They are between the ages of four to twelve. He had not approached me, but I have seen him looking at you. He is not a young man, but he is good and will provide for you. I am sure that if I ask him, he will be happy to wed you." Paini could not believe that her father was thinking of marrying her off to an old man. She sobbed and said, "No, I'd rather be a spinster than marry a man I don't love." Her exasperated father said, "It is not your fault that you are forever barren, but we have to accept the fact. I won't be there to provide for you forever. As your father, I command you to marry this man if he accepts my proposal." With that he dismissed her and sent her to bed crying. She cried until she could cry no more. Slowly, she began to see her father's point of view. He had supported her and protected her. It was now time to pay him back. Her happiness did not matter anymore. She would obey him like a good daughter should.

Thus, while Malam was away, Patamavenu offered the shopkeeper, his daughter's hand in marriage, confiding in him that she was medically proven to be barren. The shopkeeper, a Chinese in his late forties, was overjoyed, and promised to love and care for her for as long as he lived. He could not believe that he would marry the most beautiful girl in the village, and also one so young. He had four children from his late wife, and he was not interested in having any more. If he had his way, he would marry her immediately, but Patamavenu, wanted his daughter to have some time to get used to the idea, so the marriage was planned to take place in two months time. Meanwhile, Mr. Shih was quite fond of the supervisor, and they became good friends as time went by. When Patamavenu confided in Mr. Shih about the betrothal of his daughter to the shopkeeper, Mr. Shih agreed that it was a good idea. He knew the shopkeeper personally, and felt that he would take care of the young girl well. Thinking that all the problems between the young people were solved, he asked Patamavenu, "I shall be celebrating my son's birthday in three weeks time. I would need a lot of help with cooking and serving the guests. Do you think your wife and daughter could help out during the preparations? Miriam, Hamid's wife will be there also. Then later on in the evening, all of you should join us as invited guests." Patamavenu said, "Why not. I am sure Suji would like to get to know your wife better, and I haven't seen Hamid for sometime. I only hope that when Paini sees your son, she doesn't break down again. She has to learn to accept her fate and realize that she is now someone else's fiancée." To that Mr. Shih said, "I hope the same for my son."

CHAPTER 9

Malam was greeted joyfully by his parents. He looked well and happy, and his father secretly hoped that a woman was behind this well-being of his son. He did have to wait too long to find out, because at dinner that same evening of his return, Malam said, "Well, am I still getting a big birthday party?" "Of course," his mother replied. "Preparations have been made, and we have invited some of your father's friends and associates. It is up to you now to invite your friends. The party is scheduled for next Saturday evening." Malam looked pleased and said, "Good. Will it be too much if a friend of mine came a day before the party and spend a few days at our house. I met her in Penang and we became quite close." Mr. Shih's heart swelled with happiness, but he tried to be as calm as he could when he said, "Of course son, any friend of yours is welcome to stay as long as he or she likes. We shall prepare your brother's old room and make it beautiful enough to accommodate a princess." Malam laughed at that last sentence. Then he mentioned a few others in his list of friends. Although he would never join their troop again, he would like all his acting friends to be at the party. Then they talked about his vacation and the things he saw and did in Penang. There was something that Malam had decided to do, but he would wait until after his birthday to tell his parents. He wanted to buy a small apartment and live on his own. He felt he was too old to be living with his parents, regardless that he was still single.

Gina drove down to Malacca in her Benz, two days before the party. Mr. Shih could not believe his eyes when he saw her. His son had a good eye for girls. Besides that, she seemed so learned and polished. He was so glad he had the room renovated and beautifully furnished. She did look like a princess. Then when he saw the two young people together, he was sure that they were made for each other. Gina received a very warm welcome from the Shih family and felt almost immediately at home. Malam had kissed her affectionately and said, "Thank you for coming. You are the best birthday present, I ever had." That evening, Malam took Gina out to the most exquisite restaurant in Malacca. After that, they went to a night club and danced until the early morning hours. Gina did not go directly to her room when they came back to Malam's house. She spent the rest of the morning in Malam's room. They made love, and she slipped back into her room before anyone woke up. Malam did not go to work on Friday. Instead, he took Gina sightseeing. Gina was impressed with the historical town of Malacca, especially with the Portuguese architecture in the structure of the churches and run-down fortresses. She also liked the traditional costumes worn by Mrs. Shih and the other Nyonyas. The Baju Kebaya was worn with so much grace and feminine charm. The outfit consisted of a blouse, made of plain, sheer – almost transparent material, worn over a camisole, and pinned downwards at the front with specially decorated kerongsang, (which are actually a cross between pins and buttons), and a printed sarong (a long skirt) held in place by a beautifully designed metal belt. With the Baju Kebaya, the Nyonyas wore hand-sewn fabric slippers, embroidered with beads and silken threads. Gina decided to have the costume and slippers tailor-made for her before she left Malacca.

Malam's birthday was on Friday, and his parents wanted to spend that evening quietly with him and Gina. They had dinner at home and then listened to some music. Then Gina gave Malam his birthday present. It was a Swiss watch with his name engraved at the bottom with the words: with love, Gina. Mr. and Mrs. Shih said that their present would come the next day. Then before going to bed, Mr. Shih said, "By the way, please leave the house as early as you can tomorrow, because it will be full of helpers. We don't want you both getting in their way. Just make sure you come back in time to get ready for the party." Gina offered to help, but Mrs. Shih shook her head and said, "You will be helping us if you keep this young man away from the house tomorrow." Thus Malam decided to take Gina south towards another beach resort just outside Malacca. They too decided to retire early that night, but they both went into Gina's room. Malam spent another wonderful night with her, and when they got up, his parents were still fast asleep. Malam went into his room, ruffled his bed, and got ready to take Gina out for breakfast near the beach.

They found a beautiful and romantic spot on the beach. They went swimming and snorkeling, but most of the time just lay on the beach, under a tree to avoid the direct rays of the sun. They laughed and joked a lot with each other. Gina was lying on her back and her eyes were half shut, when she took Malam by surprise with her question, "Malam, where do we go from here?" Malam who was lying on his side with his right hand supporting his head, and looking admiringly at the beautiful girl beside him, sat up suddenly. So far he had taken everything for granted. Gina's question came too soon and too suddenly. He did not know what to say, and Gina, still with her eyes half closed continued, "I love you, but something is holding you back. Will you tell me what it is?"

Knowing that he had to give answers, Malam said, "My dearest Gina, you are right, my heart is not completely free to love you like you deserve. I had hoped that by the time I see you again, I would be free of an unreciprocated love, but somehow I cannot feel that freedom. I am very fond of you and I enjoy every minute with you. It is so easy to tell you now that I love you, but when I say it, it must be wholeheartedly, and my heart is not yet whole." Gina sat up too and touched his face saying, "My love for you is strong. I will wait for you to be ready." Then looking at her watch she said, "We had better start getting back or your mother will start worrying." Malam kissed her gently and said, "Thank you for being so understanding." Then they walked hand in hand towards the car. Onlookers looked at them admiringly and enviously. They portrayed a happy couple, madly in love with one another.

When Paini was told that she and her mother would help Mrs. Shih with the cooking, she was very reluctant to go. She knew that it would be hard to control her emotions, if she came face to face with Malam again. Nevertheless, her father convinced her that she should be strong, and remember that she was promised to be married to someone else. She felt that he was right. This was the test of her strength and acceptance of her fate. She was also prepared to go as a guest to the party. She had sewed another new dress for the occasion. It was a simple long dress, which hung loosely on her body. The material was again blue, which happened to be her favorite color, but this time without any prints. She had learnt how to apply some make-up, and as she was putting it on, she did not notice her mother entering the room. Suji looked at her daughter and thought, "She is so beautiful. Any man would be proud to be seen with her. God, please give her the strength to go through what destiny has in store for her." Then she said aloud, "Paini, Hamid is here to take us in his new car. You look beautiful." Paini smiled, but her heart was sad. Her beauty had cost her dearly. Hamid had left Miriam at the Shih's house to help Mrs. Shih with the last minute preparations. As promised, he had come to take the Patamavenus to the party. When he saw Paini, his heart went out to her. She was so beautiful and unique. He had met Gina, but Paini's innocent beauty outshined her elegance. He wished he knew why Paini and her parents would not accept Malam into her life.

Once more the party was held in the courtyard of the Shihs' residence. The weather was perfect, and the whole courtyard was colorfully lighted. Besides all the home-cooked meal, that was laid out, like chicken curry, roasted pork, different kinds of vegetables, fruits and Nyonya cakes, there was a pit to barbeque satay, pieces of meat on sticks, and a noodle stand also ready to take orders. A bar was set up in a corner of the courtyard with all kinds of alcoholic and soft drinks. There were two young men attending the bar. Tables and chairs were placed along the wall, and in the middle was an erected stage for the live band, and a space was made for dancing. There were not as many guests as there were at Malam's farewell party. Most of them were very close friends of the Shih family and Malam. By the time the first guests arrived, Malam was ready to greet them. To please his father, he wore a white shirt with a colorful tie and a pair of black pants. Gina was already in the courtyard, chatting with the bar tenders explaining to them how to mix a drink for her. She had on a light green silk cheongsam, a Chinese long dress with a high collar. The high slit at the side exposed one of her beautiful long legs. Her shoulder long hair was combed to fall on one side of her face. She was a picture of exquisite beauty. Soon the courtyard was filled with the guests, and Gina was the center of attraction among the young men. Malam was also with the guests and standing beside Gina, when he saw his friend Hamid walking in. Then there was some kind of hush, and Gina was no more the center of attraction as Paini and her parents came into view.

Malam's heart stopped beating. At first, he thought it was a flicker of his imagination. He knew that Hamid's wife Miriam was a good friend of Paini, but he could not associate the relationship between his family and her family. He also knew that his father had signed a full partnership with Mr. Lee and that they had hired a new supervisor, but he never suspected that the new supervisor was the father of his forsaken love. When he saw the guest list, none of the three names were on it, although his father did mention that he was going to invite some employees. Like everybody else, Gina too was taken aback by the young and beautiful newcomer. Then she saw Malam's reaction and her quick mind guessed that, whoever the girl was, she was the reason that Malam could not fall in love with her. She quietly moved away from Malam to observe him from a distance. Meanwhile, Paini had seen Malam looking in her direction, but she turned away quickly to go towards Miriam who was sitting with some other friends. She was flushed, but her resolve to be strong remained. Malam just stood there like a man in a trance, then his father nudged him, to say that he should begin the party by making a welcome speech. Malam got control of his emotions and went up to the podium, but not before gulping down the whisky which he had been sipping slowly before Paini's appearance. He looked calm as he stood there, and said loudly and clearly, "Dear friends and relatives, thank you for coming tonight to help me celebrate my birthday. I know that you are all eying the goodies and I could hear some stomachs growling. So, please help yourself to the food before you." He spoke first in English and then in Malay. His father had expected him to make a special announcement, but when Malam got off the stage, without saying anything more, he was very disappointed. He looked in the direction of Gina and saw that she was alone, sitting on a high stool and sipping a drink from a long glass. He too had noticed Malam's reaction when Paini walked in. He sincerely hoped that it was not a mistake to invite Patamavenu and his family. He turned his gaze towards the table where Paini and her parents were sitting, and saw that she was acting quite normal. Then when he saw his son heading towards the direction of Gina, he decided that he should concentrate on his own friends and the young people should solve their own problems.

The music had started and when Malam was close enough to Gina, he asked her, "Will you open the dance with me?" Gina smiled and answered, "Sure it is me you want?" Malam felt hurt, but took her hand and guided her to the floor. They danced for a few minutes and slowly a few couples joined them on the floor. Malam just held Gina tightly to him. They did not say anything, because both of them were deep in their own thoughts. Malam hoped that the girl in his arms was the girl in his heart, but his heart was not beating for her. Gina thought to herself, "Malam will never be free of her to love another woman." Gina buried her face in Malam's broad chest and tried to enjoy the moment with him. Her heart was breaking, but she would not settle for second best. When they stopped dancing, Malam's eyes searched for Paini, but she was gone and so were her parents. Hamid and Miriam too were not to be seen. Malam felt stupid and decided to pull himself together and concentrate on his special guest. But when he turned round to look for Gina, she was dancing with one of his bachelor friends. She was talking and laughing with him as they danced. She was never alone again after that. Either she was with a group of men or dancing with one of them. Out of politeness and hospitality, Malam danced with a few other girls, and then he sat himself at the bar and started to drink quite heavily.

Malam was still drinking when the last of his guests left. His brothers had left with their wives much earlier to return to their children. Mrs. Shih too had retired early, but Mr. Shih was still around. He wanted to talk to his son, but when he saw Gina going to him, he too went to bed. The bartenders were clearing up as Gina took a seat beside Malam and said, "You know that drinking will not drown your sorrows. Come take a walk

with me." Malam took a last gulp of the remaining whisky in his glass
and got off the high stool. He almost stumbled, but Gina held on to him.
Then she decided that Malam was too drunk to walk. Instead, she guided
him to his room and helped him on to his bed. She removed his shoes and
said, "Try to sleep now. I will see you at breakfast." She kissed him on the
forehead and left the room. Malam did not protest. He was too drunk to
care and he fell off to sleep almost immediately. He got up to a knock on
his door, but his head felt so heavy that he groaned. Then his father came
in and said, "Gina had left for Penang this morning." Malam forgetting his
headache, jumped up suddenly, "What are you talking about?" His father
looked very severe and repeated what he said. Then when the words sank
in, Malam said, "Why didn't you wake me up?" His father's serious face
was expressionless when he answered, "Well, you could have been more
considerate of her last night instead of drinking yourself to uselessness.
Anyway, she did not want us to wake you up. She has written you a letter."
Mr. Shih handed Malam an envelope and left the room without saying
another word.

Left alone, Malam continued sitting on his bed for sometime, staring at
the envelope in his hand. Then he willed himself to get off the bed and
rushed into the bathroom. He poured buckets of cold water on his head
and dressed up as quickly as possible. Then he rushed down and asked his
mother who was clearing up the breakfast table, "When did she leave?"
His mother looked at her son sadly and said, "It is too late to catch her.
She left about two hours ago. Why don't you sit and sober down with a
cup of coffee?" She handed him a steaming cup of black coffee. Malam
took it into his room and placed it on his bed-side table. Then he sat on
his bed and tore open the envelope. There was a page of carefully and
neatly written letter from Gina. He read: My dearest Malam, I wanted
to leave before you got up. This is the best way to say goodbye without
causing more complications and pain than necessary. You have never lied
to me about your feelings, and I respect you for that. I know now that as
long as you do not exploit your feelings for that beautiful girl, or pursue
her until you know that you have no chance, your heart will never be free
to love. I implore you therefore to do just that. You cannot go on living
a dream. Either you make it come true, or let it die completely. If our
destiny lies with one another, you will find a way back to me. Until then,
I send you all my love. Gina. Malam felt sad, but she was right. He was
still very much in love with Paini. He liked Gina very much and under
normal circumstances, he would have fallen in love with her and would
have asked her to be his wife. But his heart belonged to someone else. He

crumpled the letter, threw it into the wastepaper basket, and then decided to have a serious talk with his father. He had to know why Paini and her parents were at the party.

Confronted by his son, who demanded answers to his question, Mr. Shih was forced to tell his son his original scheme. However, he kept his promise to Patamavenu about Paini's condition. Malam was angry and said, "You interfered once and almost destroyed my life. Please keep out of my affairs in future. By the way, this is also the time to tell you that I shall be moving out. I have decided this sometime ago. It has nothing to do with my present feelings. I have looked at some apartments and found one that I could easily afford to buy." Mr. Shih was quiet. He also felt that it was time for his son to live on his own. But Mrs. Shih, who had been quiet all this time, intervened and said, "Son, you have no right to speak to your father this way. He did what he did because he loves you. His intentions were good, and he thought he could make up for what happened in the past." Her sudden outburst shocked both the men. Then Malam looked apologetically at his father and said, "I am sorry." His father nodded and said, "I too am sorry. But, I do not regret my actions in helping Patamavenu to get the job. He is one of the most hardworking men, and Mr. Lee is grateful for it. There is another thing you have to know, Paini is betrothed to marry in two weeks. Her fiancée is Mr. Liew Ah Sang, the widower. "What?" Malam looked shocked. "He is old enough to be her father." Then his mother intervened again, "Yes, I feel sorry for the poor girl. I too could not believe it when her mother told me. But Malam, please try to forget her and give yourself and Gina a chance. Gina was very sad when she left this morning. You will both make a wonderful couple."

When Paini saw Gina in Malam's arms she could not control herself anymore, and her father saw the signs of a breakdown, so he immediately excused himself and his family, and asked Hamid if he would be kind enough to take them home. Not only Hamid, but Miriam too saw the anguish in the eyes of both Paini and Malam. She decided to go along to comfort and talk to Paini. Once in the privacy of their cottage in the plantation, Paini's tears started to fall. Miriam accompanied her to her room and said, "It is okay to cry. I know you love Malam as much as he loves you. So why are you marrying another man. Tell me and let me help you." Paini felt that if she did not say anything now, she would die with her secret. Miriam had proved to be a good and trusting friend, so between sobs, she told Miriam what had happened to her when she was fourteen years old. Miriam listened with pain and sympathy for this young girl. No wonder her father was so protective of her. But he was wrong in saying that she could never have a normal life. Miriam knew of women who were happily married and could not conceive any children. She put her thoughts into words, "Paini, you still have a chance for your prince. You must tell him the truth. His love for you will overcome his longing for children. Malam has loved you for a long time, but you never gave him a chance. It is not too late." Paini looked sadly at Miriam and said, "It is too late. He has found a girl who is beautiful and educated. They looked like they were made for each other." Miriam shook her head and said, "Oh no, he could not take his eyes from you. You were the one who turned away from him." Paini had stopped crying, so Miriam kissed her on the forehead and said goodbye.

Paini stayed awake for a long time, and when she finally fell asleep, she dreamt of her prince again. Only this time, it ended beautifully. She managed to reach out to his extended hand, and he pulled her onto his horse, and they rode together into the sunset of Pataya Beach. It was Sunday the next morning. Patamavenu had time to sit for a long breakfast with his family. When they were drinking their coffee, Paini said, "Father, I am going to break off my engagement. You said that I cannot marry a young man because I can never beget him children. I don't think it is fair to marry someone who I can never love. I am now eighteen years old, and I think it is time I start thinking for myself." Her father was speechless with shock, whereas her mother was secretly proud of her daughter's courage. Seeing that her father was still without words, Paini continued, "I love one man, and if I cannot have him, then I will never marry." Patamavenu was about to say something when Suji, his wife, touched his hand warningly. She looked at her husband pleadingly and said, "Our daughter has been obedient and respectful to us. All she wants now is to make her own decisions. We have to respect that. You have to see Mr. Liew and break off the engagement." Patamavenu got up and said, "I can't talk now. I am going for a long walk and I hope that when I come back, you both will regain your senses." With that angry retort, he left the house and walked towards the row of rubber trees, mumbling to himself, "Women of today. Gone are the days when they obey and serve you without questions."

After the confrontation with his parents, Malam decided to run, firstly to get rid of the alcohol in his body, secondly to be close to Paini, even if he could not see her. This time, he drove his car right to the office of the plantation. He looked in the direction of the cottage and he felt the heaviness of his heart. He could not bear another rejection, so he got out of his car and started jogging away from the cottage. At first he ran slowly, then as his thoughts were filled with failure and loss, he began to jog furiously, heedless of time, distance and direction. He ran and ran until he could run no more. He felt as though his lungs were going to burst, and his legs would not carry him anymore. He bent down to gasp for air and to hold his aching side. Then when he caught his breath again, he straightened up and realized that he was no more in the plantation. He was in the jungle. He had lost the path and he was surrounded by heavy shrubs and wild trees. It was still part of the Lee's property, but this area had not yet been cleared. He did not have his watch with him, and he was not sure how long he had been running. He looked back at the direction of where he came from, and saw that the high rubber trees were quite a distance away. He could not run anymore, so he had to walk back. He had to be careful, because the tropical jungle was a habitat for dangerous and poisonous snakes. The unkempt grass and weeds were almost touching his knee and it was hard to see what crawled underneath them. He found a big stick and started to beat away the tall grass as he walked back towards civilization. Then, which was typical of the tropical weather, it began to rain without any warning.

Malam hurried his steps and decided to go in another direction. The plantation seemed nearer that way, but he would be closer to the cottage. In this case he had no choice. The rain was getting heavier and he was drenched to the skin. He started to run, but amidst the rain he heard some kind of groan. He stopped in his tracks and listened more carefully. He heard the groan again, and it was distinctly the sound of a human being. He went towards the sound but saw nothing, then he was about to go away when he heard, "Help me," in Malay. It came from under the deep slope that led into the river that provided water for the whole plantation. He was at the border of the jungle and the plantation, but he still had to go through thick shrubs towards the sound. When he found his way to the edge of the slope, he saw the twisted form of a figure lying on the bank of the river. The slope was very steep, and it would be very hard to climb down because of the rain which had caused it to be slippery. But Malam, heedless of the danger, could only see a man desperately in need of help. He began to go down with his face towards the slope and holding on to shrubs and plants. He slipped once or twice, but managed to find his footing again. Finally he was at the river bank, and he saw that it was Patamavenu. The man was wearing a sarong, which had come off his waist and was loosely spread around him. One of his legs was under him, and there was blood pouring out of his forehead. Malam went to him and asked, "Is your leg broken?" Patamavenu winced with pain when he tried to pull his leg from under him. Then Malam said, "Hold still. First I have to stop the flow of blood on your forehead. The rain is causing it to flow easily. I shall have to tear your sarong." Patamavenu could only nod. He was so close to unconsciousness due to the immense pain in his leg. Malam tore a strip off the sarong and carefully bandaged the wound on the forehead with it. Then he looked under the sarong and was shocked to see that Patamavenu's body was very twisted, and blood too were oozing out of a big gush at the shin. He said as calmly as he could, "This will hurt, but I will have to lift you up a bit and try to get your leg straightened out." There was no answer, and he thought it was better if the man had fainted. Patamavenu was quite a big man, so it took Malam a lot of effort to unpin his leg from under him without causing more damage. Then he saw something which sent shivers through his body. It was still raining heavily, and as the rain washed the blood away, Malam saw something white protruding from the shin. He knew that it was the shin bone. He looked at the man and saw that he was still unconscious. He was glad to know that he was still breathing. He had learnt some first aid when he took his driving license, so he decided to apply his knowledge as best as he could. He looked for a stick, and found one stable and quite straight. Then he placed it beside the broken leg and tore more pieces of the sarong. Then he tied the stick tightly to the leg, starting above the knee so that there was no way for the knee to bend. As he was doing this, Patamavenu regained consciousness and began to groan in great pain. Malam knew that he could not leave this man alone while he ran for help. The huts of the laborers were a long way off, so he had to carry the man. He knew that he would not be able to get up the slope, so the only way was to walk along the dangerous river bank, which was muddy and slippery. Malam looked at Patamavenu, and seeing that he was now fully conscious, explained, "Your leg is broken but I think the stick will hold it in place. I will have to carry you until we find help. You have to put your arms around my neck and hold me tightly. I shall lift you up with both my hands. Are you ready?" Patamavenu said, "I may be able to hop with my other leg if you support me." Malam shook his head and said, "You have lost a lot of blood. Now get hold of my neck." Patamavenu did as he was told, and Malam gathered him up in his arms. He felt the weight and almost stumbled, but he gathered every bit of strength he had and started walking with the man. After ten minutes, he too was at collapsing point, but thankfully, the rain stopped as suddenly as it started. He needed to rest, so he gently placed his burden on the ground, and lay beside him, breathing heavily.

Both men laid there by the river for sometime, one in great pain, and the other completely exhausted. Then Malam sat up and because the rain had stopped and the air was clear, he could see the outline of huts about ten minutes away. He thought that it would be faster if he ran for help, but when he saw Patamvenu in his anguish, he could not leave him alone. So once again he carried the man and walked towards the hut. It was easier this time without the hazard of the pouring rain, and as they approached the huts, the slope began to even out. Even before Malam reached the hut, some of the laborers had seen them and came running. They recognized their supervisor and relieved Malam of his burden. Then Malam said, "My car is at the office. Four of you should carry him, but make sure not to move that wounded leg. I will have to drive him to the hospital immediately." Then when they were at the car, Malam asked one of them to come along, and instructed the others to let his family know about the accident and that he would be in the Malacca General Hospital. Tired and drenched as he was, Malam drove fast but carefully towards the hospital. As Patamavenu was placed on the emergency bed, he held Malam's hand and said, "Thank you. I owe you my life." Malam assured him that all will be well. Then he turned to the man who accompanied them and said, "Please stay here until his family shows up. I have to get back and change out of these wet clothes. I shall come back later to check on him. Malam handed him some money and said, "Take a rickshaw home when his family arrives. Thank you for the help."

What happened was that Patamavenu, angry with his family, had decided to take a longer walk than usual. When he came to the end of the plantation, he decided to check how far the estate went into the jungle. He walked along the slope to see how far the river went. Then when it rained suddenly, he turned around to head for home, but the sudden downpour blurred his sight and he was closer to the edge of the slope. He was hurrying, when he stumbled on a protruding root, and fell headfirst down the slope. He hit his forehead on a sharp stone and fell hard. He tried to use his leg to break his fall into the unknown depth of the river, when he twisted it badly. He felt such severe pain that he was unable to do anything. He thought he was going to die, when he heard the patter of footsteps and that was when he made an effort to call out for help. He did not expect the runner to hear him through the rain. He became hopeful, when the sound of running footsteps stopped. At first he did not recognize his rescuer, but when he heard the voice, he knew it was Malam. Before he fainted, he thought to himself, "Is this my punishment for rejecting a good man and causing him so much pain?"

CHAPTER 10

Malam was not able to get back to the hospital that day. He was in a sorry state when he got home. His mother was shocked when her son walked in drenched in a mixture of water and blood. She called to her husband who was taking a short nap, although Malam wearily tried to assure her that it was not his blood. When Mr. Shih saw his son, he too was shocked and asked, "Are you alright? Did you have an accident?" Malam shook his head and said, "Let me shower and clean up, then I will tell you what happened." With that, he left his anxious and bewildered parents staring after him. After he had cleaned himself and donned dry clothes, he felt better, and knowing that his parents were impatient to know what happened he came down and joined them in the living room. He told them what happened. Before they could ask any questions, he said, "Now, I have to get back to the hospital." But as he stood up, he felt nauseous and sat down suddenly. His mother noticed it and said, "Well, there is no more running around for you. You look as pale as a sheet of white paper. Your father will go in your place. Let me help you to your room." Malam did not argue for he felt very sick and feverish. The strain of the morning's incident and the rain had taken over. His mother tucked him in his bed and felt his forehead. She said, "We have to call the doctor. You have a very high fever." Even before the doctor came, Malam was fast asleep.

Meanwhile, Mr. Shih went to the hospital. When he got there, Paini and Suji were waiting outside the operating room. They were both in tears and when they saw him, Suji ran to him and was on her knees before he could stop her. She said, "Your son saved his life. If he did not show up, the doctor said that my husband would have bled to death." Mr. Shih pulled her up and gently said, "How is he?" Then Paini, who had shyly moved towards them said, "They have to amputate his leg. It was so broken that they could not do anything more for it." Then she added, "Please thank your son for saving my father's life." Then she pulled her mother away and they sat down, and comforted each other. Mr. Shih felt that the two women wanted to be alone in their pain, so he sat in another corner and waited. He looked at Paini and realized that her beauty was not just superficial, but ran very deeply. No wonder his son was so bewitched. He saw beyond those physical good looks. Mr. Shih waited for another one and a half hours before the operating surgeon came out of the swinging door and went towards the patient's family. Mr. Shih joined them and introduced himself. The surgeon said, "Mr. Patamvenu is now stable. The operation was quite successful, but he need to rest. We are transferring him into the intensive unit so he should not have any visitors for at least twenty four hours. Please go home now and come back tomorrow." Mr. Shih offered to drive the women home. They could not refuse him. No one spoke until they arrived at the cottage in the plantation. Then Mr. Shih said, "Malam could not come because he got very sick when he came home." When they were out of the car, Paini said, "Please tell him that we will never forget his help."

When Mr. Shih arrived home the doctor had left, and his wife told him that Malam had caught a very bad cold, and should stay in bed for the next few days. Mr. Shih went into his son's room and saw that he was not asleep although his face was red and flushed with fever. "Son, we are so proud of you. The doctor said that if it was not for you, Patamavenu may not have survived. Nevertheless, his leg was so broken that they had to remove it." "Oh no!" Malam exclaimed, "How is he now." Then Mr. Shih repeated what the doctor said and added, "Paini and her mother are very grateful to you. Now, try to sleep and get well yourself." He wanted to say more, but his son was too ill at the moment. So he left the room without another word, keeping his thoughts until his son recovered from the bad cold. Meanwhile, he went downstairs and told his wife about Patamavenu's condition, and they both discussed the future of the supervisor. Mr. Shih agreed that without a leg, he would not be able to do the same job. That would also mean that they would not be able to stay in that cottage any more. It would be very hard on the family. Then Mrs. Shih came out with an idea, "We could help them to rebuild their old hut and employ Suji as a help in this house. You and I are getting old and I think it is time for us to relax and enjoy our old age. She could come in three times a week. I also hear that Paini is quite a tailor now. We have to recommend her to our friends. Together they could earn enough money to live like they are now." Mr. Shih looked at his wife approvingly, but said, "The Patamavenus are a very proud family. They would not accept our help in rebuilding their old home. We have to think of how to do it, without making them feel that they are receiving some kind of charity. Meanwhile, let us concentrate on our son getting better."

Malam's fever lasted four days, and his cold was getting better but not completely gone. However, he felt he should pay Patamavenu a visit. His father decided to go with him, and Malam was glad for the company. He did not feel well enough to confront any emotional turbulence should he come face to face with Paini. When they arrived at the hospital, they found Patamavenu alone on his bed. He was now in a long hospital room with ten male patients on each side of the wall. He tried to sit up as he saw his visitors, but Mr. Shih put a restraining hand on his shoulder and said, "No, don't get up. How do you feel today?" Patamavenu stretched out a hand to Malam. Malam grasped it in both his hands and said, "I am so sorry about your leg." "Don't be. You saved my life. I shall be forever in your debt." Malam shook his head and said, "Someone else would have done the same thing if he was in my shoes." "Oh no," Patamavenu insisted, "He would not have carried me all the way like you did. You risked your life and health for me." Then Mr. Shih intervened and said, "Get well soon and don't worry about a thing. If you need anything, just let us know. Remember we are friends, and friends help each other." Patamavenu wanted to say something, but he saw his daughter and wife approaching. Malam followed his gaze and his heart began to race as he saw Paini. She had also seen him, but kept her face down. Mr. Shih then made the first move and said, "Well we will leave you now with your loved ones. I shall come back soon and visit again." Then he guided his son towards another door to avoid the confrontation. Once outside, Mr. Shih said, "Son, there is something I have wanted to tell you. Let us go to the coffee shop over there." He pointed to the hospital cafeteria, and they went inside and ordered a cup of coffee each.

Malam was very withdrawn as Mr. Shih started to say, "I am breaking my promise by telling you this. When all this started, and I realized how madly in love you were, I tried to help you by talking to Patamavenu. He told me something in confidence which changed my mind about you and Paini." Mr. Shih did not finish talking, when they heard a voice saying in Malay, "Please let me tell him myself." The men were surprised as they saw Paini coming up to them. Both got up, and Mr. Shih immediately excused himself, saying that he would pay for the coffee and wait in the car. Paini looked at Malam and smiled sadly saying, "Shall we go for a walk?" Malam was speechless, but his heart was beginning to fill with happiness. Paini had finally approached him. He got up and they walked side by side, close to each other but not touching each other. They were quiet until they found a bench and unconsciously, both sat down at the same time. Then Malam found his voice and said, "Paini, if only you know how long I have waited for this moment." He looked at her with so much love in his eyes, and his lips were so close to hers that they almost met when she moved away and said, "Malam, I have loved you since the day you appeared on stage as the prince, but I had to run away from you because I am not worthy of you." Malam wanted to take her in his arms, but she resisted and continued, "But, I know that was wrong of me. It hurt you because you thought I rejected you. Now, it is time for me to tell you the truth." Then without shedding a tear, she told him of the incident that happened four years ago. She left no details out, and Malam listened with mounting anger at the rapist, wishing with all his heart that he could lay his hands on him right then. When Paini finished speaking, Malam pulled her up and hugged her, burying her face with passionate kisses and said, "My dearest love, don't look back into the past. There is now only the future. I love you with all my heart and I cannot live without you. I don't care about not having any children, I want you. Say you will marry me." Paini thought she was going to faint in the arms of her prince. The joy and happiness of his words filled her so that she felt she was floating on a cloud. She returned his kisses and said, "I love you with all my heart, my prince. Yes, I will marry you." Malam carried her up and danced with joy heedless of the onlookers. The world belonged to him and Paini.

Malam radiated so much happiness that Mr. Shih had to push back his disappointment that he would never have grandchildren from his beloved son. But, Mrs. Shih was happy for her son and asked, "Have you set the date?" Malam simply said, "As soon as possible." His mother winked her eye and said, "Unlike your father and I, and your brothers, where our marriages were match-made, you have broken the tradition of finding your own wife. But I hope you will still have the engagement and wedding according to our custom." Malam did not care what tradition his parents wanted to have, as long as the wedding took place soon. Mr. Shih went to the hospital to consult with Patamavenu who was also glad for the young couple. It was he who persuaded Paini to talk to Malam that day at the hospital. He also saw the radiance in his daughter's face when she came back, and he knew that they were right for each other, regardless of the past and the impairment. He had sent word to Paini's fiancée to break off the engagement. Mr. Liew was a true gentleman. He accepted the break-off without any hard feelings. Patamavenu also thought that a traditional wedding would make give his daughter a feeling of normality. However, the eager lovers must wait until he was well enough to attend the wedding. He could not imagine, being in the hospital on his only daughter's big day. It was no question that Malam and Paini would wait for Patamavenu to get well. However, Malam wanted to be engaged immediately, and they all agreed that an exchange of rings could be held at the cottage without Patamavenu's presence. Hamid and Miriam would act as relatives of Paini, and be there with her mother to receive the party of the suitors when they came. The date of the engagement was set for Saturday, a week after the declaration of love between the young people.

Mr. Lee, Patamavenu's boss came to visit him and to assure him that things were not as bad as it seemed. He said, "Of course you would not be able to continue to work for me, but you have been a good worker and will be compensated. Your family can stay in the cottage until your old hut is renovated. That is part of the compensation package." Patamavenu could not thank Mr. Lee enough, but what he did not know, was that Mr. Shih had agreed to help in the compensation. Mr. Shih made his friend promise never to reveal that to Patamavenu. When Mr. Lee left, Patamavenu lay back on his pillow and thought. He was now fifty five years old, and as a family, they were never able to save any money for situations like this. He accepted his handicap, but he could not accept that he could never earn money again for his family. Then he thought of his daughter, and was glad that her she would never have to suffer shame and poverty again. He was sure that Malam would love and protect her forever. Then he thought about his wife, Suji. She had shown a lot of strength and independence for the last few weeks. He hated to admit it, but he knew she had to bring the money in this time. Without Paini, they would not need much. He was glad he had made that decision never to sell their tumbling hut. It would be livable again after the renovations, and again, without Paini the hut would be big enough for the two of them.

Meanwhile Malam took Paini on an exciting shopping spree. First they went to a jewelry shop to look for engagement and wedding rings. Paini was ready to settle for the cheapest, but Malam told her that she was worth all the jewels in the world, and they came out with three rings. For the engagement Paini had a big diamond ring. She had never seen a diamond before, and when it glistened on her finger as she tried it on in the shop, she felt like a real princess. Both the wedding rings were golden bands with small diamonds implanted around them. Then they shopped for fine materials. Paini wanted to sew her own engagement and wedding dresses. Finally, they went to a man's tailor. There Malam had his measurements taken for an exquisite wedding suit. They were so happy that everywhere they went, they radiated happiness. Whenever Malam looked at Paini, he thought his heart would explode with the love he had for her. Paini felt the same way about her prince. They were both impatient to be united forever. No matter how hard it was, Malam restrained himself from being more intimate than kissing with Paini. He would not soil her. To him, she was pure, and he would wait for their wedding night to consummate their love.

Then the day of the engagement arrived, and at the set hour, Malam's parents, his brothers and their wives and a spokesman specially appointed for the occasion went to Paini's cottage. Before they entered the home, the spokesman first asked for 'lisensia' (Portuguese for permission) to do so. Then they got the verbal consent from Paini herself, agreeing to marry Malam. Malam was then presented to Paini and her mother and 'relatives', which were Hamid and Miriam. Malam gave them two bottles of spirits. Malam was again overwhelmed by Paini's beauty. She had sewed herself a Baju Kebaya in pink silk that complimented her firm and petite figure. Her sarong was black silk with pink flowering bordering the hem at the foot. She wore pink silk slippers with black beads beautifully sewn in a pattern. She had sewn them all herself. Miriam had helped her with some light make-up. The spokesman had to nudge Malam out of his reverie to continue the proceedings. Then Malam gently slipped the engagement ring onto the fourth finger of her left hand, thus making the engagement official. Then there was a 'mesa de cha' (tea – party) for all those present. According to the custom, the engagement did not grant the man the liberty to take his fiancée for outings. He was only allowed to pay court at the girl's house on Saturday and Sunday, and that too in the presence of a chaperone. But in this case, no one could impose that on this newly engaged couple. So immediately after the tea party, Malam and Paini went to the hospital to visit Patamavenu to receive his blessings. He too had good news for them. "The doctor said that I should be able to go home in two weeks time. The hospital will also provide me with a wheel chair. So my dears, knowing how impatient you both are, go ahead and set the date for your wedding." Again it was customary for the wedding to take place six months after the engagement. But Malam and Paini could not wait that long, so unanimously, they agreed that they would like to marry in a month's time.

While waiting for their wedding, Malam took Paini to see the apartment he had bought for them. It was not very big, but new and modern. It belonged to a two-storey complex which held six other apartments. Each apartment had its own garage, and Malam had bought an apartment on the first floor in consideration of Patamavenu's handicap. It had two large bedrooms with a living room that goes out into a small fenced yard. There was an attached bathroom to the master bedroom, with modern facilities, and another guest bathroom between the living room and the other bedroom. The kitchen and dining room were open to the living room, but facing the road. To Paini it was their palace. Malam would move in earlier, and Paini would join him after their wedding. Meanwhile, the renovation of the hut was underway. It was so rundown that almost everything had to be torn down. The roof was replaced with tiles, and new wood took the place of rotting wood. The whole interior and exterior were repainted white. The floor too was repaired. Then the old kitchen was replaced with modern equipment. Windows were also changed, and a larger doorway was made to allow easy assess of a wheelchair. It cost as much as building a new house, but Mr. Shih had generously donated a lot of money for it. He had also replaced the worn down furniture with new. The workers worked hard, and completed it before Mr. Patamavenu was ready to move in. The Shihs, Hamid, Miriam and some of the plantation workers helped Paini and her mother to move into their old but much improved home. It was still a one bedroom home, but Paini would only have to spend about a month in her old bed in the kitchen. Suji and Paini had seen the renovations being done, so they were not as surprised as Patamavenu, who arrived in his wheel chair in a big hospital van. His wife and daughter were waiting at home to greet him. All he could say was, "What have I done to deserve this." His voice choked with emotions and Suji said, "You do deserve this and much more. You are a wonderful man and I love you." Paini went to him and said, "Welcome home father." Then she wheeled her father inside his new home. He knew at once that his compensation would not have covered everything. Someone else was behind it all. He could guess, but he was silently grateful and secretly thanked the man in his heart.

As was customary, Malam and Hamid went from house to house to give verbal invitations. This was considered to carry more weight than invitation cards, unless the guest was someone from out of town. Malam felt it only fair to let Gina know of his impending marriage to Paini, so he sent her an invitation card, with a short note to say that he would understand if she turned down the invitation. Gina did turn down the invitation but very honorably. She sent a crystal vase as a wedding present accompanied by a note to wish the couple all the happiness they deserved, and a side note to Malam to thank him for his understanding about her being unable to come to the wedding. That was the last contact between Malam and Gina. Malam still wore Gina's birthday watch on his wrist. Then came the day that Malam had dreamt and longed for since the day he set eyes on his beautiful fiancée. That day was a Saturday in the month of May, 1925, a few months before Malam reached his twenty-ninth birthday, and Paini twenty two years old.

On the wedding day, a make-up artist was appointed to paint Paini's face. The bride was supposed to look different from everyone else, thus Paini's face was painted into a mask with exquisite care. Her mouth was crimson and her cheeks were adorned with rouge. Her eyebrows were plucked into two thin lines, and then darkened with black charcoal. Her eyes too were rimmed with the black charcoal, and extended in thin lines an inch away towards her ears and ending in triangles, which were filled in with coppery green that colored her upper eyelids all the way to her enhanced brows. Paini was not allowed to look at herself in the mirror while the artist was at work. Then when she was finished, she handed Paini a mirror and the poor girl almost fainted. She saw a sinister face staring back at her. "Oh no," she cried, "I cannot let Malam see me like that." Her mother came running in when she heard her daughter moaning and grumbling. "Paini," she said, "You look different but as stunning as a bride should be. Malam will love you more than ever." Reassured, Paini allowed her hair to be handled by another specialist. Her hair which was normally straight and long, was plaited and studded with semi-precious pins. Then she finally donned the costume she had carefully sewn herself. It was also a Baju Kebaya, only this time the outside material was of white lace lined by shining white satin material. Her sarong was of hand-woven silk, also white, with gold trimmings at the base. Her white silk slippers were beautifully decorated with small gold beads. Then, as was customary, she was bedecked with gold and ancient jewelry that her future mother- in-law presented her. Then Paini was ready to be taken to the Buddhist temple where the nuptial vows would take place. Miriam and her mother would accompany her in the rented limousine, while her father would have to go in a wheelchair accessible van, and that too was rented for the occasion.

The temple that was chosen for this very special occasion was the Cheng Hoon Teng Temple. It was the temple of the Green Merciful Clouds. It was one of the oldest and finest examples of traditional Chinese temple architecture in Malaya. Designed in a typical southern Chinese style, which emphasized the roofline and formal arrangement of halls and courtyards, the temple had been the center of the Chinese community since it was founded over two centuries ago by Malacca's Kapitan China, a distinctive title and position created by the Dutch, as the political boss of the Chinese trading community. The finely proportioned front entrance was flanked by a pair of guardian lions, which symbolized filial piety, and moon windows that opened into the courtyard. The wooden plank at the entrance was intended to force an automatic bow. Inside the spacious main hall was a thirty-inch bronze image of Kuan Yin, the idealization of womanhood and infinite piety. To her right was an image of Ma Cho Po, Guardian of the fishermen. To her left were red-faced Kwan Ti, God of

War, Literature and Justice. Behind the altars were beautifully lacquered tables and elaborate woodcarvings. The halls behind the main temple were dedicated to Confucius, and filled with ancestor tablets of all the Kapitans China, who served as heads of the Chinese community in Malacca.

All relatives and friends who had come to witness the union of Malam and Paini were already waiting in the temple. Malam and Hamid were outside waiting for the bride and her family. Mr. Patamavenu's van arrived first, and Hamid helped him out and wheeled him into the temple. Then he went out and was in time to greet the bridal car. When Paini stepped out of the car, Malam had to control his amusement at her painted face. He saw Paini's warning eyes and went to her whispering, "You are still my beautiful princess." Then he took her hand and waited for Hamid to escort his wife, Miriam and Suji into the temple. Then at the sound of a gong, the couple walked in. They went before the altar and knelt on two cushions in front of the monk. Everyone had a lighted joystick in their hands and prayers were chanted in Chinese, which Malam could not understand. Then a bigger joystick was handed to the couple to hold together. The monk burnt it and placed a yellow piece of cloth on their joined hands. He held their hands together and chanted more prayers. Then he bade the couple to stand up and turn to the crowd to bow. He had to translate what he said into the Malay language as Malam could not understand Chinese. Then without knowing it, they were told that they were now husband and wife. Unlike European weddings, they were not allowed to kiss. They were to lead the party outside the temple doors. The bridal limousine was waiting to take them to the Shih's residence, where the celebrations would continue. They were accompanied by Hamid and Miriam. The limousine had to take a round about way to give the guests and relatives time to get to the house before them. Malam held tightly on to Paini's hand, and both would have hugged and kissed each other if not for their chaperones, who were warned to make sure that they behaved themselves until they were in the privacy of their bridal room.

Everyone was already at the Shih's residence when the newly married couple arrived with their best friends. The tea ceremony awaited them. Paini had to serve tea to her parents-in-laws and Malam's brothers and their wives. Then it was Malam's turn to pay homage to Paini's parents in the same way. Then the big dinner began. The Shihs had catered food from one of the best Chinese restaurants, who also provided tables and chairs. It was set in the courtyard with tents in case of rain. There were ten round tables for one hundred people. Each table had a bottle of European brandy and it was a ten course dinner. During the dinner, numerous toasts was proposed and honored commencing with Malam, who raised his glass to his wife and said, "To my beautiful wife who makes my life complete today. I vow to protect and love her until the end of my life". Then it was Patamavenu's turn to say something. In his wheelchair, he jokingly said, "I have lost a leg, but found a son worth a thousand legs." Mr. Shih stood up raised his glass to the couple and said, "Let us drink to the newly-weds and wish them a life of happiness." When Hamid stood up, with a glass in his hand he simply said, "A toast to the two most wonderful people I know." Some relatives and friends too toasted the bride and groom. When dinner was over, the guests continued to drink until the early morning hours, unaware that the bride and groom had slipped off and driven to their new apartment.

Outside the door of their apartment, Malam unlocked the door and carried his bride into her new home. Once inside and with the door locked, they began to kiss each other tenderly, and started moving towards the master bedroom. Paini smiled when she saw how beautiful the bridal bed was. Mrs. Shih had hired an interior decorator to design the bed sheets and pillow cases. They were red and white with rose petals spread all over the bed. The material was made of fine silk, and on the bed laid a pink silk night gown for the bride. As Malam led Paini to the bed, he could feel her shivering. He knew that he would have to be patient and give her a lot of time. So all he did was to touch her face lovingly, kissing her once in a while and whispering, "I love you so much. I will never hurt you. Trust me and relax in my caresses." His dialogue with Paini had always been in Malay for that was the mutual language that they both knew. He never stopped telling her how much he loved her and slowly, he could feel the tension leaving her body as she started to return his kisses. Then he slowly began to remove all her jewelry and unpinned her hair to let it fall loosely around her. She then stood up and told him that she will come back. She took the nightgown with her when she went to the bathroom. While waiting for her, Malam undressed and went under the sheet to wait for her. He was not going to force her tonight. He will know when she was ready for him. It was sometime before Paini came out of the bathroom. Malam had dimmed the lights, but he could see that she had removed her makeup and was now wearing the nightgown. She looked like a fairy, and he was so overwhelmed with longing for her.

Paini shyly slipped under the sheet beside him and he began to touch her face tenderly tracing her eyebrows, her nose and lips with his finger.

Then she turned towards him and began to caress his face as well. They were soon buried in a sea of love and without realizing it, they were both caressing each other passionately, and when Malam felt Paini's moist and warm genitals, he knew that she was ready for him. As gently as he could he penetrated his manhood into her, and then she too began to match his gentle movements. Their hunger and love for each other were finally quenched and Paini felt that she was reborn. After that, Malam continued caressing her until they both fell asleep in each other's arms tired but contented. They got up together the next morning and started kissing each other. At first it was gentle then passion overcame them and they made love again. They did not want to get out of bed, but they knew that soon their parents would be banging at the door to demand breakfast. That was also part of the custom that the newly-weds should wait on their parents the next day. Malam could not wait to go for their week-long honeymoon in Singapore.

Just as Malam and Paini were ready, they heard the insistent ringing of the doorbell and Paini said in panic, "We have nothing prepared yet." But Malam kissed her and said, "Don't worry. My mother has everything arranged." He looked at his watch and continued, "In fifteen minutes the doorbell will ring again to announce the caterer who will bring our breakfast in. This is not traditional but we are beyond that." Together they opened the door to admit their parents. Patamavenu had left his wheelchair and had crutches instead. Malam helped him to a chair, while Paini prepared coffee. Then in less than fifteen minutes, their breakfast arrived and the couple served their parents as best they could. It was a happy gathering with much laughter on all sides. Mr. Shih looked at his happy son and thought to himself, "All the time wasted in pining and unhappiness. If only I had not thought of myself, and my longing for grandchildren from him, I could have saved him all the heartaches by breaking my promise to Patamavenu. I am sure he will forgive me, now that he too can see they are meant for each other." Then aloud he said, "So when will you both be leaving for Singapore? You know Malam, your brothers are doing quite well and I am sure they would not mind if you took more time off." Malam looked at his father and said happily, "I would like that very much. Maybe, we will stay on for two weeks. We shall leave early tomorrow morning." Then before they left, Suji took her daughter aside and said, "I don't have to ask you if you are happy. I know you are and we are too. Mrs. Shih has offered me a job to help her with her house chores and I accepted. Your father is getting stronger each day, so don't worry about us. Go and have fun." She kissed her daughter on

103

the forehead and left with the other three who were already waiting in the car.

Singapore was a diamond-shaped island of two hundred and forty square miles just south of Malaya. As Malam and Paini drove along the bridge and over the Straits of Singapore, Paini became excited. She had never left Malacca since they migrated from Thailand, and now she was almost in another country. Although Paini never went to an English school, Malam felt that she was very intelligent and witty. Even though she could not speak English, she understood a lot of it and she could speak more languages than Malam. She intrigued Malam with her curiosity, and keenness to know more about Singapore. So as they entered Singapore, Malam explained to her how Singapore got its name, since his beautiful wife was so into princes. The Prince of Palembang, who claimed direct descent from Alexander the Great, landed at this trading post in the thirteenth century, and encountered a strange animal. It was swift with a bright red body, a black head and a white breast. It was larger than a he-goat. Although it was most likely a white tiger, the prince called it a lion. Thus Temasek the 'Sea Town' became Sing Pura the "Lion City". Singapura was the Malay name for Singapore. At the end of the story, Paini looked at her own prince and smiled at him. Malam had purposely chosen the Raffles Hotel, where his parents had stayed while awaiting his return from England. As they signed in, Malam could see that Paini was overwhelmed with the luxury of the hotel. She had every reason to be. This splendid hotel was more famous than Singapore itself. The Raffles was constructed in a French Renaissance style by the Sarkies brothers, three shrewd Armenians who also ran the Strand in Rangoon and the E&O in Penang. Of course, Malam also told his wife about the tiger story, and the first Singapore Sling, promising that they would have a taste of it at dinner that night.

When they were in their honeymoon suite, Malam teasingly asked Paini, if she would like to explore the town. Paini went to him and started unbuttoning his shirt saying, "Yes I would like to explore, but not the town. They stayed in their room the whole day enjoying their overwhelming love for each other. They only got out to have dinner in the hotel restaurant. When they finished their dinner, Malam took his wife to the bar where the tiger was supposed to have been, and ordered two Singapore Slings. Paini, who had never tasted alcohol in her life, not even at their wedding, was quite drunk after only a few sips. Malam, who enjoyed occasional drinks, did not realize how strong the Sling was, especially for one who was not used to spirits. He found out from the bartender the creation of the Sling. It was a revolting combination of gin, cherry herring, Cointreau, Benedictine, pineapple, lime juice and Angostura bitters. When Malam saw that Paini was almost falling asleep on the stool bar, he gulped his down, and half carried her to their room. She felt so light in his hands and his desire to protect her became an obsession. She was fast asleep when he laid her gently on their bed. He undressed her and his longing for her beautiful body made it hard for him to sleep. However, he allowed his wife to sleep peacefully. He just put his arms around her and finally fell asleep himself.

Thankfully, Paini got up the next morning without any hangover. She looked at her husband, whose arms were still around her, and thought to herself, "I am the luckiest woman on earth." Then she moved towards him and planted a gentle kiss on his forehead. Malam stirred, opened his eyes and asked, "How do you feel, my love?" Paini did not answer him but began to kiss him on his lips and they made love again. After they had lain for a few minutes to catch their breaths, Malam said, "Let us get up and explore the city. There are so many things to do and see here. I shall order breakfast while you get ready." He kissed her and shooed her off the bed before he could feel tempted to have sex again. So after breakfast, they were out on the streets. Malam decided that it was easier to walk through Orchard Street, than to drive. It was one of the busiest streets, with lots of shops and led to Colonial Singapore on the water-front. It was a recreational square, surrounded by the Esplanade, where British architecture could be seen in government buildings, hotels, sports clubs, and churches. It took them a full day to see everything there and also to shop. Malam showered his wife with almost anything she touched, until she stopped him and said laughingly, "Don't spoil me too much. I may not want to be unspoiled again." Malam took her in his arms and said, "As long as I live, you can have what your heart desires."

For the rest of their stay in Singapore, they made love in the night and morning, and in between they went shopping and sight-seeing. Malam showed his wife everything there was to see in Singapore, and Paini would never forget those two wonderful weeks for as long as she lived. Malam had taken her to the Botanic Garden, which was the second largest in the whole of Asia, where she saw so many varieties of orchids that she never knew existed. Then there was Emerald Hill, where she saw the pre-war homes and shop houses. They also visited a few temples and churches built in the eighteenth century, not forgetting the Raffles Museum. By the time their honeymoon was over, Paini felt that she knew Singapore better than her home town in Pattaya and Malacca. Their car too was packed with all kinds of materials for sewing, exquisite Chinaware, and presents for their family and friends. Paini was sad to leave Singapore, and Malam promised her that they would revisit Singapore on their first anniversary. He winked his eye and said, "We will do everything all over again." She laughed and the couple headed for home, more in love with each other, and completely contented, forgetting all the heartaches in the past.

CHAPTER 11

Malam, now a happily married man, continued to work side by side with his two brothers. Cheah his other brother had also joined the business. Knowing that Paini enjoyed sewing, he bought her a sewing machine. She was also interested to learn English, not only to speak but to be able to read and write. Malam was all for it, so he hired a personal tutor for her. It was hard for his parents to hold a conversation with him in Malay, for he had grown up in their household with English, so very often, they would start off in Malay and then change to English. Paini had never complained, but she would not get into the conversation for fear of interrupting them. Malam knew that and appreciated her for it. There were schools for adults, but Malam was very protective of his wife. Besides, they had enough money to provide Paini a tutor. She was a quick learner, but she refused to speak English to Malam. She was sentimental of the fact that their first conversation and words of love were in Malay. It was, however, comforting for Malam to know that when in the company of his English-speaking friends, Paini was not completely left out. She understood almost everything, but when she had to say something, she would do it in Malay. When Malam was at work, Paini would clean the apartment, go to the market to buy fresh food everyday, and do some sewing. Then an hour before Malam comes back she would cook all his favorite food. Her tutor came in twice a week in the afternoons, and when she had no classes, she would spend her time sewing and making clothes for herself, Malam, her parents and parents-in-law. Their weekends were committed to visiting their parents. They were still blissfully happy.

Two years after their marriage, when they were having dinner at Malam's parent's house, Mrs. Shih had something to say. At first she did not know how to put it without hurting their feelings, but Malam made it easy for her by saying, "Chin's daughter is quite grown up now. She dropped by at the office with a young man. Well looks like both of you will be great grandparents soon." Then Mrs. Shih saw the opportunity and said, "There is a young unmarried girl who just gave birth to a baby girl. She wants to give up her child for adoption as the father of the child cannot be traced. She knows that there is no way she could bring the child up on her own. Both her parents are very old." Malam was shocked that her mother could bring up the subject so easily. He looked worriedly at Paini, but was surprised to see that her eyes were lighted with excitement. He put out his hand to touch hers and she squeezed it and smiled. Then Malam said, "Mother, I know where you are getting at. Can we leave now? We will talk another time." Mr. Shih had noticed Paini's excitement and he was secretly happy. He dismissed them casually saying, "Well these young people have better things to do than sit and talk with old people like us. Don't look like that. I was just joking." With that he said goodbye to them.

Paini was very quiet in the car, but Malam could see that she was very excited. Knowing that his wife would not impose her wishes on him, he had to bring up the subject that his mother started, but he decided to wait until they were at home. When they were inside their apartment, he took Paini into his arms and looked into her eyes and asked the question that Paini was hoping for, "Do you want to adopt a child?" Paini kept her voice under control when she replied, "Only if you think it is time for us." Malam, still holding her said, "This is your chance to be a mother. If you are ready, so am I." Then Paini lost control of herself and shouted in glee, "Oh Malam, nothing will make me happier than to have a child. A new-born baby will make me feel like she is our very own." Then she kissed her husband and her eyes became wet with tears of happiness. Then Malam whispered in her ears, "As long as I don't have less of you." He carried her into their bedroom and showed her what he meant. Their love-making was as wonderful and exciting as on their wedding night. After that, Paini felt that it was right to let her parents know of their decision before making further enquiries about the baby girl. So they drove to visit Patamavenu and Suji. They were happy with the news, but they warned the young couple not to be carried away in case it did not work out. Then Malam and Paini went back to the Shih's residence for the second time that Sunday. It was a happy Mrs. Shih who said that she would contact the young girl and make an appointment for them to see the baby.

That same evening Mrs. Shih telephoned them and said excitedly, "The mother and baby are still in the hospital. But you both can visit anytime tomorrow. The mother seemed happy that you Malam, are going to adopt her child. She was one of your greatest fans when you were an actor." When Malam passed the good news to Paini, she said, "I don't think I can sleep tonight." "Oh yes you will, I will make sure of that." He kissed her and after they made love, Paini fell asleep in his arms. But she woke up earlier than usual the next morning, hoping, but not demanding, that her husband took the day off so they could go as early as possible. Malam woke up from the sweet aroma of hot coffee, and winked at his wife saying, "I shall call the office to tell them I will be late." Paini looked so happy that he knew getting her back into bed would not be a good idea, so he got up to get ready. It was eight o'clock in the morning when they arrived at the hospital. The nurses were not too happy because the baby was not yet fed or changed, but Malam used his charms and they were taken to the ward where the mother shared the room with six other women. She looked so young and frail that Paini felt a great compassion for her. Suddenly her happiness was not important anymore. She could never take away the only possession that this little girl had. Malam sensed a foreboding when he saw the excitement fading from his wife's face, to be replaced by a deep sorrow. He put his arms around his wife's tiny shoulders and said to the girl, "We have to go out for a short while. We will come back." Then the girl said, "Please don't let someone else take my child." Her voice sounded mature and pleading. Malam led Paini out of the ward and into the waiting room. He was glad that no one else was there. He tilted her face to look at her and asked tenderly, "What is wrong?" Paini moved away towards the window and stared out. Then she said in a very solemn voice, "I was a coward when I got rid of my baby. I have no right to take her child away from her. She is so young and alone. Yet, she carried the baby to full term. I feel ashamed of myself." Malam's heart went out to his wife and he hugged her saying, "When you adopt this child you will make up for the one long gone. She is sure of a good life with us. If we do not take her, someone else will, and there is no guarantee for the child's future. The past is behind us. Let us give the baby a future. We will compensate the mother so that she too can lead a better life." Paini's eyes were still very sad, but she knew that her husband was right. The girl would never be able to raise the baby on her own. She was also sure that she would love the baby very much, and that the baby would have a good life with them. Nevertheless, she could not help comparing her cowardice to the young girl's courage. Then she took her husband's hand and said, "We will do it." Hand in hand they walked back to the ward. The nurse had already brought in the infant and the mother was holding the child in her arms. She looked sad, but when she saw Malam and Paini coming in, her face lighted up, and she handed the baby to Paini.

As soon as the baby was in her arms, Paini felt that she was meant to be a mother after all. She fell in love with the infant, and eyes glistening with joyful tears, showed her to Malam who fell in love with the child as well. Then Paini spoke in Chinese to the mother, for she was Chinese and her Malay was not very powerful. "Have you given her a name yet?" The girl shook her head and said, "No, because I will not be changing my mind about giving her away, so it is best for her new parents to name her. Please don't give her back to me. I must not get too attached to her." Then she beckoned to the nurse who took the baby away from Paini, who was already quite unwilling to part with the precious bundle in her arms. The girl looked earnestly at Malam and Paini and said, "All I want is enough money to leave Malacca and find work somewhere where no one knows me. I promise you that you will never see or hear from me again once you have the legal documents." Malam could not understand what was being said, so Paini translated everything to him. Then, knowing that the girl would understand him, he said as slowly and clearly as he could, "We will take care of your child like she is our own flesh and blood. We thank you from the bottom of our hearts for giving us this chance to be parents. I will see to it that you have more than enough with which to start a new life." Before they left the girl, to go to the administration office where the adoption formalities would take place, Paini bent down and hugged the girl, her voice full of emotion as she said, "You have made me whole again. Thank you."

It was easy for rich people to adopt babies those days, and that same day, the baby was theirs, and Malam and Paini named her Ai Li. The baby had to stay in the hospital for another week and the natural mother was discharged that same day on her request. Malam had gone to the bank and had given her a generous sum of money. It was much more than she expected. She said that it was best that they did not try to find out her name, so they could never lie to Ai Li about who her mother was. Malam had also transferred the baby to a first class ward and paid extra for the infant to have special care.

The parents of Malam and Paini were overjoyed with the news, and that same night they all went to a restaurant to celebrate and toast the new parents. Paini went to the hospital everyday, and spent hours with the baby while Malam was at work. Then she would go in the evenings with her husband and sometimes their parents would come along too. Then came the great day when Ai Li was allowed to go to her new home. The spare room was well furnished for an infant with pink curtains, a blue cot and white sheets. There were stuffed toys on the cot and all over the room. It was the year of 1926. The small apartment was filled with Malam's whole family, including his nieces and nephews, and Paini's parent to welcome the new addition. Two week old Ai Li was a beautiful infant and fitted wonderfully into the Shih family. When she was fed and laid to sleep, the family celebrated her home coming with red eggs, yellow rice and chicken curry, as was the custom. It was a perfect family gathering, and Mr. Shih felt no more remorse that he could not get a natural grandchild from his beloved son. Malam and Paini looked so happy and contented, and that was enough to last him his lifetime. When it was time for everyone to leave, Suji, Paini's mother, offered to stay and help with the baby for the first few days, but Paini refused her, saying, "Malam and I need to do this on our own. She is ours to love and cherish, no matter how difficult it may be." Ai Li slept on and off and had to be fed almost ever four hours for the next few days. Although Paini insisted that Malam slept on in the nights, he would get up with her whenever he heard the baby crying. He would go to work looking tired but happy. As promised, they both still found time to enjoy their love.

It was like happily ever after for Malam and Paini until Ai Li turned two years old. They were in the midst of getting ready to celebrate her second birthday with their family that Saturday afternoon, when Malam received a phone call from the hospital to say that Patamavenu was admitted into the hospital and was under intensive care. They left Ai Li in the care of Miriam and rushed to the hospital. They met a tearful Suji outside the intensive unit. She explained that for sometime, her husband had been complaining of great pain at the joint where his leg was removed. He also had constant headaches, but he warned her not to let Paini know of it. He said it would pass. That morning, he cried out in great pain and when Suji saw how red and swollen his stump was, she rushed him to hospital in a taxi. By the time they got there, Patamavenu had a stroke and was unconscious. The doctors were now trying to revive him. Paini tried to comfort her mother, while she herself was greatly distressed. She was so buried in her world of happiness that she failed to notice that her father was unwell. The wait for news from the intensive unit was so long, that Malam got impatient and demanded to know what was happening. The nurse just told him to sit and wait, and the doctor would come out soon. The doctor did show up a few minutes later, but his face was so grave that Malam wished he could protect his wife from whatever news the doctor had to give. The doctor asked first if they were the direct family of the patient, and Malam introduced all three of them. Then the doctor said, "We did all we could, but he is gone. The pain in his leg was so great that his heart could not take it." Paini fainted in her husband's arms and Suji rushed into the room crying hysterically. No one could stop her and before they knew it, she threw the sheet that covered his face and started kissing him and shouting, "Don't do this to me. Please come back or take me with you." By now Paini had recovered and joined her mother at her father's bed. They cried and hugged each other. Malam thought it best to leave the two women in their grief for a short time, while he rang his parents up to tell them the bad news, and to cancel the birthday party. Then once all the paper work was done, he took the women to Suji's cottage.

By now, Paini had regained control of herself for she knew that her mother needed her. She told Malam to get Ai Li and pack some clothes for them, so that she could spend the night with her mother, but Malam thought that it was better for Suji to get out of the house of memories. He suggested that Suji went with them back to the apartment, and together they could plan the burial. Suji was too weak to argue, so Paini packed her mother's clothes and they drove back to the apartment, and while Paini stayed with her, Malam went to get his daughter back. Hamid and Miriam also came back with him to the apartment in their own car. Shortly after, Mr. and Mrs. Shih showed up. It was a sad day for all of them. Paini put on a brave front, but she felt that there was now a gap in her happiness. What she regretted most of all was that she never had a chance to say good-bye to her father. He died so suddenly, and the only comfort she had was that he did not have to suffer anymore. Miriam offered to take care of Ai Li until after the burial, which normally took place two days from the time of death. But Paini could not bear to part with her daughter. Ai Li was a great comfort for her loss. Then Malam and his father went to the hospital to make arrangements for the funeral.

Patamavenu was not a religious man, and as a free thinker, there was no special ceremony. The doctor confirmed that the cause of death was a massive heart attack, so no autopsy was performed. His body was cleaned and wrapped in white sheets and brought to his house. Paini and Suji washed his corpse once more and dressed it up with the suit that he had on the day of his daughter's wedding. A stocking was put over his only foot. Then he was laid in his open coffin on a low table in the living room for twenty-hours so that relatives and friends might pay their last respects. Patamavenu had made many friends, and lots of people came by to pay their homage to a good man. Patamavenu was fifty seven years old. Suji had stopped crying and accepted her loss as bravely as she could. Paini's heart was heavy with sorrow, but her little daughter, unaware of the tragedy, kept her occupied, and she was thankful for that. The bereaved mother and daughter were dressed completely in black and Malam wore a white shirt with a black arm band. They would dress like that for one whole year, for that was the period of mourning. Malam, Paini and Suji took turns to keep vigil during the night, while Ai Li slept peacefully in the bedroom, on her own bed that her parents brought along.

The burial ground was about two miles away, and it was Suji's decision to walk along side the hearse that would transport the body of her husband to his final resting place. Paini wanted to accompany her mother, so did a few close friends like Hamid and Miriam. But because of Ai Li, Malam had to drive and his parents went with him in the car. When they arrived at the site, Malam began to feel uncomfortable. He tried to fight back the feeling, but the tragedy of the past came back. He realized that this was also the site where Aminah was buried. He had his daughter in his arm and he remembered the curse. He held her tightly and possessively, but his hands were shaking. Cold sweat was covering his forehead, and his father noticed that Malam was not himself. He took Ai Li from him without any resistance from his son, and handed Ai Li to his wife. Then he asked, "Malam, are you alright?" "No father, I feel sick. Can you look after Ai Li for a while? I need to catch my breath." By now the pallbearers had laid the coffin into the ground. He saw his wife in tears, and she was so much in pain that she did not notice that he was not near her. He was grateful for that, but at the same time, he could not go to her for he was losing himself in the past. There were no words said at the funeral. Everyone took turn to throw flowers or earth onto the coffin. Only when he saw that his wife was quite hysterical when it came to her turn, did he pull himself together and went to her. He allowed her to bury her face in his chest. He too had tears in his eyes, but no one knew that those tears were for the girl who killed herself long ago because of her love for him.

After the funeral, Malam was not the same again. He was withdrawn and not as lively as he used to be. At first Paini did not notice it as she was also sad and depressed, missing her father very much. Then she began to have a sense of foreboding when Malam took many trips out of town, and came back late. She also noticed something out of the ordinary. At nights Malam would creep into Ai Li's room and touch her gently without waking her up. He did that like two or three times a night breaking his own sleep to check on her. One night, when Paini heard him getting up, she pulled him down and said, "Ai Li is fine. You need to rest." Malam still went and checked on her, and Paini felt that it was time to find out what was happening. She was wide awake and sitting up when her husband came in. "Malam," she began, "You are worrying me. Please tell me what is wrong. You have not been yourself lately." Malam sighed and said, "Go to sleep. I just want to make sure that Ai Li is safe." Paini shook her head and insisted, "You are troubled, and as a wife who loves you dearly, I have to know why." Then Malam got up and went into the kitchen to pour himself a drink. Paini followed him and was shocked that he was drinking a glass of whisky in the middle of the night. She sat down and said, "Please talk to me. Was it business that took you out of town so often?" Malam looked at his wife and realized that he had been unfair to her. He finished the whisky in his glass and said, "Dearest Paini, something happened when I was very young. I thought I had left it all behind me, but I was wrong." Then he told her all about Aminah. Paini listened with compassion and when he added, "The curse of her mother kept ringing in my ears. She said that I would lose two children, and I feel so afraid for Ai Li." Paini put her arms around him and said, "Aminah's mother was hurting so much from the loss of her daughter that all she wanted was to hurt you. But I am sure she did not mean a thing she said." Then Malam stood up and pulled his wife towards him. "You and Ai Li mean more to me than my own life. The reason why I was away so often was because I want to take you and Ai Li away from Malacca. I sincerely feel that the further away we are, the safer Ai Li will be. It is late now. Let us go to bed and I shall tell you more when I get back. I have to leave early and will be back late tomorrow. Then we will talk." Before returning to their room, they went to check on Ai Li. Malam kissed Paini's hair and whispered, "We did the right thing two years ago. She is so beautiful. So are you."

Paini was getting worried for it was close to midnight and Malam was not home yet. He would normally call her on the phone if he was delayed at the office. She wanted to call her father-in-law, but decided against it remembering that Malam did mention about returning late. Then, just as she was dozing off on the sofa in the living room, she heard the engine of Malam's car. She jumped out and ran to open the door, while he was trying to find the key. She hugged him so tightly that he said laughingly, "Hey, you are choking me." Paini let go and pouted. "Where did you go? Why didn't you call?" Malam seemed to be in a happy mood as he said, "Let me settle down first and I will tell you everything." As he took off his shoes, he asked, "Is Ai Li alright?" "Of course," Paini replied. "Now don't change the subject. I am waiting to hear what happened?" He sat down and asked, "Do I get a drink?" Paini poured him his favorite whisky. He slipped a little and said, "Come dearest, sit on my lap." Paini did as she was told and he said, "Well, I drove to a town called Klang in the State of Selangor. I had been going there for the last two weeks looking at new plantations on the outskirts of that fast developing town, and I found one that I would like to buy. I would like to produce my own rubber and export the raw material to the European markets. So many cars are being produced, that rubber is in great demand. That means we will start a new life in Klang." He looked at his wife, who was quiet and expressionless while he was talking. He asked cautiously, "You don't like the idea do you?" Paini said quietly, "I will go to the ends of the earth with you. But I cannot leave my mother alone. She is so lonely and it will break her heart if I too left her." Malam responded, "I have thought about that. We can persuade her to move with us. There is nothing left for her here in Malacca. We are the only family she has. I have also looked at some houses and I found a beautiful one by the Klang River. It has four bedrooms." Paini looked thoughtful as she said, "I will still move with you if my mother refuses to join us. I came here and left my past completely behind. I want the same for you." Malam hugged her and said, "I will help you to persuade your mother."

Malam's parents were shocked when Malam told them of his decision. Mr. Shih, who was now sixty two years old, was ready to hand his business to his three sons. He had hoped that between the three of them, the Shih Enterprise would continue for generations to come. But as usual, he never forced his sons into any commitment, so he decided to sell his partnership in the Lee plantation, and give Malam the money to buy his new plantation. He would also give part of Malam's inheritance to him, so that Malam would have enough to start his new venture. Chin and Cheah did not like the idea either, for Malam was really good at his job. Nevertheless, they had to let him go. To his mother, Malam said, "I shall make it a point to come back once a month for a long weekend. That way you will not miss Ai Li too much." Mrs. Shih added, "And we will also try to visit you as often as we can. But promise us that you will always be there for the Chinese New Year and for your father's birthdays." Malam promised to do all that and more. He would also return for her birthday. The biggest obstacle was Suji. Malam was sure that his wife would never be happy to be so far away from her mother. He had to get Suji to make the big move with them. Suji was broken hearted when Paini relayed the news to her of their decision to leave Malacca. When she was asked to join them in the move, she sobbed and shook her head saying, "My husband's body is still warm in his grave. I cannot leave him alone. I have to visit him everyday to tell him that I love him." Then Malam said as gently as he could, "Patamavenu has gone to another world. He does not need you as much as your daughter does. You know your husband well. Think of what advise he will give you if he could." Suji looked at Malam and said, "Paini has you and Ai Li. He has no one but me." Then Paini intervened and said, "Mother, no matter where I am, I will always be his daughter. So he has me too. If you do not want to join us, I will be sad, but I will come and visit you as much as possible. I love you." Suji was quiet for sometime. Then little Ai Li tugged at her grandmother's black blouse and said, "I love you Grandma." The few words that she could speak were in Malay, although she was raised to understand both English and Malay. Suji took her in her arms and said, "I love you too, my little angel." Then she turned round and said, "Please give me time to think." Paini hugged her and they left. In the car, Paini's eyes were wet when she turned to Malam and asked, "Do you think she will change her mind? I will never forgive myself if anything happened to her when I am not here." Malam took her hand and pressed it reassuring her, "Well, I have not signed any papers yet regarding the plantation and the house. We will not move if she does not come along." Paini looked at her husband solemnly and said, "No, as I have said before, my place is with you. Our happiness will only be complete if we leave the past behind."

So for the next few days, Malam spent a lot of time in Klang. For the first time since they were married, Malam stayed away from home. He had to do a lot of negotiations to get a good deal for his new plantation, and also to purchase the house by the river, and to get it ready for his family to move in. It was a tired but happy Malam who returned home after five grueling days in Klang. He told his wife that they could make the big move anytime she was ready. Meanwhile, he had a lot to do to set up his office, and he would have to be in Klang by the following week. Paini had missed him terribly and decided that she would start packing and be ready to go with him the same time. Thus they only had two days to get ready, and with professional help they did it. The night before they left, Malam drove Paini and Ai Li to Suji's cottage to say goodbye to her. To their surprise, Suji had packed two suitcases and was ready to leave with them. Paini was overjoyed and hugged her mother saying, "You are the most wonderful mother in the world." Suji simply looked at Malam and said, "You are right, this is what my departed husband would expect of me. I have made arrangements for someone to stay in this cottage without having to pay any rent. All he needs to do is to look after my husband's grave." Malam thanked her and added, "We will come back at least once a month and you can always visit his grave." Then they drove to the Shih's residence together, had dinner there, and said their goodbyes without much ado.

Klang was situated west of Kuala Lumpur, and the town would end at Port Swettenham, where sampans came and went. As they drove from Kuala Lumpur towards Klang, Malam pointed to the tin mining areas, and explained that beside rubber, tin was also Malaya's main export. Then as they entered Klang, they had to cross the Klang River which separated the town into two parts, the North and the South. This muddy river also ran through the city of Kuala Lumpur giving the capital its name. The word Kuala Lumpur meant the city where two muddy rivers met. As they crossed the two-way bridge, Malam pointed to their new home on the northern bank of the river. It was a wooden house on brick stilts. Even before they reached it Paini was in love with it. It was surrounded by high shady trees which gave it a romantic atmosphere. She knew she was right to trust her husband to find something nice. As Malam pulled in front of the house, the brick staircase that broadens towards the main door was impressive. Then Malam told Suji and Ai Li to stay for a short while in the car. Paini followed him as he opened the door. Once the door was open, he scooped her into his arms and carried her into the completely furnished living room. He kissed her and said, "Welcome to your new home. May this house bring us everlasting happiness." Then Ai Li, followed by Suji came in. It was obvious from the happy sounds they made that they loved the house. The professional movers had already brought the furniture the day before, and Malam had also bought new ones to furnish the rest of the big house. Malam was good at business, and managed to make money on the sale of their apartment in order to buy this house at a very good price, for the house was twice the value o their apartment.

Malam's new plantation was off the road towards Kuala Lumpur. It would take him half an hour to get there, and the same time to get home. So every morning Paini would get up early to prepare his breakfast, and cook lunch for him to take to work. For the first few weeks, she and Suji were busy unpacking boxes and sewing curtains for all the many windows in the house. Suji was a great help with Ai Li, so that when Malam came home in the evenings, he and Paini could spend a lot of time together. True to his promise, they went back to Malacca once a month, and spent Friday and Saturday nights at the Shih's residence. Paini and her mother would take a taxi to Patamavenu's grave on Saturday morning. Suji was glad to see how well kept her husband's burial site was. She had never regretted her decision to be with her daughter. Seeing how big the house was, Paini would have difficulty to do house chores, cook and look after Ai Li. She did not feel lonely anymore as Ai Li began to become talkative. The child seemed to be able to speak three languages, for Paini had started speaking to her in Chinese as well. Ai Li loved to be outside, and Malam had to put up a fence to prevent direct access to the river bank. Nevertheless, she was never allowed to be out of the house on her own. They were a very happy family, and Malam's business was doing very well. Soon, he bought another car, and hired a part-time driver to take his family wherever they wanted to go while he was at work. He wanted Paini to take up driving lessons, but she was too nervous. Besides, everything was in English, and Paini had given up learning English when Ai Li came into her life.

Malam also kept his promises by going back to Malacca for both his parents' birthdays, and also to celebrate the Chinese New Years with them. It was on his father's sixty-fifth birthday that Malam began to feel uneasy. Chin's eldest daughter had married and begotten a son. When Mr. Shih held his first great grandson in his arms, there was so much pride in his face that Malam suddenly felt remorse that he could never give his father that feeling. Then his niece teasingly said to him, "Uncle, behold your great nephew, and handed the baby to him. Malam saw the great likeness to his father in the baby's features. He was sad as they returned to Klang. Paini knew that something had upset her husband, and she could guess why. However, there was nothing she could do about it, except to make a suggestion. A few days went by, and although Malam tried to act normal, he could not hide his discontentment from his wife. One night when they were in their room she said, "Malam, Ai Li is now five years old and will be going to pre-school soon. Wouldn't it be nice to have another child? Maybe, we could get a boy this time." For once, Malam could not understand how his wife could talk about adoption as easily as having a baby. He could not control the anger and frustration in his voice when he answered, "A boy would be great but it will be better if he has both our blood." As soon as he said those words, he regretted it and immediately apologized. But it was too late, Paini ran out of the room in tears. That was their first quarrel after seven years of marriage. She was sitting alone in the dark kitchen and staring out towards the river. Malam approached her and gently put his arms around her saying, "Paini, I promise you I will never speak to you that way again. I don't know what came over me." "Oh you do," Paini retorted without looking at him. "Since we returned from your father's birthday, you have been longing to have a son of your very own. I am sorry, I cannot fulfill that wish of yours." Malam went on his knees and pleaded her to forgive him. She gave in and as they walked back into the room, he said, "We will talk about adopting another child soon. He kissed her forehead and they went to bed.

The longing for a son of his own never left Malam, but because of his great love for his wife, he compromised to adopt a boy. But boys were hard to come by. So they decided to keep on looking instead of settling for another girl. Malam loved Ai Li, but like all business men during his time, sons were important to carry on their father's business. Time went by and there were still no boys to be adopted. Although Malam did not show any more signs of depression, Paini was quite desperate. With Ai Li at pre-school during the day, she and Suji had lots of time on their hands. Even though Paini did a lot of sewing and helped her mother with housework and cooking, she still missed having a child in the house. She sometimes wondered if Malam would settle for another daughter, but never stop the search for a boy. She knew of many baby girls waiting to be adopted. She decided that she would wait another month, and if the results were still futile, she would talk to him about it. Malam had more or less given up on the adoption idea, when Paini suggested they adopt a baby girl instead. As gently as he could, he said, "Let us wait another year. Ai Li would be attending regular school and she would be too busy to be jealous of another girl in the house. It would be different if it was a boy." Paini knew that her husband was just making an excuse. He did not want another girl, so she had to be contented with his answer for the time being.

CHAPTER 12

Meanwhile, Mr. Shih's health was getting bad. He was diagnosed with acute Tuberculosis. On hearing this, Malam went home every weekend. Sometimes he would take his whole family with him, and sometimes, he would go on his own. Whenever he went alone he spent precious moments with his father. Each time he saw him, his father seemed to get worse, and Malam could not bear to leave him. One weekend when they were together, Mr. Shih said, "Son, you have chosen your destiny and I have accepted it. You too must accept it." Malam was puzzled because he had never told his father of his longing. But his father had always managed to read his son's mind. That was the last advise Mr. Shih gave his son. When Malam brought his family the following weekend, Mr. Shih was too sick to talk. Malam's mother was in tears when she said, "Stay on if you can. I don't think he will get out of his bed anymore." True enough, Mr. Shih died on Monday at the age of sixty five. He left behind his wife, three sons, three daughters-in-law, six grandchildren, one grandson-in-law and a great grandson. He was a very revered man in his neighborhood. He had donated a lot to the temples and Buddhist associations, and it was one of the biggest funeral processions that followed the hearse carrying his body to his final resting ground. He was buried in an upgraded cemetery on one of Malacca's hills. After the funeral, food was served in the same courtyard where all the big family celebrations took place. This time, not only the females wore black, even the males were in complete black. Malam felt a great loss, and part of his sorrow was that his father had to accept that he would never be able to have a grandson from Malam. Malam and his family stayed on a few days to make sure that his mother was alright. It was during this time that he noticed the growing friendship between Suji and his mother. He talked to his brothers about it, and they all came to one conclusion. As long as their mother intended to stay in that big house, she should have a companion, and Suji would be the most suitable. Malam discussed that with Paini before he made the proposal to the two older women. Paini was all for it. She knew that since Ai Li was away at pre-school in the mornings, Suji was quite restless. She was sure that Suji and her mother-in-law would be happy together. When Malam approached his mother about the idea, she smiled and said, "Suji and I have talked about it. She said if Paini can manage without her, she would love to move in with me." That was settled then. So Malam, Paini and Ai Li returned to Klang without Suji. They promised to come back in two weeks with her belongings.

As synthetic rubber became more and more popular, Malam decided to grow palm trees, and bought more land to extend his plantation. Many immigrants from India, Siam and China came pouring into the State of Selangor because it was Malaya's richest and most developed state. It was home to the largest port in the country, Port Swettenham, now known as Port Klang, and to many of the country's largest industrial operations, like tin mining and rubber and oil palm plantations. Malam employed many of the immigrants. His overseer took charge in hiring the field workers, while he himself chose the people who would work closely with him in the office. That being the case, Malam hardly knew any of the workers on the plantation, in the storehouses and packing stations. However, if there was any problem with the workers, the overseer would consult Malam before he made the final decision of terminating the employment of the trouble maker. Thus one day, his overseer came to his office and complained that there was a girl in the packing department who was very hardworking and good at her job. But, because she was very attractive, the other male workers were easily distracted, and were not working as hard as they should. She did not do anything to tempt them or to discourage them. So, it was a difficult situation to handle. He could not sack her because she was doing a good job, but at the same time, her presence was causing her male colleagues to be lax in their jobs. Malam wanted to know if it was possible to transfer her to another department where there were more females. The overseer shook his head, so Malam said, "Well send her to me first thing tomorrow morning, and I will check to see if she could work in the office as a delivery girl or something."

Malam's face was buried in his account book when he heard someone say boldly but in broken Malay, "Sir, you wanted to see me." Malam looked up and for a moment he thought he was hallucinating, for before him stood the image of Gina. But as he looked more carefully, and noticed her simple clothes and no make-up on her face, he realized that she was the unconscious trouble-maker in the packing department. He could understand the unrest she was creating. Even though she had on loose pants and blouse, her voluptuous figure was visible with every slight movement of her body. Even without any make-up, she was as beautiful as Gina. She was a little slimmer and a little shorter, but still taller than most Chinese woman. Her eyebrows were more arched than Gina's, giving her an aristocratic look. Her full unpainted lips would tempt any men to want to kiss them. Malam had to shake himself into reality, and felt ashamed that he had been staring at her for so long without saying anything. Unconsciously, he pulled a chair for her to sit down and when he was back behind his desk, he said as formerly as his voice would allow, "What is your name?" The girl replied, "Ah Leng." "Well Ah Leng, I was wondering if you would like to work in the office instead of in the packing house." It was obvious that Ah Leng was not a timid girl for she replied, "But, what can I do here. I went to school for a short while in Canton and can read and write some Mandarin. Other than that, I don't know any trade." Her Malay was broken, but she managed to express herself quite well. That gave Malam an idea and he said, "Well, you come from Canton, so I presume you speak good Cantonese, and you can speak and write Mandarin. I have a lot of Chinese clients, who could hardly speak Malay or English. You can work as a translator as well as keep the office clean. I shall double your pay." Ah Leng could not believe her good fortune. She would be able to boast to her parents that she had a job as a translator, but not mention the cleaning part. She said eagerly, "When can I start?" "Tomorrow," said Malam and dismissed her immediately, for he was finding it difficult to stay focused in her presence.

Ah Leng left Malam deep in thoughts. Malam's longing to have a son of his own had never left him, and seeing the beautiful Chinese girl made his longing greater. He could imagine the beautiful children that would come out of her womb. He hated himself for those thoughts for he was still very much in love with his wife. Nevertheless, he could not go home directly after work that day. He called up one of his business associates, who was more a friend than just a colleague and said on the phone, "Chew, shall we meet at the club in half an hour? I just need someone to talk to." Chew, who never refused Malam anything, agreed. After two drinks of pure whisky on the rocks, Malam looked at his friend and asked, "Do you know that my wife is unable to give me children?" Chew shook his head and was about to ask about Ai Li, when Malam cut him off saying, "We adopted Ai Li when she was an infant. I trust that what I am going to tell you will be just between us. But before I go on, I have got to call my wife and tell her that I shall come back late tonight." While he was off to make the call, Chew ordered more drinks and as the men drank, Malam told him about how his first yearning came at his father's sixty-fifth birthday, and no matter how much he tried, he could not get rid of that feeling of failure to produce his own son. Then as Malam became more intoxicated, he told his friend about his encounter with Ah Leng and his feelings towards her. Chew, who was still very sober said, "Malam, you are a rich man. You can buy anything you want. Make a business deal with Ah Leng. Tell her all you want from her is for her to conceive your child. Pay her any amount she asks for." Malam shook his head saying, "How can I do that without hurting Paini?" Chew answered, "Paini knows of your longing. I am sure she will be hurt if you sleep with another woman, but if you assure her that it is only until you have your child, I am sure she will understand." Malam felt his friend had a point there, but right now, he knew that he could not make any decisions. He would give it a serious thought when he was sober. Paini was not very happy when her husband came home late and drove under influence of alcohol. But, like a good wife, she tucked him in bed lovingly and said nothing.

Malam was quite anxious to get to the office the next day, although he did not feel well. He hated to admit it to himself that Ah Leng was the reason for the anxiety. She was already at the office preparing coffee for the staff. When Malam walked in, he noticed that his male employees were livelier than before, and then he saw Ah Leng and his heart skipped a beat. She was lovelier than the day before. She had a pretty printed dress and walked in high heel shoes which added two more inches to her height. She had a touch of lipstick and looked like a model. No wonder the men were all trying to get her attention. She definitely had his. He controlled himself, and simply said to his staff of four men and three women, "This is Ah Leng and she will be a translator for our Cantonese and Mandarin-speaking clients. She will also help to clear up your mess." Then he walked quickly into his office to hide his flushed face. He hardly left his room that day, and he could not bring himself to work as usual. Although, his office was closed and he could not see the workers outside his room, he could feel Ah Leng's presence, and hear her high heels, even though his other female employees too had high heels. He felt he was losing himself and he had to do something about it. So he left the office earlier than usual. He managed to avoid Ah Leng as he left hurriedly for his car.

When Paini and Ai Li greeted him happily, all thoughts of Ah Leng disappeared. He looked at both of them and felt proud of his beautiful family. Paini was just as beautiful as when he first laid eyes on her and Ai Li was getting prettier every year. He spent a quiet evening with them, and it was he who tucked in Ai Li that night. For some reason, when he said goodnight to his daughter, she held his hand and said, "Papa, it would be nice if I could have a little sister to play with." Malam kissed her forehead and left the room puzzled. That was the first time she ever brought up the subject of another sibling. However, he did not give it much thought until he went to bed with Paini. He still enjoyed every bit of her when they made love. Then after their love-making that night, Paini snuggled into his arms and said, "Malam, maybe it is still too soon after your father's death to talk about an addition to our family. But I am afraid that if we wait, we may lose this chance." Malam sat up immediately and Paini could feel tension in his body. "Please don't be angry. If it is too soon, then we won't talk about it." It was too late. Malam wanted to know what she meant by them losing a chance. "Well, there is a pregnant lady looking for someone to pay her hospital bills, and then later adopt her child. The sex of the child is unknown, but it could be a boy if we are lucky." Malam managed to relax, for she had given him the opportunity to talk about Ah Leng. He needed a drink and some time to formulate his sentences without hurting his precious wife. So he got up, went into the kitchen, poured himself a glass of whisky and drank it all in one gulp, then he came back into the room and took his wife in his arms as he said, "Paini, my love, I remember that I told you long ago that all I wanted was you. I did not care if we had children or not. Somehow as we grow older things changed. When my father died, I regretted that he never had a chance to see my child. In fact, the longing to have my own son came when I held my grandnephew in my arms. I love you so much that I tried to suppress my yearning. But I have found a solution, where I could have my own child." Paini was quiet, but he could feel her body tensing up. He still held on to her as he continued, "It may hurt you, but as far as I am concerned, it would only be a business transaction. I have found someone who will be suitable to bear my child. I will have to sleep with her until she conceives and that will be the last I will ever touch her again. I shall pay all bills and upkeep, while she is carrying my child. Then I shall give her as much money as she wants for the baby." Paini was now sobbing, and all she said was, "Please leave me alone." Malam knew that he could not withdraw what he just said, so he left the room and spent the rest of the night in another room. Before he fell asleep, he vowed to himself that he would not do anything without his wife's approval.

The next morning, when Malam woke up from a troubled sleep, the driver had already taken Ai Li to Kindergarten, and Paini was back in her room. She locked the door and left Malam's change on the sofa in the living room. Malam tried to talk to her, but her response was, "Please go to work. I need to be alone." Malam had no choice, but to leave. She had already prepared his breakfast, but there was no lunch packet for him to take to work. He had his breakfast, but before he left, he knocked on the door and said, "Paini, I will not do anything to hurt you. Please be there for me when I come back this evening." There was no answer so he said, "I love you," and left for work. He did not want to see Ah Leng, so he made a beeline for his office without his usual 'good morning' to his employees. He was glad that there was a lot of work waiting for him on his desk. Since he set eyes on Ah Leng, he had neglected some important matters, and this morning he decided to bury himself in those matters and hopefully, when he got home, things would be normal. But, he still felt Ah Leng's presence close by and by noon, he decided to leave his office and go home for lunch. Just as he was leaving, someone knocked on his door. He asked gruffly, "Who's that?" Then the door opened to admit his wife with his lunch. She closed the door behind her and said, "Please forgive me for behaving so badly." Malam put his arms around her and said, "It is I who should beg your forgiveness. I love you and I am supposed to protect you and not hurt you." Paini put her fingers to his lips and said, "Eat your lunch and we will talk tonight. I love you." Then she left as suddenly as she came in. Malam felt much happier, and was able to complete his work without any disturbing influence of Ah Leng.

That night, Malam was once more overwhelmed with love for Paini as they made passionate love. He decided then that whatever his heart desired was right beside him. He could not sleep, and noticed that Paini too was wide awake so he wanted to tell her that they should go ahead and check on the pregnant lady. But before he could say anything, Paini said, "Malam, you are a wonderful husband and father. You have made me very happy. It is now my turn to make you happy. You have my blessing and permission to fulfill your heart's desire. Do what you must, and your child will be just as much as mine." Malam felt an ache in his heart for his wife. Her unselfish love filled him with shame. He had to make immediate amendments so he said, "No, my love. My heart's desire is to love and cherish you. We will go ahead and adopt another child." Before he could go on, Paini intervened and said, "No, only a child from your seed will complete our family. I will not forgive myself if you deny yourself that. I am now begging you to go on with what you have to do to achieve that." Malam was speechless. He knew that his wife meant every word she said. If he denied her this, she would live in guilt and that would mar their chance of happiness. There was nothing more he could say, so he kissed her goodnight and tried to fall asleep. It was a sleepless night for both of them. Malam was troubled and uneasy with what he had to do the next day, and Paini's heart was breaking because she had to share her husband with another woman. She knew who the woman was. She had seen her, and knew in her heart that the relationship between her husband and that woman would last longer than he thought.

When Paini saw that her husband had not taken the lunch box that she had packed for him, she knew that he would be going out for lunch with his future mistress. She decided to take Ai Li with her to Malacca and spend a few days with her mother and mother-in-law. When the driver dropped them off, Paini told him to inform Malam that they would stay on until he was ready to take them back. Mrs. Shih and Suji were pleasantly surprised by the visit. Paini's explanation was that Malam had a lot of work to do, so she decided to take a short vacation. She also said that he would come and get them when he had more time. Suji believed her daughter, but Mrs. Shih knew that something was wrong. Anyway, she was happy to see her granddaughter again and said, "Stay here as long as you like. It is wonderful to have young company again." Then to Ai Li, she exclaimed, "My, you have grown up so fast!" She decided that when everyone was fast asleep, she was going to call her son and have a serious talk with him. There had never been a case of infidelity in their family and she hoped that he would not be the one to start it. Paini was glad that she came back to Malacca, instead of staying at home and feeling sad and depressed. She saw how well her mother got along with her mother-in-law. She went with her mother and Ai Li to visit her father's grave. Subconsciously, she wandered towards Aminah's grave and said quietly to the spirit of the girl, "You lost your life for your love. I am lost, but I will live for my love." Her heart was heavy, and she felt that the weight would never be lifted.

Meanwhile, Malam unaware, that his wife and daughter had left for Malacca sat in his office thinking of what Paini had told him. He felt he had no choice. Either way, Paini would be hurt. If he went on with his original plan, she would be heart broken, and if he did not, she would never forgive herself. Then he thought of himself and what he really wanted. He wanted to have a son of his own flesh and blood, and that was it. He sent for Ah Leng. When she came in, he began to weaken in his resolve to make his proposition as business-like as possible. He avoided her eyes and simply asked, "I have not brought my lunch with me. I was wondering if you would like to join me for lunch." Ah Leng did not show any surprise. It was obvious, that he was not the first person to have asked her out, even though he was the big man. She answered, "Tell me where and I will join you there." Malam could see that she knew how to be discreet and he was thankful for that. He mentioned his clubhouse and gave her money to take a taxi there. Ah Leng informed a colleague that she had asked permission from the big boss for the afternoon off and will not be back until the next morning. She was waiting outside the club when Malam arrived half an hour later. As he approached her, he was again fascinated by her good looks and wondered why she was still single. From the records of his employees, he had found out that she was twenty-two years old, and normally, at that time girls her age were either married or engaged. She was not married, but he was not sure if she was engaged. Well, he would find out soon enough. As they entered the dining room of the club house, a few heads turned. Malam wondered whether it was curiosity or her looks that drew the attention. He presumed it was the latter.

She had no scruples about ordering the most expensive dishes and Malam admired her confidence. As he watched her eat, his longing for her became more physical than he wanted. He was not sure of himself anymore. He felt an overwhelming desire for her body, thus forgetting the reason for asking her out. However, she made it easy for him when she asked still in broken Malay, "Sir, why do you want to see me?" Her direct question came as no surprise, for Malam was beginning to realize that she was not lacking in self confidence. He decided to give just as direct an answer. "I want you to conceive my baby." "And how am I supposed to do that?" "Simple," Malam said. He really liked her boldness. "Sleep with me until you conceive. I will pay for everything, and when the baby is born, you give it to me for an amount of your say." She looked him in the eye and said, "No money in the world can buy my body. Thank you for the lunch and I am giving you my resignation right now." She got up and left with her nose in the air. There were a few taxis waiting outside the club house. Malam was just in time to see her take off in one of them. He felt like a fool staring after the disappearing vehicle. He could not believe that instead of being angry, he was hurt and felt jilted. He drove back to his office frustrated. He could not concentrate on anything else, but Ah Leng's beauty and temperament. He did not like to think that he was falling in love with her. How could he when he was still deeply in love with his wife? He knew that whatever it was, he was physically attracted to her, and he hungered for her. Then his thoughts went back to Paini, and he decided that he would end this craving once and for all. It was good that Ah Leng would not come back to work for him. Time will remove this physical desire for her. He would go back to his faithful and wonderful wife, and beg her forgiveness for his egocentricity.

But alas, just as he was about to leave the office, his wife's driver, who just returned after a long drive, informed him of the whereabouts of his family. He got into the car and was about to drive to Malacca himself, when Paini's words came back into his mind. She had said that if he did not fulfill his desire, she would always blame herself. She had now cleared the path for him and made it easy for him. There was no turning back. He had to go through with it. His desire for Ah Leng returned, and he went back to the office, got out the records of his employees and found her address. He drove to her place. It did not surprise him to see that she lived in a fairly good environment. Her house was small but in better condition than most of the homes of the other laborers. It was obvious that her parents did have some money when they left China. It was Ah Leng who opened the door in answer to his knock. She was still dressed in the same attire she wore at work and did not seem the bit least surprised to see him. Before he faltered, Malam quickly said, "Let us talk." She put her finger to her lips to warn him not to say anything more. She nodded and said, "Wait in your car." She shut the door after her and was out in a few minutes. She entered the car and said, "Drive now." She did not want the neighbors to talk. Both of them were quiet until they arrived in Port Swettenham. Then Malam said, "We need to be alone to talk. Would you allow me to get a room in one of the respectable hotels here?" Ah Leng answered, "If your intentions are noble, why not?" Then Malam drove to an exclusive hotel and got them a room. Once inside the room, Ah Leng sat on a sofa there with her legs crossed and said, "So what other proposition do you have in mind? I did not accept the first. Let us hear the second." Malam who was known for his eloquence seemed to be lost for words. So Ah Leng decided to help him. "You already have a daughter, so why are you looking for another woman to conceive a child for you?" Then Malam had to explain that his daughter was adopted because Paini was medically proven to be barren. "So now you want to have an heir to your wealth, am I right?" She did not wait for his reply but continued to say, "A man as rich as you can marry as many wives as he like. He need not have to pay a woman to bear his child." Malam could not believe his ears. "I am happy with one wife. I don't need more wives." Ah Leng shrugged and said, "Then I can't help you. So please send me home now." As she stood up, Malam lost his mind and grabbed her saying, "Can't you see that I am crazy for you. All I want right now is you." At first, Ah Leng was rigid, then her body softened against his and they were kissing and embracing each other hungrily.   Actually Ah Leng had fallen madly in love with Malam that very first morning when she reported at his office. She had managed to keep her emotions under control until this moment. Between embraces and kisses, words of love were being exchanged, but as she felt the softness of the bed, she said, "Stop. We cannot make love without being married." Malam was beyond control. His hunger for her unheeded her words, and he was still undressing when she got up and slapped him hard in the face.

That brought him to his senses, but did not quench his desire. He rubbed his sore face and said, "I thought you said you love me." "Oh yes I do," Ah Leng said, "But that does not give you the right to take my body. If you love me, then marry me and I promise to give you as many children as you want. Go home and think about it, or better still discuss it with your wife. I am prepared to be your second wife, she should be prepared to remain the first. Now, please take me home and only come to me when you have made up your mind." She looked at herself in the mirror and made sure that she did not look disheveled. Malam needed more time to cool down. Finally, they left the room and Malam drove her home. He was very frustrated, but he knew for sure that he was now mentally and physically attracted to the woman beside him. How could he ever face his wife again. He had betrayed her. The promises that he made to her were all just words. He had vowed to cherish, love and protect her forever. He had broken them, and in a way, he was glad that his father was not alive to see what a weakling his favorite son was. When he arrived home, his house was in complete darkness. It was about ten o'clock at night. He never felt so lonely in his life. He was not sure if his loneliness was because of the absence of his family or Ah Leng. He poured himself a glass of whisky and decided to drink himself to sleep that night. But just as he wanted to take a sip, the phone rang. It was his mother on the other line. "Where have you been? I have been trying to call you for an hour. Don't tell me it is work. I called the office and they said you left early." Malam was quiet for sometime then he asked, "How are Paini and Ai Li? Can I talk to them?" His mother told him that they were sleeping and she demanded to know what was happening. Malam managed to convince her that it was a small misunderstanding and that tomorrow being Friday, he would drive down, spend the weekend and bring them back on Sunday. Then he decided not to drink after all. Fortunately, he was so exhausted that sleep came quite easily.

Malam went to the office the next morning to inform his secretary that Ah Leng had tendered her resignation, but then he saw her at the coffee counter. He was secretly pleased, but he did not show it. He was not going to change his mind about going to Malacca, so he entered his room to sign some papers and was about to tell his secretary that he would be off for the weekend when his phone rang. It was Paini. Her voice was soft and full of love as she said, "Please don't come. You have to finish what you started. I love you and will be there for you." Before Malam could protest, she hung up. He was lost. He was not sure how far she expected him to go. But, he would not commit himself to Ah Leng's wishes without letting his wife know of the price she had to pay. He had to speak to Paini, so despite her phone call he drove to Malacca. He arrived there in the late afternoon and was happily greeted by his daughter. On hearing her daughter's shouts, Paini came out and greeted her husband with a stiff hug. He hugged her tightly and said, "I came because I am lost. I need your help." His mother too was quite cold towards him. But Suji seemed friendly enough and asked him if he was hungry. Malam said he was not and asked her to look after Ai Li for a while. Then he turned to Paini and said, "We have to talk. Let us drive somewhere where we can discuss our future in peace." Paini nodded and got into the car.

Malam drove to a park and found a seat in a secluded area. Then he held Paini's hands and said, "Paini, I don't want to lose you, and if wanting a child meant losing you then I am not going to have it." Paini said, "I meant everything I said. You cannot ask me for more than my blessing and permission. I will never leave you, no matter what happens." Then Malam felt he should tell her the ultimate truth. "Will you be able to accept a second woman in my life? There is no other alternative but to marry the woman who will bear my child." Paini turned her face as she replied, "I expected that. I have seen her and I know that is what she would demand. You have given me eight years of happiness. That will last me a life time. You have a big heart and I know that you will still love me. Yes, I will never leave you." Malam wished that the earth would open up and swallow him. He was so undeserving of this wonderful woman. He would have given everything to go back to the time when his heart belonged only to her. Now it was too late. Paini would never forgive herself if he backed out now. His eyes were wet when he kissed his wife on the forehead and said, "Thank you for loving me so unselfishly. You are my first great love and will remain so till the end of my life." Paini kissed him and said, "So are you."

It was harder for the two older women to accept Malam's decision to take a second wife. His mother wept and between sobs said, "I am glad that you father is not here to see all this." Suji was sad for her daughter, but she said, "If Paini can accept it so can I." Paini and Malam had decided that she would stay on in Malacca until it was time for him to wed Ah Leng. It was customary for the first wife to receive the second into the household through a tea ceremony. Without Paini's presence the marriage cannot take place. So, Malam drove home alone on Sunday. His feelings were mixed. At one point, he felt he could not go through with it no matter what Paini said. And then the thought of Ah Leng brought desires into his body that he never thought could be possible. Finally, the idea of having children of his own overcame all other thoughts. He would marry Ah Leng, but she had to abide by certain conditions. She would have her own room in the same house and the relationship between her and Paini would be like sisters. Paini would always be the elder sister and Ah Leng should give her due respect. He knew that normally the second wife could demand a separate house for herself and should get it. He was determined that either Ah Leng agreed to his terms or despite his desires, he would not marry her.

When Malam met Ah Leng on his way to his private room, he gestured to her to join him. Once the door was closed behind them, he pulled her to him and said, "Will you marry me?" Ah Leng was prepared with her answer. "Do you love me for myself or do you see me as the future mother of your children?" "You know how I feel about you. It is yes to both your questions. I love you and I do hope to have children with you," Malam said. "Will you live with me?" was Ah Leng's next question. Then Malam let go of her and sat behind his desk. "No, you will come to live with us. You must understand once and for all, that falling in love with you did not mean that I am no more in love with my wife. I still love her dearly, and I cannot explain how this is possible. Only if you will accept to live in the same house and regard my wife as your elder sister, can there be a marriage between us." "I see," said Ah Leng with her head down. For the first time, since they had contact with each other, Malam saw no arrogance in her answer and look. He felt warmed towards her and got up to go to her. She too had pulled a chair to sit down. Malam pulled her up again and said gently, "Ah Leng is it not enough that I love you and want you to be my wife?" She sighed, "I will say yes to your proposal, because I too love you and I don't want to lose you. I know that I will have to share you with someone all my life, but you are a great man with a heart big enough for more loves than one." He took her in his arms and kissed her tenderly and passionately. They planned to be married in two weeks under the Chinese custom of second marriages. Meanwhile, Malam dated her every day after work, taking her to the best restaurants in town and buying her beautiful clothes. They kissed and touched each other passionately, but abstained from the ultimate act of sex.

Malam had not called or talked to Paini since he left Malacca, but he knew he had to update her with the latest development, so he left a pouting Ah Leng to drive back to Malacca that weekend. He warned her that he would be bringing his family back, and they would not meet until the day of the wedding. But before he left, he and Ah Leng had made all arrangements for the wedding. Ah Leng had chosen the room that was Malam's office until then. She herself had decorated the room and made it into a bridal suite. She had expensive taste, but Malam indulged her. She locked the room and handed the key to Malam. He was not to open it until they returned from their honeymoon. The wedding was on a small scale. Only the relatives were invited. That meant Ah Leng's parents, her teenage brother and sister, Malam's mother, his brothers and their family. Paini and Ai Li would be there to welcome the newcomer into their family. But Suji had decided that it was not appropriate for her to be present. The marriage would not be recorded in the Registry of Marriages, but would be witnessed and sanctioned by a monk, and witnessed by all present. The tea ceremony was the highlight of the union, and it would be followed by a ten-course dinner in a Chinese restaurant. After that, Malam and Ah Leng would go on their honeymoon for a week. Ah Leng had chosen to go to Penang, and Malam unwillingly obliged her. He did not want to cross path with his ex-girlfriend, whose resemblance to Ah Leng was what triggered it all.

It was a sober Paini who came out to greet her husband when his car pulled up in front of the Shih Residence. Ai Li had an exciting day and was already in bed. Paini knew that it was time to go back so she had already packed most of their belongings. Malam felt a tinge of guilt when he saw that Paini had lost the happiness that showed whenever he came back from work. But he did not expect that anymore. He had chosen another path, and even though she would still be there, things would never be the same again. His mother had finally accepted her son's decision and welcomed him home. When he was alone in the room with Paini, he asked her, "How did Ai Li take it?" Paini replied, "I told her that I was adopting a sister, and that she would be like another mother to her. At first she was upset, but I managed to convince her that our family will increase, and now she is looking forward to many brothers and sisters." Once again, Malam felt undeserving of this wonderful woman. Then he told her of the arrangements he made with Ah Leng and about the wedding ceremony. He knew that Paini's heart was breaking as he talked, but she kept on a brave front. There was no more turning back. They all had to go through with it. She agreed to return home with him that Sunday. When Malam made love to her that night, she submitted to him dutifully. He felt it, but nevertheless, he still had a lot of lust and passion for her. His love for her was not any less than when they first met.

Malam was thirty six year old when he married Ah Leng, who was twenty two. The tea ceremony was held in the house by the river, the future home of the new bride. It was the saddest day of Paini's married life, but she hid her feelings well, when Ah Leng served her tea and called her 'big sister'. She gave her husband's new bride a gold necklace and said, "Welcome into my family, younger sister. May we all live in harmony and serve our husband well." It was only when she could escape into the privacy of her room, on the pretence of powdering her face to get ready for dinner, did she allow the tears to flow non-stop. She was still sobbing when she heard her mother-in-law at the door, saying softly, "Paini, please let me come in." She dried her tears and opened the door to admit the older lady. Mrs. Shih knew that Paini had been crying. She closed the door behind her and held her daughter-in-law tightly. She knew no words could comfort Paini, but she said, "Paini, you are the best wife a man could ever have. Malam knows that, and he will always love you more than her. You have earned the highest regard in our family, and to me you are the only daughter I will have from Malam." Paini had stopped crying and said, "No, you love your son. You must also love what he loves. I am just being sentimental. Please forgive me. We have to leave for the restaurant soon." Mrs. Shih left the room, but her admiration for Paini overwhelmed her love for her son. She could never love Ah Leng, even if the girl gave her grandchildren. She wondered whether this would have happened if her husband was still alive.

CHAPTER 13

It was obvious from Ah Leng's disposition that they had had a wonderful honeymoon. Paini greeted them with a show of warmth, although her heart ached. If she could have helped it, she would rather be in Malacca when Malam returned with his new bride. Unfortunately, Ai Li who was now six years old, would be attending school that year and Paini had to prepare her for it. Ai Li was happy to see her father and her new mother, and laughed when her father carried Ah Leng into her new room. Paini held back her tears and went into the kitchen to prepare food. Then she allowed the tears to fall. She was unaware that Malam had come into the kitchen and was looking sadly at her. When he saw the tears, he went to her and put his arms around her saying, "Oh Paini, nothing has changed between us. I still love you." Paini disentangled herself and said softly, "I know that you will always love me. But things have changed, and it will take me more time to get used to it. Welcome home, husband. Now, let me prepare our dinner." Malam stopped her and said, "Ah Leng will help you once she has unpacked. That is how it should be and will be from now on." Then he went into Ah Leng's room and said, "Dear, if you are done packing, could you go and help Paini with the dinner?" "Sure," Ah Leng replied, but she took a long time to unpack, and when she was done, dinner was already waiting.

Malam was still awake and sitting in the living room when his wives retired to their respective rooms. Paini had closed her door, but Ah Leng left hers ajar. Malam realized that Paini was so right when she said that things had changed. He would never be able to sleep in her room every night from now on. Well, it was time for him to discipline himself. He would spend a week in Paini's room, and then the next week in Ah Leng's and so on. This week was Paini's turn, so he turned the doorknob and entered her room. She was still awake and was surprised to see him. She sat up and shook her head saying, "No, you have to spend your nights with her until she conceives." Malam held her and whispered, "I want to be with you. So hush." Paini was defenseless as her husband made love to her gently and with as much passion as before. She was contented, and decided never to doubt his love for her again. He was a big man with a heart, big enough for more than one love. She would never be sad again, even if he was spending the night in the next room with her new sister. Malam too was contented, and he hoped that Ah Leng would accept his divided attention and love. If she showed signs of anger tomorrow, he would explain to her. He had to make sure that there was immediate harmony in his household of two wives. He had no reason to worry. When he woke up the next morning, both his wives were in the kitchen chatting and preparing breakfast. Ah Leng did not show any signs of disappointment, instead, asked him if he slept well. He smiled at her and said he did.

It was also Ai Li's first day of school. Malam had insisted that she went to the Klang Convent which was run by European nuns. It was a very reputable school for girls. He had briefed Ai Li that she should learn everything they taught her, except their religion. She was not to repeat any of their prayers. She had to remember that she came from a staunch Buddhist family. He took her to school that day, and on the way, Ai Li who now spoke very good English asked, "Papa, is Second Mother going to give me a little brother?" Malam laughed and said, "I hope so, but it always takes some time to make one. You have to be patient." When he left his daughter at the Convent, he drove to work thinking, "Well, maybe Paini is right. I should spend the nights with Ah Leng for sometime. That does not mean that I cannot go into her room once in a while. Oh, I am so happy to be loved by two women at one time, and to be able to love them both just as much." Everyone in his office could see the radiance on their boss's face. They were already informed that Ah Leng would not be working any more, because she was now the second wife of the big man himself. When Malam checked his accounts, he could see that his business was expanding, and he decided to expand his house with the expectations of many children. That afternoon, he called an architect to discuss the extension of his house by the river to two more bedrooms.

Three months after the wedding, Ah Leng broke the good news to Malam that she was pregnant. Malam was overjoyed, and so was Paini. The two women had become very good friends and because of Malam's fairness, they had no reason to be jealous of one another. He spent more nights in Ah Leng's room because they all knew the reason for it. He gave them equal amount of cake money to do whatever they liked. They both shared a full time chauffeur and a car. Malam used to buy lots of jewelry for Paini and he continued to spoil both his wives the same way. Malam could not wish for a more harmonious family. Ah Leng was also very good to Ai Li, and the little girl loved her second mother, but not as much as she loved her own mother, Paini. Ai Li too was thrilled about the imminent addition to the family. So was Mrs. Shih, Malam's mother. They had not gone back to Malacca since the wedding, but Mrs. Shih and Suji were not disappointed. It was hard for both of them to accept Ah Leng. However, they welcomed the good news with joy, and told Malam that they should bring the baby to visit them. Malam promised that they would celebrate the one-month old celebration of the infant in Malacca. He wanted to present the baby to the rest of his family, and especially to the spirit of his father.

Meanwhile, Malam's house was being renovated and extended. The two women had to put up with the noise and disorder for two solid months, but when it was finished, it was bigger and more spacious. The living room extended towards the back, and two bigger bedrooms with a shared bathroom were built after that extension. Paini decided to keep her old room, which was smaller than the new one, but Ah Leng moved to the new quarters. Ai Li too kept her room beside her mother, and Ah Leng's old room became Malam's office again. Thus the sleeping quarters of the two wives were separated by the kitchen and dining room. The guestroom was untouched and was sometimes occupied by the chauffeur, whenever he was needed in the late hours of the night to drive Malam back from a drinking party. Paini had managed to persuade Malam never to drive under the influence of alcohol. Since Ai Li had started going to school, Paini had developed a new interest. She enjoyed going to the movie houses, which were getting to become popular. Her favorite films were from India, especially the ones in Tamil, as she knew the language very well. She never missed any of them. She would tell Ai Li the stories of the movies she saw every evening when tucking her in. Ah Leng showed an interest in sewing. One of the first things that Malam had bought Paini was a sewing machine. Ah Leng asked Paini to teach her, and soon she could sew baby clothes. Malam came home every evening to enjoy his favorite meals prepared by both his wives. He had a tendency to show a bit more attention to Ah Leng, but that was understandable as she was pregnant. Paini was not at all affected. In fact, she too began to spoil Ah Leng as she became bigger and more advanced in her pregnancy. She did not allow Ah Leng to do any housework. Malam noticed that, and decided to employ a daily housekeeper.

Malam's son was born in 1934, in the house by the river. A renowned mid-wife, Madam Teoh delivered the baby in Ah Leng's room. Malam was overcome with pride and love when Madam Teoh placed the naked and bloody infant in his arms. He raised it over his head and said proudly, "Here is to my father and my grandfathers. Bless my son Shih Teh Ik." 'Teh Ik' is the Hokkien words meaning 'Number One". Then he handed his son to be washed and cleaned. He then bent to kiss Ah Leng saying, "Thank you my love." Once the baby was washed and dressed, he was handed to Paini, whose eyes were filled with tears of joy for her husband whose desire was now fulfilled. She kissed Teh Ik on the forehead and said, "Welcome into our world son." Then she handed Teh Ik to Ai Li and said in Chinese, "Behold your brother." By now, Paini spoke to Ai Li in two languages, sometimes in Malay and other times in Hokkien. Then Malam called his mother and she too was overjoyed for him. He told her to inform his brothers about the birth, and to ask their help to prepare the big celebration in one month's time in the Shih Residence in Malacca. The invitation should extend to all friends and relatives. He was so proud that he felt the whole world should be informed. When he went to the office the next day, he called a restaurant to cater food for all his office staff, and food packages for the laborers in the plantation and warehouses.

For the next few days, Malam went to work radiating happiness every where he went. Meanwhile, his brothers, their wives and Mrs. Shih were in the midst of preparing and sending out invitations for the big party. Then three weeks later, Paini called Malam at the office. "Malam," Paini's voice sounded tearful and that sent a shiver down his spine. "Come home now. We need you." He put down the phone without saying anything and rushed to his car. He drove like a madman. He saw the car of the family doctor on the driveway when he arrived home. He jumped out of his car and rushed into his house. Paini was hugging a hysterical Ah Leng, while the doctor was trying to give her a sedative in the form of an injection. Without saying anything Malam rushed into Ah Leng's room. He let out an agonizing cry when he saw that his baby was completely covered with a blanket. The doctor had followed him into the room and said that the baby died in his sleep, and there was nothing he could do. Malam uncovered his son and carried him in his arms, shaking him and willing him to cry out. But the infant remained cold in his arms. Paini came into the room and gently took the dead child from her husband and laid it back into its crib, covering it again with the blanket. She hugged her husband and allowed him to weep bitterly on her small shoulders. Then Ah Leng, who was still sobbing joined them, and they hugged each other and comforted each other in this great loss. Fortunately little Ai Li was still in school. When she got back, her parents had collected themselves, and were able to break the bad news to her gently. Ai Li was just as heartbroken. For the last three weeks, Teh Ik was the first person she would see, when she came back from school. She loved him dearly and never stopped talking about him in school. But no one suffered more than Malam. To him the curse of many years ago had struck its first chord.

For many days after that it was a pathetic Malam who went to work late, because he drank himself to sleep every night and it was even more pathetic when he came home. He was listless and moody. He had no appetite, even though his favorite food was laid on the table. He spent his nights in his office drinking and falling asleep on the couch. If not for his faithful accountant and assistant manager, his expending business would have suffered. They knew that he was going through a mourning period and they pulled all the resources they had to run his business for him. Thus his business survived, but his family was breaking apart. Ah Leng was very irritable, because of her husband's neglect, and Paini began to feel the strain of trying to keep peace in the house. It was getting worse, especially when Malam came home late after some heavy drinking at the club, and stumbled into one of his wives' room demanding sex. Ah Leng would scream at him and push him out of her room. But Paini would simply turn away and allow him to fall asleep on her bed.

It went on like that for a few months until Mrs. Shih answered Paini's call for help. She asked her son Chin to drive her and Suji to Klang for a few days. Chin, knowing of his brother's pathetic situation decided to stay on and help. After all, he was the eldest and Malam had always respected him. When Malam did not come home on the day they arrived in Klang, it was Chin who found him at the clubhouse, drinking all alone at the bar. He was too drunk to be surprised to see his brother. However, he went home with Chin willingly. It was when he saw his mother's stern and disappointed look that he managed to sober up a bit and said, "Hi Mother, why didn't you tell me you were coming?" His mother glared at him, handed him a cup of hot steaming coffee and said, "Drink this and we will talk." Chin looked at their mother and shook his head. "Let us get him to bed and tomorrow, when he is sober, you can talk to him." Paini and Ah Leng were still up, and Paini told Chin to help him onto her bed. Ah Leng just went into her room and shut the door after her. Malam went to sleep almost immediately, while Paini sat on her bed and looked sadly at her husband. She still loved him as much as before. If only the past would stay buried.

The next day was Saturday, so there was no school for Ai Li. Paini had arranged to take Ai Li and Suji for a long shopping spree. She would suggest that Ah Leng came along. She thought it best for the brothers and their mother to be alone. Ah Leng agreed to go along and before Malam got up, his wives and his daughter were gone. He was surprised to find his mother and brother alone at the breakfast table. His mother did not look angry anymore and he was relieved. He sat down, and Chin poured him a cup of coffee saying, "Your wives have taken Ai Li and Suji shopping." Malam just grunted and drank his coffee quietly. He was beginning to feel ashamed that his mother saw him in the same situation that he was many years ago, when he was a teenager. The shame was a start of some awakening in him. Mrs. Shih detected some remorse, and was glad for that would make her work easier. She put her hand out to Malam and touched his saying, "Son, we know what you are going through. Losing your son does not mean it has anything to do with the curse. Many babies have died that way." Malam pulled away his hand and buried his face in both of them. He said fiercely, "If it was a co-incidence, why did it have to be my very first born?" Then Chin said, "Would it have made a difference if it was your second or third? Would you feel differently?" Malam could not answer him. Then as tears began to gather in his eyes, he looked at his mother and said, "Tell me how can I stop blaming myself for what happened long ago?" His mother replied, "Convince yourself that it was not your doing that caused the girl to commit suicide. It was the decision of both your father and her father. Your future is here in this house with your two wives and daughter, and many more daughters and sons to come. I was wrong about Ah Leng, but I do think you did the right thing. She is very fertile and loves you enough to give you as many children as your heart desires." Malam looked at his mother gratefully and said, "Once again you have rescued me. I thank you for coming and opening up my eyes. I promise you that I shall never let you down again." It was a different Malam who greeted his family when they returned home. Paini looked at her mother-in-law gratefully. Ah Leng too felt appreciative of the older lady who now had a gentle smile for her. When it was time, Mrs. Shih, Suji and Chin left a happy family to go back to Malacca, after extracting a promise from them to spend the next Chinese New Year in Malacca.

It was a happy Ah Leng who welcomed her husband back into her room and even though he spent more nights with her than with Paini, his first wife never complained, and when Ah Leng became pregnant again, they felt the same joy and happiness as before. A year later, Ah Leng gave birth to a baby girl, delivered by Madam Teoh in the same room. Malam was just as proud to have a girl and named her Jo Lin. Only this time, he made sure that at no time should she be alone. There had to be someone by her crib to check on her once in a while as she slept. A maid was hired to help with the new baby and the house chores. Then when Jo Lin became two years old and as healthy as can be, Malam began to relax and the memory of the curse faded. Ah Leng conceived again and David was born in 1937, followed by John in 1939. They were both born in the same house and delivered by the same mid-wife. Malam had decided to give his future children English names, since he spoke only English to his children. They would still be registered under Chinese names in their birth certificates. As his family increased, Malam decided that it was time to build a mansion. He began to look for a big piece of land on the other side of the river and closer to his plantation. He had also worked out the plan of the house with a number of architects. Then something happened and Malam had to give up his plans.

The warehouse where bales of rubber waiting to be exported were kept was burnt down, destroying other warehouses and part of the plantation with it. Malam suffered a great loss especially when the importers had paid for the rubber in advance. The insurance only covered the destroyed buildings and that was not enough to repay the importers and rebuild the warehouses as well as reshaping the destroyed land. It would take a long time to be able to produce the same amount of rubber that was destroyed. Malam's business was at a great risk. To make matters worse, it was also a period of economic regression in the country. It was hard to get loans from the bank. The Shihs in Malacca wanted to help, but because of the regression, the Shih Enterprise was not doing too well. Malam had no choice but to sell his business at a loss. He would rather do that than to declare bankruptcy. Remembering how his ancestors started their business, he decided to start an import and export enterprise. With the little money that he had left, he could only start with a small shop and on a small scale. He found an old building close to his house, but on the other side of the river. He bought it and turned it into a merchant shop. He started with basic foods like rice, flour, sugar and wheat. In the beginning, he could only hire a man to help him, and there were many other things that his family had to give up. They gave up the maids, sold the extra car and the chauffeur was the only employee in the shop. Even though Malam lost his fortune, he was still a happy man. His family was more united than ever, standing by him and supporting him in this new endeavor. The business was slow but steady, and as long as he could support his family, he was satisfied.

It was when Ah Leng announced that she was again with a child that Malam felt he had to speed up his business somehow. He decided that while running his own business, he would also work as a consultant to other businesses, especially the new ones. With his qualifications and talent, Malam was in demand, and was earning more money than the profits he got from his import and export business. Soon, he had enough to expand his shop, and began to add more commodities to import and export. As his business grew, Malam continued to be a consultant and when his third son Gary was born in 1940, he was once more a rich man, not as rich as before, but rich enough to return some of the luxuries his family had to give up. He bought them a new car and hired another chauffeur, because the old chauffeur was good at his job, and Malam wanted to keep him at the shop. As Malam's shop grew in size, he began to dream of buying another plantation and was looking around for one, when the idea was disrupted by news that the Japanese were invading Malaya. That threw the country into chaos. People tried to sell their businesses, afraid that the war would destroy everything they owned, but Malam held on to his and when the Japanese invaded Malaya on December 8, 1941, Malam was still running his business.

Malam was glad that he did not own a rubber plantation during the Japanese occupancy. Because a war was on during the whole occupation period, the Japanese Government concentrated on its military position, and paid little heed to the economic development of the country. The two major industries, rubber and tin came to a standstill. They regressed. Tin dredges were destroyed or left to rust and rubber trees were cut down to give way to tapioca plants. Malam's old plantation was in fact used as a Japanese camp to hold prisoners. The newly restored warehouses were the prison camps and the compound was fenced off by barbed wires. Any one trying to escape would be shot or tortured till they died. The Japanese allowed Malam to carry on his business, with the condition that he supplied them with the best imported Siamese rice. The other reason that his business was not interrupted, was because it transpired within south East Asia. The Japanese Government tried to discredit the Allied Powers like Britain and the United States, and destroy their influence on Asian people. They did not know then that Malam had voluntarily got himself involved with the British intelligence, to report Japanese activities through radio communications. In fact none of his family was aware of this secret assignment of his.

The Japanese treated the people under their rule with no respect, and those who did not comply would be harshly punished or put to death. One of the first things they did was to restrict movement of the people. Everyone had to be registered, and certificates were issued. They also received 'banana notes' to be used as currencies during the occupational years. The notes were so called because it had pictures of banana trees printed on them. There was widespread food rationing, and food ration cards were issued so that there would be enough food for everyone. But this proved useless, as there was not enough food because the Japanese took most of the supplies for their soldiers. This resulted in poverty and caused severe economic problems. Healthcare was also jeopardized as most of the medical supplies were sent to military bases. Many people died of diseases, especially from tuberculosis, which was pervasive because of poor sanitation.   Children were forced to learn Japanese and sing Japanese songs. The curriculum of the education system followed very closely to that of Japan. Singing of the Japanese national anthem was compulsory before school commenced. In this case, Malam was thankful that Jo Lin had not yet attended school.

 Worst and most feared of all was that the Japanese soldiers were plundering homes and raping young girls. Malam feared for his daughter Ai Li, who was now fifteen years old. It was good that the Japanese had shut down most English oriented schools and the Convent was one of them. Ai Li need not leave the house at all. But that did not mean that she was safe from the Japanese. They would march into a house unannounced, and demand food and look around for young girls to quench their sexual appetites. Interfering parents would be shot at once. While Malam was worrying about his daughter, his old chauffeur, now his assistant in his shop came to him one day and said, "Sir, I know it is not my place to ask you this favor, but I am very desperate. I have an eighteen year old daughter, whose fiancée ran into the jungle to join the rebels and was killed by the Japanese. I am afraid that if I do not do anything for her, she will fall prey to the Japanese soldiers. You are a good man and I beg you to take my daughter into your house." Malam did not know what his employee wanted of him so he said, "I too have a teenage daughter and I am also worried about her. Every time, there is a knock on our door, she runs and hides under the bed. Nothing has happened so far, but one day, it could be Japanese soldiers and they would turn the house upside down to satisfy their animal instincts." The man spoke pleadingly, "I know, what you mean. But you are a good man and if you marry my daughter, the Japanese may leave her alone, because they are more interested in virgins." Malam was shocked at the man's proposal. "My second wife will never accept it." "But," the desperate father continued to plead, "This is a period of war and we are all trying to survive. Please take my daughter. You don't have to marry her. Just make sure that she is not a virgin when the Japanese get her." Malam could only think of one possibility. This man had been very loyal to him. He had to help him so he said, "Send your daughter to my house tonight. I will treat her like my own daughter, and I shall find a way to hide both the girls should the Japanese soldiers show up at our house." The man said, "Thank you. I know that you will protect her well."

Malam had prepared his wives about the appearance of the girl that night. Paini liked their old chauffeur very much and was willing to help. Ah Leng was reluctant, but as usual had to give in to her husband. Earlier that day, after the conversation with his assistant, Malam had purchased an old sampan. He tied it to one of the mangrove trees by the river. He had cut a hole in the fence bordering the river. If the Japanese appeared at the door, the two young girls could run out the back way, get into the sampan and row out until they could hide under the bridge. It was too late to teach them how to row, and although the river was deep, the currents were not strong, so the girls would be able to use their common sense on how to row to safety. It was late that night, when there was a soft knock at the main door. Malam need not look out of his window to see who his night visitors were. The Japanese would not knock. They would bang the door with their rifles. He opened the door quickly to let his employee and the young girl in. All the children were fast asleep, except for Ai Li. Without even looking at the girl who was introduced as Cheng Mee, Malam told Ai Li to take the girl into her room. Ai Li put her arms around the shivering girl and said, "My name is Ai Li and you are gong to share my room." As they walked away, Malam noticed that his daughter was taller and bigger than Cheng Mee. Cheng Mee's father shook Malam's hand gratefully and left quickly. Paini went to Ai Li's room to help settle the newcomer, and Malam followed Ah Leng into her room. He could feel her disapproval, so he decided to pamper her that night. Ah Leng had seen the girl's face and was seething with jealousy. The girl was small in size, but she had a face that would capture many hearts. She wondered if her husband had noticed that. Instead of going directly into her room, she led Malam into the room where her three children slept. Seven year old Jo Lin slept on a bed in one corner, and David and John had their beds in another corner. Gary, who was just a year old, was still sleeping in a cot in Ah Leng's room. Malam was not aware that it was Ah Leng's way of reminding him that she had given him all these children.

Meanwhile, Cheng Mee lay in bed afraid and alone. She had been living in fear since the day her best friend was raped and brutally beaten up. Three Japanese soldiers had seen the girl hanging clothes in the back of her house. They moved up slowly without her noticing them. When she saw them it was too late. Afraid to cry for help, in case her parents came running out and would be shot by the soldiers, she allowed them to drag her into the jungle. When they found out that she was not a virgin as they expected, they beat her up. Nevertheless, they satisfied themselves with her and left her naked and bloody to find her way home. She was too ashamed to face her own parents, so instead of going home she went to Cheng Mee, hoping that the girl would be alone. She was lucky that Cheng Mee's brothers were out in the fields planting tapioca plants for the

Japanese. Only Cheng Mee was at home. She tended to her wounds and put her to bed. That night, when her parents came to look for her, they found her in the bathroom dead. The soldiers had raped her with hate and anger, and had caused her to die of internal hemorrhaging. From then on, Cheng Mee's brothers stayed in the house to protect their little sister. Cheng Mee was the only girl and her two brothers were two and three years older than her. Her mother died when she was seven years old and she became the young mistress of her home cooking for her father and two brothers. The three men loved her dearly. Before he brought Cheng Mee to Malam's house, her father explained, to her, "I would rather see you married to an older man than have the Japanese defile your body. My boss already has two wives, but he has a heart of gold. He has refused to marry you, but will protect you like he protects his daughter. But if for some reason, you feel that he likes you, do not reject him." Cheng Mee could not believe that her father was willing to give her up to a man old enough to be her father who already had two wives. But then, the fate of being a third wife was better than the fate of her poor friend.

Even though she was the last to fall asleep the night before, Cheng Mee woke up before anyone else. She was moving around in the kitchen, hoping to make herself useful by preparing breakfast for the whole family, when she heard the door to Ah Leng's room opening. It was Malam. Since the time he got involved with British Intelligence, he would leave the house very early to get into his office when everyone else was asleep. Then after his secret report, he would return to have breakfast with his family. He saw Cheng Mee pottering around and said, "Child, go back to sleep. It is only six o'clock in the morning." When Cheng Mee turned round to wish him good morning, he saw her clearly for the first time. He was stunned by her beautiful face. Except for her fair skin, she could have been Paini's younger sister. She had the same sad look as Paini when Malam first saw her. Her features were not Chinese at all. Her eyes were round and her small nose had a high bridge. Her lips were not as full as Paini's, but they were well curved. Her short curly hair was blue-black. She was about four feet six inches tall, and weighed around ninety pounds. When Malam realized that he was attracted to her, he pulled himself together and tried to speak as casually as he could. "If you can't sleep, you can dig out some tapioca in our garden and boil them. My wives will get up soon and they will help you with the rest. I have to go to the office now and will be back in time for breakfast." He left Cheng Mee hurriedly.

Left alone, Cheng Mee could not get rid of the excitement she felt when Malam looked at her. She had heard that he was handsome, but she never thought that he could be so attractive and youngish looking. She had never been interested in any man before. Like most girls of her culture and upbringing, she would wait for her parents to find her a good husband. She was also of the Baba and Nyona heritage, but unlike Malam, her ancestors migrated to Penang, which was also another flourishing port during the period of the Dutch and Portuguese settlement. She had gone to an English school until she was twelve years old, so besides Hokkien, she could speak English and Malay quite well. Malam had spoken to her in Malay as he did with his wives. If he treated her like his daughter, he would have spoken English to her. She was secretly happy that he did not do that. Then when she heard Gary crying, she knew that Ah Leng was awake, so brushing all thoughts of Malam from her mind, she went to the backyard and dug out some tapioca.

Besides tapioca, Paini and Ah Leng had labored to grow lots of vegetables and sugarcanes. They had a fenced up area where they reared chickens and ducks. Most of them however were taken by the Japanese to feed their own soldiers. Like everyone else, Malam and his family had to live on the rations the Japanese provided them. Even though they grew their own vegetables and reared their own poultry, they could hardly make use of them themselves. They would get into trouble if the Japanese came and there was not enough to provide them with. Tapioca was different. It was easy to grow, and there was an abundance of it in the backyard. While Cheng Mee was digging up the tapioca, Paini joined her and kindly asked her how she slept. Cheng Mee felt touched by her kindness, and wished that the second wife was just as nice. She had already felt Ah Leng's hostility last night. The woman had looked at her with unfriendly eyes, and did not welcome her into the house as Ai Li and Paini did. While Paini helped her with the tapioca, she asked in Malay, "How should I address you and the other mistress of the house?" Paini thought for a while, and felt that Ah Leng would not accept the word 'sister', so she said, "Call me by name and address my younger sister as 'madam', unless she says otherwise. "What about Sir? Can I call him Sir like my father does?" Paini smiled and said, "That is fine. Well we have enough tapioca for the day, but before we go back into the house, I have to show you something." Malam had instructed Paini to tell Ai Li and Cheng Mee about the sampan, so Paini showed Cheng Mee where the sampan was, and explained to her what it was for. Then she added, "If the situation arises, and you have to make use of the sampan, do not come back until you see one of us standing on this bank and waving a big white towel."

Paini and Ah Leng had questioned Malam about the reason for going to his office so early, and then coming back for breakfast, instead of just going after breakfast. He had to lie to them about wanting to set his accounts straight, so that the Japanese would not accuse him of hiding anything from them. He was not very clear with his explanation, but his wives knew better than to question him further. That morning, as most mornings, he removed the Japanese flag that was pinned to the wall in his office and took out a radio transmitter from a dug-out hole in the wall. He relayed to his British source that the Japanese had taken over the newspapers and radio stations and the broadcasts only consisted of Japanese songs and slogans. Most of the teachers in schools were Japanese, and they spoke very lowly of the British. Only Japanese and Asian films were showed in cinemas. Then when he was done, he replaced the flag and sat down at his desk and allowed his thoughts to wonder back to his morning encounter with Cheng Mee. No wonder her father feared for his daughter. Her untainted beauty would attract not only the Japanese, but any men who saw her. He shuddered to think about her under the mercy of the Japanese soldiers. Not only did he develop a sense of protection towards her, he had also developed a great desire for her. Then he reprimanded himself and decided to forget that he even thought of Cheng Mee that way. She was really young enough to be his daughter.

CHAPTER 14

As the Japanese Occupation of Malaya continued, poverty and sicknesses prevailed. Food rations became less, and medical supplies were hard to come by. The Japanese became more violent in plundering houses at random, so women tried to make themselves as ugly as possible, some dressing as men, and some painting their faces in black coal. Word reached Malam's household that the Japanese were getting close to their area and they would show up anytime soon. Malam had avoided looking at Cheng Mee, but he still felt her presence. He was aware of Ah Leng's aloofness towards the girl, so he tried his best not to look at Cheng Mee, but whenever he spent the nights with Paini, he would discuss the relationship between the young girl and his second wife. "Well, my dear husband, you cannot blame Ah Leng for being jealous. Cheng Mee is quite a beauty and you do feel some attraction towards her. Am I right?" Paini was so direct that Malam blushed, but answered almost immediately. "I am fond of the girl, because she is the daughter of my faithful employee. As long as she is under my roof, I will have to protect her. I only hope the idea with rowing off in the sampan works. I don't know if I can live if anything happened to our daughter or to her." Paini looked at her husband affectionately and thought to herself. "He has a heart big enough to love more than one." Then she promised her husband, "I will keep an eye to make sure that Ah Leng's hostility does not become too obvious. Cheng Mee may just run off and endanger her life in the process."

One night, Malam had more work to do at his shop. He had informed his wives not to wait up for him as he would be back very late. He got back after midnight and was sitting in the kitchen with a glass of whisky in his hand, when he heard a soft voice behind him saying in English, "Sir, can I talk to you?" He turned around and saw Cheng Mee. She was fully dressed in a sarong and a loose Chinese blouse. "Why are you dressed up? You should be in bed." "I am always ready to run out in case the soldiers come." Then Malam saw the fear in the girl's eyes, and was overcome with the desire to protect her from all harm. Unconsciously, he extended his hands out to her and she came to him. At first it was a gesture to comfort her, but as she moved into his arms, he forgot himself, and indulged himself in the joy and pleasure of her warm and small body. She too responded to his touch, and soon they were looking into each other's eyes with love and desire. Malam kissed her gently on her forehead, but she moved her lips to meet his, and soon they were kissing and stroking each other. In the midst of their passion Cheng Mee said, "Take me before the soldiers do."

147

Those words jerked Malam to reality and he pushed her aside. He could not believe that he almost made love to her. Then he said, "Cheng Mee, I will not have you unless you love me and I love you. I will die before I allow the soldiers to touch you. Right now, I am tired and confused. What happened just now was my fault. Please go to sleep and trust me." Cheng Mee looked at him and said sadly, "Under normal circumstances, I will still want you. I do love you." Then she walked towards Ai Li's room leaving Malam staring after her. He could not go to either wife's room that night. He went into his study and thankfully fell asleep quite easily on the sofa.

For sometime now, Malam had less and less information for the British Intelligence as the Japanese were very secretive in their moves. Since they captured Singapore, they made Singapore their headquarters to plot and plan strategies. Malam's business was also jeopardized, as rice became more expensive and scarce, and people began to eat tapioca as their stable food. Meanwhile, as movement was restricted, and most telephone wires were destroyed, Malam had no news about his family in Malacca. He was not aware that the Japanese had invaded his mother's home, and used it to house some of their officers. They kept the two women in the house as servants to cook and serve them. In the process, from lack of nutrition and hard work, Mrs. Shih succumbed to ill health. They allowed her eldest son Chin to take her to his home, but they held on to Suji, who at age fifty was still strong. However, Suji did something brave and lost her life in that process. Poultry and eggs were brought in for Suji to cook for the Japanese officers. She knew that her friend needed good food to survive, so she smuggled a chicken and some eggs to Chin's house. She was caught in the act and was shot on the spot. Mrs. Shih was devastated, but did not know how to get word to Paini. With a lot of begging and pleas, the Japanese allowed the Shihs to perform a decent burial for the brave woman. She was buried beside her husband. Paini never knew of the fate of her mother until after the Japanese were defeated.

As the Japanese continued to make the lives of its occupied people miserable, Cheng Mee was facing a different kind of misery at Malam's house. As Malam spent more time at home, it was hard for him to hide the fact that he had feelings for her. Ah Leng saw the way he looked at Cheng Mee, and noticed the tone of voice, he used when he talked to her. She began to make Cheng Mee's life miserable, and that created disharmony between her and Paini. Finally, Cheng Mee could not bear to be the cause of the quarrels between Malam's two wives, so she decided to leave. Early one morning, when she thought everyone was fast asleep, she dressed as a boy, painted her face black with ash, and tied a cloth over her short curly hair. She tied her clothes in a bundle and left the house to go home. She knew that it was dangerous, but she kept away from the main roads, and hid behind bushes each time she heard voices. It took her about three hours to reach her home. Her brothers greeted her happily, but her father was angry that she took such a big risk. She explained to him why she could not continue to stay with his boss. "His second wife hates me and fights a lot with Paini, who is kind and nice to me." Her father asked, "Has the second wife a reason to be angry?" Cheng Mee decided to tell the truth. "I have looked at your boss as a prospective husband. I am sure that I could learn to love such a man as he. I think he also likes me." Her father did not say anything but his eyes were questioning. Cheng Mee knew what the question was. She shook her head and said, "That is why I respect him. I have offered myself to him, but he will not take me, unless I become his wife. But I know that is not possible. So please find another man to marry me before the Japanese get me." He looked at his daughter's smeared face and smiled secretly thinking to himself, "No matter what she does to her face, she is still beautiful. There is no problem to find a man for her, but to find the right one will be hard." Aloud, he said, "But until then, we have to hide you, and I don't know how. You must not show yourself outside this door, until I think of something."

When Ai Li ran to Paini's room and announced that Cheng Mee had left the house, Malam who had spent the night with his first wife, was alarmed. "If anything happened to her, I will never forgive myself." He jumped out of bed, dressed hurriedly and went out to his car. Fortunately, when the Japanese started claiming properties from the rich people, they had left Malam one car. He got into it and drove to his assistant's house hoping with all his heart that he would find Cheng Mee unharmed in her father's house. When one of the boys opened the door to Malam's insistent knocking, his first question was, "Is your sister here?" Then Cheng Mee who was sent into hiding came out of her room, her face still smeared, and in boy's clothes. At first Malam could not recognize her, but when she said, "I am sorry sir," he went to her without thinking, and hugged her in relief. Then realizing where he was, he let go of her suddenly and said, "That is not nice of you to just run away like that." Then Cheng Mee's father intervened, "She did not run away from you. She ran away from your second wife." Malam sat down and said, "I am sorry. It is my fault. I should have kept my feelings within me." It was too late for him to retract those words. Then his assistant sighed and said, "Sir, if you love my daughter, marry her. You only need the first wife's permission. The Japanese are not leaving any stones unturned." Malam looked at Cheng Mee and realized that his love for her was not just lust. He had the same desire to cherish and protect her as he had for Paini many years ago. He went on his knees and asked her, "Cheng Mee will you be my wife?" Cheng Mee pulled him up and said, "I am the one who should go on my knees and thank you for wanting me. Yes, I will be your third wife, not because I am afraid of the Japanese, but because I truly love you."

Malam knew that Ah Leng would never accept his decision, but at this point, all he cared about was Cheng Mee. He would first talk to Paini, and based upon her answer, which he was sure was going to be positive; he would break the news to Ah Leng. Before he left, he promised to come back later in the day to pick Cheng Mee up. He told her not to change her disguise until they got to his house. Paini could sense her husband's mounting excitement as he asked her to go into her room with him. Once the door was closed behind them, Malam took Paini's hands into his and said, "Paini, I want your permission to marry again." Paini withdrew her hands and stood at the window looking out of it. "We are in the midst of war and difficult times. How can you think of marriage?" Malam replied, "It is because of the war that I have to marry Cheng Mee almost immediately." Paini sighed, "It makes no more difference to me if I have one or two sisters. I will give you my permission, but I am afraid that there will be no more harmony in this family." Malam knew what she meant. Ah Leng would never accept Cheng Mee, but she had to accept his decision. If she made life miserable for everyone, she would have to leave. Malam hoped not, for he still loved and appreciated her for the children she had given him. He wondered if wanting and loving more than one woman at a time was a weakness or a capability. He was sure that he had never stopped loving Paini, when he met Ah Leng. The same went for Ah Leng. He still loved her, despite his feelings for Cheng Mee. Paini had mentioned that he had a heart big enough to love more than one. She was right. Those thoughts took away any guilty feelings he might have had towards his two wives, and gave him the courage to approach Ah Leng.

"No way!" Ah Leng screamed, when Malam relayed his intentions to marry Cheng Mee. "If she comes back to this house, I will leave," she threatened. Malam tried to soothe her, "Ah Leng, marrying Cheng Mee will not reduce my love for you. I love you and will always appreciate you for our children." "You will destroy my respect and love for you, if you marry again." Ah Leng's last sentence made Malam very angry. "How can you say that when you married me, despite the fact that I still loved Paini?" Ah Leng retorted, "It was different. Paini could not bear you any children." Knowing that it was useless to go on arguing, Malam ended the conversation by saying, "Paini has given me permission to take Cheng Mee as my third wife. I am going to pick her up and we will have a small tea ceremony tonight to seal the pact of marriage." He left Ah Leng in hysterical tears. The children and Paini overheard everything, and Ai Li was comforting the tearful Jo Lin. Paini had the crying Gary in her arms, while David and John played with their toys quietly. When Malam came out of his room, Jo Lin ran to him and said, "Papa, please don't hurt mother." He squatted down to be at eye level with his eight year old daughter and said, "Darling, I love you all and nothing will change that. I hope you will understand when you grow older." He kissed her forehead and nodded at Paini, who returned the nod, then left to bring back his future bride.

When he returned with Cheng Mee who was still disguised as a boy, Ah Leng had left with Gary. Paini told Malam that they were at Ah Leng's parents' house. She added, "Let it be. She will come back when she is ready. For the sake of the children, let us hold the tea ceremony quietly in my room only with Ai Li as witness." Paini did not tell Malam that Ah Leng had approached her and begged her to stop the marriage. "Big Sister, I beg you to help me stop Cheng Mee from entering our lives," Ah Leng had pleaded. Then Paini without trying to be unkind said, "I could not stop him from marrying you. How could I do that now?" In her heart she added, "The more the merrier." In a way Cheng Mee, was glad that Ah Leng was not around. It was hard enough to feel Jo Lin's hostility towards her as she entered the house. David and John were still absorbed in the games and acted very indifferently. Paini did her best to make the guest room as presentable for Cheng Mee as was possible during the wartime. Cheng Mee had showered and was getting ready for the ceremony with Ai Li's help, when Jo Lin walked in. Ai Li was about to shoo her out of the room when Cheng Mee said, "It is alright. Let Jo Lin says what she wants to." Encouraged, Jo Lin, her eyes filling with tears said, "My brothers and I will never call you 'mother'. We have only two mothers, 'First Mother' and our mother." Cheng Mee smiled kindly at the little girl and said, "I understand that I cannot be your mother. Call me what you like, but I want to be your friend. I love your father and so I also love his children." Without another word, Jo Lin left the room, collected her two brothers and locked themselves up in their room. She was fuming, and she wanted to hurt her father. She should be attending school at this age, but her father wanted to hold back for as long as possible. She would insist on attending school the next day, and learn to sing all the Japanese songs the school taught. That way she would spend less time at home.

In January 1943, two years after the Japanese defeated the British and invaded Malaya, Malam married his third wife. It was a very quiet ceremony in the privacy of Paini's room. Sixteen year old Ai Li was the only witness as Cheng Mee served Paini tea in reverence. Paini sat on an armchair and Malam and Cheng Mee stood before her. Malam was in the same suit he wore when he married Ah Leng and Cheng Mee had a simple kebaya and sarong on. Ai Li had a tray with a teapot and a cup. Cheng Mee poured the tea into the tea cup, went on her knees and handed the cup with two hands to Paini saying, "Big Sister, with this I pay you respect and thank you for accepting me into your family. Paini sipped the tea and handed the cup back to Ai Li. Then when Malam and Cheng Mee knelt together in front of her, she placed her hands one on each of their heads and said, "I accept you Cheng Mee as the third wife to my husband, and sister to me and his second wife. Malam, I shall continue to serve you as your wife. I wish you both as much happiness as I have." Her voice choked on her last sentence. Malam got up and kissed her and said, "My beloved wife, I shall always love you and only death can separate us." Then he pulled Cheng Mee up, kissed her too and said, "I pledge you my love and protection." The ceremony ended without any big meal. When Ah Leng's children did not come out of their room at dinner, which was again tapioca in different forms, baked, boiled and fried, Ai Li took their food into the room for them. That night, Malam and Cheng Mee consummated their love, while Paini cried herself to sleep. Even though she had resigned herself to her husband's multiple loves, she could not help feeling a sense of loneliness and loss. Her husband at forty seven was still as handsome as he was when she first saw him. She was sure that this was not his last marriage.

"No, you are not going to school yet," Malam told his daughter when she said that she would like to attend school. "I am eight years old and Ai Li went to school when she was seven," Jo Lin argued. Then in tears she told her father, "I miss Mother. If you don't let me go to school, then let my brothers and I go to live with her and Gary." That jolted Malam to reality. Ah Leng and his little son Gary had been gone for over a month and he had not missed them. He felt guilty and promised Jo Lin, "I am going now to bring back your mother and brother. There can be no more discussion about going to school until the Japanese make it compulsory. By the way, since you are now a big girl, we shall move your bed into Ai Li's room. Would you like that?" Malam knew how to get around his children. He knew that Jo Lin had looked up to Ai Li, and would be thrilled to sleep with her older sister. He was sure that Ai Li would have no objections. If she had, he would ask her to do that as a favor for him. Jo Lin was thrilled, and forgetting her anger, ran to her room to get her things ready. Before Malam left to bring back his second wife, he talked to Ai Li, who said, "That will be nice. I can start teaching Jo Lin some reading and writing." He kissed his adopted daughter. She had always been a good girl and he had never regretted adopting her. He loved her as much as the children of his own flesh and blood. Now the big problem was to reason with Ah Leng. He hoped that he can convince her that he still loved her. He had made up his mind that if she came back, he would spend the whole week in her room. Gary was old enough to move in with his brothers.

Malam had no need to worry. Ah Leng had been expecting him to come much earlier. She had missed him terribly, although she greeted him coldly when he knocked at their door. But when Malam said, "Ah Leng, we all missed you, especially me. Please come home with me now." Her coldness melted and tears filled her eyes as she replied, "Why did you wait so long to come?" Without another word, she ran to a room and collected her ready luggage while Malam played a little with his son. Gary too was happy to see his father. Ah Leng was given a very warm welcome by Paini and all the children. Cheng Mee kept to her room. Paini had already organized another tea ceremony between Ah Leng and Cheng Mee. At first Cheng Mee was reluctant. She had said, "What do I do if Ah Leng refuses my tea?" Paini answered, "If Ah Leng comes back, it also means that she accepts you. I will be here to support you so have no fear." Malam felt appreciation and admiration for his first wife. He truly felt unworthy of her. Ah Leng agreed to the tea ceremony and it was held in the living room. This time the whole family was there to witness it. She took the tea from Cheng Mee and said just one word, "Welcome." But she did the most unexpected thing, when she told Cheng Mee to sit on her chair and commanded all the children including Ai Li, to pour tea each and hand it to Cheng Mee. She told them to call her 'Third Mother' each time she took the cup from them. Malam was overwhelmed with pride and happiness as he watched his children in turn, obediently pour tea into a cup and hand it to Cheng Mee calling her 'Third Mother' each time. Cheng Mee in turn kissed them on their foreheads. When Malam was alone with Ah Leng that night, he told her, "I shall never forget this wonderful gesture." Ah Leng said, "I did it because I love you with all my heart." He spent the whole week with her, and she was glad to be part of his life again. As the people of Malaya continued to suffer under the reign of the Japanese, harmony returned to Malam's house. Ah Leng was not hostile towards Cheng Mee, but neither was she friendly towards her. It did not bother Cheng Mee too much because Paini was kind and loving towards her. Malam was fair to all his three wives and divided his attention and time equally.

The sampan was left tied to the mangrove tree and there was never a need to make use of it. The Japanese did not bother Malam's family because he was supplying them with imported rice. He spent less and less time in his shop as the economy in Malaya sank lower and lower. He still contacted the British once in a while, but there was nothing much to report. One day, in July of 1945 Malam went to his shop very early, but did not return home for lunch as he normally did. At first, his wives thought that he had more work than expected, but when he did not show up at dinner, they began to worry. It was too late and dangerous to send anyone to the shop to check on him, so they sat down and waited. Then when it was close to midnight and he had not returned, they were desperate. There were no men in the house, and although a curfew was not declared, not even men would dare to attempt to go out so late at night. The Japanese were trigger happy and would simply shoot anyone on sight. There was nothing they could do but go to bed and hope for the best. But it was a sleepless night for the three wives and for Ai Li. Ai Li was sleeping on the same bed as Paini and she could hear her daughter sobbing. She sat up in bed and said, "Don't worry, I shall sneak out tomorrow to find out what happened. Maybe, he had to entertain the Japanese in his shop so that they do not bother us. He may be quite drunk and decided to sleep in his office." Ai Li hugged her mother and whimpered, "Let me come with you." "Oh no," Paini replied. "You have to stay and help your mothers look after your younger sister and brothers."

As soon as it was light, Paini dressed up in the clothes that Cheng Mee wore once to disguise herself as a boy, smeared her face with black coal, and was about to leave the house, when she saw Ah Leng also disguised the same way coming out of her room. Cheng Mee and Ai Li were also up. "Looks like we both have the same idea," Ah Leng commented. "Yes, well we had better get going before it is bright and the soldiers could see through our disguise." Cheng Mee knew that it was hers and Ai Li's responsibility to stay back and look after the children, so she said, "Please be careful." So together, Paini and Ah Leng left to search for their husband.

They passed a few Japanese soldiers, who thought they were some young boys going to work in the fields. Although the shop was not too far away, it took them an hour to get there on foot. When they saw that the door was wide open, and there were no lights on in the building, their fear made them forget that they could be watched. They ran into the small building calling their husband softly. Even without switching on the lights, they knew that the shop had been ransacked. The sacks of rice, flour, sugar and all major foods were gone. The shop floor was strewed with other smaller items. Then Paini went into Malam's office where he kept his books and accounts. The door was ajar and she pushed it open, and her stifled scream brought Ah Leng running to her. Everything was in a big mess. Papers were strewed on the floor, pictures frames were smashed to pieces. Then slowly as they looked at a broken radio, they began to realize that the Japanese had ransacked the office. There was a gaping hole where the Japanese flag used to hang. In the midst of fear that the worst had happened to Malam, both the wives realized that they and their children were in immediate danger. Paini whispered to Ah Leng, "We have to get out of here immediately." Ah Leng nodded and whispered in return, "We have to get everyone out of the house before the Japanese get there. It was obvious that Malam alive or dead was in the hands of the Japanese. They were not sure what he did, but it must be something wrong, especially as the Japanese had banned the use of radios. Without any thoughts for themselves, they ran as fast as they could towards home. They were lucky not to encounter any Japanese.

There was no time to waste. They quickly explained to Cheng Mee what happened. Ah Leng decided to take her children and hide at her parent's house. Paini had no relatives, so Cheng Mee offered, "We can use the sampan and row to my house. I know that my father has not gone to the shop for sometime now. I am sure he does not know what has happened. He and my brothers will be able to help look for Malam." Paini felt grateful and agreed. They packed as little clothes as possible but made sure they took all their jewelry with them. Before the Japanese invasion, Malam had always been very generous with his wives and gave them expensive jewelry for every special occasion. Ah Leng left almost immediately with her children. There was no need for disguise as long as she carried Gary in her arms. It would be a long walk to her home. If they were confronted by soldiers, there was no way for the soldiers to associate them with Malam. However, Paini, Cheng Mee and Ai Li had to disguise themselves as men and boy. Being in the sampan, even if it was light, it would be hard for the Japanese to see through their disguise, as long as they kept in the shadows of the early morning. It may be light before they reached their destination, but if they kept away from the shore they would still be unrecognizable. So finally the sampan was put to use. Good luck was with Malam's family. They managed to arrive at their destinations without any harassment from the soldiers. Cheng Mee's father was shocked to hear that his boss was missing. He never knew that Malam had a hidden radio. The Japanese Government had banned the possession or use of short-wave radio because they did not want the Malayans to listen to broadcasts of the allied powers. To be caught in possession of one of them would mean instant death. However, they all refused to think that Malam had been killed.

From their hiding places, the wives sent feelers out for any information of their beloved husband. It was also at this period, when the wives felt closer to each other. They wished they could be together to comfort each other, and to give each other hope that Malam was still alive. Friends and relatives tried to help, but no one could find out anything. Then when the Japanese were defeated in August 1945, and the British returned to Malaya, Malam's family returned to their home. They were unprepared to see the condition of their once beautiful and well kept house. All the furniture was stolen, taken away, or destroyed. The clothes that they had left behind were also gone. The doors and windows were broken, and rain that came in through them had destroyed the expensive wooden floor. The only usable equipment was the kitchen stove and some old cups and plates. The expensive China was gone. They were completely disheartened, but before anyone of them could decide to return to their parents' house, Paini said, "We can rebuild our home. Malam had given us the means to do this. We are still one family and we shall stay here and await his return." Even as she said it, she had lost all faith that he was still alive. However, she felt responsible for the family she had adopted through her husband's marriages. Cheng Mee hugged her and said, "Yes, I will help you and stay with you for as long as you want me to." Ah Leng added, "I shall also stay for as long as there is no proof of Malam's death, I shall never give up hope." Paini was touched. These two women loved the same man the same way she did. She wanted to be able to assure them that their husband was only missing, but she could not. The Japanese had shown no mercy to people who went against them. They were tortured to death, shot, or beheaded. She shuddered at the thought that her husband might have met his death at the hands of the Japanese.

The Japanese had left Malaya in chaos and poverty, and the people had lost confidence in the British and were wary of foreign influence due to the Japanese propaganda during their occupation. Many rubber trees were destroyed, and tin dredges were rusting away. The British returned to Malaya at its economic decline. The Japanese had taken away assets from the rich, and only a few were lucky enough to still keep their own homes. In the case of Malam's family, although their house was almost destroyed, his wives had managed to protect their expensive jewelry. They pawned their jewelry to furnish their house and bring it back to livable conditions. The Japanese had destroyed many telephone lines, and there was no way to contact families living far away to find out if they had survived the war. The British however brought back some order and soon telephones lines, were reinstated. When that happened, the first thing Paini did was to call Mrs. Shih and her mother, but that line remained dead. Then after many attempts, she managed to contact Chin, Malam's eldest brother. Paini thought her news was bad, but when Chin told her of her mother's death, she broke down. Mrs. Shih, whose own health had been getting worse, tried her best to comfort her daughter in law. "She did not suffer. We managed to bury her close to your father. And I know in my heart that my son is still alive. A mother would sense it if her son died. Be patient, he will show up one day." However, Paini was so distraught that she had forgotten to tell her mother-in-law of Cheng Mee. So before the line went dead, Cheng Mee took the phone from Paini and introduced herself in the Chinese dialect that she was brought up with. Mrs. Shih was quiet for a while, then in the same dialect she said, "Welcome into the family. Have faith that your husband is still alive. Give Paini all the support she needs." Then the old lady hung up, not because she did not want to continue, but she was very weak, and the news that her son married again during the Japanese Occupation was a bit heavy. However, from the way Cheng Mee spoke, she knew that she was a good girl. She accepted her new daughter-in-law in her heart.

Paini cried the whole day and no one could comfort her. All she could think of was that she had lost the two people she loved the most. Paini wished that she could have faith in her mother-in-law's instinct that her husband was still alive, but the war was over for more than a month now, and there was still no trace of her husband. However, she now had the responsibility of her husband. She had a big family to look after, and even though Cheng Mee did not mention it, Paini had noticed the morning sicknesses that she went through. Paini was sure that Cheng Mee was now with a child. After another sleepless night, Paini decided that there was no time for mourning the dead. The living needed her and she would look after them as her husband would have done. There were a lot of repairs to do in the house, and now that most of the jewelry was gone, she had to find other means of bringing in some income. There were five children and three adults to feed. She was sure that she could depend on her two younger sisters. The most important thing was to convey to them the hope that her mother-in-law tried to give her. She looked at the wedding band on her finger, kissed it and said to herself, "Malam, please come back to us."

CHAPTER 15

That morning, just a month before the Japanese were conquered, Malam had decided that he was going to destroy the evidence of his connection with the British Intelligence. He left early without informing any members of his family. He drove his car as close to his shop as he could without having to stop at any check posts that the Japanese had installed. From that point, he had to walk another ten minutes. As he approached his shop, he had an uneasy feeling, when he saw some soldiers standing outside the shop. It was about six in the morning, and his shop was not expected to be opened until eight. However, he bowed to the Japanese soldiers and was about to unlock the door, when he noticed that it was open. Before he could turn away, he was pushed roughly into the building and rough hands grabbed him, pulling him into his office. It was lighted and two Japanese officers were waiting for him. He saw the gaping hole, where his radio transmitter was hidden, and he feared the worst. He would have been taken out and shot immediately, if not for the intervention of one of the officers who had befriended him, and regarded him with respect. The officers exchanged harsh words with one another in Japanese, and it was obvious that Malam's friend was of higher rank than the other one. However, he approached Malam and smacked him hard on the head and said just one word "Traitor." Then Malam's hands were tied tightly behind his back, and he was led to a waiting truck. Two soldiers sat beside him, one on each side, while the officer sat in front with the driver. No words were exchanged as they drove towards the jungle.

It was a rough ride and Malam knew where they were heading. His head was still hurting from the hard hit of the Japanese officer who had saved him from immediate death. They were taking him to one of their camps in the jungle, probably the one for local prisoners. He was full of fear, but not for himself. He hoped that his family would not be implicated, or else they would all be tortured or put to death, as he felt sure that was his fate. He hoped with all his heart that once they found him missing, they would all go into hiding. At whatever cost, he must never admit that he was an agent for the British. He would stick to the story that he kept the radio out of pure curiosity, and all he wanted was to know what was happening in the world. However, the penalty of disobeying the Japanese meant death, and he could only hope for a quick one. It was very hot and the two soldiers sat closely to him. Malam's tied hands were beginning to hurt him for they had been driving for over an hour. Still no one talked, and Malam knew that if he opened his mouth to say anything, the soldiers would slap him.

He closed his eyes tightly and prayed, "Dear Lord Buddha, please keep my family safe. Punish me for my foolishness in endangering their lives but don't let any harm come to them." For the rest of the uncomfortable journey, he could only think of his three wives and children. He loved all of them equally, especially his wives. He thought fondly of each one of them, and had no regrets that he married them all.

After the tedious drive through wasted rubber plantations and the thick tropical jungle, the truck finally came to a halt. Malam was surprised to see that the prisoners in the fenced camp were mostly Europeans. They had brought him to the camp for the prisoners of war of allied forces. As soon as he was out of the truck, he was nudged at gunpoint towards a small wooden construction with a zinc roof. It was about four feet wide and less than five feet in height. It was some kind of torture chamber where the prisoner could not stand or lie down. There was no opening, and the prisoner would have to endure the immense heat that would penetrate the zinc roof. Malam's hands were untied and before he could massage his swollen fingers, he was pushed roughly into the hut. He was trying to squeeze in when the door was rudely shut and locked, throwing him off balance. It was sometime before he could get himself in position in the tiny space. He managed to sit and pull his legs towards his chest. That was the most comfortable position that the space would allow him. Malam knew that after sometime his body would start cramping, and there was no other way he could shift or straighten his joints. He could smell the foul scent of the sweat of the other unfortunate prisoners like himself. He wondered if the Japanese would leave him to die this way. If so, his Japanese friend did him no favor. A bullet in his head would be a much easier death than dying in this sweat house. He buried his face in his hands and cried not for himself, but for his beloved family that he might never see again.

Malam was beginning to feel his body cramping up and he began to shift his position with great aching pains. There was no way he could stretch his body or limbs to the fullest, and the heat in the boxlike hut was draining him of any energy he had. His mouth was dry, and he was more thirsty than hungry, although he had not had anything to eat since the night before. It must be late afternoon as the tropical sun was at its worst. There were some cracks in the wood that allowed some light and air in, but not big enough to let him see outside. However, he could hear voices and people moving around. The torture hut was in a fenced up area, thus no prisoners could get close to comfort the poor victim. Soon Malam was beginning to feel great pain in his limbs, and his throat was constricted, and breathing became an effort. He had no idea how long it would take him to die but he hoped it would be soon. He nauseated, but there was nothing in his body to vomit out, not even saliva. The heavenly bliss of unconsciousness finally overcame him, and he felt himself drowning in hot water. He felt his body burning, but he could not let out any cry of pain. Then he saw his father stretching out his arms and pulling him out of the sea of hot water. Then he could breathe again, as he felt cold water splashing on his body.

The door to his small prison was opened and a Japanese soldier had thrown in a bucket of water on him. When Malam opened his eyes, he was pulled out by two rough hands. He felt as though they were breaking his bones as he was dragged out. When he tried to get on his feet, his knees gave way and he fell heavily on the ground at the foot of the soldier. Two other soldiers came and held him by his armpits, and pulled him with his feet dragging along the earth towards the camp's headquarters. Malam was still not fully conscious, and he was unaware of his surroundings or the time of day. He never realized that he had been unconscious for many hours, and when they pulled him out it was the morning of the next day. Prisoners were getting ready to be marched into the fields for hard labor. They looked at Malam with sympathy and pity, especially those who had been in that sweat hut before. Twenty four hours in the torture chamber could easily break a strong man, and hardly any men had survived after three or four days in the extreme heat without food and water. They shrugged their shoulders as they marched with heavy tools on their shoulders, in a single file towards another hard day of labor. Japanese soldiers hemmed them in with guns, ready to fire at anyone who disobeyed their orders. As Malam became more conscious, he could feel the pain in his body as the soldiers continued to drag him. Once they reached the small building which was supposed to be the headquarters, Malam felt a cool breeze which brought him to complete alertness. The comfortable breeze was the result of the ceiling fan. He managed to stand up and the soldiers stopped holding him. Seated at a table were two Japanese officers, but there was no sign of his friend who had saved him from immediate death.

In broken English, one of the officers said, "Are you ready to talk?" Malam tried to speak, but his throat was so dry and his lips were so torn that he could hardly get a word out. The officer who spoke to him said something in Japanese, and one of the soldiers gave Malam a metal cup half-filled with water. Malam took it and drank so fast that he started coughing and choking. But when he recovered, he felt much better, and seeing that the officer was still waiting for an answer, Malam whispered, "What do you want me to say?" "Who were you working for?" Malam replied, "No one." The officer walked towards him and slapped him, almost throwing him off balance with the impact. Malam stood his ground and said, "I kept the radio to listen to news of what was happening in the world." "Liar," shouted the officer and slapped Malam again. Malam felt blood in his mouth and kept quiet. "I am going to ask you one more time and you had better tell the truth. Are you a British agent?" Malam shook his head. The Japanese officer spoke in Japanese and the soldiers who brought Malam in, tore his shirt and tied his hands to a supporting wood at the ceiling. A few seconds later, Malam felt his skin tearing as a bamboo rod hit his back. Malam winced in pain, but as the blows continued, he screamed with whatever voice he had left. Each blow became more agonizing than the last and at the twentieth stroke Malam fainted. However, he was quickly revived with another bucket of cold water. But he fainted again at the next stroke. Then when he was revived again by the same method, he hung limply wishing for death. He hardly heard what the officer said. The officer wanted to know if he was ready to talk. When he received no response from Malam, he shouted some command in Japanese, and Malam was released from the rope that held him. He fell heavily onto the floor and immediately he was pulled up and dragged outside. The two officers followed and the one who questioned him drew out his sword.

When the soldiers forced Malam onto his knees, Malam knew that he was going to be beheaded. The feeling that he was going to meet his end made him fully conscious. He could see the sun reflecting on the sword, and he prayed that it was sharp. But just as the officer raised his sword the sound of screeching tires could be heard and he heard a familiar voice speaking in Japanese. Malam looked up and saw his friend approaching. Words were exchanged, and Malam was ordered to stand up. Once more, he was saved from immediate death, but as he was led to a small fenced area where he could see some holes in the ground, he was not grateful to his friend. He knew what those holes were for. His hands were tied behind his back and his legs were also tied together and he was lifted and put into the pit. He was buried with only his head above the ground. The raw wounds on his back would make work easy for the worms to gnaw into his body. His friend came close to him and whispered in excellent English, "Maybe, two or three days in this pit will open your mouth, that is if the worms and ants and the heat have not finished you up. Goodbye and good luck. He left Malam and marched into the building where he was joined by the other two officers. Two hours later, Malam saw him leave, and wondered if he would come back before Malam perished in this grave. Even though his words and voice sounded harsh, there was a kindness in his eyes that Malam could not decipher.

Malam was unable to move any part of his body. His tormentors had made sure that the earth that filled up the hole was firm. He was buried naked from the waist upwards and he could feel the agonizing pain on his torn flesh from the beating. The sweltering sun added to his discomfort and agony. His mind became disoriented, and he was not able to think properly. He tried to picture his loved ones, but he could not stay focused. Insects were beginning to attack his sweaty face and he could feel the little creatures in the earth gnawing his wounds. The camp was quiet and after a few hours, Malam felt life draining away from his body. He became more and more disoriented and his mind was playing tricks with him. His body underwent spasms, and there were times when his head felt disconnected to his buried body. Finally, the oblivion of unconsciousness overcame him and he felt no more pain or discomfort. He felt his body being lifted by clouds towards a moving ship, where a beautiful dancer performed only for him. She saw him on a cloud above her and blew him a flying kiss. Malam wanted to go down to the ship, but the cloud moved on and he saw another beautiful girl crying. He wanted to comfort her, but again his transport continued its journey. Then, he saw an older man who said something, but Malam could not hear his words. The cloud stopped moving and the older man waved him away, a gesture to show him to go back. Then suddenly, Malam heard voices and he began to feel immense pain as he returned to consciousness. The prisoners of war had returned from a hard day's work and they were all about the camp. Malam could hear them, but not see them, because he was buried in a way where he faced the other side of the fence. His own hole was fenced off, so that no prisoners could get close enough to him to offer him water, or words of comfort, without getting punished by the Japanese. However, someone was singing a song, and in between, Malam heard these words, "Hang on, it will all be over soon." Those words did not belong to the song, but Malam thought it was his way of comforting Malam, to say that soon Malam would die. Malam was sure that he would not survive the night. His throat was hurting and his body felt like it was tattered and torn. His face was covered with insect bites, and the skin was completely sunburned. He could hardly keep his eyes open and his mind focused. He tried to think of his family, but his thoughts kept fading away. His head became heavier and heavier, and finally he was lost in a pit of darkness where nothing existed, not even himself.

Meanwhile, in retaliation for the attack on Pearl Harbor, the Americans bombed Hiroshima on August 6, 1945, forcing the Japanese to surrender, thus also ending their occupancy in Malaya. The Japanese left all the prison camps very suddenly, and the victorious British and allied forces drove into the camps with their military trucks to free all prisoners. When the prisoners from Malam's camp were about to leave, someone decided that Malam who had been left for dead for the last three days should have a decent burial. It was then that he realized that Malam was unconscious but still alive. Immediately, the earth that held his body down was removed, and Malam was gently lifted from his grave. They cleaned his sores and wiped his face with clean water, but he could not be revived. A helicopter was sent for, and Malam was transported to Singapore to the best military hospital. With great care, Malam regained consciousness, but was unable to remember anything. He had amnesia and did not even know who he was. However, he was treated as a hero and had the best care possible. The British tried to find any family connection by sending his pictures all over Malaya, but no one claimed him. Malam stayed in the hospital for a month. His physical recovery was complete, but he was still amnesic, and the marks left by the bamboo rods, although completely healed, were visible. Luckily, Malam suffered only memory loss. He was still able to speak Malay and English very well. It was obvious to the people who cared for him that he was a man of high standing. The doctors felt that if Malam could be taken to places, he might find something familiar to jolt a little of his memory back. Thus, a British officer who had grown very fond of Malam, decided to make it his job to help him. His name was Captain John Stevens. Thus when the doctor certified that Malam was in no more need of medical treatment, Captain Steven's family took him into their home. Malam did not want to waste anytime in finding his identity. One thing he was sure of, was that the given name of Tom was not his. So a week after his release from the hospital, John took leave from his wife and two daughters, and drove with Malam across the causeway to Peninsular Malaya.

As they drove over the causeway, John looked at Malam and said, "Tom, do you realize how difficult it will be to find your heritage? We don't even know whether you are a Malayan. We made that presumption because you speak the language like a native. If we are right about your nationality, we don't know your race. Your looks are quite deceiving. You could be Malay or Eurasian. But your habits and behavior do not conform to that of a Malay man." Malam looked at his friend and smiled. "I appreciate what you are doing for me John, and I hope that I will find some places that will look familiar. The doctor did say that this amnesia is temporary." John nodded and thought, "This is no ordinary man. His English is excellent, and now that he is fully recovered from the terrible ordeal, he is also very distinguished. I will not give up on him." Malam was very quiet as they drove into Johore Bahru, the capital of the state of Johore Bahru. He tried to concentrate on the city, as they drove to a hotel. John decided that they should spend a few nights in each big city. He would expose Malam to the public by going to crowded places, and then they would also visit places of interest. But it was futile in Johore Bahru, nothing was familiar to Malam, and no one recognized him. John was sure that if Malam had lived in Malaya, he would have been brought up in a big town. He was definitely not a country boy, so after three days and nights in Johore Bahru, they drove along the coast to Malacca. Again, Malam was silent, and John knew that the poor man was trying his best to concentrate, so he too kept quiet. As they entered the city, Malam showed signs of agitation, and John kept his fingers crossed. John was posted to Singapore long before the Japanese Occupation, and he had taken his family to visit Peninsular Malaya quite often. Malacca was one of his favorite spots due to the multiple cultures and historical buildings. He was very familiar with the places of interest.

It was around noon when they arrived at Christ Church. It was a bright red church built in 1753 for the Dutch, but was now used by the Anglicans. John decided that it was too early to check into a hotel, so he parked the car at the church, and suggested that they walk through Malacca's 'Red Square', which was a collection of salmon-colored buildings that formed the finest Dutch architecture in Malaya. It was still quite unspoiled by the Japanese, except for the beautifully proportioned clock tower in the park. The Japanese had replaced the old English clock by a Seiko model. John knew of a nice restaurant in the park, and he hoped that it was now reopened for business. He took Malam, who was very engrossed in his thoughts, into the park towards the restaurant. It was open, and they found a table by the glass window. Once seated, John felt concern, when he saw how pale Malam was, so he asked, "Are you alright Tom?" Malam's reply was quite brisk when he said, "Don't call me Tom, that is not my name." Then he softened his voice and continued, "I feel some connection to this city, but nothing seems familiar. It is getting to be so frustrating. I don't even know how old I am." "Well, judging from your looks, you could be in your thirties." John was honest in his estimation. Although Malam was close to being fifty, he did look much younger. When the waitress came to take their order, Malam surprised John by ordering something without even looking at the menu. He felt that they were getting somewhere. They now knew what Malam liked to eat and drink. He decided to have the same dish, and like Malam, he ordered a glass of whisky on the rocks. After a hearty meal and two glasses of whisky, John wanted to know if Malam would like to rest. "Oh no," said Malam, "Let us walk a little bit more. Even as we sit here, the connection that I felt when we drove into the city gets stronger."

When they left the restaurant, unconsciously, Malam's footsteps took him towards Malacca's old city hall. John was observant, and decided to just follow Malam instead of being the guide himself. The old city hall which was called the Stadthuys was constructed by the Dutch between 1641 and 1669. It was their oldest surviving building in the East. Originally used as the residence of Dutch governors and their retinue, it was now used as government offices. With John by his side, Malam just looked at the hall from the outside, and continued to walk, leaving the Red Square behind. His footsteps led him to climb steps to the top of Residency Hill where part of the Formosa Fortress still remained. The Portuguese had built this fortress to guard their homes, churches and shops. All were destroyed by the British, except for St. Paul's Church which housed the corpse of St. Francis Xavier, a Jesuit missionary, also known as Francis of Assissi. The hill had been converted into a burial ground, and when Malam saw tombstones, he stood still. John noticed his intensity and said softly, "Are you alright?" He decided not to use 'Tom' anymore. Malam's tensed face broke into a smile and John felt relief. "I was lost for a moment. I don't understand why I felt some kind of emotion here. These are graves of people who died many years ago. If you don't mind, I would like to check into a hotel now and take a short nap. My body is not tired, but my mind is." John was agreeable, so they walked back towards the car, and John drove to a quiet hotel outside the city. He felt that Malam needed some quiet and peace.

In the privacy of his room, Malam allowed his tears to flow. Somehow the burial grounds gave him a feeling of overwhelming sadness, and he had great difficulty trying to keep his emotions within himself. He wished that he knew the reason for that feeling. One thing was for sure, they would have to spend more time in Malacca. His body had not found any familiarity, but his spirit felt very involved in this city. Since his physical recovery, all he knew about himself was that he was taken into the prison camp to be interrogated and tortured. He was left to die buried with his head above the ground. It was a miracle that he survived the three days in the scorching heat without food and water. Like all prisoners of war, he was decorated and compensated with a large sum of money. But without an identity, Malam did not really feel alive. He had no emotions until today. He was glad to feel the deep painful sadness. He cried and cried until he could cry no more. Then he washed himself up and took a nap, his mind filled with unclear pictures. An hour later he got up, and was ready to go out to explore for himself. At first, he thought he would do that on his own, but if he got lost, it would be hard to find his bearings. After all, John had made it his business to help him. He owed it to John to guide him in this search. He knocked on the door of his friend's room. John was ready, and suggested they have tea and some cookies in the hotel lobby before they went exploring.

John drove back to Christ Church where parking was convenient. He had decided that they should be in the busiest part of Malacca. Maybe someone would recognize Malam. He was also sure that somehow, Malam's heritage was in this town. They walked the opposite direction, where they crossed the bridge to Malacca's old town, a crosshatch of narrow streets, perhaps more fascinating than any historical attractions. Here they encountered the different races of people, Malays, Tamils and Chinese. It was the old Nyona ladies dressed in the traditional sarong kebaya that attracted Malam's attention. His agitation caused John to feel more confident that they were on the right path. Somehow, people just stared at them, but no one seemed to recognize Malam. They passed many emporiums, some of them were under renovation, those that the Japanese had partly destroyed. Then they came to Heeren Street, where the narrow alley was flanked by Peranakan ancestral homes. Most of these homes were used by the Japanese officers as offices and residences. It was obvious that the Japanese had misused them, for more renovations were going on. Malam became more excited and agitated as they walked through the alley. Suddenly, he stopped, and John felt Malam stiffening as he looked at a huge house. The once beautiful home was almost falling apart. The huge red door was barred with a rod across it. The windows were slightly ajar, but hung in hinges. No one was renovating that house, although it must have been the most gorgeous and beautiful of all the houses there before the Japanese Occupation.

John asked Malam, "Do you want to go closer for a better look?" Malam did not answer him, but walked towards the house and climbed the stairs. John did not follow him, but when he saw that Malam was trying to unbar the door, he had to intervene. John had read a sign that said that it was private property and that violators would be prosecuted. "My dear friend, why don't we get permission to go in," John said when he was close to Malam. "No, I have to get in right now. There is something about the house that is drawing me like a magnet." John shrugged his shoulders and helped Malam with the heavy wooden rod. The door was not locked from the inside because the lock had been broken and as Malam pushed the door open, it scraped heavily on the marble floor. A huge empty space awaited them as they walked in. There was not a single piece of furniture in sight, except for torn curtains and broken glasses on the once beautiful marble floor, which now had huge cracks in it. Malam walked right into the kitchen and to the unkempt courtyard in a daze. In silence John followed him. Malam seemed to know his way around. John was close to him as he took the steps and entered one special room. There was a bed with a tattered mattress. Malam went to it and just sat down. Then he began to cry unashamedly. John knew that this was Malam's home. He put his arms around the distraught man and said, "Do you remember anything?" Malam sobbed out, "No, that is the problem. All I know is that this house is familiar. Oh John, do you think, I will ever be able to get back my memory?" "Sure you will," replied his friend. Then they heard voices downstairs and John felt that they were in trouble. He looked at Malam and noticed that his friend was unaware of the noise downstairs. So he decided to go down on his own and explain the situation.

There were two men; one of them was a Malay policeman and the other a distinguished looking man in his late fifties or early sixties. When they saw John, they were surprised to see that a white man had broken into the house. Before they could say anything John said, "I am sorry that we broke into the house. But we have a good reason." When the older man spoke, John was surprised to see a great resemblance to his friend upstairs. The man looked much older and was much fairer in complexion, but he definitely had Malam's features. He was not as good looking as Malam, but the resemblance was undeniable. John gathered his wits and in answer to the man's question of what business they had in the house, John said, "I have a strong feeling that if you go upstairs and see my friend, you will know the answer. Just be very careful. He has a loss of memory." Without hesitation, the older man rushed upstairs. John and the policeman followed him, and they were in time to see the two men looking at each other. Malam looked lost, but the older man had tears in his eyes and they heard him whisper, "Malam." It was Chin, Malam's eldest brother. He went to his brother to hug him, but Malam pulled back. Then John intervened and said, "Give him some more time." John went to Malam and put his arms around Malam's shoulders and said, "I think we have found your family." Malam refused to leave the room, so they left him there, and all three went downstairs. Chin introduced himself to John, and there was no doubt in John's mind that Chin was the brother of his friend. Chin suggested that they take Malam to his house to meet his mother. Maybe that would help Malam. But John had another idea. He explained, "This morning when we were at the cemetery at the Formosa Fortress, Malam felt a great connection. Maybe we should visit China Hill and see what happens." Chin thought for a while and said, "That is where our father was buried. Yes, I think we should try that. My mother is very frail and sick, and Malam's situation may not help. It would break her heart if her beloved son could not recognize her."

John went upstairs alone and found Malam, still sitting on the bed, but with his hands cupping his face. John said, "Malam, the man who called you this name is your brother. You are home now. Everything is fine. We need to make another stop before we go to his home." Malam stood up and said, "I wish I could remember him, but I don't. I feel that I belonged in this house, but I don't remember living here." However, he went down and allowed his brother to hug him and to welcome him back into their lives. Chin was careful not to say too much. It would only bring more confusion. The policeman took his leave, and Chin invited John and Malam into his car. They did not tell Malam where they were going, and Malam did not ask. John sat in front with Chin and Malam sat behind. As they approached China Hill, Malam became agitated again. John looked at Chin, who acknowledged his look with a nod. It was a way of telling each other that they were doing the right thing. China Hill was a huge Chinese graveyard which held over 10,000 burial plots. Its elevated location was supposed to block the winds of evil, and give the spirits an unobstructed view of their descendents. There was a modest temple at the base of the hill with a dirty but famous well. According to legend, it would ensure the return of any visitor who drank its water. Chin drove close to the temple and parked the car. Even before he could switch off the engine Malam was out of the car. Chin was about to open the door when John held his hand and said, "Let him alone. He has to find himself without our help." They both sat in the car and watched Malam climbing up the hill with a sense of direction to where he was heading.

Malam himself was not aware of why he was heading in one direction. Just before he reached the top of the hill, he stopped in front of a beautiful and grand marbled grave with white fencing. He saw the picture of the deceased and his eyes were fixed on it. Suddenly, he began to shake vigorously and held his head with his hands. Chin and John saw him shaking and holding his head as if he was in great pain, so they rushed out of the car and reached him in time before he collapsed. Malam fainted in Chin's arms. John and Chin tried to revive him, but Malam was completely out. Then without saying anything to each other, they carried him down towards the car. Malam had lost a lot of weight, so it was not difficult for both the strong men to carry him down. When they were close to the well, John dished out a pail of water, soaked his handkerchief in it, and put it on Malam's forehead, while Chin rubbed his chest and was about to do artificial respiration, when Malam opened his eyes and blinked. He saw his brother and said, "Brother." John knew then that Malam had recovered from his amnesia. Malam then acknowledged John, and when he managed to stand up, he hugged his brother, and John stood aside and witnessed the tearful, but joyful reunion of two brothers. Malam looked towards his father's grave and said, "Let us go and pay homage to our father. It was he who saved my life. He did not allow me to succumb to death." John said that he would wait by the car. As he watched the two brothers walking up towards the spot where Malam stood before he fainted, he felt relief and happiness for his friend. He never thought that his job would be over so soon. He will say goodbye to his friend tomorrow and return to his family.

CHAPTER 16

John witnessed another emotional scene as mother and son hugged each other. He was again thankful that it did not take them too long for Malam to find his family. It was obvious that Mrs. Shih had held on to life in the hope that she would see her son, before departing to join her husband in another world. She was so weak that she could hardly sit up, and her voice was merely a whisper. The tears of joy were so overwhelming, that John could feel the wetness in his own eyes. Malam's mother whispered in his ears, "I prayed that I would live long enough to see you. Now, you must go back to your family. They have suffered too much." As soon as he recovered, the first thing on Malam's mind was his family and Chin had convinced him that they were alright. There was no way to contact them on the phone as the line had been cut off. Chin had promised Malam that after his reunion with his mother, they would drive immediately to Klang. Cheng the other brother was there too, and he welcomed his younger brother as emotionally as Chin. Now that Malam was in good hands, John decided to take his leave. But before he left, he got all the information he needed about Malam's part in the British Secret Service. Malam was due more than the compensation he received. John will put in a report to his headquarters in Singapore. Malam went out alone with John to his car. He took his friend's hand, grasped it tightly and said, "No words can express my gratitude. I shall never forget you and I promise you that I shall keep in touch." Then he hugged the captain and John drove off. He was right about his friend. Malam was no ordinary man, and on top of everything, he had three wives.

It was very hard for Malam to take leave of his mother. He had the feeling that he might not see her again. However, Mrs. Shih insisted that he went as soon as possible. When he kissed his mother goodbye, she whispered, "I am so proud of you. Goodbye my son, give my love to your family." Malam felt heavy, but his mother was right. His family had suffered long enough not knowing whether he was alive or not. Hopefully, they were still together. He got into the car with Chin and they drove towards Klang. On the way, Chin explained to Malam about how Suji died, and why they never bothered to renovate the house. "The Japanese had defiled our home by executing Suji in it. We cannot live there anymore. You know that mother is very ill and may go any time now. It was a miracle that she lasted that long. She was the one who gave us all hope that you are still alive. I will only put up that house for sale when she is gone. Heaven knows how we will all need that money. The Japanese had taken a lot

171

from us, and although the British had returned us most of our property, there are still losses and debts to be paid." Then he looked at his brother and smiled, "But the greatest gift that no money can buy is your return. Once more, welcome back my little brother." Malam nudged him and jokingly said, "Thank you big brother."

They drove for many hours and Malam told Chin about his involvement with the British; how he reported the activities of the Japanese in Selangor, the downfall of the economy as the Japanese were more involved in their wars than looking after their occupied lands, the move of the headquarters to Singapore to plan their strategies, and finally, their attempt to raise hatred among the people for the British. He had difficulty in talking about his torture, so he was brief about that. However, he told Chin about the dream he had of their father. "I am very sure now that if he had not shooed me away as I was sitting on my cloud and drifting to him, I would have died in that pit." Chin nodded and said, "Isn't it strange that the spirits of our ancestors are always with us. I am sure he must have come into mother's dreams to give her so much hope that you were still alive." They were quiet for a while then Malam asked, "When was the last time you saw my family?" "I had no chance to see them as mother is very weak. But after the war ended, Paini called, and almost gave up on you. Mother managed to convince her that you will return soon. Then I called her, and she said that she was trying to keep the family together, and selling all the jewelry you had given them. She did not ask for help, so I gathered that they must have managed. Lately, we tried to call your home again, but were informed that the phone line had been cut off. I gathered that it was too expensive to pay the phone bills. I would have gone to check on them if not for the problems we are facing. We are trying to set up our business again, but somehow it is now a bad time for people are waiting in line to get loans. But I have confidence in your first wife. She is a resourceful woman, and will find a way to keep the family safe and well-cared for." Malam hoped with all his heart that they would all be there when he arrived. They were now entering the State of Selangor. They should be in Klang before mid-night.

Malam's three wives had almost given up on ever seeing him again. However, they decided to stay together for as long as they could keep the house by the river. They had no more jewelry to pawn, so they began to make Nyona cakes, and started selling them to restaurants and on the roadside outside the house. However, the income from the sale of the cakes was hardly sufficient. They now have three school-going children who needed money for books. At first, they tried to reduce their electric bills, but even that did not help, so they had to give up electricity completely and started using kerosene lamps instead. Thus, there was no way they could communicate with anyone as the phone line was also cut off. Then Ai Li, who was now sixteen years old, decided to help and against Paini's wishes, she gave up school and looked for employment as a help in some rich household. She was hardworking and was able to bring enough money home. Meanwhile Cheng Mee's pregnancy was confirmed. She was now in her fourth month. She had decided that if Malam never survived, she would at least have a part of him with her. Her child would be the memory of the short and wonderful love she had with her husband. Ah Leng too was doing her part. She reared chickens and ducks for sale. She was glad that whatever happened, Malam had left them a wonderful house. One day, they would bring it back to its old glory. Like the other two, her faith in her husband's return was beginning to diminish.

As they approached the town of Klang, Malam became excited. He saw his shop before they crossed the bridge to his home. He shuddered when he remembered what happened. It was too dark to see the condition it was in, and he was thankful for that. But as they approached his home, everything was dark. His anxiety grew. Chin reassured him that it was almost midnight, and everyone was sleeping. Malam's fears disappeared when he took a few steps and stumbled on some shoes outside the door. Chin was beside him as he braced himself before he knocked on the door. At first, his knock was gentle, and when he heard no sounds, he knocked harder and then he began to panic and started banging on the door. Chin stopped him and they heard some movement, and through the cracks they saw a light coming through. As the light shifted, they knew that someone was holding a torchlight or a lantern and moving towards the door. Malam froze when he heard a familiar voice asking in Malay, "Who is it?" He could not answer, so Chin replied, "Paini, is that you. It is Chin." They heard the latch and the door opened to a disheveled and sleepy Paini. At first, she did not see two men and so she asked, "Chin, what are you doing here so late?" Then she held the lantern higher, and almost dropped the kerosene light when she saw the second man. Chin quickly took the lantern from her hands as she collapsed in Malam's arms. This time it was Chin's turn to witness the emotional scene. Malam hugged and kissed Paini, who just sobbed in his arms.

The commotion woke the others up, and soon more kerosene lanterns lighted the whole house. Paini moved away as she saw Ah Leng rushing towards her husband. Ah Leng too cried, but the tears were of joy, and Cheng Mee who was now five months pregnant stood shyly close by and only moved when Malam extended his hands to her. Then while still embracing his second wife, he engulfed his young wife and kissed her. Then it was Ai Li's turn. She was the only one who spoke, "Welcome home father. We all missed you." Malam said, "I missed you all too." Then he saw Jo Lin, pouting away. He bent down and put out his hands to her, but she shook her head and cried, "Why did you leave us alone for so long?" Malam shook his head and went to her. Gathering the fighting girl in his arms he said, "I did not leave you. I was taken away. Then I was lost. It took me sometime to find myself and when I did, I came back immediately." That explanation seemed to satisfy his daughter. She returned his kisses. Then Malam hugged his oldest son and said, "I am sure you have been looking after all the girls." David nodded proudly. Then Malam gathered John and Gary one in each arm and smothered them with more kisses. Ah Leng then sent the three boys to bed. They were not willing, but Malam promised them that he would explain everything to them at breakfast the next morning. Then he looked at Chin and said, "I think you too would like to retire. You have a long drive back tomorrow." Chin nodded, and said that he would just rest on the sofa in Malam's office. But Paini insisted that he should have something to eat before he retired. Cheng Mee was already preparing coffee in the kitchen, and warming up some cakes that were to be sold the next day. Chin saw the Nyonya cakes and did not hesitate to accept the invitation. As they all sat down to drink coffee and eat the delicious cakes, Malam told the story of his capture, leaving out the gory details of his torture. He told them of his amnesia and how his good friend helped him regain his memory. Ai Li and Jo Lin were so proud of their father's heroism, but his wives were more concerned for his well-being. They knew the Japanese well enough, and were sure that Malam did not reveal too much of what they did to him. They hoped that Malam would tell them one day. Right now, the important thing was that they had him back, and they felt whole again.

Chin had about five hours of sleep, but he was ready to leave early, and when Malam was alone with him by his car, Chin said, "Mother has seen you, so I think she is ready to go. Take care of your family first, and if God willing, you may have a chance to see her once more." Malam held his brother's hand and replied, "Yes, I will have to make sure that the electricity and phone lines are reinstalled, so that we can keep in touch often. I have enough money to see to all that. I shall also look for a car, and will drive down to visit as soon as I can." They hugged each other and

Chin drove off. Malam wasted no time in having everything reinstalled. He even stopped his wives from selling any cakes, and Ai Li from going to work as a maid. He was back and he would take care of them again. The compensation money that he received would be sufficient for them to lead a normal life for sometime. He was also sure that the British Government would pay him for the services he had rendered. John had assured him of that. A few days later, he bought a car, and he wasted no time in taking Paini with him to visit his mother. The car was not big enough to contain his whole family, and after all, Paini was the closest to his mother. Besides, Cheng Mee's pregnancy prevented her from taking long journeys. As usual, no one contradicted Malam's decision.

Since Malam came home, he had spent the nights only in Paini's room. She had seen the scars on his back, and as she traced them with her fingers, her tears flowed, but she did not question him about them. Malam appreciated her for it, and taking her in his arms, he said, "The Japanese were very cruel to me, but I have left it all behind, so talking about it will only make me relive those pains. There is so much ahead for us. We have to move on, and I promise you that we shall get there where we were before the war." The reason that Malam had not gone to the rooms of his other wives, was because they did not have the kind of understanding and patience as his first wife. When he returned from Malacca, he would go back to the routine of moving from one room to another. But before he did that, he would ask of his wives not to question him of his captivity. He had told them what they needed to know. Since the phone line was installed, he had talked to his brother almost every day. His mother was definitely fading away. She was totally bed-ridden and was unaware of many things. Malam knew that if he wanted to see his mother again, he would have to drive down soon. So six days after he was back with his family, he and Paini were on their way to Malacca. On the way, Paini was very quiet, and Malam knew that she was very sad about the way her mother died. He tried to comfort her. "Suji was a heroine. Chin told me how she tried to help my mother. But, I am sure that she is now very happy to be with your father. When our financial situation improves, I shall build both your parents beautiful graves. Our lives have to go on. Let us move on but preserve their memories in fondness and love." Paini looked at her husband with wet eyes and smiled, "I am grateful and filled with happiness to have you beside me. To think that I almost gave up on you is unforgivable, but your mother gave me courage and hope." Malam took one hand off the wheel and gave her a tight squeeze.

Mrs. Shih was aware of the presence of her youngest son and his first wife, but she was unable to acknowledge them. On the second evening of their visit, the old lady died in her sleep. Malam found her with a smile on her lips the next morning. His sorrow of losing her was replaced by the comforting thought that she wanted to join her husband. He held her limp body and kissed her before he went out of the room to say, "Mother is gone." Chin had already ordered a coffin a month ago, and the funeral was planned immediately. It was a simple ceremony with the attendance of a few friends and relatives. She was buried beside her husband, and Chin and Cheng assured Malam that her grave would be as grand as their father's. After the funeral, instead of joining the others for a reception, Malam took Paini to her parents' graves. Paini was about to protest when Malam said, "Don't worry, I have come to terms with the past. I shall also visit Aminah's grave. I shall never forget her, but I don't blame myself for her death any more." As husband and wife stood before the graves of Suji and Patamavenu, Paini was filled with a determination that no matter what her husband did, she would stand and support him. She shed no tears as she remembered what her husband said on the road a few days ago. The past should only be memories to cherish. Life should go on. Then when they were at Aminah's grave, she saw calmness on her husband's face and knew that he meant every word he said. She spoke to the spirit of the dead girl in her heart. "Thank you for forgiving him. He never meant to hurt you. May you rest in peace."

Malam and Paini then went back to Chin's house to thank friends and relatives for attending his mother's funeral. Then, when everyone went home, Chin said to Malam, "I know that you and Paini would like to leave as soon as possible, but before you do so, Cheng, you and I should meet in my office." Malam nodded, and as Paini helped her sister-in-laws to clear up, the three brothers had a conference. Chin started the conversation by explaining to Malam that the family business was not doing well at all. The Japanese had left the country in regression, and there was nothing to sell except the business complex that the family had owned for a few generations. Then they have the house, which was in very bad shape. Someone had made them an offer. It was not good, but neither was the condition of the house. If Malam agreed, they would sell both the buildings and split the money into three. With whatever they would receive from that, both Chin and Cheng would start a small business separately. Malam was sure that by the time the British paid him, he would have more money than the two of them put together, so he offered, "You both have always been there, and I know the expenses incurred due to mother's health is not small. I would like you both to share the inheritance. I have been well compensated as a prisoner of war, and I know that I will get much more once John sends in the report of my involvement with the British Intelligence." Chin and Cheng looked at each other and were about to protest, when Malam said, "Call it a loan if you must, but I shall not expect payment until your business is established." Then Chin went to his desk and brought out a big box from the drawer. "This is mother's jewelry. She wants Paini to have it. Suji died because of her and she would rest in peace if Paini accepted it. Knowing your wife, she may want to share it, but you must make her keep it. If you promise us that, then we will accept the loan." Malam looked into the box and knew how valuable the jewelry was. Chin was right about Paini. He will keep the box until they got home. Then he would persuade Paini that it was his mother's last wish that she inherited her last belongings. All said and done, Malam drove home with his wife.

Malam wasted no time in repairing his house. He had a new kitchen installed and bought furniture to replace what was stolen. In no time at all, his house was at the grandeur it was before the Japanese Invasion. Then, when a generous check arrived from the British Consulate, he decided to check on his shop, which was still standing by the other side of the river. Everything inside it was destroyed, but Cheng Mee's father with the help of his sons, managed to clear the rubbish that was left. Malam decided not to continue the business, but also not to sell the building. He would have it repaired and keep it locked for sometime. He had enough money to go back into the rubber and palm oil business. At this point the land where the rubber trees were destroyed was cheap, so Malam took advantage of it and bought a few acres. He knew that growing rubber would not bring in much revenue, as synthetic rubber was getting very popular. So he used most of the land to grow oil palms. He did grow some rubber trees, but unlike oil palms they would take years to be productive. It would also be a few years before he could start harvesting oil from the oil palms, but the generous amount he received for his services would bridge the gap. He started with a few employees, and erected a long wooden building, partitioning a part of it to use as his office, and the rest to store equipment and other necessities for his new plantation. He trained his daughter Ai Li to be his secretary and typist. Ah Leng offered to help, but he felt she should stay home to look after the children, especially now that Cheng Mee was close to delivery.

At the beginning of 1946, Cheng Mee gave birth to a still-born baby boy. Malam was distraught, and only Paini knew that he was thinking of the curse of so many years. Somehow, he never mentioned it, and when Paini saw how he tried to comfort his young wife, she felt that the curse was now over with the loss of her husband's second child. Cheng Mee mourned the death of her son for many days. Malam gave her all his support by spending the nights with her, regardless of the mounting jealousy of his second wife. At this point, Ah Leng had missed her last period. She did not mention it before, but after seeing that Malam was paying more attention to Cheng Mee, she decided to break the news to her husband. Malam was happy, but nevertheless, he would be with Cheng Mee until she got over some of the pain of her loss. Cheng Mee was sensitive to Ah Leng's feelings, so one night, although her heart still cried for her dead son, she said, "Dear husband, I am glad that you are with me for so many nights, but Ah Leng now needs you. Her child will replace this loss." Malam could see that Cheng Mee was still hurting, but she was right. He had two other wives and he had his responsibility towards them, so he went back to his routine of spending equal time with each of them.

When Malam gave Paini the box of jewelry from his mother, she begged him to keep it in the bank. She had experienced hard times and she felt that one day, the precious jewels would come in handy. That would also eliminate any jealousies, if no one else knew about it for the time being. Malam appreciated his wife for her decision, but decided that if he had more money, he would try to retrieve all the jewelry that his wives pawned, to make ends meet during his absence. Malam was smart to invest some of his money in the European market. The economy there picked up faster than in Asia after the Second World War, and after Alex, his fourth son was born in November of 1946, Malam's returns from his investments made him almost as rich as he was before his rubber plantation was burnt down. Thus Malam kept his promise, and managed to buy back almost all the jewelry for his wives. For the pieces that could not be retrieved, he replaced them with better and more expensive ones. While waiting for the revenue from his estate, he continued to invest his money, not only in Europe, but also in America. That paid off, and he was able to buy another big car and also employ a chauffeur to go with it. He would have liked to have some maids help with the children and house chores, but his wives felt that the house was crowded enough to have more people around. That was when Malam decided that once his plantation flourished, he would build a mansion, the biggest in Klang for his huge family.

178

Even though Malam was quite rich, it would take sometime before he would have enough to build the mansion of his dreams. However, the urgency to have a bigger house came when in 1947, Cheng Mee gave birth to a healthy girl. Malam named her Lily. Malam wanted to hire a nurse-maid to help Ah Leng and Cheng Mee with Alex and Lily, but Cheng Mee did not want to share the caring of her precious daughter with anyone else. However, Ah Leng wanted help so a help was employed to help with the children and the housework. Then Malam decided to extend his existing home towards the back, by building more rooms to accommodate the maid and the children. He immediately consulted an architect, but since the house had been extended before, the architect advised him that only two more bedrooms could be added. There were already six bedrooms including his office. So Malam decided that he would make the two new rooms into his office and own bedroom. He would invite his wives to spend the nights with him, instead of him going into their rooms. Since unemployment was still a great problem, Malam's rooms were ready within a month. Paini still maintained her room, Ai Li moved into Malam's old office; Cheng Mee kept Ai Li's room and slept there with her daughter. Ah Leng kept her room with Alex's cot close to her bed. The other three boys shared a room and Jo Lin had her own room. The room closest to the kitchen was occupied by the nursemaid. When Malam saw how packed the living and dining room was when everyone was at home, he wished the business with his plantation would pick up soon. However, he was satisfied when he saw how happy and harmonious his family was. They had survived the hard times together, and that had bonded them to each other more than ever.

Malam went to his little office in his plantation every morning during the weekdays and would return by six o'clock in the evening to have dinner with his family. Now that they had two cars, he would take his family on outings during the weekends. His children loved going to the Morib beach about an hour's drive from Klang. Sometimes when it got too hot, Malam would take them to the hills. Malam was a disciplinarian, and his children grew up to respect him and their mothers. Malam loved all his children but he was particularly fond of Jo Lin, much to Ah Leng's delight. He was more tolerable of her pranks than that of any of the others. He had emphasized that he would not tolerate lies, cheating and stealing, which were normal among children. Anyone caught with such 'crimes' would be severely caned; the number of strokes would depend on how serious the act was. Jo Lin had got away with it quite often but not the three older boys. It always hurt Ah Leng, when one of her sons was punished, and she would pout the whole day, refusing his invitation to spend the night with him in his room. That did not deter her husband from continuing his art of disciplinary action whenever he saw it fitting. This was how Malam ran his household. Whenever and wherever, his wives or children needed to go, the chauffeur and the extra car were at their disposal. Malam was the one who would send his school going children, Jo Lin, David, John and Gary to school, before going to work. The chauffeur would bring them home.

Finally, Malam's patience was rewarded. His oil palms began to bring revenue, so he employed more workers to help with the production and refinement of the palm oil. It started as an internal market where he sold his oil to soap factories, and companies that produced commodities for the food market locally. Then gradually, he began exporting his produce to other countries in South-East Asia, then the whole of Asia. As his plantation expanded, he began to explore the markets in Australia, Europe and America. He was almost a millionaire before his rubber trees began to produce latex. He was too busy getting rich that he laid aside his plans to build his dream mansion, but he never neglected his family. He was always home in time for the family dinner, and kept the weekends free to spoil his family. Because of the demand for cooking oil, he had to keep his office open during the weekend, but by then, he had employed an assistant to help with the work. By now Ai Li, who had learnt how to keep accounts under her father's supervision, was promoted to be an accountant. Her father had trained her so well, that she could match her skills with that of a qualified accountant. Spoilt by his daughter's integrity as a secretary, Malam had a difficult time finding someone to replace her. He had a few, but had to fire them, because they did not meet his criteria. Malam was getting desperate, because Ai Li had too much on her hands in accounting to help with secretarial work, so he asked his assistant, Mr. Yap to send out word that he was looking for a qualified and experienced secretary.

Actually, Mr. Yap had been waiting for this opportunity. His fiancée had just finished a secretarial course. She did not have the experience, but he would offer to train her if Malam gave her a chance. The only problem was that Malam did not like to have his employees related to another in anyway, so he decided not to mention the relationship between them. So when Malam asked him to help, he told Malam, "I have someone in mind. She is my neighbor, and she has just completed her secretarial course with outstanding grades. She has no experience, but because I am close to her family, I would put in extra time to teach her. I can assure you that she is very intelligent and hard-working. Just give her a chance." Malam liked his assistant and if he felt that this girl would meet the criteria, he would give it a try, so he said, "Okay, arrange an interview as soon as you can and we shall see if she is what you say she is. By the way, has she a name?" That last sentence was said jokingly, and Mr. Lee smiled and answered, "Loh Keng Yi."

CHAPTER 17

Keng Yi was born on October of 1931 in a small village in the State of Johore. Her parents migrated from China in the late 19th Century. Being both uneducated, the Lohs earned their livelihood by working as laborers in small factories. However, their poverty did not prevent them from having children. Their first born was a boy, and then they had five more girls, Keng Yi being the fourth child. At birth, she was already betrothed to a cousin, whose family was quite well off. He was only five years old when the parents made the arrangements. That meant that once she turned five, she would have to move in with the family of her fiancé. The fifth child had the same fate, but they decided to keep their youngest daughter. Keng Yi's early years were difficult and she very often felt hungry. When she became five years old, her parents were glad to hand her over to her new family, hoping that her life would improve. Unfortunately, that was not so. Her new family not only had a son, but they also had a very spoilt daughter, two years older than Keng Yi. It was she who made Keng Yi's life miserable. She bullied the little girl and treated her like a servant. She told her mother lies about Keng Yi stealing her things and destroying them. Her mother believed her, and Keng Yi was often beaten and sent to bed hungry.

The positive thing about moving into this family was that Keng Yi was allowed to go to a proper English school. The parents of her fiancé would like to have an educated daughter-in-law. However, although she attended the same school as the other girl, she was not allowed to go in the car with her. Keng Yi had to walk about half an hour each way. As the boy grew older, he began to see the unfairness, and he disliked his sister and parents for treating Keng Yi so badly. He had developed a great fondness for his future bride and began to see that she was growing up to be a beautiful girl. His intervention did improve Keng Yi's life. The bullying was not so obvious, and the parents tried their best to be as fair as they could without upsetting their daughter. Keng Yi was very intelligent and brought home better grades than her cousin. She did not get any praises from her guardians, but her fiancé's appreciation of her good work made up for it. She saw in her fiancé a big and caring brother, and in her young mind, she wished that he was truly her brother.

The Japanese invasion rudely interrupted Keng Yi's third year of Primary School. But when the war was over, Keng Yi begged to go back to school. Her cousin, however, had no intention of going back, so her parents thought that Keng Yi too should forget the idea. Fortunately for Keng Yi, the boy who was then nineteen years old, managed to persuade his parents to allow her to go back to school. Keng Yi had four years to catch up, but like most of her classmates, whose schooling was also interrupted, they started from where they left off. Keng Yi was about four years too old for the class, but her intelligence and hard work had its results, and she managed to skip a school year each time to a higher level. In three years, she was on a par with girls her age. Meanwhile, her fiancé had gone to College and there he fell in love with another girl. He had known that there could be no romantic attachment between him and Keng Yi. She was now a very beautiful teenager, but his feelings for her were that of a brother. His parents were reasonable enough to accept his decision to marry the girl of his choice, but they would not support Keng Yi anymore. She would have to go back to her parents, or look after herself. Keng Yi was only fifteen and had another year to complete her secondary school. Her ex-fiancé, her cousin decided that Keng Yi was his responsibility, and that she could come to live with him and his future wife. He had finished college and had a good job in a law firm in Kuala Lumpur, the capital of the Nation.

That one year with her cousin and his girlfriend was enough to make up for all the sufferings that Keng Yi had undergone while living with his parents. They were both so good to her, treating her like an equal. When they got married, Keng Yi was the bridesmaid. When Keng Yi finished her last year of school with flying colors, Tan, her cousin and his wife Mei who was also working, suggested that Keng Yi should continue college education. They would loan her the money. But Keng Yi knew that college education cost a lot of time and money. She wanted her independence as soon as possible, and they had done enough for her financially. However, she had enquired about a secretarial course, which would not take longer than two years, and would not cost too much, as they offered the students to do some part-time typing for a fee. Tan was happy to loan her some money to start her off, and he insisted that she continued to stay on with them.

It was at the school of Commerce that Keng Yi met Yap. He was a part-time teacher there, and he could not take his eyes off the beautiful, but shy Chinese girl. It was not acceptable for a teacher to have a relationship with a student, so Yap decided to quit his part-time job and look for something that paid enough for him to start courting girls. When he heard that Malam was looking for an assistant, he wasted no time in applying.

He was hardworking and had a degree in marketing. Malam liked the young man and employed him almost immediately. So on his last day at the school, he approached Keng Yi and said, "I shall not be teaching here anymore. I would like to talk to you. If you would wait for me after classes, I will walk you home or walk you to the bus-stop if the bus is your means of transport." Keng Yi was taken by surprise. It was the first time in her life that any man had approached her so directly, although she was used to admiring glances from the opposite sex and cheeky comments. She did not know how to react to Yap's approach. However, due to her respect for the teacher, she waited for him. Her heart skipped a beat as he approached with a gentle smile. She had caught him looking at her quite often, but when he saw her looking back, he would move his eyes elsewhere. He had always approving smiles for students who did well, but this was a special smile. It was a normal gesture for Keng Yi to smile back. That smile gave Mr. Yap courage to tell her what was in his heart. Keng Yi normally took the bus, but if she had an escort, it would be nice to take a walk. "I am glad that you waited for me. So which direction do we go?" Keng Yi replied, "It is about half an hour's walk to my place. But I could also take the bus, which is just a block away." Yap took her books from her and said, "It will be a pleasure to have your company for half an hour."

For the first few minutes, Yap was very quiet, and then he pulled Keng Yi to the side of the road and under the shade of a big tree. "Keng Yi," he started to say, "I have been in love with you for over a year now. I have had to restrain myself for professional reasons, but now there is no more holding back. I would like to date you and get to know you better." Keng Yi was speechless, but at the same time, she could feel the excitement of romance rising in her. Seeing that she was blushing, Yap felt that he was being too pushy and he might just lose the girl, so he quickly said, "You don't have to give me an answer now. You have two days to think about it. I shall call on you on Saturday evening to take you out to dinner. If you feel you would like to go out with me then be ready, or else I will understand and I shall not bother you any more." Keng Yi still did not say anything as they walked on. Then when they reached her home, she looked at Yap and said, "Thank you for the invitation. I shall be waiting for you on Saturday." Then she just ran as fast as her legs could carry towards the door. She left Yap gaping after her, but with a heart full of joy. He was half running and half skipping as he went back to the school to collect his bicycle. He was in seventh heaven. What he never knew, was that like all the other girls, Keng Yi had a crush on him. He was good-looking and charming. Keng Yi could not believe her ears when he professed his love for her.

Keng Yi could not restrain her excitement so she decided to confide in Mei. She was just as excited for her ward, and went out shopping on Saturday morning with her to buy her a new dress and a matching pair of high heel shoes. As the hours got closer, Keng Yi could not contain herself and was dressed early. She had never put make-up before, so Mei helped her to put on some light make-up. Tan thought he saw an apparition, when Keng Yi came out of the room for his opinion. He jokingly said, "Thank God, I am happily married, or I shall definitely reconsider you as my wife." His wife pouted with humor added, "Well, you are stuck with me. Just wish your beautiful cousin good luck." When the door-bell rang, Keng Yi ran into her room and closed the door on the suggestion of the older girl. Her cousin-in-law opened the door and could not help thinking, "My, he is good-looking. No wonder my little cousin is so excited." Then aloud, she said, "Come in. Keng Yi is getting ready." Yap introduced himself and he was about to sit down, when the door to Keng Yi's bedroom opened. Yap was taken aback by the striking beauty that stood at the door. He had never seen Keng Yi in a dress and high heels before, let alone the make-up. He was more in love with her than ever. Keng Yi on the other hand found Yap more attractive in his colored shirt than the white ones that he used to have at the school. When she approached him, he was still taller than she was, but not too much because of her three inches heels. All Yap could say was, "The blue color becomes you." He had more to say, but not in front of her guardians. Yap had borrowed his father's old car and he was going to drive down to a seaside restaurant in Port Swettenham. They had to drive through Klang to get to the port. He wanted to show Keng Yi where he would be working next. Since the drive itself would take two hours both ways, Yap asked Keng Yi's cousin if it was alright for Keng Yi to be home after midnight. The cousin felt that Yap was a reputable man so he gave his consent.

As they drove, the conversation was easy and unrelated to their feelings for each other. Yap knew that Keng Yi would complete her course in a few months time so he asked, "What are your plans when you are done with school?" Keng Yi had a ready answer, for she had made a few enquiries and had sent in her résumé to some banks and some law firms. She did not only learn shorthand and typing, but she had taken extra classes in political science. She replied, "Two banks have asked me to reapply when I am finished and there is a law firm that have asked me for an interview. If

185

they will accept me, I would rather work for them than in the banks." Yap had always known that behind the shyness was an ambitious person. Then the opportunity arose when Keng Yi asked him about his new job. "You are the main reason why I did not want to teach in the school anymore. As I have told you before, I had been in love with you for a long time. As a teacher I cannot do anything about it. Secondly, I was not earning enough doing part-time work. I am now in my mid twenties and would like to marry and settle down." Keng Yi blushed and looked down at her hands. Yap touched her gently and said, "I am not rushing you. You are the first girl that has won my heart. I would like us to date more often and hope that one day you will learn to love me too." Keng Yi surprised herself when she said, "My one wish is to be able to look after myself. I need the time to be independent. I don't want to get married yet." "Take all the time you need, but be my girlfriend for now." Keng Yi nodded and felt herself warming up to the young man beside her. It was dusk when the entered Malam's property. There was a road leading to the long building and he pointed to Keng Yi saying, "I shall start work in that office on Monday. It is an honorable position, and I shall be assistant to the big man himself. The pay is good, but there are weekends that I will have to work." Then he went on to explain that he had to move to Klang once he was established in his new job.

Yap then drove to a nice Chinese restaurant. Many eyes were turned in Keng Yi's direction and Yap felt proud and confident of his girl. He allowed Keng Yi to do the ordering, and he was glad that she was very fond of sea food. That was the first thing they had in common. Yap told a lot about himself and his upbringing, hoping that Keng Yi would do the same. But he began to realize as she left out many details, that she did not have a happy childhood. It made him all the more determined to look after her and give her the best he could. They had a long and satisfying dinner. Once more the conversation was light hearted and full of humor. Yap was very entertaining and made Keng Yi laugh a lot. Then just after midnight, they arrived at her residence. Yap was too much a gentleman to kiss her goodnight on the first evening. But secretly, Keng Yi wished that he would. She was falling in love for the first time. She would be eighteen when she graduated as a secretary and she was still a virgin and had never been kissed before. She went to bed that night wondering how the first kiss would be like. Before Yap left, they had made another date for the next weekend if he did not have to work. That was the second of many dates and finally, Keng Yi accepted Yap's proposal of marriage, except that the date for their nuptial union would be in three years time.

Keng Yi wanted to live on her own and pursue a career before she started a family. Yap was agreeable, and they were engaged a month before Keng Yi's graduation. Yap had moved to Klang, and wished that Keng Yi's new job would also take her in that direction. Fortunately for him, Keng Yi did not get the job at the law firm, so after her graduation, she send out more applications, and that was about the time that Malam needed a secretary very badly.

Yap knew that because of her moral standards, Keng Yi would never move in with him. She would find another apartment. But it was enough to be able to see her everyday. It was getting more difficult for him to see her on weekends, as Malam needed him almost every weekend as his business expanded. Keng Yi had also mentioned that she missed him, so he was sure that she would accept this job if Malam found her suitable. He was a little worried about his boss's reputation for beautiful young girls, but he had confidence that Keng Yi was strong enough to ward off any advances the boss might make. When he told Keng Yi of the open position, she was excited, not because the job appealed to her, but because she would be close to her fiancé. Then jokingly she warned Yap. "Help me find an apartment close enough for us to see each other often, but far enough so that you won't come knocking on my door in the middle of the night." Yap smiled and said, "I have always respected your wishes. I only wish that I don't have to wait that long to make you my wife. But my happiness is almost complete now that I will be able to see you almost everyday." Yap made an appointment with his boss to meet Keng Yi on a Monday morning. He told Keng Yi to take a bus to Klang and he would pick her up on his way to work. "Dress smartly but not sexily," he said with a smile. In her studies, she was also well informed of how to dress up for an interview, and her cousin had made sure she had a few appropriate clothes for such occasions.

When Malam first laid eyes on Keng Yi, he could not believe that he was reliving the emotions of yesteryears. It was like the first time when he saw Paini, as a young actor on stage. It was love at first sight for him all over again. At fifty two, he felt like a silly teenager, but he could not help himself. His heart stood still and he felt light-headed as though he had had a few drinks. If Yap had been in the same room, he would have taken Keng Yi out immediately, but unfortunately for him, he did not go into the enclosed office with her. The look of admiration and longing on Malam's face was so obvious, that Keng Yi herself felt like running away, but she felt some magnetic power holding her back. Thus, they both looked at each other without saying a word, Keng Yi standing and Malam sitting behind his huge oak desk. It was Keng Yi, who first recovered and broke the spell by saying, "How do you do, Mr. Shih? I am Keng Yi and I am here for an interview." Her voice brought him down to earth and he felt ashamed of himself. Regaining his composure, he stood up and went to her. "Thank you for coming. Please take a seat." He gestured to the chair in front of his desk. Then he went back to the seat and decided to be businesslike, although it took a lot of will-power to do that. "From your résumé, I can see that you have just graduated from the School of Commerce. I guess that you have no working experience." Keng Yi was about to say something when he continued, "Nevertheless, I always like to give people a chance. Can you start tomorrow?" Malam had to get rid of her as soon as possible. He was afraid he might frighten her away. He needed some hours to recover from his emotional turbulence. Keng Yi too was glad to be dismissed. She had more questions to ask, like the salary and work compensations, but since he did not wait for her reply, she thought that she would return home and that would give her time to think. At that moment she was confused with the feelings that the older man had stirred in her.

Yap who had asked permission to send Keng Yi to the bus station was excited, that Keng Yi had got the job, but he was puzzled to see that she was in a world of her own. She was uncommunicative and when he asked, "So, shall we start looking for an apartment today?" She simply answered, "I don't know yet." He asked her about the interview, but she was again vague until he lost his patience, and stopped the car on the side of the road. Then in a louder tone he said, "Keng Yi, I don't know what happened in that room, but I don't like the way you are acting. Maybe, you should not take the job." That alerted Keng Yi and she retorted, "Why not? Nothing happened in the room. I was just surprised that I got the job so easily and that he wanted me to start tomorrow." Yap was satisfied with the answer and thought that he could take the credit that she got the job. Then Keng Yi went on, "But I cannot start tomorrow. I need time to find an apartment or a room. I won't be able to be on time if I have to travel from Kuala Lumpur everyday. I don't want to start on the wrong footing." Yap said that he would talk to his boss. He explained that his boss was a very understanding man and a few more days without a secretary would not hurt him. When they arrived at the bus terminal, Keng Yi got out of the car and thanked Yap without giving him a kiss. The young man was very hurt, but he forgave his fiancée thinking that she was excited about the new job. He drove to the plantation with the intent of telling his boss that Keng Yi could only start work next week. Malam was no longer in the office. Yap thought that he must have gone home for an early lunch.

When Keng Yi left him, Malam sat on his chair and stared at her departing back. His mind was in turmoil. The girl was certainly beautiful, but he had seen enough beautiful girls, so beauty alone was not the reason for his emotional turbulence over this girl. This was the second time that he fell in love at first sight. The first was many years ago when he was very young. He could not believe that it could happen again in his middle-age. He knew that if he was in his right mind he should not hire her, but he could not bear the thought of never seeing her again. He tried to dismiss her from his mind and concentrate on his day's work, but that was impossible. He kept on seeing her composed and elegant face in front of him. She had it all, beauty, intelligence, confidence and dignity. There was however sadness about her that added to her appeal. Malam knew that the day of work was over for him. He had to go to his club and spend some quiet time on his own. He had also decided not to go home for lunch. He could not face his wives with the emotions stirred by another woman. Thus he spent his afternoon at the club, drinking his favorite drink of whisky on the rocks. But he was careful not to get drunk. He wanted to get back to his office before going home for the evening. There was nothing he did that could remove Keng Yi from his mind. So he called his office to talk to Yap. "Your recommendation was good. I like everything about the girl and I told her that she could start tomorrow," he said to his employee. "Thank you Mr. Shih, but it is not possible for her to start tomorrow. You see, she is living in Kuala Lumpur and she will have to find somewhere to live in Klang before she could start. She has asked me to tell you that she would like to start next Monday. She wants the job very much, so she hopes that you will not mind." Malam was very quiet on the other end. He was beginning to miss her. It would seem like a lifetime to wait until next week. However, he composed himself and replied, "tell her, I don't mind. By the way, I have decided not to come back to the office today. I am meeting some clients at the club. Hold the fort for me and if anything important turns up, you can get hold of me at the club." He hung up the phone. Knowing that he would not be able to see her tomorrow was very upsetting. His resolution of being careful about his drinks and going back to the office weakened.

The bus journey back to Kuala Lumpur was an hour. Keng Yi hated herself for the thoughts that occupied her mind as she sat in the bus and looked out of the window. She had heard from Yap that Mr. Shih was a very distinguished looking man, but he never told her that he was also a very tall and handsome man. As she went through an unhappy childhood, she too had dreams of a prince coming into her life and taking her away from all the miseries that she had faced. That day, she faced her prince. The only difference was that he was an older man with three wives. She could feel the pain in her heart as she realized that he was beyond her reach. She thought that it would be best for her to reject the job. Then again, it would mean that she would never see him again. That pain would be more intolerable than the pain she was now experiencing. Then she thought of her sweet and gentle fiancé. Maybe marriage to him would put her in her place once and for all. But alas, it would not be fair to Yap, unless she could get the romantic thoughts of his boss off her mind. She debated with herself and decided that she would take the job, and maybe, after knowing him for sometime, he would become as ordinary as any other man. Meanwhile, she would try to stay as aloof as she could towards her boss, and give her fiancé undivided attention. She knew that she did love Yap, but Yap had never stirred such feelings of desire in her. She dismissed those thoughts as that of every young romantic school girls, who dreamt of princes and romances. As the bus arrived in Kuala Lumpur, she concluded that she had behaved like a silly romantic teenager.

Malam was quite intoxicated when it was time to go home to join his family for dinner. He decided to leave his car at the club and called for his chauffeur to take him home in the family car. Only Paini noticed the change in her husband when the driver brought him home. Though he felt light-headed, he was still composed and managed to greet his children and wives as usual. However, he was strangely quiet and decided to spend the night alone in his own room. He retired early saying that he had a bad headache and that he would have to go to work quite early. Ah Leng pouted, for she expected to spend that evening with him, but he ignored her and went to his room early. Sleep did not come as easily as he thought. The amount of alcohol that he had did not erase the longing for the girl he met today. He tossed and turned in bed. Then shortly before midnight, he heard a knock on his door. He pretended to be fast asleep, as his unlocked door was opened. Then he heard the soft voice of his first wife, "Malam, I know you are awake. Can I come in?" Malam sat up and said, "What time is it?" He looked at the clock and continued, "Why aren't you asleep?" Paini replied, "I know that something is bothering you and I would like you to talk to me about it?" Without an invitation, she sat on his bed and smiled at him. He saw that smile and realized that he had never for a moment stopped loving this woman. Then he felt ashamed of his new feelings and looked down at his hands. He was not going to hurt her anymore so he said, "I had a little too much to drink. That is all. However, you can sleep with me if you like." He moved aside and Paini snuggled beside him. He put his arms around her and the peace that he found with her proximity made him fall asleep almost immediately.

Paini lay beside him contented and glad that she was still madly in love with her husband, although she had to share him with two others. She was sure that her generosity would have to be extended. She had gone through enough to see the tell-tale signs. She would be hurt, but she was sure the other two would suffer more than her. She smiled to herself as she thought of the tantrums Ah Leng would throw. However, she would not refuse her husband anything. His love for her is forever, no matter how many more wives he would have. She was his first true love and that is one position that no one could take away from her. She lay quietly in his arms, until sleep finally overcame her. She made sure that she got up early enough to leave his room. She did not want to upset Ah Leng, especially now that she suspected that another woman had come into her husband's life. Thus, after just a few hours of sleep, she got up, looked at her husband who was snoring quietly, and left his room without disturbing him. She went back to sleep for another hour before everyone else got up for breakfast. She was glad to see that Malam was himself again the next day. He chatted happily with his children and kissed all his wives, before he drove off with the chauffeur to collect his car at the club. However, she did not dismiss the thoughts that there was now another woman in his life.

Malam went to work as usual. His business was expanding as his rubber trees were also ready for producing latex. He was very short of staff, and many of his old employees were employed one after the other. He needed a secretary urgently, but he would wait to see if Keng Yi showed up at all the following week. Meanwhile he kept his daughter Ai Li busy with accounting and filing documents such as sales and orders. Ai Li was very industrious and stayed late to help her father. She would be glad when the new secretary showed up. She had not had the opportunity to be present at the interview, as she was on an outside job taking orders. If she had been around, she would have noticed something. Malam was able to keep his emotions under control, and even Paini was beginning to doubt her intuitions. The only time he brought her name up was on the Friday before he left for the weekend. He called for Mr. Yap and asked, "Well, has Keng Yi found an apartment here?" Yap said, "Yes, and she is looking forward to starting early on Monday." There was an immeasurable joy in Malam's heart. He was afraid that he might have frightened her away with the intensity that he showed when they met. Although he had kept his feelings well to himself, there was not a moment when the girl was not on his mind. His longing to look on her beauty and hear her voice was immense. He had told himself, that it would be enough just to have her close to him and see her everyday. He must not reveal his feelings to her or to anyone else. This would be his secret.

Yap was a happy man. He had spent his evenings looking for an apartment that was close to his own, and affordable for Keng Yi. When he finally found one, he drove to Kuala Lumpur and brought Keng Yi to see it. Keng Yi was very agreeable, and when he took her home again, she said, "Yap, let me stay on my own for at least one year, and then if you still want me, we can get married after that." Yap was overjoyed. He would have married her immediately, but he knew how important it was for her to feel independent. He answered, "My dearest Keng Yi, you have made me very happy by just moving to Klang and close to me. I love you very much, one year will seem like a life time, but it is better than three years. Yes, we will plan our marriage in a year's time." When Keng Yi saw how happy she had made Yap, she felt that she had done the right thing. No man could love her like he did. She only wished that she felt the same way about him, but time will change all that. She had erased her romantic notions about her future boss. She would work hard and make her fiancé proud of her. Mr. Shih was a married man with three wives and she was engaged. She looked at the small diamond ring on her finger and vowed to be true to it. Yap would come for her on Saturday to help her move to Klang. She was very excited, and that worried her. She was not sure of the cause of her excitement. Was it because of being close to Yap, or was it because she was about to start a whole new life on her own? She dared not even think of the third possibility but it was there. Could it be because she was going to see the man who seemed to draw her to him like a magnet?

Malam had briefed his daughter Ai Li of the duties that Keng Yi would relieve her of. Normally, Ai Li would cycle to the office and be there before her father. But her father had told her to come a little later as he had to discuss matters of pay and vacation with the new girl. Somehow on the day of the interview, those subjects were not brought up. Malam realized that he had dismissed the girl so fast and she too was glad to get away quickly. He had to be as business-like as possible on her first day. That night, Malam again decided to be alone in his own room. He was thankful that none of his wives made any demands. Somehow, sleep would not come as he tossed and turned on his bed. He tried hard not to think of his new secretary, but the more he tried, the more he seemed to long for her. Likewise, Keng Yi too was having a sleepless night. She could not get the picture of her new boss out of her mind. When weariness finally overcame her, she dreamt of him and woke up feeling guilty and lowly. Then she tried hard to fall asleep again, but the same dreams would come back and she seemed to savor them. She was in his arms and he was showering her with kisses, when she was rudely awakened by the alarm clock beside her bed. She sat upright, bit her lips and vowed that she was not going to have any more romantic thoughts of Mr. Shih. She was ready when she heard Yap's car at the driveway. She ran downstairs and greeted him so lovingly that he was gladly surprised. Even though his fiancée had hardly any make-up on except for a light touch of lipstick, she was a sight to behold. He wished that he could let all his colleagues know that she belonged to him, without jeopardizing their jobs. "Maybe later," he told himself. Then he realized that he had not told Keng Yi that they were not supposed to be attached to each other in their working environment. He looked at the beautiful girl beside him and said, "We have to keep our engagement a secret for the time being. Mr. Shih is against employing people who are related to each other, unless they are his relatives. You will be taking his daughter's place. She is very nice and she will help you to settle in." Secretly, Keng Yi was pleased that no one should know of her relationship to Yap, especially her boss. Then she looked down in shame for the pleasure she just experienced. Poor Yap, if he had not been so blind in his love, he would have seen the inevitable.

Chapter 18

Keng Yi started her first day in the middle of May, 1948. It was the day that she would remember as long as she lived. Malam was already at his desk waiting anxiously for her appearance. He stood up as soon as he heard a knock at his door. He reminded himself that he was just going to meet his new employee, and that the topic should be business associated. But as soon as the door opened and Keng Yi stepped in, his heart began to beat uncontrollably. She was more beautiful than the first time he saw her. She was as petite as all his wives, at five foot and weighed around a hundred pounds. She had a white shirt on tucked into a yellow printed skirt which covered her knees. She wore a pair of two-inch black high heel shoes. Her professional appearance, added to her vivacious beauty, broke down all the resolutions that Malam had made the night before. Keng Yi, however, was stronger in that aspect. She was also appalled by the feeling that Malam's presence stirred in her, but she did not deter. As Malam did not say a word, she started by saying, "good morning Mr. Shih." That brought Malam back to reality and he apologized, "Oh, I am sorry. Please take a seat," and he himself sat down. Malam could not believe that he could control himself throughout the meeting. Keng Yi could not believe the pay, he had offered her. She had no working experience, and she was getting as much as her fiancé. She did not care about the vacation time, but he was even very generous with that. He simply told her that he was flexible, and if she needed more time than ten days a year, all she needed to do was let him know a week in advance. When she smiled her acceptance of his offer, he became vulnerable again, and before he lost his control he dismissed her and said that his daughter would be there soon to help Keng Yi. "Meanwhile," he said, "Ask Mr. Yap to show you around. Your desk is just outside my door. You can also browse through the log books. Ai Li will tell you what your duties are." He stood up and Keng Yi knew that it was a sign of dismissal. She left the room but not before she said, "Thank you so much. I will not let you down." Malam wished the earth would open up and swallow him. The pain of not being able to express his feelings for her was becoming unbearable.

Once outside his door, Keng Yi allowed herself to weaken. Instead of going out to look for Yap, who was giving the supervisor of the laborers some instruction, she sat down at the desk outside Malam's office, and let down her defenses. She was now very sure that she was not only attracted by the good looks of her boss, but she was very much in love. She also knew that he felt the same way for her. She cupped her flushed face with her hands and thought, "If only he was not married and I am not engaged. He is the prince that I have been waiting for." Then she heard Yap coming in, and her reverie of thoughts was broken only to be replaced by guilt. Thankfully Ai Li also came in almost at the same time, so she was not alone with Yap. Keng Yi felt more ashamed than ever when she realized that the daughter of her prince was a few years older than herself. He was really old enough to be her father, so how could she even have romantic notions of him. She dismissed her thoughts as she and Ai Li got to know each other. Both of them liked each other, and Ai Li could not help but say, "My you are a beauty. I hope you will not distract our male employees from their work." She looked at Yap and winked jokingly at him. Then she continued, "Well, we have to get started." The day went fast, ending with Keng Yi typing out a few letters that Malam had dictated to her. Ai Li was pleased to see that Keng Yi was a fast learner and very intelligent too. Her English was flawless and her typing speed was very good. However, she detected some discomfort in her father's face, when she had to interrupt him once, while he was dictating to Keng Yi. He looked kind of embarrassed when his daughter popped into the office without knocking. She had done that almost all the time. But it was the first time when he said in irritable tones, "Don't just bust in. Knock first." Ai Li hoped with all her heart that it was just one of his bad days. She did not allow herself to see other possibilities.

Keng Yi was kept very busy the first few days. She spent a lot of time with Ai Li learning all that she had to learn. She had no time to be distracted by the presence of her boss. Once in a while, she had to go into the office when he needed her to type out a letter. Her heart would beat faster than normal, but that was as far as it went. Malam on the other hand found her presence distracting, but he was in control of his emotions. His behavior towards her was kindly but business-like. He did not allow his feelings for her to rule his mind. He was the usual husband and father at home. His business was catching up very fast, and as more people were hired as field workers and office clerks, he had to extend his office building so he bought more acres of land to grow more oil palm. The rubber trees were productive enough, but it was his oil palms that brought in a lot of revenue. He then decided that it was also time to build the mansion of his dreams. Although after the births of Alex and Lily, and with his wives showing no more signs of fertility, his house by the river were getting too small as his children grew and wanted rooms of their own. His mansion would have at least ten bedrooms. Thus, he found an architect, and together they looked for a piece of land in the suburbs of the growing town of Klang.

Malam saw a three-acre lot with plenty of fruit trees growing wildly. At first he was skeptical about the location as it was opposite a huge Chinese cemetery. But after consulting with some mediums, his fears of bad luck were dispelled. He knew that it would take at least a year to finish building his house, so he made his architect start work immediately. The first foundation was laid in June 1948, a month after Keng Yi came into his life.

Meanwhile, Malam's two brothers in Malacca were not doing too well in their own businesses. They were not that young any more, and their children were all grown up, so they decided to sell their businesses and retire. Some of their children found employment at their uncle's plantation. One of them, Kok Seng, caught Ai Li's eyes. He had applied for a teacher training college, but it would be another year before he got accepted, so instead of waiting he decided to earn some money. He was about twenty one years old, just a year older than Ai Li. He too was attracted to Ai Li, who unlike her mothers was quite tall. While Malam and Keng Yi subdued and hid their feelings well, the two young people flaunted their interest for each other openly. Malam was not very happy about the relationship, and complained to Paini. Paini, on the other hand was glad that Ai Li finally found someone, and that someone was Kok Seng. Paini had always liked him when he was a little boy. She managed to convince her husband when she said, "Ai Li is very much our child as the others, but she is adopted, and there is no blood relationship between the two of them. Kok Seng is a very nice boy and we cannot hope for a better son-in-law." Malam gave in but said, "Well, he will always be my nephew first." Thus it was with her parents blessing that Ai Li was engaged to Kok Seng. They would get married in three years when he graduated as a teacher.

It was at the engagement party that Malam gave, that offset the subdued feelings between him and Keng Yi. Malam had a big tent erected outside his home, and all his office workers, close friends and business associates were invited. His brothers and their family also came for the engagement party. It was normal for Yap and Keng Yi to come together. When Keng Yi stepped out of the car, Malam could not help but look in their direction whilst he was talking to an old friend. He felt a pain in his heart as he saw how beautiful she was in a flowered chiffon dress. However, he controlled himself and greeted them both with a smile. Keng Yi was nervous when she met all his three wives. She thought that all of them were very beautiful, especially the oldest one. Paini was in her forties, but she still looked very young and appealing. Paini too had noticed Keng

Yi and thought the same way as she did. She felt that Keng Yi's beauty was outstanding. Not only was the girl beautiful, she was well educated and dignified. The thoughts and suspicion that she had dismissed came back. That did not make her hostile towards the girl. In fact, she liked Keng Yi and was very nice towards her. Cheng Mee too admired the secretary, and she could see why the young Yap was so devoted to her. Ah Leng's attitude was very obvious. She decided immediately to dislike the girl. She even complained to her husband that Keng Yi should be more selective in the way that she dressed. Malam just looked at her and said, "She looks nice in the dress. This is a party and not an office."

As the evening wore on, Yap's closeness to Keng Yi began to upset Malam. Yap thought that it was not necessary anymore to keep their betrothal a secret. He had his arms around Keng Yi most of the time. He was so proud of her. There was much talk about how beautiful all of Malam's wives were, but his fiancée outshone them all. Malam began to seethe with jealousy, and tried as he could, he was not paying any more attention to his friend's chatter. His eyes were on the young couple and he began to drink heavily. Paini was observant of her husband, and she thought it best to separate Keng Yi from Yap. She looked for her daughter, but she was too engrossed in Kok Seng, so she decided to go to Keng Yi herself. It was out of respect for Paini that Yap quickly removed his hand from Keng Yi's shoulders when the older lady approached them. Paini asked Yap, "Hope you don't mind giving me your chair. I would like to get to know Keng Yi better." Yap got up and joined his colleagues. Keng Yi smiled as Paini sat down beside her. "Ai Li looks so happy," she started the conversation. Paini nodded and asked Keng Yi about herself. It was a very normal conversation. While they talked, her eyes would check on her husband. She was glad that he was now surrounded by his two brothers. That would occupy him for sometime, and his brothers would make sure that he did not drink too much. She also caught Ah Leng looking at Keng Yi suspiciously, and she thought to herself, "My dear Malam, please don't do anything foolish to destroy the harmony of your home."

When Paini left Keng Yi to check on some other guests, Yap did no come back immediately. Keng Yi felt she needed to be on her own. She had noticed Malam's agony when he saw how intimate Yap was towards her. Her feelings were stirred, but she thought it best that he knew that she was not free. She got up and walked to the back towards the river bank. Because of her heels she was not able to reach the edge of the river, but she found a dry spot and sat down on it. She noticed that there was a sampan tied to a mangrove tree. She stared at it and allowed her thoughts to wander. She was thinking that it would be best if she married Yap as soon as possible. A voice interrupted her thoughts. "The sampan has been sitting there unused." She got up and turned around to see her boss with a glass of whisky in his hands. "I am sorry. I don't mean to frighten you," he continued to say. Then he went on to explain, "I had it tied to the tree during the Japanese Occupation. It was supposed to be a mean of escape for Ai Li and Cheng Mee. Thank God that they never needed to use it." Keng Yi found her voice and said, "Yes, I know how it was when the Japanese were here. I had to hide in ditches and run into bushes whenever they came near our area." Malam came closer to her and said, "I am so glad that nothing happened to you." He stood very close to her, and even with her heels he was one head taller than her. She looked up into his intense eyes and felt that the world stood still. He then said in a voice that she had never heard before, "You are very beautiful and you are driving me insane." Keng Yi thought she was dreaming, but the touch of Malam's hands on her face brought her back to reality, and she ran as fast as she could away from him. Malam stared after her. Somehow, he did not feel guilty for expressing his feelings. He looked at his empty glass and said to himself, "No, I am not drunk. I had to let her know before I go insane with jealousy." He looked at the running river for another few minutes before he turned back to join the party.

Keng Yi, feeling flushed and hot, was glad that Yap was alone waiting for her. She went up to him and said, "I would like to go home now." Yap looked surprised, and seeing how red her face was asked, "Have you been drinking?" Keng Yi grew impatient with him and said, "No. Please take me home now. I don't feel well." Yap believed her and said, "We will have to thank our boss and explain to him that you are not feeling well." "That is not necessary. There are so many people here, he won't notice our absence." Keng Yi was so insistent that Yap had no choice but to leave with her. He was glad that he had parked his car at the side of the road, quite a distance away from the house. Keng Yi was very quiet on the way home, and when Yap insisted on coming into her apartment, she said, "Sorry Yap, but I have a headache and would like to go to bed immediately." Yap tried to kiss her on the lips, but she offered her cheeks instead and ran up the stairs to her second floor apartment. Yap stood outside the door hurt and confused. She was missing for sometime from the party and he wondered where she was and what had made her so upset. Her changes of mood were getting to him. They had been together for almost a year, and she had not allowed him to touch her intimately. They most she did was to kiss him, sometimes passionately, but more often lightly. However, Yap still loved her very much, and he concluded that they should not wait to get married. He would come over the next day, which was a Sunday and propose. If she lost her job at the plantation, she could apply for a new one at a bank. Many new jobs were opening, and with her skills and good looks she would have no problems. Besides, Malam was very generous and had given him a very good raise. He would have enough to support a small family.

Keng Yi went directly to bed, and let out all the pent up emotions in pools of tears. There was no more denying her love for Malam. She had thought that Yap was her first true love, but she now knew that she was wrong. She had never felt this way for Yap. She would have melted in Malam's arms, and would have given herself completely to him without reason or questions. She cried bitterly because she felt the hopelessness of this love. Malam had confessed his feelings, but that did not change the fact that he already had three wives. When there were no more tears left to shed, she sat up in her bed and made some very painful decisions. First of all, she was going to break up her engagement. She could not marry a man she did not love. Secondly, she was not going back to work. Seeing Malam and not being able to have him would eat her heart out. She would ask her cousin to help her with the rent, together with some money to go back to the place of her birth. She would find a job there and start anew. Fresh tears began to roll at the thought that she would never see Malam again. She wondered if she would ever get over him. However, her mind was made up, and she started to pack up her clothes and what ever belongings she had. Yap could keep the furniture that they had bought together. She would send the landlord the money for the month's rent.

In the early hours of the morning, she wrote Yap a letter, telling him that she did not love him. She begged his forgiveness and thanked him for all that he had done for her. She took off the engagement ring from her finger, and sealed the envelope with the letter and the ring. Then she wrote Malam a letter of resignation. It was as official as it could get. She wrote that due to personal reasons she had to tender her resignation. She also mentioned that she was aware that since she did not give enough notice she would forfeit her pay. She addressed him as Mr. Shih, and signed off in her full name of Loh Keng Yi. As she wetted the seal with her tongue, she allowed it to linger. Then when it was finally sealed, she put it close to her chest and said solemnly, "Goodbye my handsome prince. It was a wonderful encounter, but alas we are not destined to be together. For the first and last time I will say, 'I love you with all my heart'." She hardly slept a wink. So at about 6.00 am, she pinned both the letters on the door outside her apartment. She was sure that Yap would come on Sunday to take her for breakfast. In her letter to Yap, she told him to hand the other one to Malam on Monday. With a big suitcase, she walked to the nearest bus stop to take the earliest transport to the big terminal, from where she would take the bus to her cousin's house in Kuala Lumpur. Her eyes were swollen from crying and she was exhausted. Thankfully, she fell asleep throughout the one and a half hours journey to Kuala Lumpur.

Tan and Mei had a baby girl and they were happy to see Keng Yi. But when Mei noticed that there was something bothering Keng Yi, she told her husband to take the baby for a walk in the pram. When they were alone Mei asked, "You don't have an engagement ring anymore. Did you break up with Yap?" Keng Yi broke down in Mei's arms and poured out her heart to the older girl. She told Mei everything about Malam and her feelings for him. Mei listened quietly, and when Keng Yi stopped sobbing, Mei said, "You did the right thing. You will never be happy if you married Yap. As for your boss, you should get away from him as far as possible. First of all, he is too old for you, and secondly, he already has three wives. You deserve a better life. You are beautiful, intelligent and hardworking. One day, you will find a man of your caliber and you will fall in love again. You feel a lot of pain right now, but distance and time will heal all that." Being able to confide in Mei released a lot of tension, and Keng Yi felt much better. Mei suggested that since she has stopped working after the baby was born, she would drive Keng Yi to the State of Johore. She too would like to visit her parents. She would spend a few days with the baby there. If Keng Yi did not feel comfortable with her birth parents who had given her away, Mei's parents would welcome Keng Yi into their home until she found a job. When Tan came back with the baby, Mei told him about their plan to go to Johore in two days time. Tan had no objection, for he too had detected that something was wrong. He was sure that he would find out what it was about soon. Meanwhile, Keng Yi kept herself busy by helping Mei with the baby, and writing her résumé and letters of applications. Once they arrived in Johore Bahru the capital of Johore, she would find the right companies to send her letters too. She had visited her birth parents before she moved to Kuala Lumpur and they had welcomed her, so she was sure that they would not mind if she stayed in their humble home until she found a job. No matter how hard she tried, the ache and longing in her heart for Malam, did not lessen and the two nights were sleepless nights.

When Yap found the two letters on her door, he was afraid to open his. He expected the worst, and true enough his fears were realized when he saw the ring in the envelope. He was devastated. He could not believe that she could change her mind so quickly. He wanted to drive to Kuala Lumpur immediately, but in her letter she specifically stated that he should not try to contact her. He knew that the letter to Mr. Shih was a letter of resignation. He was too naïve and innocent to think that his boss was the cause of Keng Yi's change of heart. However, he made it his obligation to ring up her cousin to see if she had arrived safely. Mei had answered the phone and cordially thanked him for his concern. Yap did not even dare ask if he could speak to Keng Yi. He was sure that he would be rejected, and the pain that he was undergoing was great enough without the rejection. He spent the Sunday feeling miserable and lonely, hoping against hope that his phone would ring and that she would be on the other line. But his phone remained silent, and he went to sleep broken-hearted. He got up the next morning with a new resolution. He was still a young man, and he was sure that the right girl would come into his life one day. Keng Yi had said that she did not love him and she meant every word of it, so there was no point waiting for her to come back to him. He was thankful that they had managed to keep their betrothal a secret. At least no one would know that he was a jilted lover.

Malam however had been looking forward for Monday to come. He had restrained himself from thinking of Keng Yi after the party and dedicated himself to his family. It was easy for him, thinking that he would be seeing her again on Monday. He was shocked when Yap came into the office telling him that Keng Yi was not coming back. As he tore open the letter and saw that it was an official letter or resignation, he quickly dismissed Yap and locked the door after him. Then he sat down and tried to read between the lines, but there was nothing there. He felt his whole world crumbling around him. Once again, he experienced the hopelessness and anguish of many years ago, when Paini's parents first rejected him. He went to his private cabinet and was about to pour himself some whisky, when he was overcome with a determination. He locked his cabinet again, composed himself and unlocked his door. He paged for Yap to come into his office. The young man looked forlorn and Malam asked him, "Is there a connection between you and Keng Yi?" Yap said sadly, "We were engaged, but she ended it yesterday. I am sorry for not being open about that." Malam was not angry. In fact, his heart soared for he was now very sure that Keng Yi reciprocated his feelings. "Do you know how I could get in touch with her?" Yap nodded and innocently gave him the address of her cousin in Kuala Lumpur.

Monday was a very busy day, and Malam had a lot of meetings to attend. He looked at Keng Yi's notes and smiled to himself. She was very efficient and was a great secretary. He would get her back not only as his secretary, but as his wife. He could not deny himself anymore. He loved her with all his heart, and he was ready to risk everything for her. He could never be a whole person again if she was not by his side. He was still looking at the appointment list when Ai Li knocked at his door. She looked very unhappy and asked, "Father, what happened? Why did Keng Yi resign so suddenly?" Malam told her not to worry. They had a lot to do today and he assured her that everything would be back to normal. Ai Li was not convinced. She was very sure that her father had something to do with the girl's sudden decision. She had also noticed the distress and sadness on Yap's face when he told her that Keng Yi was not coming back. Somehow, Ai Li knew that Yap and Keng Yi were together. They came to work together, and left for home together. She had also seen them at some restaurants and at her party, they were very intimate. Her father's reassurance did not ease her feelings, instead, she had a foreboding that she was getting another mother. She could not imagine a girl, younger than her being her mother. "Well," she thought to herself, "I will not let anything destroy my new found happiness." She looked at Kok Seng, who looked back at her, and a smile of love passed between them. Her worries disappeared and she started to do two jobs again, moving from her desk to that of Keng Yi's. It was indeed a busy day; Ai Li, Yap and Malam had no time to think about the girl who made such an impact in their lives.

That evening Malam came home exhausted. Even though his mind managed to put all thoughts of Keng Yi aside, his heart was still full of her. As he sat down at the head of the dinner table with his huge family, he looked at them all. They all seemed to be happy and contented. He watched his wives helping the younger children with their meals and felt that he still loved all of them just as much. However, there was emptiness within him, and he knew that only Keng Yi could fill up that hole. That night, he chose Paini to sleep in his room. Only she would be able to help him make the big decision. She had always supported him, and he hoped with all his heart that she would continue to stand by him. Paini had a strong suspicion that something big was going to happen, so when her husband started to seduce her, she pushed him gently away and said, "You have something to tell me. Let us get it over with." Malam was thankful for her intuition, for it was more a duty than an urge that he began to make his approach. He sat up in bed, and looked at his wife who was lying on her back. She encouraged him to start the conversation. "My dearest Paini, what I am about to tell you does not mean that I love any of you less. I am in love again, only this time the love for this girl brings back the past with you. I have the same longing and pain of many years ago. I shall never be whole again unless I have her." He paused and waited for his wife's response. Paini took her eyes off her husband and turned on her side. Tears were gathering in her eyes as she said, "This time, I alone cannot make the decision for you. The other two have also loved you faithfully. Together we have gone through a lot when you were in the hands of the Japanese. But think carefully before you approach them with this topic. Be prepared for Ah Leng's wrath." She got up, kissed him on the forehead, and left his room without looking back.

Alone in his room, Malam paced the floor. For the first time in his life he was angry with Paini. She did not give him her support as he had hoped. According to custom, he need not get permission from the others to remarry. Paini was the one who held the key to unchain his heart, and allow him to bring Keng Yi into the family. When he thought of her, his desire for her closeness and presence almost made him insane. Then shamefully, he realized that at this moment, she meant more to him than all his three wives and children put together. If they would not accept her into their lives, then he would find a separate home for her, and he would spend more time with her than anyone else. Malam was beyond reasoning with himself. He decided not to confront his family yet. He would go first thing in the morning to convince Keng Yi of his love and desire to make her his wife. If Keng Yi loved him as much as he loved her, she would be persuaded to come back with him. He could not imagine how her rejection would destroy him. He could not think anymore. The busy day at the office, and the emotional strain finally wore him out, and he slept without any dreams.

When Paini was alone in her room, she allowed her tears to flow. She surprised herself that she was miserable, not because her husband was getting another wife, but because she was jealous. She had always held on to the memory that she was the first true love in Malam's life, but she could sense that Keng Yi, although not his first love, might be his greatest love. Keng Yi was extremely beautiful, well educated, intelligent and very dignified. Paini knew that none of them could compete with her qualities. Her husband had finally found his match. Her heart ached as those thoughts went through her head. Then somehow, the overwhelming love for her husband took over, and she began to rationalize. His mother had once said that her son had a big heart with enough place for many loves. His love for her did not decrease when Ah Leng and then Cheng Mee came into their lives. He had been good to all of them, and no one had complained about him being unfair. Ah Leng was disgruntled once in a while, but that was because she was too demanding. Paini went to the bathroom outside her room, washed her face and looked at herself in the mirror. Then she spoke softly to her reflection, "It is your fate to share your prince with other princesses. Be grateful that he still loves you and will continue to do so until the end of time." She decided that even if the other two disagreed, she would give him her permission to take a fourth wife. Even though she was still jealous of Keng Yi, she gave her the credit that she would be his very last love. She did fall asleep, and for the first time after many years, she saw her prince on the white horse. She was sitting on her favorite rock on the beach in Pataya. He swooped her into his arms and they rode into the clouds. He left her on a big cloud, rode off and came back with two more women. Then he waved them goodbye. Paini started to cry, thinking that he would never come back. Her sobs become hysterical and she woke herself up by the sound of her own sobbing.

Meanwhile, Keng Yi was getting ready to leave for Johore Bahru. Mei had to cancel her plans of driving her because her infant child was having a slight fever. So the other alternative was for Keng Yi to go ahead on her own by bus, and Mei would join her later. Keng Yi wanted to leave as soon as possible. She was afraid that she might give in to her longing and break her resolution. Her heart was heavy with immeasurable sorrow, and she felt that only distance would give her the strength to go on living without her 'prince'. She was glad that Yap did not try to contact her, which meant that he had accepted the break-up quite well. She wondered about how Malam had reacted to her sudden resignation. Maybe he blamed himself for professing his love to her. It could also be that he was quite drunk when he said those things to her and was now glad that he would not ever see her again. It should not matter what he thought, but somehow, she wished that he had meant what he said. She pulled herself together and left her room to enter her cousin's car. He drove her to the bus terminal where she caught the express bus to Johore Bahru. As the bus moved south, she thought to herself, "I have to put the past behind me and look ahead." However, her heart remained heavy, and no matter how hard she tried, she could not erase the picture of Malam's handsome face from her mind.

Malam had decided before he went to sleep, that he would drive down to Kuala Lumpur and beg Keng Yi to come back with him. He got up earlier than anyone else, and wrote a note to Ai Li with instructions to cancel all his appointments in the morning, and postpone them to the afternoon. He called his chauffeur to be early to send his school-going children to school. Before any of his wives woke up, he was already on the road towards the address that Yap had given him. If Keng Yi would have him, he would simply announce his desire to marry her. If Paini would not give him her permission, he would still marry Keng Yi, but he would not bring her home. Instead, he would find an apartment or house for both of them, until his wives came to their senses. At this point, Keng Yi mattered more to him than anything else. He had seen how Keng Yi looked at him, and he was full of hope. But when he arrived at the cousin's house, his hope turned to anxiety and apprehension. What if he saw only what he wanted to see? Keng Yi was so much younger than him. She could have any man she wanted, so why would she want one old enough to be her father and already married to three women. Then the doubts were replaced by the fact that she had broken off with a young man after the night he opened his heart to her. She must have realized that she could not love Yap because she had fallen in love with him. That gave him the courage to knock at the door of the house.

A disheveled Mei opened the door, thinking that her husband had returned from the bus terminal. When she saw a distinguished gentleman at the door, she almost slammed the door in his face, not because she was afraid of him, but because she was ashamed of how she looked. Malam however had a way of making people feel at ease, and when he smiled and introduced himself, Mei could see why her cousin-in-law was so much attracted to the man standing at the door. This certainly was no ordinary man. As Mei explained to the devastated Malam that Keng Yi had taken the early bus to Johore Bahru, her husband returned. His instinct told him who the owner of the limousine was. Mei had explained every thing to him, and when he saw how forlorn and unhappy his cousin was as she said goodbye to him, he could not understand why she was hurting herself so much. It was hard for him as a man to give advice to a female, but if Keng Yi had asked him for it, he would have told her to simply follow her heart. This man in his house with his wife had done exactly that, and hopefully, it was not too late for him. Looking at his watch, the bus must have left about half an hour ago. He went in, and after introductions were made, he said, "You have a fast car, you may still be able to overtake the bus." His wife looked at him and an understanding smile passed between them. Tan could also see that Malam was someone special, and regardless of his age and number of wives, whomever he loved was also just as special. If it was Keng Yi's destiny to be his fourth wife, then she would return with him, otherwise, it was just not meant to be.

Malam drove with a speed that would lead to a high fine if his car had been stopped by the traffic police. But all he could think of was Keng Yi. Then just as he saw the end of the big bus, he heard the siren of the police car. Even that did not slow him down, but as the police car caught up with him and the siren became more insistent, Malam had no choice but to pull to the side of the road. Frustrated, he saw the bus disappearing in a cloud of dust. He buried his face into the steering wheels and thought to himself, "There goes my life." Luckily for him, the policeman recognized the important man in the car. "Sir," the policeman spoke in Malay, "you are violating the traffic speed." Malam looked up sadly and recognizing the young man as the son of one of his workers, he said, "I am sorry, but the woman who holds my life in her hands is in the bus that is now far away." The officer could see the despair on Malam's face, but he had to do his duty. He could not allow Malam to drive on at the same speed, but remembering how well his father had talked about his boss, the officer decided to help. He asked Malam the name of the woman that Malam was talking about. When Malam told him, he made Malam promise to wait in his car. He would try to overtake the bus and see what he could do. With renewed hope, Malam watched as the siren went on again, and the police car shot off at a speed as though it was after a criminal.

It was sometime before he saw the tail of the bus and when the bus driver realized that the police car was trailing him, he pulled aside wondering if he had gone over the speed limit. The passengers too were worried, but Keng Yi who was so deep in thoughts, was not aware of the commotion. As the bus covered the miles southwards, her heart became heavier, and there was a point where she thought that she should stop the bus and hitch-hike back to where she had left her heart. Then she heard someone calling her name. Surprised and shocked at the same time, she put up her hand to identify herself to the policeman. He beckoned her to get off the bus. She hoped that nothing had happened to her niece, because when she left, the niece was having a fever. The officer said something to the bus driver and he nodded. The bus driver would see what Keng Yi would decide to do. The officer looked at Keng Yi and thought to himself, "No wonder the poor man was so devastated. I too, would not let a girl like that slip out of my life so easily." Then to Keng Yi he said, "I have come to beg you to go back with me. The man you left behind has nothing to live for without you." At first Keng Yi thought that he was referring to Yap, but his next sentence, "Mr. Shih risked his life trying to overtake this bus," brought unshed tears to her eyes, and she allowed her heart to take over her mind. She simply said, "I have my suitcases in the bus." The driver had already got the suitcases out of the compartment in the bus and handed them to the policeman. He smiled and said, "Good luck," to Keng Yi before he drove off." As Keng Yi got into the police car, her heart was soaring. Princes came in different forms. Malam was older than most and married three times, but he was her prince, and she loved him with all her heart.

CHAPTER 19

For the kindly policeman, it was like the ending of a fairy tale. When Malam saw the police car returning, his heart was in his mouth. He could not imagine how his life would be if the officer returned alone. But as the car drew close and he saw his beloved in it, he got out of his car, his heart throbbing so fast, that he thought he was going to faint. Keng Yi too did not wait for the car to stop completely. She was out of it and both ran towards each other at the same time. There were no words exchanged as they embraced each other. Malam lifted Keng Yi and kissed her with all the passion that flowed, unaware of the officer who said, "I wish you both the happiness of a lifetime." They did not even hear his car driving off. They were in a world of their own. Even the hot sun burning their skin, as they stood by the side on the road, did not bother them. Finally, they managed to pull themselves away from each other, and Malam took hold of Keng Yi's hand and led her towards his car. They just held on to each other's hands as Malam drove to the nearest hotel. Still, no words passed between them. They were just contented to feel each other. In a trance Keng Yi followed Malam into the lobby of a very posh hotel on the outskirts of Kuala Lumpur. Malam asked for the most expensive room, and when they were inside the room, he kissed Keng Yi again. It was an automatic reaction as they both moved towards the bed. Then for the first time Malam spoke, "My dearest love, let us just enjoy being with each other." Keng Yi caressed his face and said, "Take me now." But Malam, still kissing her said, "I will, but not now. I want you to be my wife first. Will you marry me?" Keng Yi replied, "Yes, oh yes. But I want you now." Malam could not resist her, and as his manhood penetrated her virginity, he was sure that this was definitely the last love of his life. He felt the years melting away. His love for Keng Yi equaled, if not more than, his love for Paini. They lay beside each other panting but contented and happy. Malam's voice was soft and full of tenderness when he asked, "Did I hurt you my love?" Keng Yi nodded but replied, "The pain was blissful. I love you with all my heart." It was the happiest and most fulfilling day of her entire life. Her prince was everything she had dreamt of.

It was the first time that Malam made love to his future wife before the customary nuptial agreement, but he felt no regrets, and looking at Keng Yi's happy face, he was sure that she too felt the same way. Her smile reaffirmed his thoughts and he felt so much love for her that he made love to her again. Then he knew, that he should get back to his office, do some work and talk to his family. He wanted Keng Yi to stay in the hotel until he finalized all the plans, but Keng Yi said, "Take me back to my apartment. I am sure that the landlord will give me back the key. I'd rather stay there and be closer to you than in this hotel. I don't want to go to your home yet. Take me back only when you are sure that all your wives will accept me. I have felt unwanted when I was a child, and I don't want to feel that way again." Malam kissed her and was hurt to know that she had suffered before. He will make sure that she would never have to feel pain again. He agreed to do that, but told her that he would spend all his nights with her.

When they arrived at Keng Yi's apartment, Malam was unwilling to leave her, but Keng Yi insisted that he had to go about his business. She also suggested that she went back to the office as his secretary. But Malam felt that she needed to rest. He would love to have her back the next day. Before he left her, they made love again. Then he left reluctantly, promising to be back that night. Left alone, Keng Yi wondered what Yap would say when he found out that she was to be Malam's wife. She thought of Ai Li's reaction. Could they remain friends? There were a lot of risks involved in this relationship. What if Malam's wives never accepted her? She knew that she would never allow him to give up his family for her. If that was the case, she would be contented just to be his mistress. She loved him too much to run away. She would also continue to work as his secretary and that way, she would see more of him than any of his wives. Her fate was sealed. She belonged to Malam whether they were married or not. She could never live without him. With Malam's love, she would be able to face Yap's anger and that of all those who would not accept their relationship. She started unpacking. Malam was hardly gone for an hour but she began to miss him already. She shrugged her shoulders and told herself to get used to such situations. Whatever pain she went through when he was not around would be worth the ecstasy and joy when he was with her.

By the time Malam got to his office it was late afternoon and Ai Li had cancelled all appointments. When he did not show up after lunch, she was worried for no one knew where he was. When he finally showed up, Ai Li was surprised to see her father in such a good mood, but instead of being happy for him, she feared that something was seriously wrong. She was now old enough to confront her father, so she entered his office and closed the door behind her. "Father, where have you been? Mother has been so worried when she did not see you this morning." Malam looked at his daughter and said, "I had to do something for myself. I am glad that you cancelled all my appointments. Get home early today because I have something to tell you all." "I'd rather hear it now," Ai Li said with an intensity that surprised her father. "Well, then take a seat." Ai Li sat down and waited for her father to begin. He took a deep breath and began, "From the first day that I laid eyes on Keng Yi, I fell deeply in love with her. When she found out my feelings, she tried to run away. But I could not let that happen. I know that I can not live without her. I went after her as she was on her way to her place of birth. I manage to get her back. You see, she feels the same way about me. I want to marry her as soon as possible." He looked hard at his daughter's sad face. Then he continued, "I know what you are thinking. I did fall in love with Ah Leng and Cheng Mee, but the love I have for Keng Yi is very similar to the first love of my life, which was your mother. I have to be honest with you. I may even love Keng Yi more than anyone else in my life." Ai Li stood up and said, "That is now between you and the rest of the family. I would like to leave home and move in with Kok Seng. I don't want to hang around and see the unhappiness this relationship will cost. I shall continue to work for you until Kok Seng becomes a full-time teacher." Malam realized that he had already lost a daughter. He wondered how many more members of his family were going to leave him before the night was over. Like Keng Yi, he was prepared to make sacrifices so that they could be together.

When Paini woke up and found her husband gone, she felt that she had let him down. When she called the office and found that he had not returned after lunch, she knew that he had gone to his new love. She felt it her duty to inform the other two women of their discussion the night before, but she changed her mind. Her husband should be the one to tell them. However, she would stick to her resolution of giving him permission to remarry. When Ai Li had called her to say that Malam had come into the office, she decided that all the children should be fed early and sent to bed. Jo Lin made a fuss about not seeing her father, but a little bribe finally persuaded her to eat with the rest of her siblings, and then to retire to her room and stay there until sent for. Paini explained to Ah Leng and Cheng Mee that Malam had important matters to discuss with them. She had to lie that she did not know what it was about. Ah Leng thought that it was about the mansion that was now under construction. Cheng Mee had a different opinion. She wondered if her husband wanted more children. She was not happy that after Lily was born, she did not feel that she was as fertile as before. She had lost her first child and she would love to have another one. As for Ah Leng, she already had a handful, and she was not that young anymore. All three of them waited anxiously for their husband to get home. Paini was more anxious than the others, for she wanted her husband back and she needed to let him know that no matter what happens she would stand by him.

Malam unable to resist seeing Keng Yi again went back to her apartment. She was overjoyed to see him, but her unselfish character persuaded him to return home to his family. So all he got from her was a loving hug and a short kiss. As he drove his car towards home he dreaded to think of how the environment would be when he said his piece. When he arrived home, he was glad that all his children were in their rooms. He could hear music from a record player coming out of Jo Lin's room. His heart was heavy for he knew that she would be very hurt. Of all his children, he loved her most of all. At age thirteen, she was turning out to be a beautiful young lady, and in many ways she reminded him of himself when he was young. She pouted whenever she did not get her way. She was also independent, and could entertain herself with music and books like he did when he was a child. She too had a beautiful and melodious voice. There were times when he showed her more favoritism than the others and he would be reprimanded by his wives. She was the last person he wanted to hurt, but he believed that she would also learn to accept Keng Yi with time. Well, he would cross that bridge when he came to it. First of all, he had to confront his wives with the news of his new love.

He greeted them the same way, kissing each on their forehead. When they were seated for dinner, it was Ah Leng who started the conversation. "When will our new house be ready?" she asked. "I hope sooner than what the architect predicted," was Malam's reply. He looked at his other two wives and saw that they were very quiet. He decided that he would not bring up the topic until after dinner. He would invite all of them into his room, which was far away from the children's. That way, whatever commotion occurred, the children would not hear it. He kept the conversation at the table as casual as he could, but it was only Ah Leng who was conversant. Then as his wives got up and started clearing, he said, "I would like to talk to all of you in my room. Once you are done here in the kitchen, please come. I shall be waiting for all of you." Whenever Malam addressed his whole family, he would use the Malay language. When he talked to his children, it was English, but to all his three wives, alone or together it was Malay. Ah Leng and Cheng Mee looked wonderingly at each other. But when they looked at Paini, she avoided their eyes and simply said, "let us finish fast. We don't want to keep him waiting too long."

Malam had drunk two glasses of whisky before his wives joined him. He had taken three chairs from the dining room, and when his wives came in he gestured to them to sit down, while he stood with an empty glass in his hand. He drank to steady his resolve but not to be drunk. He looked at all three of them, and thought to himself that he still loved them just as much. Then he braced himself and began to talk. "My dears, I want you to know that I still love all of you. I have not neglected my duties as a husband and father. If any of you think otherwise, please tell me now." He paused and when no one answered he continued, "I have fallen in love again and I am going to marry one more time." Before he could go on Ah Leng screamed, "No! I will not accept it!" She looked at the other two for support, but got none. Cheng Mee's eyes were welling with tears and so were Paini's. Ah Leng got out of her chair and went to Paini saying, "Don't give him permission. Think of all the things we have gone through." Then Paini stood up and went to her husband. She looked up at him and said, "You are right. You have been a good husband and father to us all. You have worked hard to make our lives comfortable. Your mother was right when she told me that you have a big heart, big enough to love as many as possible. I will not stand in your way. If it is Keng Yi that you are talking about then she is welcome to join us." Ah Leng left the room without another word. Then Malam looked at his youngest wife and asked, "What about you, Cheng Mee?" Cheng Mee just looked at her folded hands on her laps and in a tearful voice said, "When you married me, you hurt Paini and Ah Leng. Somehow they got over the hurt. It will be the same for me." Malam went to her and hugged her saying, "Thank you. I will never stop loving you." Then he took Paini in his arms and kissed her. "You will always be my first love." "I know," was her reply, but in her heart she knew that no matter what he said, Keng Yi was the most valued person in his life right now. Then she continued, "Leave Ah Leng alone for now. I will see what I can do to help." She kissed him and left the room with an ache that she hoped would not stay for too long.

Malam could not wait to go to Keng Yi. As he passed Ah Leng's room, he could hear her sobbing bitterly, but he hardened his heart and just passed by without hesitating. Ai Li had not returned from work and that worried him a little. He did not like the idea of her living with a man out of wedlock. But, she was a young woman now and he had no right to control her life. All he could do was advise her to be careful and not to conceive until she and Seng were legally married. He knew that he had hurt her and his three wives. Even though Paini had given in to him, he sensed the agony she was going through. Cheng Mee too was heartbroken even though she put on a brave front. His greatest worry was Ah Leng. He wondered whether she would ever forgive him. It would be terrible if she decided to leave him. He could not bear to be parted from any of his children, especially Jo Lin. There was still some hope that Ah Leng would remain. She had always been materialistic, and he was sure that she would not be satisfied with whatever compensation she would get from him. Being his wife, she had more security. Anyway, he was going to prove to his three wives that he still loved them, and Keng Yi was no intruder. He would not treat any of them differently. He would be as fair as possible where his nights were spent, although he knew deep in his heart that it would be hard. Right now, all he wanted was to be with Keng Yi for always.

Keng Yi greeted Malam as though they had been parted for a long time. He gathered her in his arms, and as they entered her bedroom, he whispered in her ears, "We have to be careful. I don't want you to get pregnant before we are married." Keng Yi smiled and said, "Does it matter? Our child will be the fruit of the greatest love on earth." Then as he gently put her down on her bed, she touched his lips with her fingers and said, "Don't worry. I am at the end of my cycle. Tonight could be the last evening to consummate our love for the next seven days." Laughingly, Malam teased, "Then there is no time to waste." He felt that he could go on making love to her until they collapsed. He had never felt this way since he first married Paini. She made him feel young and alive. Then as he lay beside her and watched her sigh with contentment, he decided that he was going to make her special. He would wait until his mansion was ready and she would be his first and last bride in the house of his dreams. Their child would also be the first to be born there. He would be so discreet that none of his wives would notice the difference. Then Keng Yi turned over and placing one hand to support her head, she asked the important question, "How did your wives react to our love?" Malam had no choice but to tell her everything. He wished he could hide Ah Leng's strong objection from her, but she would find out on her own. Surprisingly, Keng Yi was supportive of Ah Leng's behavior. She said, "I would feel the same way if I was in her shoes. Well, I shall continue to stay in my apartment and work as your secretary. You can visit me some nights, but I will be content that I shall be seeing more of you than the others." Malam was sad when he said, "Some nights are not enough for me. I want you by my side all the time. But we will marry later whether Ah Leng likes it or not. You are going to be my first bride in my new house. I hope that the mansion will be ready before the end of this year. As long as you are not in my home, I shall come to you after dinner every night." Keng Yi protested saying,

"You have a reputation of being a fair man. I don't want you to change even though I would welcome you whole heartedly every night. Your wives must know that you still love them." He kissed Keng Yi tenderly, then his desire for her returned and they made love again. It was on Keng Yi's insistence that Malam reluctantly went home that night. He would come back and take her to work the next morning.

It was late in the night when he got home. All his children were fast asleep and when he looked into Ai Li's room, and saw that it was empty, his uneasiness returned. Unhappily, he presumed that she decided to spend the night with her fiancé. He was not sure whether all his three wives were fast asleep, but all the doors to their rooms were closed. He was exhausted and was thankful that no one noticed his return. He went to bed and slept fitfully until the next morning, when he woke up to the usual sounds of his children getting ready for school. Jo Lin greeted him happily but complained that he did not come into her room to say good-night. Ah Leng ignored him completely, Cheng Mee pretended to pay full attention to Lily, and only Paini talked to him, but she tried to be as casual as possible. When she asked him if he was coming back for lunch he replied, "No, I shall be having lunch with Keng Yi at the club." He wanted his wives to get used to the idea that there was now another woman in their lives. However, he did feel some regret when Jo Lin asked, "Who is Keng Yi?" He had to be careful with his answer so he told her that she was his secretary and that they have to discuss business. Ah Leng made an unpleasant sound and went back into her room. Ai Li, who came home just before everybody was up, came out of her room, simply wished everybody good morning and without any breakfast cycled to work. It was then that Paini brought up the subject of Ai Li's decision. "You must not let her live with Kok Seng before they are married. He is just renting a room, and soon he will leave Klang to study in Kuala Lumpur. If Ai Li went along, she won't be able to work for you. How will they live?" Malam assured her that he would talk to Ai Li and they could find a solution, if she still insisted on moving in with Kok Seng.

Keng Yi was ready and waiting for Malam when he arrived. She did not want to tempt Malam by inviting him into her apartment, so as soon as she saw his car pulling in, she came out, kissed him lightly and said, "Let us go to work." She had already made up her mind of how she was going to confront both Yap and Ai Li. Surprisingly, Ai Li greeted her with, "Nice to have you back." Yap, naïve of the reason for her return, went to her, and was going to give her a hug when Keng Yi moved away and said,

"Can we go somewhere quiet to talk." Hurt and unsure of himself, Yap just shrugged and Keng Yi led him towards the back of Malam's office where the coffee maker stood. There was a table and some chairs, and at that time the morning, there was hardly anyone around except for the four of them. Keng Yi started making coffee while Yap sat down, still looking hurt. As the water boiled, Keng Yi sat beside him and started, "I came back because of Mr. Shih. He was also the reason why I decided to quit. But do not misunderstand me when I say that he was not why I broke off our engagement. I am very fond of you, but I can never love you the way you deserved to be loved." Yap looked down and never said a word, so Keng Yi continued after a short pause. "I knew the true meaning of love when I first set eyes on Mr. Shih. At first it mattered that he was older and already had three wives, but the love I have for him knows no bounds. So when he came after me as I was on the bus to my hometown, I knew that I could never run away from him. So here I am." Yap got up, and with a voice drained of emotion said, "Good luck," and walked out.

Malam knew that Keng Yi had to talk to Yap, so he left them alone, but he was glad that his daughter did not show any animosity towards Keng Yi. He decided that he would postpone talking to her that day, as he felt that Keng Yi's return would cause enough excitement in the office when the rest of his employees arrived. But he felt that it was obligatory for him to talk to Yap, so when he found out that Keng Yi had finished speaking to his assistant he sent for him, but Yap was at his desk writing a letter of resignation. He could not bear to be in the same office with the two people who according to him had betrayed him. So instead of appearing personally before Malam, he sent the office boy with the letter, and left the plantation for good. Keng Yi never saw him again. She felt sorry but not for what she did to him, but for Malam who had lost a trusted and hard-working assistant. She came into Malam's office and said, "I shall help you as much as I can. I am not worried about Yap, for I know that he will find another good job somewhere else." Malam took her in his arms and whispered in her ears, "Your nearness to me is all I need. I will find another assistant. Maybe it is all for the best that he left." She kissed him and told him that as long as she was in the office, she would be his secretary, and that this would be the last time that they would have any tender moments at work. Malam smiled with agreement and they both went about their business. They went to the club for lunch that day and almost everyday after that.

Malam spent alternate nights at home and with Keng Yi. Ah Leng never left the house as there were no more discussions about Malam bringing Keng Yi in to live with them. However, she still would not accept Keng Yi as his mistress, so she did not speak to him or even serve him. Whenever he was at home, she would be in her room sewing or playing with her children. Paini was feeling the strain of the broken home unbearable, and she tried to talk to Ah Leng. "Ah Leng," she said, "as long as we do not accept his wish to remarry we have less than half of him. He does not come back for lunch anymore, and he is only home every other night. Our husband has a lot of love to give and we have learnt to share him. Let us accommodate him and you will see nothing much will change." Ah Leng glared at her and said, "You are too blind to see that he loves only this woman. He will not be fair anymore. If he is still the same person, he would have been home more often. There are three of us here and only one of her. Besides, he spends the whole day with her at the office and at lunch. It is time that I tell Jo Lin about her father. She may be the only one to get him back for us." Paini was exasperated. She felt that it was unfair to use an innocent child for their means. But she said, "Well have it your way. When he comes back tonight, I shall tell him that it is time for him to bring Keng Yi home. Cheng Mee and I want him back." That was the end of the conversation. Ah Leng was determined to make life as difficult as possible for the whole family if Malam married again. Cheng Mee too felt the same way as Paini. She loved Malam very much and missed him. When they were together she expressed her feelings to him. "I really don't care if you marry Keng Yi. I will treat her like a younger sister." Malam convinced her that he would marry Keng Yi but not until the mansion was completed. When they made love, Cheng Mee felt that Malam's love and desire for her had not changed, and she was sure that it would remain the same even after his marriage to Keng Yi. Like Paini, she too would like to have him home every night.

Malam was unable to prevent his daughter Ai Li from moving in with his nephew. But he made them a good offer so that they could set an earlier wedding date. He offered Kok Seng Yap's position, which meant that he would be getting more pay than that of a qualified teacher. Thus Kok Seng need not go into a teacher's college and they could get married as soon as possible. The couple was overjoyed, and they planned to get married within the same year. They rented a small but comfortable house in Klang. Ai Li convinced her mother that she would not get pregnant before the wedding. Paini was reassured to know that her daughter would not move too far away. Meanwhile, Malam was pushing his architect and the builders to complete his mansion. He could not wait to make Keng Yi his wife. He hated to think of her as his mistress. Although Keng Yi told him that she was taking precautions, he was still afraid of her conceiving. He wanted their child to be legitimate. They have been together for over six months and Ah Leng was still hostile towards him, and never sat down to have meals with the family when he was around. Jo Lin was beginning to be difficult and would not go near her father. Although Ah Leng did not keep her threat of telling her about Keng Yi, she was old enough to guess that her father was seeing someone else. It hurt him to see her moving away from him, but for the time being there was nothing he could do to change the situation.

Malam's business was doing very well, so he was able to push the builders with more money to finish up his mansion at a faster pace. He was getting anxious and impatient to marry Keng Yi. Meanwhile, Ai Li and Kok Seng had set the date for the wedding, and Malam intended to give them a grand ceremony, as grand as his when he married Paini. Since they did not live in Malacca, and according to the wishes of the couple, it would be a modern white wedding. Paini was excited because there was no greater joy for her than to personally sew her daughter's wedding gown. Malam had decided to rent the whole clubhouse for the day. It would be expensive, but with his wealth Malam could afford anything. The big day finally arrived, and there was no question that Keng Yi would be at the wedding. It was her decision not to mingle with Malam's immediate family, but to be among the close friends and relatives. The nuptial agreement took place in the Registry of Marriages in Klang, followed by a luncheon among family, close relatives and good friends. Malam insisted that Keng Yi join them for that occasion much to the disgust of Ah Leng. Keng Yi tried to make herself as unnoticeable as possible, but Malam openly kept looking in her direction. She had told Malam the night before that she would not be at the main table, and if Malam insisted, she would not attend the luncheon. Malam was quite agreeable because he had to give his wives due respect. Their places were beside him according to their ranks, Paini would be directly on his right, followed by Ah Leng and Cheng Mee. The married couple sat at the head of the table flanked by their parents. To have Keng Yi sitting beside Cheng Mee would be exposing her to Ah Leng's anger. However, when lunch was over and the guests began to mingle with one another, Malam was at Keng Yi's side all the time. Ah Leng saw that and with a huff left the clubhouse followed by a tearful Jo Lin.

Thankfully, the guests were having such a good time that no one noticed the exit, except for Malam, his two other wives and Keng Yi. Keng Yi took Malam aside and said, "I shall be leaving soon and I shall not be attending the party tonight. Today is Ai Li's big day; let us not spoil it for her." Malam was angry with Ah Leng so he said, "No my love, I cannot bear not to have you around me. I could make you my wife anytime, but we decided to wait. Paini and Cheng Mee had told me they would welcome you into the family. If Ah Leng wants to behave badly, it is not your fault." But Keng Yi was determined, and she begged Malam to be reasonable. He could come to her after the party was over, no matter how late it was. Malam was unhappy, but he knew that Keng Yi would not change her mind. He would send her back, rest at her place and attend the dinner party and then return to her. He decided that he would have a serious talk with Ah Leng the next day. Either she accepted Keng Yi as part of the family or he would ask her to leave without the children. He looked around for his sons and saw that they were happily playing outside with their cousins. Alex, the youngest boy, was with Paini. He glanced in her direction and saw an encouraging smile. Cheng Mee was busy with Lily and seemed undisturbed by Ah Leng's actions. He felt a deep and sincere love for both his wives and all his children. He only wished that Jo Lin, the apple of his eye would not have gone off with her mother. But he knew that was Ah Leng's way of punishing him, using her own daughter for her means. When luncheon was over, he went over to Paini and said, "Paini, since Keng Yi has decided not to come to the dinner tonight, I am sending her home and will only be back here in time to greet the guests. Please make sure that Ah Leng attends the dinner for Ai Li's sake." Paini nodded and replied, "I am sorry that Keng Yi won't be there, but I think she has made the right decision. I will try my best to make Ah Leng come to terms with the situation." Then just before Malam took off, she kissed him on the lips and said, "I love you." He smiled and replied, "Me too." Paini is one woman he would always respect and love until the end of his life.

When the rest of Malam's family returned home, Jo Lin was sitting on the steps pouting. Cheng Mee handed her daughter to Paini and sat down with Jo Lin. She put her arms around the sad and forlorn child and said, "Jo Lin, you know that your father loves you very much." "No," was the tearful reply. "He loves that woman now and he spends all his time with her." "Yes, he does love the woman, but he still loves all of us. It is like when he has a new child, he loves the baby, but he does not stop loving the other children that are already there. His love for you did not become less when your brothers were born. It is going to be the same way. He will not love your mother or me or First Mother less when he marries again. He is a big man with a big heart and there is place in his heart to love many." Jo Lin looked at Cheng Mee and said, "But if that is so, why is my mother always crying." Cheng Mee was glad to see that Jo Lin was beginning to soften so she had to choose her words carefully. "Well, it is always hard for the older wife to accept the new one. First Mother cried a lot when your father decided to marry your mother. Then your mother was also angry and hurt when he married me. But when she realized that he did not stop loving her, she was happy again. We are all very hurt that your father has found another woman, but we know that he will still love all of us. As long as your father is not married to Keng Yi, he will not be home every night. He has to share his time with all of us. But after they are married, you will see him everyday. You will like that won't you?" Jo Lin's eyes brightened, then looked sad again when she said, "I miss him so much." Cheng Mee kissed her on the forehead and said, "Everything will be as it was, I promise you."

After Paini had put Alex and Lily to sleep, she knocked at Ah Leng's door before letting herself in. Ah Leng was lying in bed, pretending to be fast asleep. But Paini knew that she was awake, so she sat on the bed and said, "Ah Leng, for the sake of all our children, we should talk." Without bothering to open her eyes, Ah Leng muttered, "What is there to talk about. You both seemed to be contented that our husband is committing adultery." This time, Paini was quite angry, but she managed to control her temper and continued to say, "I accepted you without much ado. You made a big fuss when he wanted to marry Cheng Mee, and you are doing the same thing again. You of all persons should know how vulnerable Malam is where love is concerned. He will marry Keng Yi whether you like it or not. If you refuse to accept her you are going to be on the losing end. If you give in to him, he will appreciate you for it." Paini paused to give Ah Leng a chance to say something, but she just lay still. Assuming that she was digesting her words, Paini went on. I have never felt that he loved me less when he married you. The only difference was that I had to share his time. Tell me honestly, did you feel that he neglected you when he married Cheng Mee?" This time Ah Leng sat up and looked Paini in the eyes saying, "Are you blind? It is different this time. All he cares for is to be with her. Mark my words, when she moves in, she will be sharing his room every night." Paini sighed and said, "Ah Leng, we are women, and as we grow older sex is not our main focus. Men are different. Sometimes, I am grateful that there are two other women to help me with his urges." Ah Leng's answer to that was an inaudible sound. Paini was not finished. "If you want to remain in this house with your children, you should show Malam that you will accept his bride-to be. You will never be able to take the children away from him. Even if you could, the children will not have the benefits of a good home. Think about it before he himself throws you out. By the way, you had better be there at the dinner party. Keng Yi will not be there." Paini left the younger woman in anger and in deep thoughts.

Chapter 20

It was exactly a year after the first foundation was laid, that the great house was finally completed. Malam's chief architect was a European, with great experience in building European homes in South East Asia. This magnificent structure incorporated Chinese and European elements, with a great touch of Baba Nyona heritage. It was a classic example of Straits Chinese architecture. The ten thousand square foot home stood on a three-acre land, with scattered fruit trees in front, and a regular orchard towards the very back of the land. The fruit trees were seasonal except for the coconuts. Almost all known tropical fruits like rambutans, mangosteens, mangoes, guavas and durians could be found in the orchard. A part of the orchard had succulent sugar canes growing. Between the mansion and the orchard were small but comfortable wooden huts built for the servants. Two outdoor badminton courts were erected in front of the house. These courts were flanked by light poles to enable night games. Tall and shady trees protected the courts from the wind. The front portion of the property was fenced by a brick wall with a huge and heavy iron gate. The driveway divided into a one thousand square foot garage and the porch of the mansion. The rest of the property was enclosed by an iron fence. The body of the splendid mansion was brick. The main door opened into a huge ballroom with wooden floor and four concrete pillars. There was a raised platform with an exquisite piano in a corner. Rich furnishings and the base of a spiral staircase completed the grandness of the ballroom. Separated by a wooden wall and a swinging door was the huge dining room, with an expensive oak table and chairs. There was a bathroom between the dining room and the ballroom. There was also another staircase leading upstairs. Then to the very back of the house was the big modern kitchen with a breakfast area. There was another bathroom in the kitchen. The second floor had a large family living room flanked by five bedrooms; two bigger ones on one side with a bathroom between them, and the three smaller ones on the other side. The third floor too had a bathroom, but with only four bedrooms as the house narrowed towards the top. However, the corridor between the bedrooms was furnished with desks and chairs for the school-going children.

The mansion was one of a kind in the whole of Klang and it symbolized wealth and class. At its completion, Malam stood outside the main gate and stared at it for a long time. He felt that his life was almost complete. There was just one more thing to do, and that was to marry for the very last time, a woman he had loved and cherished for over a year. Keng Yi had made it possible for him to be a good husband, father and lover. Although she longed to have more of him, she wanted him to remain fair and just. On her insistence, Malam spent every fourth night with her. It was hard for him, but he still loved his three wives and Ah Leng was beginning to be more accommodating. His children too began to feel that their father had returned to them. Jo Lin was again the happy, slightly spoilt teenager. Malam did not take his family for weekend outings as often as he did before Keng Yi came into his life, but he made it up by taking his wives to the movies once in a while. Everyone seemed contented, and great preparations were being made for the big move. By now, not only had his plantation staff increased, he had also hired two maids and a gardener cum driver, besides the chauffeur who would only work during certain hours. He did that just before the move, so that his wives had more help in packing and looking after the younger children at the same time. After the wedding, none of his family had seen Keng Yi except for Ai Li, who was still working with her father. By now, they were great friends and Ai Li was sure that Keng Yi would fit into their family with no problems. Her only worry was that Ah Leng might never accept her father's fourth, and she truly believed, his very last wife.

The weekend of the great move arrived. The wives had their respectful rooms. Paini had the other larger room that was separated from Malam's by the bathroom. Ah Leng and Alex moved into one of the smaller room, and Cheng Mee and Lily had the other one. It was understood that the last room on the second floor would soon be occupied. The three older boys occupied the same room on the third floor, Jo Lin had her very own room beside her brothers, and the last one on the third floor was reserved for guests and relatives. The maids and the gardener occupied the wooden huts at the back of the house. Malam had made sure that if there was any need for more space, an extension was possible from the side of the house towards the garage. As Malam looked at his big and spacious room, all he could think of was Keng Yi beside him on his huge oak bed. The thought made him long for her all the more, so he made up his mind to propose to her within the same week. Except for Paini, he had not bought any of his other wives engagement rings. But, he wanted Keng Yi to have one, so to be fair to the other two, he took them to the jeweler's to let them choose their own diamond rings. It was not surprising to him that Ah Leng chose the most exquisite and expensive one. Cheng Mee was humble in her choice, but it looked nice on her finger and she was very appreciative of her husband's generosity. Then the next day he went on his own and bought a beautiful solitaire for Keng Yi.

A week after Malam and his big family moved into their new mansion, he proposed to Keng Yi. He took her out to a very exclusive club in Kuala Lumpur, where formal dressing was required. He had booked a special table in the most romantic corner of the dining room. A live band was playing love songs, and there was a marbled floor for dancing. Keng Yi wore a light green cheongsam with a slit long enough to allow easy movement. Her shoulder length hair was combed towards the back, to expose a pair of jade earrings hanging from her dainty ears. With high heel shoes to match her attire, she was a picture of elegance and beauty. Malam was quite jealous of the male eyes on her as they entered the room, although he himself attracted quite a few females in his light beige suit of English wool, and a light shirt unbuttoned to expose his strong neck. Keng Yi was petite compared to Malam's height, but they made a beautiful couple, even though it was obvious that there was a big age difference between them. Malam was fifty three years old and Keng Yi was just eighteen. As their table was the only one with a bunch of red roses in a crystal vase, it was obvious that Malam had specially ordered them. There was also a bottle of imported Champagne in a bucket filled with ice cubes. There was no need for a menu for Malam knew exactly what to order. The waiter wanted to pour the Champagne, but Malam stopped him. He wanted to do it himself.

As Malam handed the filled glass to Keng Yi, he said, "Before we drink it, I have something to ask you." He dug into his coat pocket and produced a small red velvet box. He flipped it open and Keng Yi gasped when she saw the glittering ring inside it. She was speechless as Malam continued to say, "My dearest love, will you marry me?" At the same time, he got up and went to her side of the table and knelt in front of her. Keng Yi was oblivious of the approving stares of the other guests. All she could see was her prince. Tears of happiness welled in her eyes as she got up, pulling Malam up with her and said, "Oh yes, I will. I love you with all my heart." It was only when she heard applause that she blushed and realized that they were not alone. Malam did not give her a chance to feel shy. He acknowledged the applause and made a gesture to the band. They played 'April Rose' and he guided her to the dance floor. They were the only couple on the floor and with Malam's strong arms around her, Keng Yi glided like a princess from a fairy tale. They dined, wined and danced to all the wonderful love songs that the band played. It was an evening to be remembered not only by the couple, but by all onlookers. They had never seen so much love in their lifetime. For the first time since Malam started his family, no one else mattered but the woman in his arms. They went back to Keng Yi's apartment long after midnight, intoxicated with passion and love for each other. As they made love, Malam felt his years melting away. Keng Yi fell asleep, contented and happy in the arms of her one and only true love.

The next day was Sunday so as they had breakfast together, they made plans for the ceremonious union. As a child and in her dreams of her prince, Keng Yi had always pictured herself in a white flowing gown with flowers on her head, but she knew and accepted that it was not possible to have such a wedding with Malam. Nevertheless, the joy of belonging to Malam completely made the planning and arrangements exciting. Malam would send for Keng Yi's birth parents to give her away. All known relatives and friends of Keng Yi would be invited to witness the union. It was Malam's wish to have the celebrations in his mansion. The ceremony would start with the presentation of tea in the presence of a monk who would bless the union, then to be followed by a sumptuous dinner and dance in the ballroom of the great house. Then Malam and Keng Yi would drive off to an island off the west coast of the Peninsular for a week long honeymoon. The date had been set for the end of June, two weeks after the proposal. Meanwhile, Keng Yi would continue to live in her apartment. Malam would love to be with her every night but he knew he had responsibilities towards his family. The sudden thought of them jolted him to realize that he had a big barrier to overcome when he got home. He had to let his wives know of his intentions. The only fear he had was that Ah Leng would create a big problem. However, when all was discussed and planned, they made love once more, and his heart was heavy when he left Keng Yi to go home. The only comfort he had was that he would see her again at his office early the next morning. Their goodbye kiss was long and lingering. Malam would have stayed on, but Keng Yi knew that he had a difficult task ahead, so she hurried him home.

His three wives were getting ready to prepare lunch when Malam arrived at his home. Before he got into the big house, he ordered his chauffeur to take his children for a matinee. He then gave Jo Lin some money and said, "There is a nice movie for children. Take your three brothers with you. After that you all can go for ice-cream. The driver will take you to the cinema and pick you up after the show. Treat him to an ice-cream too." Jo Lin was pleased. This was the first time her father had given her such a responsibility. She gathered David, John and Gary, and all four of them hopped into the waiting car. His wives had a foreboding. Malam never liked his children to witness any arguments. Paini knew what was coming, Cheng Mee had long resigned herself to this day, and Ah Leng, who also knew what was in store, was prepared to oppose her husband's wishes as strongly as she could. Paini made sure that the maids took the youngest children, Alex and Lily to the playroom upstairs. She advised them to stay put until she sent for them. With all his children out of sight, Malam sat on his chair at the head of the dining table, and told his wives to do likewise in their respective places. Then he began, "It is no secret that I have been having a relationship with my secretary. I love her very much, and it is time now to make her a part of my family. Paini, you have more or less given me permission to marry her. Do you still feel the same?" Paini nodded. Then he looked at Cheng Mee and asked, "What about you, my dear? Will you be able to accept Keng Yi as your younger sister?" Cheng Mee said softly, "If you love her, I shall also learn to love her." Then Malam took a deep sigh before he addressed his second wife. "Ah Leng, I do not expect your approval, but I demand respect for my wishes." By saying that he gave Ah Leng no chance to object, but she still had to have her say. She stood up and in angry tones said, "I have given you sons, but you have abused me by first marrying Cheng Mee, and now you expect me to keep quiet and let you hurt me again. I cannot stop you from this stupidity, but I will never accept that woman to be a part of my life." With that she stormed away and went upstairs to her room. Malam was undisturbed by her rude exit. Instead, he got up and went to his two other wives, who were sitting side by side. He put his arms around their shoulders and said, "My love for you will not be any lesser. Thank you both for your support." Then he kissed them on the foreheads, and told them the date of the official ceremony.

The following week was very busy for Keng Yi. With the help of her cousin Tan and Mei, his wife, she managed to trace her natural siblings. She had an elder brother, two sisters older than her, and two younger ones. Like her, the other two younger sisters were given away. However, they did marry into the adopted family as planned. Keng Yi sent out letters of invitation to them, explaining who she was, and her wish to be reunited with her family. The weekend before the wedding, Malam drove her to her birth place and met her parents. He made them happy by offering them a very large sum of money as dowry for their daughter. They felt honored that their daughter whom they had given up still loved them and wanted them to give her away. Arrangements were made about their trip and stay in Klang. Since the journey to the State of Johore was long and tedious, Malam and Keng Yi spent a night in a hotel there. Johore was so close to Singapore that it brought back wonderful memories of his time with Paini. It also reminded him of the time he lost his memory. He had told Keng Yi all about his past, and when Keng Yi caught him in a pensive mood, she allowed him to ponder undisturbed. For Keng Yi, his future belonged to her even though it meant sharing him with three other women. This man had so much to give, and a little part of him was enough to fulfill all her dreams. She looked at the thoughtful man beside her and felt overwhelming love for him. She too was impatient to belong to him, and she wished with all her heart that she would be able to bear him a child. Like most young girls at that time, the greatest fear that Keng Yi had was infertility, for it was considered a curse.

A few days before the wedding, Keng Yi's family arrived in Klang. Malam had reserved rooms for them in one of the upgrade hotels in Port Swettenham, and rented two cars with chauffeurs at their disposal. Keng Yi had taken one week off from work, and had more or less begged Malam not to visit her at that time. Mei, who had left her daughter with her mother-in-law, spent that week with Keng Yi helping her with the preparations. For the first time, Malam gave the task of choosing the dinner menu to his fiancée. He also left it to Keng Yi to plan the wedding procedure, advising her not to exclude the tea ceremony for her sisters-to-be. Keng Yi tried to make the whole wedding as close to a white wedding as possible. At least a part of her childhood dream would be fulfilled, when she would dance in the arms of her husband and prince, until it was time for him to take her away to paradise. She had carefully had a beige cheongsam tailored with pink flowery embroidery at the hems and slit. The slit started from above her thigh. She bought a pearl necklace and pair of pearl earrings to go with the beige cheongsam. Keng Yi did not want a make-up artist. She wanted to look like she did when Malam first set eyes on her, with a touch of lipstick and some rouge. Her two-inch high heel shoes, which were also beige, matched her whole attire. Beige was very close to white, and that brought her even closer to her dream of a white wedding. When Keng Yi dressed up for Mei's approval the night before, her best friend and cousin-in-law felt sad. Keng Yi looked like a princess herself, and deserved much more than a man who already had three wives. Malam's age did not matter as much, for he had a youthful look about him. She kept that tinge of sadness to herself, and allowed Keng Yi's radiant happiness to influence her. She took Keng Yi's hands in hers and said, "I wish that you will always be as happy as you are today." Keng Yi laughed and said, "Don't be silly, no one can be as happy as the day of her wedding. The important thing is that I have no doubts of my love for Malam, and I am aware and ready for all problems and obstacles that I have to face. Don't worry about me, my dearest friend. Our love will survive until death parts us." Mei believed that Keng Yi meant every word she said.

Meanwhile, Malam missed Keng Yi terribly, but he had his own problems at home. Ah Leng had threatened to leave him taking all her children with her. Somehow, a lawyer made her realize that she had a lot to lose. First of all, her marriage to Malam was not official, which meant that he need not give her any alimony. Secondly, he was the legal father of her children. Without a marriage certificate, she would not be able to hold on to her children. Malam on the other hand was still very nice to her. He begged her to stay, saying that he still loved her, and he would not hold it against her if she did not want to attend the tea ceremony or for that matter, even the wedding. Ah Leng thought about everything, and decided that for the sake of her children she would stay, but would abstain from the whole ceremony. She was adamant to let everyone know that this was an unacceptable marriage. She was now in her late thirties, and she decided that she would never share Malam's bed again. Malam was quite hurt when she told him of her decisions, but he understood her and thanked her for staying on. He felt that she had every right to be hurt and he hoped that one day, she could forgive him and act like his wife again. However, as the day of the wedding approached, all Malam could think of was that soon Keng Yi would be his. Nothing else mattered at this time. Paini and Cheng Mee spent their time getting nice clothes for themselves and the children for that special occasion. They were not overly happy, but they were not unhappy either. They were resigned to their destiny of sharing their husband with three other women. If he was happy, he would make them happy too, and they could live with it.

Cheng Mee's wedding ceremony was very simple, but that was because the union took place during the Japanese Occupation. Ah Leng's was grander, but still nothing comparable to that of Malam's first wedding to Paini. But the celebrations of Malam's fourth marriage were just as unforgettable as his first. It could not be less because of Malam's present status in the community. He was by then one of the wealthiest men in the district of Klang. Thus there was no question of impartiality or comparisons to the other marriages. It was an entourage that brought Keng Yi to the doorsteps of the grand mansion that was to be her future home. Malam had rented more limousines for the occasion. The first two that drove into the driveway were occupied by Keng Yi's brother and his family, and the next three were occupied by her sisters and their family. In the last white limousine was the bride with her parents, followed by her Tan and Mei in

227

their own car. Malam, in a dark blue suit with a cream-colored shirt, and a stripped black, gold and cream tie, stood elegantly and majestically at the main doorway to welcome Keng Yi into his home. As she stepped out of the car, the 'oohs' and 'aahs' of all the guests made his chest swell with pride at the beautiful woman who would soon be his to love and to cherish forever. He thanked Keng Yi's father for giving Keng Yi to him, and as she placed her hand on his outstretched arm, he felt that the whole world belonged to him. Keng Yi too trembled with an overpowering sense of wonderment. In this man, she had it all.

The tea ceremony was held on the stage of the ballroom. Paini and Cheng Mee were sitting side by side, both dressed in Sarong Kebaya. Ah Leng had gone to spend a few days at her parent's house. When Keng Yi served Paini tea, she smiled and said, "Welcome into our big family young sister." Keng Yi thanked her, and when it was Cheng Mee's turn, she just kissed Keng Yi on the forehead and addressed her as "younger sister." Unlike the other two tea ceremonies, where Malam's brothers were not involved, Keng Yi had to give them tea calling each of them "Big Brother." Malam did likewise to her parents addressing them as "Mother and Father". Then the monk chanted a few prayers, showering the kneeling couple with the smoke of burning incense. The ceremony lasted for two hours, and then congratulations were in order. Malam had also invited most of his business associates and some of his employees. Ai Li too was there with her husband. She had managed to get Jo Lin to accept their father's fourth wife quite easily. Jo Lin was behind Ai Li when she congratulated Keng Yi. Since Ai Li was older than Keng Yi, she simply addressed her fourth mother by name, whereas she had instructed her younger sister Jo Lin, who was four years younger than Keng Yi to address her as Fourth Mother. Malam was overjoyed to see his favorite child hugging his new wife and calling her Mother. He had been afraid that Ah Leng's stubbornness would affect his daughter. Paini brought the other children and introduced Keng Yi to them. David, John and Gary were not as responsive as their sister. They grudgingly said, "Mother" and ran away. It was easier for Alex and Lily who were still too young to know what was going on. They allowed Keng Yi to plant kisses on them, and they returned those kisses eagerly.

As cocktails were being served, the band arrived, followed by the food truck. Keng Yi had catered food from her favorite restaurant in Port Swettenham. It was a buffet set on a long table in one corner of the ballroom. Tables formed a large U with the bridal table at one end. The chairs were on the outside of the U, so that everyone faced the portion of the ballroom that was left for a show and dancing. There were about sixty adult guests. The children had their food in the formal dining room. Extra maids were hired to look after the children. The menu had been chosen with great care. It consisted of shrimp, oysters, fish and crabs, some cooked in elegant sauces, some served natural, some lightly grilled, accompanied by salads of lettuce, cucumber and celery laced with various dressings of the best oils and aged vinegar. There were deviled eggs, fresh crusty bread and butter. Then the variety of meats, roasted until the skin was crisp and crackled, and some cooked in curry sauces, to be accompanied by white and fried rice. On the dessert table was a huge chocolate cake decorated with small sugared white roses, honey cakes, sweet Danish pastries and all kinds of tropical fruits. Six waiters and waitresses were hired that day to serve drinks. Vintage wines from France were served beside other beverages and alcoholic drinks. While the guests wined and dined, they were entertained by the live band with English, Chinese and Malay songs. Then in the midst of dining, everyone was surprised with the performance of an Egyptian belly dancer. It was a wedding gift from one of Malam's business friends. Keng Yi held her breath as she looked at her husband and saw a sudden change in his smiling and happy face. Malam had never kept any of his past from her, and she knew that he was remembering the Egyptian girl that he had loved for a short while, and who died. She took his hand in hers and tried to initiate a gesture of understanding. Malam felt it and tightened his to acknowledge her understanding with gratitude. Malam did not feel sad, but was overcome with nostalgia. He braced himself and looked tenderly at his new wife and whispered, "I love you." The girl did two beautiful dances and then came up to Malam and Keng Yi to invite them to open the floor for general dancing.

Paini put on a brave front as she watched the lovely couple on the floor. Her heart was heavy as memories of yesteryears came flowing into her mind. She pictured herself as Keng Yi in Malam's arms. How dearly and passionately he had loved her. He still loved her very much, but Keng Yi now had both his love and passion. As other couples joined the newlyweds on the floor, Keng Yi whispered in his ear, "It is time for you to dance with your other wives." That jerked Malam's guilty conscience, for he had totally forgotten about Paini and Cheng Mee. He led Keng Yi back to the table and invited Paini to dance. Paini obliged gracefully and soon she was gliding in is arms. Her sadness was replaced by confidence, as she looked into her husband's eyes and saw that there was still so much love and longing for her. She closed her eyes, buried her face in his chest and remembered what his mother once told her. Malam had a big heart filled with enough love to give to as many as his heart desired. Cheng Mee, who never danced before rejected Malam's invitation. Nevertheless, he pulled her up gently and teasingly said, "Now is the time for you to learn from your husband." He guided her with his strong arms, and onlookers would never guess that that was Cheng Mee's first dance. Like Paini, Cheng Mee felt that Malam still loved her with the same passion he had when they first slept together. When Malam looked for Keng Yi, she was dancing with all his friends, so he danced more often with his other wives. However, Keng Yi reserved the last dance for him, and when he had her once more in his arms, he said, "It is time for us to sneak away. Paini and Cheng Mee will take care of everything." Keng Yi nodded happily. Malam told her to go quietly into the waiting car on the porch. He needed to say goodbye to his other wives.

Paini and Cheng Mee knew that Malam would be leaving for his honeymoon with Keng Yi, so when he gestured them to go upstairs they obediently followed him. At the landing of the second floor, Malam took his wives' hands in each of his and said, "I love you both very much and I will not neglect any of you. Once more thank you for your love, understanding and support. If you hear from Ah Leng, please tell her that I still love her, and will be very happy to see her when I return." Then he kissed his wives goodbye, and said that he and Keng Yi would be back in a week's time. Paini's eyes blurred as she returned his goodbye kiss, whilst Cheng Mee just said, "Have a good time. Just come back to us safe and sound. We will be waiting for you and Younger Sister." In a way she felt elated because she is no more the Younger Sister. Malam left them with a flying kiss, and joined his new wife in his car. Then off they drove into the night. They were going up north to spend a week in Langkawi Island off the North-west coast of Peninsular Malaya. However, they only drove for an hour checking into a hotel on the way. They would continue up North early the next morning to take a boat to the island. Malam carried his wife into the room, and they consummated their love for the first time as husband and wife. Once again, Malam felt the years melting away, and no one else existed for him except the young and beautiful woman in his arms. Even Keng Yi allowed herself to forget that she shared him with three other women. She felt that he belonged completely to her, and that she would love him and cherish him until death.

Langkawi Island was remote and unspoiled. It was an enormous island twice the size of Penang. Kuah, the port town, meaning 'gravy', took its name from a legendary nuptial fight in which the gravy pot landed where the town grew up. It had a picturesque mosque and some small shops. The road north from Kuah passes through serene landscapes of rice fields, rubber plantations, coconut farms, and sleepy Malay villages tucked away in the thick jungle. This road led to the cascading falls, and then onwards to the hot springs. There were many beautiful beaches on this huge island, but since it had not yet been fully developed, only one hotel was built on the most attractive beach, with a few scattered bungalows for budget travelers. The ferry from Kuala Perlis, the capital of the most northern state, left once a day to arrive in the small port town of Kuah. Other than that there were boats to hire. Most of the wealthier holiday makers would hire a boat for the duration of their stay in order to explore other beaches. The rental of the boats could come with or without their own captains.

Even though they hardly slept, savoring each other's love and passion, the newly married couple woke up early to continue their long journey to Perlis. They had another ten hours drive to Kuala Perlis where a hired boat would be waiting for them. Malam was tired but elated. He could not wait to get to their paradise island, so all they did was a short stop for lunch. Like all rich people, Malam had rented the boat for all the time that they would be on the island. As the boat chugged through clear waters, Keng Yi was in seventh heaven. As soon as they arrived at their hotel room, Malam carried her to the bed, and forgot his weariness as he expressed his deep love and longing for her. They enjoyed the peace and serenity of the island, but hardly used the boat. They behaved like all honeymooners. They spent a lot of their time in the privacy of the room. The hotel was complete in itself, with a nice restaurant and a lounge where the guests were entertained by a pianist and singer. It was an expensive hotel and quite exclusive, thus it was not as crowded as the budget bungalows. Very often they would order room service, but sometimes they would dine in the restaurant and listen to the singer singing appropriate love songs. They did take short excursions around the island, and sometimes walked along the beautiful beach in the evenings. Keng Yi was water shy, but Malam managed to teach her to swim a little.

All too soon the honeymoon was over and their boat was waiting to take them back to the mainland. Malam would have liked to stay another week, but he had pressing business to attend to and Keng Yi also felt responsible to her new sisters. She wanted to start her new life without any resentment, at least not from Paini and Cheng Mee. Malam held her hand as they stood by the edge of the boat and watched the island getting smaller. Both were strangely quiet as they were buried in their own thoughts. Malam wished with all his heart that Keng Yi would never regret marrying him. He hoped that Ah Leng would one day learn to accept her. For the first time he felt an uncanny guilt that he loved his youngest wife more than the others. His guilt increased when he felt that Keng Yi was more precious to him than his faithful and loyal Paini. Keng Yi's heart was heavy, as she realized that the week on the island would be the only time that Malam belonged completely to her. However, no matter how short that time was, it would last her a lifetime of happiness. As the boat docked at the mainland, Keng Yi had braced herself to face reality. She had chosen a man with three wives, and unlike new brides, her married life would begin with sharing her husband with other women.

CHAPTER 21

It was a pleasant surprise for Malam to be affectionately greeted by Ah Leng. However, his pleasure was dampened when she refused to acknowledge Keng Yi's greeting of, "Second Sister." Paini, Cheng Mee and all the children were happy to have their husband and father back home. They were also very nice and warm when they welcomed their youngest sister and mother into their home. While Malam was being overwhelmed by his children, Keng Yi quietly stole away with her luggage into her room. Paini had made sure that the maids had cleaned and prepared the room for her. There was a vase of fresh flowers from the garden, and she felt comforted after the coldness on Ah Leng's part. She felt that the flowers were a gesture of friendship from her eldest and third sister. If Ah Leng would never accept her, the friendship of the other two would ease her life. She sat on her bed and made a few decisions. She would continue to work as Malam's secretary; that way, she would not have to face Ah Leng as much and the important thing was that she would be close to her husband more often than the others. She would make sure that Malam remained fair and treated her like the others. She would do her part in looking after all the children when she was at home. She looked down at her stomach and hoped that she was not pregnant. She would like to get used to this new life before bringing a child into the world, which at the moment was still strange for her.

As Malam's family grew so did his business especially with Keng Yi working closely with him. Her knowledge of business was very extensive, and Malam could leave her in complete charge of his business while he traveled and took stock of the business world. Keng Yi was happy to spend long hours in the plantation, because although she tried to ignore Ah Leng's hostility, it did sometimes get to her. She had never uttered a word of complaint to Malam, and the rest of the family appreciated her for trying to keep the peace. Malam on the other hand, would have liked to spend more evenings with his new wife, but he felt responsible towards the others. He spent an equal number of nights with all his four wives. Deep in his heart, he was thankful that Keng Yi was working with him. He hated himself when he realized that he really did love her more than all his other wives. He tried not to show it and he hoped no one, not even Keng Yi herself would be aware of this biased feeling. Paini, who was now forty eight years old, still enjoyed going to the movies. No matter what was on, she would go every afternoon for a show. Then the children would gather round her in the evenings, and she would relate the stories to them. Ah Leng was into gardening and rearing poultry. She had the green thumb, and the vegetables that she grew were plentiful and enough to feed the family. She raised chickens and ducks for their eggs and also for their meat. Cheng Mee, who had learnt sewing from Paini also liked going to the movies. Sometimes, she would accompany Paini but not everyday. She loved making clothes for the children, especially for Jo Lin and Lily. Keng Yi had no time for hobbies, but some evenings, when the children were all in bed, she and Malam would play a short game of chess.

Three months after Keng Yi became Malam's fourth wife, she was shocked to find out that she was pregnant. Malam was overjoyed, and Keng Yi seeing how happy her husband was, accepted her pregnancy, but with mixed feelings. She wanted to be able to continue working for a few more years, or at least until she and Ah Leng became friends. However, she made Malam promise to allow her to work until the very last month, and then to go back three months after the baby was born. Surprisingly, when Ah Leng heard about the pregnancy, her attitude towards Keng Yi changed completely. She started by first smiling at Keng Yi whenever their eyes met, and then including her in her conversations at meal times. Malam warmed towards his second wife, and Keng Yi was finally happy to be with child. Thus Keng Yi continued to work until the end of May 1950. Ah Leng was very nice and caring when Keng Yi stayed home, although she was unable to do much with her protruding stomach. Then in the middle of June, 1950, Keng Yi gave birth to a baby girl. She was the first child to be born in the big mansion. The same mid-wife who delivered all of Malam's children was in attendance, with the family doctor looking on in case of complications. It was a difficult birth, and Malam was a nervous wreck. The labor pains started at ten in the night, and the baby was finally delivered at seven in the morning. Like the births of all his other children, the infant was cleaned and wrapped in white sheets, then handed to Malam to hold and to name her. He kissed her forehead and said, "Her name is Marlene." On official birth certificates, all his children had their Chinese names, so he wrote down her Chinese name for the doctor to register the birth. Then Marlene was handed from one wife to the next according to their ranks. While the others were fussing over the new-born, Malam went to the exhausted Keng Yi, kissed her on the lips and whispered in her ear, "Marlene to me means 'My Darling'. Thank you my love for a beautiful daughter." Keng Yi smiled and said, "It is I who has to thank you. You have made me the happiest woman on earth." Then she closed her eyes to take the rest and sleep she deserved.

A few days after Marlene's birth, Malam decided to make a big change. He wanted to make it less confusing for all his children in the way they addressed their four mothers. So he made a rule that Paini should be called 'Mak', (meaning mother in the Malay language) by all the children. They would call their respective birth mothers, 'Mother' in Hokkien, Malam's original dialect and Ah Leng would be addressed as 'First Aunt' by the other children, Cheng Mee as 'Second Aunt' and Keng Yi as 'Aunt'. Since Keng Yi spoke only English with Malam, she taught her little daughter to call her 'Mummy'. 'Papa' for Malam remained unchanged. Paini was still the head of the household in Malam's absence. Malam gave his wives equal amount of cake money each month for their personal use. Besides the cake money, Keng Yi still received the salary of a secretary, which she kept aside for a rainy day. By now Malam had three limousines and two chauffeurs. He drove one on his own, and the other two were at his wives discretion. There were always weekend outings for the whole family where all three cars were used. The children seemed to enjoy those outings, especially, when they went to the beaches that were close by. At times, when the weather was too hot, they would spend a day and night in the Highlands where the temperature was cooler.

All would have gone well if Marlene was a healthy child. Unfortunately, she fell ill quite often, and the doctors detected that she was very anemic. Malam was very distressed and fearful that the curse had returned. He would not leave her crib whenever she ran a fever, even when the family doctor was there. Keng Yi did not go back to work as early as planned, even though a new nurse-maid had been hired to look only after the infant. Even when Marlene was not sick, Malam would come back from the plantation two or three times a day to look in on her. His anxiety brought out what he tried to hide – Marlene was now his favorite child. Before Marlene came into the world, Jo Lin was the apple of Malam's eye and it became obvious to the sharp eyes of Ah Leng that Marlene had now replaced Jo Lin. That made her resent the innocent child, and her animosity towards Keng Yi returned. Malam was too absorbed in the welfare of his youngest child and his business to notice his second wife's attitude. Keng Yi felt the resentment and jealousy of the older woman, but did not bother her husband with any complaints. She waited for Marlene to get stronger, which fortunately she did when she became six months old. Then Keng Yi insisted on going back to work for Malam. By then, she also knew that Marlene's nurse-maid loved her child, and would care for her like her very own.

Meanwhile Ai Li had stopped working when her daughter was born. She was two months older than Marlene. Jo Lin, who was now fifteen years old and had two more years before she completed her secondary school, fell in love with a young police cadet. She had been seeing him secretly for over a year. When it came to light, Malam, afraid that his daughter might conceive an illegitimate child, advised the couple to get married as soon as Jo Lin finished school. Jo Lin was happy to do so for she was very much in love, but Eddy her boyfriend was hesitant. He wanted to be a full time officer before he raised a family. Malam, however, quelled his financial fears, by saying that he would support them until they were independent enough to live on their own. Malam then stressed that the young people should abstain from sex until then. He would not accept an illegitimate grandchild. Secretly, he hoped that Jo Lin was still a virgin, but it was beyond his dignity to question her. Malam's three sons, David, John and Gary attended a Catholic School. Alex and Lily, still too young to go to school, had a nanny to play and look after them. Marlene's nursemaid's duty was only towards her ward when Keng Yi was not at home. There was a cook to help in the kitchen, and a housekeeper to help with cleaning the big mansion. Besides the two chauffeurs, Malam had also employed a full time gardener to take care of his orchard and garden. The gardener's duties included the security of the house, which meant that he had to walk about late at nights to see that all the gates and doors were locked. At almost the same time that Marlene was born, Malam bought three Alsatian puppies to be trained by the gardener to be watch dogs. All the employees lived at the wooden houses behind the mansion. Each month, they had four days off, and it was up to them when or how they used their time off. They were all unmarried, but if they got married and still wanted to work on, they would have to find their own lodgings.

Eighteen year-old Mina was very devoted to the frail infant Marlene. Although Marlene was getting stronger, she was still not as healthy as a normal baby. Her immune system was not strong enough, thus, when someone in the family had a minor cold or cough, Marlene would be the first to be infected, but in her case it would not be just a simple infection. She would have dangerously high fevers and her doctor's bills ran very high. In times like that, Keng Yi would stay home, and she and Mina took turns to be by the infant at all times. Mina sensed Ah Leng's dislike for the innocent child, and kept her away from the woman. With Mina's loving care, Marlene began to get stronger and began to show signs of a lively toddler. She became more attached to her nursemaid than to her mother, and unlike all infants her first word was 'Na', short for Mina.

Keng Yi did not resent that, instead she was grateful to Mina for making it possible for her to work alongside her beloved husband. However, unless she had some urgent business to attend to in the evenings, she made sure that she was the one to tuck her little daughter into bed. Whenever Malam was home before Marlene went to bed, he would never miss kissing her goodnight, with words of endearment like, "Sweet dreams, my princess." Marlene was the only person he ever called 'princess'.

From a very young age, Marlene showed signs of being a fast learner. At age one, she could walk without help, and then a few months later, she began running. It was obvious that Marlene liked to be outdoors, and her favorite pastime was playing with the three Alsatians. These dogs were not allowed indoors, so the first thing Marlene did when she got up was to beg Mina to let her play with the dogs. Mina would have to feed her outside the house to make sure she ate well. However, she knew that family dinners were at the dining table. No matter how pampered Marlene was, she learnt from early childhood that there were rules in the house that could not be broken. As Marlene became older, she realized that there were more rules to follow, and breaking them resulted in punishments, so being the apple of her father's eyes did not exempt her from the consequences of disobedience and disrespect for the elders.

At the end of 1952 and beginning of 1953, the Shih family was enlarged by three girls. Keng Yi gave birth to another girl, Anna. At first Marlene was jealous, but when Anna had her own nursemaid, she began to accept her younger sister. That same year two more baby girls were adopted into the family. Cheng Mee, who knew that she could not have another child, persuaded Malam to adopt her niece. Her brother had more children than he could afford, so when the seventh child was born, he offered her to his sister. The girl was born a few months later than Anna and was given the English name of Theresa. A month later, late in the night, the cry of an infant was heard by the gardener. Someone had left a baby naked and cold at the gate of the mansion. When the baby was brought in, it was Ah Leng who said, "God has answered my prayers and so soon too. When Cheng Mee adopted her niece, I prayed that I too could adopt a baby girl." No one, not even Malam, could say otherwise. After the infant was taken to the hospital and the proper authority informed, the child was handed to Malam for adoption without much-ado. Ah Leng then declared herself the official mother of the child and gave her a Chinese name. It was Malam who gave her the English name of Jan, as she was found in January of 1953, although the doctor had determined her age to be two months at that time. A year later, Michael was born to Keng Yi, who then decided to stay home and look after her own son, and help the two nursemaids in bringing up her girls. She sensed that Marlene was becoming more attached to Mina than to her, so she did not want Anna and Michael to follow suit.

Four year-old Marlene was getting a bit out of hand. Because of her tomboyish ways, she had quite a few escapades. Besides scrambling with the dogs, she loved climbing trees and eating the fruits off the trees. Sometimes, she would not be able to get down as easily as she climbed up, and ended up with bruises. Mina, afraid of height, would get the gardener to help her ward get down, but stubborn Marlene wanted to prove to herself that if she could get up, she could get down. However, there was one time when she jumped down and sprained her ankle so badly, that she was forbidden to climb trees again. Then she became rebellious, and ignored the orders and had to face the inevitable punishment. It hurt Malam very much whenever he had to punish his favorite child, but he was very strict when it came to his children's conduct. He never caned the girls, instead they were sent to bed hungry, and that happened to Marlene too often. Marlene began to get difficult, and started provoking her half brothers, especially Alex. He lost his temper with her many times and would slap her so hard that the marks stayed on her face. She never reported any of the incidents to her father or mother, but one evening, when Malam was caressing Marlene's face, he noticed that her left cheek was swollen and red. Marlene did not disclose why her cheek was red and swollen, but Ah Leng said, "She was very naughty and was irritating Alex so much that he lost his temper." Malam put his favorite child down and yelled, "Alex, come here at once." Alex shivered as he stood before his father, but before Malam could say anything, he muttered, "Sorry Papa." But Malam had a cane in his hand and he commanded, "Loosen your trousers and let them fall." Alex began to cry and Ah Leng intervened, "It was Marlene's fault." Then Mina decided to tell the truth. "Alex has been bullying Marlene for a long time. Sometimes she was naughty, but more often, he would just slap her on the face. He enjoyed seeing her in tears." Ah Leng glared at Mina, but she just looked away. Malam forced Alex to bend down and gave him the cane several times with the warning, "If you ever lay your hands on Marlene or Lily or any of your sisters, this caning is minor to what you will receive in future." From that day on for as long as Malam lived, Alex never laid his hands on Marlene or any of his sisters. Also from that day on, Ah Leng resented Marlene and her mother, and she showed that resentment openly.

Keng Yi had stopped working completely and stayed home like the other three wives. She got along very well with Paini and Cheng Mee, but her relationship with Ah Leng was very uncomfortable. She would have liked to terminate the services of both the nursemaids, but she realized that Marlene would never let Mina go. The bond between the two was too strong, so she only let Anna's nursemaid go. However, she tried her best to take over the disciplining of her eldest child. She was very strict with Marlene, but that made the girl more rebellious and she always ran to Mina for comfort. Mina knew her place and never intervened when Keng Yi punished her ward, but her heart broke whenever she saw the child in tears. Since Keng Yi stayed home, Mina was allowed to go home more often, and each time she did, Marlene would brood and become listless. That worried both her parents that she took the short separation so badly. One day, Marlene went up to her father and said, "Next time when Mina goes home, I would like to go with her." It was always almost impossible for Malam to refuse his child but he had to put his foot down. His explanation was very gentle. "My darling, your place is here at home with us. Mina is only working here, and like you, she has a father and mother and she needs to spend some time alone with them." Marlene's reply was angry and hurt, "But she said, I can come along. She is my best friend and I love her most of all." Then realizing that she might have hurt her father, she quickly added, "I mean more than the others." Malam knew what she meant and smiled saying, "Ask your mother if you can go, but if she says, 'yes' it will only be one time. OK?" Marlene ran to Keng Yi who had overheard the whole conversation , decided that she should let Marlene go or her daughter would resent her.

That weekend with Mina and her family was one of the happiest occasions in Marlene's childhood. Normally, Mina took the bus home, but because Marlene was joining her, Malam, accompanied by Keng Yi drove them in his big limousine. It was a treat for simple people to see an expensive car driving into their kampong, a Malay village. Little wooden huts on stilts were scattered everywhere, with no boundaries, and in the open spaces between the homes grew all kinds of tropical fruits. There were also plots of rice fields, and as Malam drove through the small and winding road towards Mina's humble home, the workers, mostly women, stopped work to stare at the big and expensive car. One or two began to wave when they recognized Mina as one of the passengers. Marlene had never been exposed to villages like that and she was in awe of the number of half naked children running about and after the car. Even as a toddler, she was brought up to expose as little of her body as possible. Mina saw her uneasy feeling and smiled to herself. She put her arms comfortingly around the little shoulders and said, "Most of them are your age and they will be very nice to you." Marlene felt a sense of freedom and she could not wait to get out of the car.

Mina's parents came out of the house to greet their distinguished guests. They invited Malam and Keng Yi in for a cup of tea and some home-made cakes. Their invitation was accepted, mostly because they wanted to check on the hygiene of the people with whom their child was going to spend a few days. Mina had always given the impression of tidiness and cleanliness, and her house proved that she had been well trained in that aspect. Malam and Keng Yi thanked the parents, then Malam went on his knees to be at eye-level with his daughter and said, "My Darling, I shall miss you very much, but I am sure you will be very happy here. Be good and do not go anywhere without Mina. Promise me?" Marlene nodded her head happily and kissed her father. Then she ran into her mother's waiting arms and saw that her eyes were wet. "Don't cry Mummy, I promise to be good." She then kissed her mother goodbye. She was impatient to join the children outside. As Malam drove the car away, he looked in the rear mirror and saw that his daughter was already mingling with the children, some of them completely naked and some partly dressed. He looked at his young wife, who was quiet and looked a little sad. He said, "Don't worry about our little girl. She is in good hands, and you and I know that Mina loves her like she was her very own child." Keng Yi gave a big sigh before replying, "I am not thinking of this weekend with Mina. I worry about Marlene's rebellion and her tomboyish ways. Her brothers dislike her and Second Sister always looks at her with hatred. I know you love her above all, but you should try to hide this feeling from the others." Malam nodded and said, "You are right. It is hard, but I will do my best. But with regard to Marlene's rebellion, I feel that is the strength that she possesses. As a child, having a mind of her own makes it look like rebellion, but I am sure that as she grows older, that inner strength in her will come out to help her. We should not try to curb the rebellion unless it goes out of hand. At this age, you could already see that there are many who love her unconditionally, but there are also a few who hate her guts, and mostly that feeling of hate is aroused by jealousy." Marlene was the topic of conversation during the one hour drive home. Just before they arrived at the gate, Malam took Keng Yi's hand in his and assured her that Marlene would always be protected for as long as he lived. Somehow, that did not erase Keng Yi's worries about the rebellious character of her first-born.

She never mentioned it to Malam, but she had noticed that Marlene had a quick temper with a tendency to bully her younger siblings.

As soon as the car was out of sight, Marlene took off her shoes and socks and ran to join the group of curious children standing around. Her outgoing character overcame their shyness and in no time, they were playing all kinds of outdoor games. Marlene's favorite game was Hide-and-Seek. Although she was new to the area, her ability to climb trees was an advantage. Luckily, Mina was not aware that she was hiding on branches of the fruit trees, or else Mina would have to bring her indoors. Then there was 'Catching' and the little Village boys were in awe of Marlene's running speed. Whenever Mina went to visit a friend, she took Marlene along. The little girl made friends so fast that she did not miss her parents. She was so happy, and wished that she could stay in the kampong forever with Mina, where life was simple and without rules. However, the weekend came to an end when Marlene saw her parents' car driving along the small, unpaved and winding path. Her heart dropped, and it was a very sad girl who greeted her parents and said goodbye to all her new friends. If she had known that that was the first and last time in that kampong, her heart would have been completely shattered. No matter how rebellious Marlene was, she knew that her place was with her parents, so she got into the car without much ado. Mina's presence in the car did not cheer her up. Malam sensed that his daughter was not happy, and it broke his heart to see her so. She answered his cheerful questions like, "Did you enjoy yourself?" "Have you been good?" "Did you listen to Mina?" with a nod and 'Yes' to every question. She was not responsive when Keng Yi talked about her sister and little brother. Keng Yi was more determined than ever to spend more time with her daughter. Marlene seemed to be growing more distant from her.

That evening when it was time for Marlene to be in bed, she was the one who washed and bathed her. It was normally Mina's duty to do that, and bring the clean child to her parents to be tucked in. Keng Yi expected some retaliation from her daughter, but Marlene was quiet and reserved. Then she realized that her daughter had grown up very suddenly. She seemed more matured and the few words that she exchanged with her mother were very unlike a child of four. As Keng Yi removed her clothes she asked, "Did you make many friends?" "Some," her daughter replied, "and they are nicer to be with than all my cousins and the children of Papa's friends." "And why is that so?" Keng Yi asked as tenderly as she could. Her daughter's reply made her proud, but at the same time caused her some anxiety. "They are not snobbish, and do not care who has more toys. They share the little they have with everyone. I would like to spend more time with them." Keng Yi was afraid to ask her any more questions. However, when Malam came in for the normal ritual of telling his daughter a short story, and to sing one of the songs from his acting career, Marlene got back the feeling of belonging. She knew that she loved Mina, but her father was still the greatest love in her young life. She did not fall asleep in the midst of his song as she usually did. When he got up after kissing her on the forehead, she called out, "Papa, I love you." Malam was overjoyed to have his daughter back, and he sat down again on her bed and whispered, "I love you too my darling, and I am glad to have you back. The three days without you was like life without sunshine. There are times when I do not show you how much I love you, but that is to protect you. I want you to understand that." Like Keng Yi, he too was surprised to notice his child's maturity with her short answer of "I know."

That night, instead of playing chess, Keng Yi and her husband went to his office to discuss their daughter. Keng Yi started by saying, "As I was bathing Marlene, I noticed a lot of scratches on her legs and arms. It is obvious that Mina did not stop her from climbing trees. I will have to talk to Mina about it." Malam, who always liked to maintain a good relationship with his employees said, "Maybe Mina was not aware of that, or Marlene may have got those scratches from running about with the kids. Since there is no major crisis, and Marlene will not be going anywhere without us again, we should just let the matter go." Then Keng Yi decided to tell him that she felt that Marlene was closer to Mina than to herself and before it went too far, she thought that they should terminate Mina's employment. Malam was aghast, for he knew the disastrous effects it would have on his emotional child. "Oh no!' he exclaimed, "Marlene would never forgive us for that. I know what you mean, and I do feel uncomfortable about the close relationship between the two. You are at home now and you could take over Marlene's upbringing discreetly. You have started to be in charge of her personal hygiene. You can gradually transfer Mina's duties in helping with Anna and Michael. Marlene is an intelligent girl and will feel proud that she does not need to have someone with her all the time." Then Keng Yi came up with another point. "I think that you should be as strict to Marlene as you are with the others. Marlene is now four years old, and if her willful actions go unpunished, she will be harder to control later. She likes to bully Anna and the other two girls younger than her. I have sometimes smacked her on her back, but that did not curb her." Malam sighed and said, "All right. I will do my best to help discipline her. It is always painful for me to have to send her to bed hungry. It is not in me to punish my daughters physically. Well, whenever Marlene gets out of hand, she will have to stay indoors for the rest of the day. That should be a hard punishment for her, especially as she likes being outside with the dogs so much."

The rest of the family was in bed when they finished talking. Malam and Keng Yi went into her room where her three children were fast asleep. Marlene was on a single bed, Anna was sleeping on her mother's bed and little Michael was in the cot. Malam automatically went to the bed of Marlene and looked down at her with overwhelming love. He thought to himself, "She is like an angel and she will grow up to be one. I don't believe that she is as wild or rebellious as her mother and the others think." He bent down to kiss her on the forehead, and then felt Keng Yi's hands guiding him out. They adjourned to his room, and all thoughts of Marlene left them as they savored their love for each other. Malam was still fair in sharing his room with all his wives, but Paini and had very often declined his offer. Paini was contented in pursuing her hobbies of going to the movies and story telling. She also loved to cook. At age fifty-two, her sexual desires seemed to decline even though she still loved her husband. Ah Leng kept her threat of never sleeping with him again, when he married Keng Yi. Besides, she was often angry with him for his unfairness towards the children. She complained to him about every small thing, especially about Marlene's bad behavior. When she realized that Malam paid no heed to her, she decided to keep her anger to herself. Thus Malam spent his nights with his two younger wives, sometimes more often with Keng Yi. Even when Cheng Mee noticed that, she was never jealous. She was sure that had she married another man, he would not have been as nice to her as Malam was. Like Paini, she loved him dearly, and his wishes were her command. Keng Yi too had no regrets that she married a man with three wives. Her love and admiration for Malam grew with the years. He was still the prince of her dreams, and she could not imagine what her life would be if she had never met him.

CHAPTER 22

As Malam's children grew in numbers, he spent more time at home. He knew from his childhood experience that the father was always the role model for the boys. He never had sisters, so he did not presume that the mothers would be that of their daughters. Most evenings after dinner, he would gather his children round him and tell them those stories of his bygone acting days. Sometimes to his younger children's glee he would act his parts and sing some of his songs. There were also times when he made up stories to keep his children out of mischief. One of them was about the Guardian of the Sugar-cane. He always had his reasons for such stories. Sugar-cane plants were used to guard the main entrance to the house, from the eve of Chinese New Year until the next full moon. For such an occasion, the best and strongest plants would be chosen to grow to its fullest. However, John and Gary were apprehended many times when they tried to cut down those chosen plants. They were punished for disobedience, but they never quit trying. Thus one particular evening Malam told them this story. "When I was a boy of about thirteen," he began, "I loved sugar-canes and so did many of my classmates and friends. In the neighborhood where we lived, was a farmer who had acres and acres of sugar-canes. Every week, he paid helpers to help him cut the canes and take them to the open market for sale. As cartloads of canes left the farm, we kids eyed hungrily and thirstily for the juicy canes. Then one day we decided that he had too many canes to miss a few of them. So we would steal into his plantation at night and start cutting a few, and then enjoy eating them in one of our houses. Since we were successful the first time, we continued stealing the canes almost every night until one evening when..." Malam broke off his sentence and looked at the two culprits who were anxiously waiting for the rest of the story. Then he continued, "Until one evening when one of the boys was chopping at the thickest and juiciest of all the canes, his big knife did not even cause a scratch on the hard skin of the cane. He attracted our attention to it, and each of us tried in turns to bring down the cane. It was my turn when I heard a distant laughter. Everyone heard it, but we did not know where it came from. We looked around but saw nobody, so I stubbornly continued to hack at the cane. Then the laughter came again. It was louder than the first one and it came from above. We all looked up at the same time and realized that the cane that we had been trying to cut was extraordinary high. As the laughter continued, our eyes went further up and suddenly one of the boys shouted, 'Look, the sugar-cane has a face!' No one stayed back to look. We ran as fast as we could. We never stole sugar-canes ever again." That night

Gary and John had bad dreams, but they never attempted to cut down sugar-cane plants anymore.

There were many more such stories, and they always had an effect on his children. One which was specially told to make sure that Marlene, his little tomboy, did not stay outdoors when it was dark. Marlene, whose favorite game was Hide-and-Seek, was very good at hiding herself. Long after the game was over, she would still remain in her hiding place, and only when the gardener or one of the adults started looking for her, and threatening her punishment, did she show herself. Her late appearance also meant that the family dinners were delayed. Keng Yi and Malam had reprimanded her, but her reason was that she had to show that she was the best in that game. Malam's story of the Lady with the Worms erased that problem completely. This particular lady did not walk, but floated in the air, holding a covered bowl in her hand. She could not be seen unless she allowed herself to be seen. She slept during the day and roamed at night. She looked for children to feed them from her bowl. When she found a child on her own and away from safety, she showed herself to the child. She had such a sweet smile that the child automatically went to her. Then she uncovered her bowl, and when the child saw the delicious looking noodles in the bowl, she or he became hungry and the lady would feed the child and send her home. That night the child would have a very bad stomach ache, and when she or he was taken to the hospital, the doctor found out that the child had eaten a lot of earth-worms. The worms looked like noodles in the bowl. For a long time, Marlene would never eat any noodles, but the good thing was that she only found places to hide in the house whenever she played that game with her siblings or friends. Not only that, as soon as it became dark, Marlene was the first to be inside the house.

Thus Malam spent his evenings with his children telling those stories or playing some games with them. He had friends and employees coming over later in the evenings to play Badminton, and most of his older children, including four-year old Marlene, seemed to be quite talented in that sport. Unlike the earlier days when there were outings every weekend, it became a once a month affair, as most of the children were growing up and had their own school activities. Malam also made it a point to take his family to Malacca once a year, to pay homage to his parents' graves and also those of Paini's. He wanted to instill in his children that they belonged to that Baba-Nyona heritage. Keng Yi never went back to work, instead like all the other three wives, she too found a new hobby. She took up sewing under the guidance of Paini. Marlene loved new clothes and almost everyday, she had something new to wear. She began to love her mother like an ordinary child should, but her relationship with Mina was still as strong as before. Malam however was still the top of her list. She loved him dearly and enjoyed all his stories, although some of them frightened her. Malam in return spent more time with her than any of his other children. He too began to see her bad temper especially vented on the ones younger than her. He took a firm hand in that matter, and showed his disapproval in his words which had a great impact on Marlene. "That is not my daughter, it is the devil in her, that does bad things like this," was one of the reproaches he would use. It hurt Marlene and frightened her at the same time, but that did not curb her temper, and she was sent to bed very often without dinner.

Meanwhile, Ah Leng was beginning to be friendly again towards Keng Yi, and except for her resentment towards Marlene, Malam's family was living in harmony. Paini was still the matriarch in the family and was in charge of all meals and the maids. Cheng Mee and Keng Yi became close friends and shared their ideas in sewing clothes for the girls. Lily was now in school, and she was the only sibling that Marlene looked up to, although they were worlds apart in their characters. Lily was quiet, gentle and very lady-like unlike her younger sister. She was obedient and liked helping in the kitchen. She often managed to keep Marlene out of trouble in her own special way. When she sensed that Marlene was in a bullying mood, she would distract her with some exciting activity like having a game of Badminton. She also made sure that Marlene kept out of Ah Leng's way as much as possible. Whenever she saw an uneasiness brewing between Alex and Marlene, she would discreetly be the peace maker. She was well-liked by all her half brothers and sisters, but there was a strong bond between the spoilt Marlene and her. Malam noticed this relationship with great approval, and he was sure that when it was time for his bad-tempered and temperamental daughter to go to school, her older sister would keep an eye on her.

David, who was now attending a Day Teacher Training College had some good news to give. He had been selected to represent the State of Selangor in Badminton. His father was very proud of him and promised to be present for his first tournament in Kuala Lumpur. Seventeen year-old John was in his last year of Secondary School. His ambition was to be a veterinarian. That suited him very well for he always had a love for animals. Because of that, his mixed feelings for Marlene always became positive whenever he saw the way she played with the dogs, like they were her good friends. Gary was a quiet and hardworking boy. He was also good at Badminton, but his first priority was to get good grades. Alex was very mischievous and quite a bully. Since the last time he was punished for using his hands on Marlene, he never touched her again, but he used words to make her angry. However, Marlene always gave him back a taste of his own medicine with her quick mind. Alex was also good at Sports and hoped to play badminton like his eldest brother. Lily too liked playing Badminton and could not wait for Marlene to go to school to be her partner in the inter-school tournaments. Marlene had to wait another year and a half before she could go to school. But with her mother's help, she could read and write at age five. Besides her outdoor activities, she liked reading comic books. Since her mother stayed home, she became less of a bully and was not as rebellious as before. The three girls, Anna, Theresa and Jan were lucky to have each other. Since they were only months apart of each other they were never lonely. Cheng Mee was always close at hand to make sure that they learn to play well with each other.

Sometimes, Ai Li would bring her two daughters, the older one was closer to Marlene's age, but she was more attached to the gentle Lily. The younger one was also a few months older than the three-year old girls, but they accepted her company gleefully. Michael, Malam's last son, was a happy toddler, healthy and easily entertained. Mina's duties were discreetly transferred to taking care of him. Jo Lin was married in 1952 to the cadet who was now a police officer. By 1955, she had given birth to a girl and a boy. While her husband was doing his cadetship, Malam had supported them by renting a nice apartment for them, and giving them enough money so that they could maintain a reasonable standard of living. When Jo Lin's husband completed his training, he was posted to Seremban in the State of Negri Sembilan. Malam helped them buy a house there, and they made it a point to visit the Shih household every second month for a long weekend. Jo Lin loved her father dearly, and seeing a lot of her in Marlene was also quite attached to her half-sister. Marlene too liked and admired her elder sister. To the little girl, Jo Lin was the most beautiful girl in the world. However this attachment was incomparable to the bond between Lily and Marlene.

Early in 1955, Malam, at age fifty-nine began to have a back problem. Sometimes his back hurt him so much that he could hardly get out of bed. Doctors could not find the source of the ailment, so all they could do was prescribe pain-killers. Those pain-killers eased his pain, but took away his concentration and integrity in making important business decisions. With the bad economy that the country was facing at that time, Malam's business was badly affected as he was unable to give his best. Business associates and some disloyal employees were discreetly undercutting him. Malam's business was going down very fast, so he began to sell some acres of his plantation to greedy buyers at great losses. He tried to keep his financial difficulty from his family for as long as he could. He continued to let them enjoy the luxury they were used to, while he shortened the number of his staff at the plantation. He even called back his daughter Ai Li to help, but not before making her promise to keep the bad situation from the rest of the family. Ai Li, who then had two young daughters, told her father that she could work only part-time for him. Malam agreed, but somehow his losses were too great and finally, he had no choice but to confide in Keng Yi. Without hesitation, she went back to work with him everyday. When Malam's back kept him home, Keng Yi would be at the office running the whole show. For sometime the business stabilized, but too many losses had incurred and the back orders were too difficult to handle. Although Ai Li planned to work only part-time, she stayed on many more hours to help her young mother, especially when her father had to stay home. Malam's back ache had gotten worse, and with the pressure at work, he began to have headaches as well. So as Keng Yi and Ai Li struggled to stabilize the family business, Malam's failing health kept him more and more at home.

Since Keng Yi's reconciliation with her family, her relatives had made frequent visits to the mansion, and Keng Yi too visited them as often as she could with her three children. Sometimes Malam would accompany her on those visits. One of her sisters owned a coffee shop. Keng Yi was quite close to her, but never liked her husband who was a heavy drinker and gambler. One day amidst the financial problems that the Shihs were facing, he turned up unannounced at the front gate. If Keng Yi had been home, she would have refused him entry into the house. But unfortunately, she was at the plantation, and Malam was lying sick in bed. The gardener, recognizing him as one of Keng Yi's relatives, opened the gate to him. Paini was at the movie house and all the older children were at school. Marlene, who was five years of age, was the oldest child at home with her two adopted half sisters, her own younger sister and her little brother. Cheng Mee was helping Mina to take care of them upstairs, so it was Ah Leng who greeted the visitor at the main door of the mansion. Ah Leng was the only person who had some background in Mandarin, and that was the language they spoke. When she saw that Keng Yi's brother-in-law was holding a suitcase she had a bad feeling. She stood behind the half-ajar door and said, "We didn't expect you and besides, Keng Yi and Mr. Shih are not at home." The man smiled and replied, "Well, I came to see if Mr. Shih could offer me a job at this plantation. The coffee shop is not doing well, and my wife thinks her sister's husband could help." Ah Leng told him to come back later and was about to close the door when he pushed his way into the house.

There was nothing Ah Leng could do but to admit that Malam was at home but was not feeling well. She told him to take a seat while she went upstairs to see if Malam could come down. She went into the kitchen instead, and told one of the maids preparing food to get the chauffeur and the gardener to come into the house and stay in the kitchen. Then she went to Malam's room and gently woke the sleeping man. "We have an unexpected and rude visitor. Please come downstairs and handle this matter." Malam who was still groggy from the painkillers sat up with difficulty and said, "Well, help me to dress up." While Ah Leng helped him to put on his clothes, she told him who the visitor was and what he wanted. She continued, "He is not a reputable man, and I have made sure that both our man-servants are in the kitchen waiting for a command of help from you." Malam complimented her on her good thinking, but assured her that he did not foresee any problems. Before he went down, he went to the room where the children were being entertained by Mina and his third wife. He called Cheng Mee aside and told her, "Stay in the room and do not let the children out. Keng Yi's brother-in-law is here and he may be drunk." Marlene on seeing her father wanted to be with him, but he kissed her and said, "Be a good girl and help look after the others." Pouting, Marlene went back to reading her comic books.

Ah Leng helped her husband to get downstairs. She then went directly into the kitchen, while Malam went into the ballroom-cum-living room where visitors were entertained. It was obvious that Keng Yi's brother-in-law did not sit down at all. He was walking around and inspecting the expensive pictures on the wall, and the antique furniture in the huge room. Malam greeted him with a friendly voice and said in the Malay language, "This is a surprise. What brings you here?" He approached Malam who sat on the nearest chair and shook his hands saying, "Your sister-in-law sent me hoping that you could help us by giving me a job." Malam gave a big sigh and winced as he felt the pain in his back. "You know that I am always willing to help relatives, but times are bad and I have been forced to lay off many of my loyal employees. I am sorry but I cannot help you."

Ah Seng, Keng Yi's brother-in-law put on a sorrowful face and pleaded, "I cannot go back to my wife and tell her that her sister's rich husband has refused me. Maybe, with your influence, I could work with one of your associates. Please don't turn me away without any hope." Malam was getting very weary and he wanted to dismiss the man as soon as he could. "I cannot promise anything, but I shall try my best. If you will excuse me, I have to go back to bed." His next words angered Malam. "Could I stay here until I find a job?" Malam was already on his feet, but he sat down again heavily and said, "No, you have to leave right now. My chauffeur will take you to the bus station." Without hearing what Ah Seng had to say, Malam called for his chauffeur who came in immediately. He was a hefty Malay man. Ah Seng was quiet while Malam gave him the orders to take Ah Seng to the bus station. Once Ah Seng left the house, Malam called for Ah Leng, who was listening to the whole conversation in the kitchen, to help him back to his room. He went back into a very troubled sleep.

Malam was feeling much better by the time Keng Yi came home. When he saw how exhausted she was, he decided to wait until everyone was in bed before he talked to her. Keng Yi too had bad news for him, but seeing that he was looking well, she did not want to bring down his spirits. She was sure that he would go to work the next day and he would find out for himself how bad things were. Ah Leng, however, blurted out at dinner, "That brother-in-law of Keng Yi, the drunkard, invaded our home today." Keng Yi worriedly looked at Malam, who gave her a reassuring smile and said, "He was looking for a job, but I told him that we are not in the position to hire anyone at this point. Let us just enjoy our meal and spend sometime with the children before they go to bed." He gave Ah Leng a disapproving look and changed the subject to the children's day at school. The atmosphere at the table became normal as each child took his or her own turn to talk about their day. When it came to Marlene's turn, she had more to say about her day than the other children who were at school. She told her father that she had finished reading all her comic books and would like to have some more. Her father sighed and said, "I wish that there was a school that would accept my five-year old daughter who can read and write so well." Malam did try his best not to show his favoritism towards his beloved daughter, but he could never resist voicing his pride in her achievements. Marlene had often read aloud to him, and he marveled at her progress from one day to another. He was glad that she had found a new hobby. She seemed to be less of a tom-boy and did not climb trees that often. He also knew that she would one day be an athlete.

Her motor developments were far superior to other children her age. She could outrun all of them, even boys, and her skills in playing badminton were beginning to show. By now, she could ride an adult bicycle without any help, except that she was still too little to sit on the saddle and reach the paddles, so she cycled without sitting.

For sometime now, Malam had been going to bed almost immediately after dinner. This night he decided to be with his children again before they went to bed. His back was still hurting a little, but his headaches were almost gone. The children were glad for they missed his stories. However, as soon as they were all in their respective rooms, Malam gathered his eldest son David and his wives into his study. He had made some definite decisions before he went back to sleep after his encounter with Ah Seng. When everyone took their place in his home office, he looked at Keng Yi and said, "When you came back, I detected that you had some bad news for me. You can spill it out now. Everyone in this room should know what is happening to our family business." So Keng Yi with a solemn voice spoke in the Malay language, Malam's language with his first three wives. "We are now very deep in debt. We were not able to meet the deadline for the back orders and many of our buyers have pulled out. They want their money back, and the banks will not give us any more loans as our business has not been making any profit for sometime now." No one said a word. They all turned to look at Malam who had an expressionless face. It took him awhile before he got up with an effort from his armchair and said, "Well, I have been aware of the bad economy that our country is facing, and only the very hard-working companies and small businesses can survive. Unfortunately, my days are numbered. Because of my health, I am not able to do what I should have done. I have thought carefully, and instead of declaring bankruptcy, I shall sell a big portion of my plantation. I shall sell the plot of rubber trees and two-thirds of the land that grew the oil palms. With that money, we should be able to pay all our debts and still keep our house. However, we will have to dismiss all the maids and the two chauffeurs. We can only afford to keep the gardener and Mina, who will have to help, not only with all the young children, but also with the housework. The gardener will also act as a chauffeur whenever the need arises. It is obvious that with what we can earn from the little plot of oil palms, it won't be enough to maintain our present standard of living." Malam then sat down heavily and his face took on a look of deep sadness. As usual, everyone just accepted his decision without any protest. Then Paini went to her husband and stroked his head saying, "We have survived worst times before. It is alright to have less to spend. The important thing is that we still have our house and each other. We now have to concentrate on your health. Go and take a rest now." With a nod at the others, she left the room, followed by Ah Leng, Cheng Mee and David. Keng Yi stayed on.

She missed him terribly. For a few months since the first attack on his back he had not invited any of his wives into his room. But the reason for her staying back was to find out more about Ah Seng's visit, and also about the business. Malam looked at her wearily, but gave her an encouraging smile when he said, "I am sorry that I could not help your brother-in-law. This is the first time that I turned down a relative in need." "Oh no don't be sorry," Keng Yi quickly replied. "I am glad that you did that. He is a no-good, and I am sure that my sister did not send him. You did right in sending him away without any money. He would just spend it on drinks and then go back and give my sister a hard time." She paused and looked at him before continuing, "I know that we cannot save our business, but what I don't understand is why you have decided to keep a small portion of the plantation instead of selling it off completely. We will have no chance against the bigger companies. I think that selling everything and starting something completely different, no matter how small it is, is better than to continue to compete with them on a small scale." Malam told her that he had thought about it, but he would like to try for a while. If that did not work then he would sell again. Then he stood up, took her hand in his and said, "I miss you. I hope that the exercises that the doctor prescribed will help my back. I do feel a little better, and tomorrow we will both go to the office and settle everything." He kissed her good-night, but Keng Yi insisted on going with him into his room to give him a massage. Malam welcomed that and after the gentle massage that his young wife gave him, he fell into a fitful sleep. Keng Yi lay beside him, looking at his heaving form with affection. No matter what happened, she would always love this man, her one and only prince.

Malam and Keng Yi were at work very early. They went through the files and accounts together, and Malam was more certain than ever, that they could never recuperate from the losses and loans he owed his buyers and the bank by keeping his estate. Selling a big part of it at market price would cover the loans and losses. Keeping that one third of the oil palm plot and the little warehouse where soaps, oil, candles and some other household products were being manufactured, would bring in enough income to keep his household in fairly good shape if Malam worked hard at it, and he was determined to do so even if it meant breaking his back. Ai Li, aware of the decision her father had made, decided to stay home. So it was Keng Yi and Malam who made the important phone calls to some business associates, who were not affected by the bad economy of the country. Knowing that Malam was an honest man, one of his best friends bought everything Malam had to sell without much ado. Malam even managed to extract the promise from him that he would keep as many of Malam's present employees as possible. Then late in the afternoon, Malam called a meeting of his staff and explained the situation to them. They were sad, for Malam had always been a good and fair boss. Even the coolies, who worked in the fields, were sorry that Malam had to sell a big portion of his business. However, the few that he kept to help him with what he had left were grateful and they promised to give him their best. All said and done, Malam and his youngest wife left for home, sad, but contented with how smoothly everything went and how quickly and painlessly the sale took place. That weekend would involve moving Malam's office from the big building to the small factory where the small products were manufactured. His three older sons and some of his remaining staff would help.

Once established, Malam, despite his back-aches worked hard. Keng Yi and Ai Li took turns to help him with his accounting, while Malam supervised the small staff that he had, and made business contacts for his merchandise. All the wives did their part in the big household, cooking, cleaning and looking after all the children's needs. Malam still had two cars, one for himself, and the other for the use of the rest of his family. The gardener became the family chauffeur and ran errands for the family. He also took the children to and from school. Paini refrained from her favorite pastime of movie-going. All the wives held tightly to their monthly cake money that Malam still gave them, without any reduction for rainy days. None of them complained about the present situation. They were happy to have enough food on the table. In fact, Ah Leng put more effort in growing more vegetables and extended her small poultry farm. She was very industrious in that field, and soon had all the children helping her with feeding the chickens and ducks. Malam's small business was beginning to stabilize and some profits were pouring in, whilst his back aches began to bother him less. Things were looking good for the Shih family until a terrible incident took place.

One day, the gardener came rushing into the house to announce that Keng Yi's brother in law and a stranger were outside the main gate. Keng Yi happened to be at home that day, and the first thing she did was to ring up her husband. She insisted that he should come home immediately.

Before she went out to meet the unwanted visitors, she told everyone to take the children upstairs and keep them there. She had the gardener accompany her as she walked towards the gate. "Hello dear Sister-in-law," said a smiling Ah Seng in the dialect of Keng Yi's parents. Keng Yi, not returning the smile replied in the same South Chinese dialect, "My husband is not in and we are not in any position to attend to unannounced guests. So please leave now." Before Ah Seng could say anything the stranger intervened, "Ah, but this is your relative. We had a hard journey and it is not nice of you to turn us away without providing us any drinks or food." "Well, if that is all you want, my gardener will go in and pack you some food and bring you some water," Keng Yi said, and was about to turn away and walk back when she heard her husband's car arriving. She realized then that it was a mistake to call Malam, for now he was on the other side of the gate with them. The gardener was not sure what he should do, but Malam stopped the car in front of the gate and confronted the two men. "Why have you come back, and who is this man with you?" Malam looked angry and Keng Yi decided that she had to be with him. She whispered to the gardener to open the gate just enough for her to slip out, and that he should lock it up again. It was obvious that the stranger could not understand the Malay language that Malam used for Ah Seng had to translate Malam's question to him. Words were exchanged between the two in Mandarin, an alien language to both Malam and his wife. Then Ah Seng squared his shoulders and said, "We have formed a society to protect rich families from harm. With a small amount of money that you donate to help our society, we will make sure that no harm befalls any members of your family." Malam was furious. He ordered his gardener to go back to the house and call the police. Then he went into his car, opened the back hood and took out his hunting gun. "Get off my property or you will be sorry!" Keng Yi was getting worried, but Ah Seng simply said, "You don't have to be nasty. We came to help, but since you don't want it, we shall go." The two men began to walk away and at a distance, Ah Seng shouted, "Be warned!" The gardener came back with a chopping knife in his hand and said, "The police are on their way." Malam noticing that the two men had walked quite a distance away, told the gardener to open the gate and to lock it up as soon as the car was in. Then he also ordered the gardener to let the dogs out of their fenced area. "From now on, let them free all the time" he continued to say. Normally, they were only allowed to roam the whole property in the night. In the day, they were kept towards the back with a fence, to prevent them from running towards the front anytime someone came to visit. It was in this fenced up area that Marlene spent a lot of her time playing with her four-legged friends.

When the police arrived, the dogs were quickly led back into their pen. There were two of them and the older officer said, "Well, I am surprised that those fierce dogs of yours did not keep your visitors away." Malam explained that he normally kept his dogs in their fenced area at the back of the house, but he also said that they would be loose to move around the whole day and night in future. In the big ballroom, the younger officer took down notes as Malam gave details of their conversation. "What complicates matter," Malam added, "is that one of the men is my brother-in-law. He was here one time looking for employment with me. I refused him, and this time he brought a total stranger with him." Then it struck Malam's mind that the stranger was wearing some jungle attire. When he voiced this to the policemen, they looked at each other and again the older one spoke, "We are having a lot of communist activities going on. They hide in the jungle. Is your brother-in-law a communist?" Malam shrugged his shoulders and said, "Not that I know of. He is a gambler and a drinker, other than that, I don't know of any of his activities." "Well, since they did not force themselves in or use violence, there is nothing we can do. I am sure that as long as your dogs are on the prowl they will keep away. I will advise you though to keep your eyes open and your ears sharp. If you can afford it, try to get a night watchman, someone professional with a license to carry a weapon." They left with a friendly note of, "Don't hesitate to call us if they show up again."

CHAPTER 23

Nothing eventful happened for the next few days, but exactly a week after the troubled visit from the two men, the gardener was late in bringing home Gary, Alex and Lily. John cycled to school and he always came back a few minutes after his younger siblings. Malam had made it a point to be home at lunch time, and after half an hour when there was still no sign of his three children, he got worried. His first thought was that the gardener must have had an accident. He was about to drive to Lily's school, for she would be the last person to be picked up, when to his relief he saw his second car at the gate. But his relief was short-lived when the gardener came out to open the gate instead of Gary, who normally did that. He rushed out and his fears doubled when he did not see any of his children in the car. The car was still at the gate as he approached the gardener, who looked much shaken and was in tears. The gardener tried to speak but his words came out in stammers, so that Malam could hardly understand a word. By now, he was joined by his whole family. Cheng Mee began to scream for her daughter and Ah Leng cried out her sons' names. Everyone was hysterical, until Malam shouted for control. He held the gardener tightly and asked as calmly as he could, "Where are my children?" Finally the words came out, "They took them." "Who took them?" Malam was beside himself, but tried not to show his fear and emotions. "Drive the car in and lock the gate," he commanded the gardener, who shakily did as he was told. Then Malam got everyone into the house, and after the gardener drank water from a glass that Paini offered him he managed to talk.

In sobbing tones, he related the whole story of the missing children. He had picked all three of them up and as usual, they had to stop at the railway crossing before crossing the bridge. The children were happily counting the number of coaches as the train chugged by, when suddenly the back door was opened, and a strange man jumped in pushing Lily and Alex aside. Then he pointed a pistol at Gary's head and told the gardener, "Turn the car around and follow my directions carefully, or this boy will have his brains blown out." Gary was sitting on the passenger seat, and he froze as he felt cold metal on his neck. Lily and Alex began to cry, and the man shouted at them to keep quiet. The gardener had no choice but to turn the car around, and followed the directions to a lonely corner of the street where a covered truck was parked. Then, three other men jumped out of the truck towards the car and pulled the children out. When Lily and Alex started screaming, they were slapped so hard that their voices became just whimpers. All three of them were dragged towards the truck and commanded to get into the back, with the threat of a beating if anyone of them disobeyed. The first man was still in the car with the gardener with his pistol directed at him. The gardener was too shocked to say anything except to nod his head when spoken to. The man with the pistol said, "Drive back directly to your big boss and tell him that if the police gets involved, he will never see his children again." The shivering gardener could only nod as the man continued, "Tonight, at midnight, he will get some visitors. The main gate should be left ajar and the dogs safely tied up. Every member of the Shih family, including the young children and the household employees should be in the main living room. There should be as little light as possible. The door should be opened by your big boss himself when he hears our knock. These instructions should be carried out exactly as I tell you, or else we will return the heads of the two boys and the girl." Without any parting word, he jumped out of the car and jumped into the back of the truck, where the three frightened children lay, with their hands and legs tied up. The gardener did glance in their direction and saw that they were being tied up as the man talked.

Mina was told to take all the young children, Marlene, Anna, Theresa, Jan and Michael upstairs. John had his arms around his weeping mother, and Paini, with silent tears, held on to the shaking Cheng Mee, while Keng Yi stood beside her husband with the feeling that her heart had stopped beating as the gardener spoke. Malam's face was contorted with the feeling of helplessness. Then he pulled his aching back straight and told the gardener to go about his business. Then gesturing his wives to come to him, he said as he stretched out his arms to reach each and every one of them, "First of all, let us be comforted that our three children are still alive. Secondly, our young ones are hungry, so let us sit down to lunch with them, and Mina can continue to stay upstairs and play with them while we discuss our options." By now, Ah Leng had lost all control, and she pushed herself away from her husband, and with an accusing finger she shouted at Keng Yi, "It is all her fault. You should not have married her then we won't have to deal with undesirable relatives." Keng Yi, who had already felt responsible for the kidnapping, just sat down on the nearest chair and said, "I am sorry." Then her eyes began to fill with held back tears. Paini and Cheng Mee went to her and put their arms around her. With tears in her eyes Cheng Mee said, "Don't heed her. She is distraught. We must hold ourselves together, I am sure Malam will find a way to get our children back." Malam felt a great affection for his third wife who hardly spoke her mind but when she did, it was always with common sense and at the right time. At the same time he could understand his second wife's anger. Two of her sons were the victims. He went to her and put his arms around her and said as gently as he could. "I promise you that I will die before I let anything happen to our children. Come let us eat."

None of the adults could eat a morsel. John was hungry, but did not eat as much as usual. Marlene, who had heard part of the conversation, was very worried about Lily. She hoped that by being a good girl, her sister would be returned. She did not care too much about Alex or Gary. She felt that she was better off without them. When Malam saw that his younger children had enough to eat, he gestured to Mina to take them upstairs. Marlene, who would usually argue about that went quietly. She too did not have an appetite, and knowing that her father and all the mothers were sad, she was unusually quiet. She also helped Mina to get her younger siblings upstairs and played nicely with them. Even though she liked bullying her younger siblings from time to time, she loved Anna and Michael very much. As Malam watched her go, he could not help but be thankful that his darling daughter was safe at home. Since she had shown a great deal of learning ability, he had thought of using his influence to send her to school earlier than the normal age. He was really glad that she was only five, or she would have been in the same school as Lily. He could not imagine what would happen to his willful and bad-tempered Marlene in the hands of the Communists. He was sure by now that it was them who kidnapped his children for a ransom.

Malam knew that there was nothing more to be said or done until midnight. He looked at the tearful faces of all his four wives, and the sad face of his second son. He wished that his eldest son was at home, but alas there was no way to let him know of what had happened. It would have to wait until the evening. Right now, his wives expected him to say something so he said, "I promise you that I shall meet whatever demands they make, so that our children will be returned to us. Let us wait until tonight. Now I will have to go to the office and call Ai Li from there. She will have to take charge of the business until everything is settled. However, we have to keep this from Jo Lin. Her husband is in the police force, and if he finds out, it is his duty to take measures and that will endanger the lives of our children. For their sake, please remain as calm as you can. I shall close the factory early and come back as soon as I can. He stood up and went to each one of them kissing them on their forehead. Then he said to Gary, "You are the man in the house when I am gone. Make sure that no one answers the phone when it rings and that no one uses it. We may be under observation. I love you all." Then he left. When Keng Yi got up to follow him, Paini stopped her and said, "We all need to be as much together as possible. I think Malam need, some time alone to think and make some important decisions. Let us be with our little ones until he comes back." Keng Yi nodded obediently. Marlene tried to be brave, but she was hurting inside, so it would be good for Keng Yi to be around her three children. Her period was overdue, and she secretly hoped that it was nothing but the pressure of the last few months that caused the delay. Another child in the family would not be so welcomed now that they were financially unstable.

When Malam came back that evening, he was glad that the first person to greet him was his eldest son. Before this, he had never needed another man to help him carry his burden, but this time he needed David. David's eyes were red but his voice was steady, when he said, "Father, don't you think that we should inform Jo Lin's husband? You could command him not to get the police involved." Wearily, Malam replied, "One instruction that was very clear was that no police should be involved, and your brother-in-law is a policeman. We cannot take any risk. We have to follow every word if we are to see your brothers and sister again." David put his arms around his father's shoulders and said, "Well, try to have something to eat and rest. We will just have to wait until midnight. Mother has locked herself in the room and nothing I say or do will calm her." Except for Ah Leng, everyone was at the dinner table, but no one seemed to be hungry, even the little ones. No one talked. Everyone waited for Malam to say something, but all he said was, "If we are all finished eating, clear the table and go to your respective rooms with your children and try to rest. I shall wake everybody up at midnight." Then David said, "You too need a rest Father. I shall be the one to make sure that everyone is downstairs before midnight." His father looked at him gratefully and got up to go up to his room. But before he left the dining table he spoke to John. "Please try to get your mother to let you in. Be with her until then."

Close to midnight, everyone was in the big ballroom. Little Michael was still fast asleep in Mina's arms. Keng Yi carried Anna who was pining a little from having to wake up in the middle of the night, Theresa was in Cheng Mee's arms, and Paini was sitting down with Jan on her lap. David and John sat beside their mother who was groggy from non-stop crying. The gardener stood close to the half-opened door. Malam was sitting beside Paini, and he also had Marlene who was wide awake on his lap. Mina had offered to be with Marlene, but at this point, Marlene chose to be with her father. Thus, Mina sat on a chair close to the kitchen. As the minutes went by, he became agitated, but the closeness of his daughter gave him some comfort. Then without any warning, the door was pushed completely opened and two armed men walked in. They were dressed exactly the same way as Ah Seng's companion. They had heavy brown boots on, a brown tee-shirt tucked into a pair of green trousers, and a green heavy shirt unbuttoned over the tee-shirt. They were Chinese, but their complexions were dark from living outdoors. Somehow they knew that someone in the household could speak Mandarin, for they used the language without any hesitation. They commanded the gardener to close the door. He did not understand a word of what they said, so Ah Leng who was familiar with the language, got up in a daze and shut the door. Then she began to weep and asked them in their language, "Where are my children? What have you done to them?" The same man spoke, "They are safe as long as you all do what we tell you. You Madam will translate everything I say to your husband." Somehow the manner in which the man spoke brought Ah Leng back to her senses. She nodded and translated everything the man said without faltering. First of all, he demanded that they be fed. There was enough left-over from the day's meals, so Paini gave Jan to John, and Cheng Mee handed Theresa to David, as they both went into the kitchen to heat up the food.

The men ate and drank hungrily and thirstily while the Shih family and their two employees looked on. Then wiping his mouth, the man who did all the talking looked at Malam and said, "One week from now and at the same time we will come back. You will have one hundred thousand Malayan dollars for us." Ah Leng translated that and Malam answered, "How do I know that my children are still alive?" When Ah Leng repeated that in Mandarin, the communist said, "You have my word that they are safe, and that same night when the money is in our hands, they will be returned to you. We live by our word." Then as suddenly as they came in, they gestured to the gardener to open the door and they disappeared into the dark. Ah Leng began to cry saying that she cannot bear to think that her children had to spend another week in their hands. Cheng Mee too was crying, but she cried softly in Paini's arms. Malam had known what their demands would be, and had made up his mind, of what he had to do, before he went back to his office earlier that day. He stood up and said, "My dear wives, I promise you that I will meet their demand and our children will be back with us. The communists needed money to carry out their cause. They are not murderers of children. There is nothing more that we can do, but raise the money. It is a lot, but we will find a way." David escorted his mother back to her room, and the others went with the children to their respective rooms. Paini decided that Jan should sleep with her that night. Malam whispered in Marlene's ears, "Do you want to keep your father company tonight." Marlene nodded eagerly and Keng Yi smiled at her. She would have liked to be with him, but she could understand her husband's special possessiveness of his beloved child at this moment.

Malam knew that selling what was left of his plantation and his small trade would not cover the high ransom. He was sure that his wives would pawn all their jewelry and if that was not enough, he would have to mortgage his mansion to the bank. The question was how they would survive after that with no more income. At this point, nothing mattered except to raise the money so that his children could come home. He wasted no time in selling his business, and his wives without any hesitation pawned all the jewelry that Malam had given them through the years of prosperity. All they kept were the wedding rings on their fingers. The car for the family use had to be sold too to reach the big amount. Thankfully, there was no need to get a mortgage for his mansion. Even though Paini began to be more sparing with the meals, no one minded. Everyone was still pining for the three missing children. Even the young ones began to feel sad as their young minds began to realize the difficult and painful situation that the adults were facing. Mina and the gardener were prepared to help with whatever savings they had, but Malam told them that it was not necessary. He already knew that the next step had to be the termination of their services, but he would wait until the big problem was resolved before he even mentioned it.

That Friday night, which was exactly a week after the kidnapping, Malam kept himself locked in his office and counted the money. He put in exactly the amount asked for, into a shoe box. He had a few hundred Malayan dollars left, which he would use to pay up his two remaining and loyal servants. There was no big family dinner that night. The young ones were fed and sent to bed early. The adults just went in to have snacks to curb their hunger. Paini knocked at Malam's door with a tray of food, but Malam's gruff voice said, "I am not hungry." Paini left sadly and told the other women not to bother him. Then at half-past eleven that night, David knocked at his door to announce that all the wives and John were in the ballroom. He opened the door, and David thought that his father had aged tremendously over a week. He handed David the shoe box and asked if all his younger siblings were in bed. David nodded and said that they were all sleeping in Keng Yi's room with Mina to take care of them. Together, father and son walked down the stairs. David tried to support his father, but he said that he could manage the few steps. The first person to greet him was Ah Leng with the question, "Do you have the money?" Malam did not answer, but David with a disapproving glance at his mother said, "It is all in this box." Ah Leng looked at the box and acknowledging her son's disapproval went back to sit down with the others. The gardener stood exactly where he was before, and the ballroom was lighted very dimly as it was the first time. The gate was left ajar and the dogs were at the very back of the compound, so that their barking would not disturb the important but undesired visitors. The main door to the ballroom was also left ajar. There was great tension in the big room. No one spoke and Malam did not look at anyone. He just looked ahead of him with unseeing eyes. His heart was heavy, for he knew that after this night, there was nothing left for his family. All he could do now was to pray that his three children would soon be reunited with them.

Exactly as the grandfather clock in the ballroom struck twelve, two men, pushed the door open and walked in holding rifles in their hands. They were not the same people who came the last time, but they wore exactly the same kind of attire. They locked the door behind them and wasted no time in asking, "Do you have the money?" Malam needed no translation from Ah Leng. He knew what they wanted. He stood up and said, "Show me my children first." The one who spoke hit him with the butt of the rifle that caused Malam to let out a gasp of pain and fall to the floor. All his four wives got up immediately to help him, and David and John rushed to fence off the strikes when they saw the two men about to strike the four women. David handed the box and said quickly, "Here is the money." They lowered the rifles. "Tell your father never ever doubt our words when we said that the children will be returned to you once we have the money. Another mistake like this will cause him his life and that of the children." Ah Leng translated shakily, and Malam whose forehead was bleeding from the blow, told Ah Leng to tell them that he was sorry. The other man who never spoke, counted the money and when he nodded his head, his companion said, "Stay exactly where you are and your children will be running into this house in an hour after we leave." With that parting note, the two men left as suddenly as they came in. Paini then left to get some bandages for Malam's bleeding head. He was still quite groggy and they laid him on the big sofa with his head on Keng Yi's laps. Her eyes were brimming with tears, and she wondered if Ah Leng was right. Her marriage into the family brought about the contact with her brother-in-law who was obviously a communist. Her husband must have read her thoughts for he put his hand on her cheek and said, "Everything will be alright."

At one o'clock in the morning, the door burst open and three disheveled children ran in. They were crying as they rushed straight into their father's open arms. He was so overjoyed to see them that he ignored the sudden pain of standing up. Then Ah Leng grabbed her two sons while Lily then ran to her mother. Both the women shed tears of joy. They checked their children and found no trace of injury, except that they were dirty and smelt badly. Meanwhile, Paini had slipped into the kitchen and prepared hot meals. She was sure that the children were not fed well while in captivity. True enough, they hungrily ate the hot meat porridge that Paini had cooked. No one had the heart to make them talk while they gobbled their food. Then once their appetites were curbed, Malam sent them off with their respective mothers for a thorough cleaning. He warned that they should not ask them any questions tonight. They should go to bed immediately, and they could tell them what happened the next day. Paini and Keng Yi accompanied their husband to his room. They had to help him upstairs, for he could hardly walk on his own. They sat on his bed and rubbed his back with eucalyptus oil. They knew that his back was hurting him more than the cut on his forehead. For the first time after a week, Malam managed to fall asleep under the tender care of his first and fourth wives. Seeing him snug and snoring slightly, Paini left his room, and Keng Yi, because her room was occupied by the other children and Mina, snuggled beside her sleeping husband and fell into a restless sleep. She was more aware than the others of the future that awaited the Shih family after this terrible occurrence.

Malam woke up at ten o'clock the next morning, and smiled to himself when he felt Keng Yi's body close to him. The wound in his head was not bleeding anymore, and although he still felt some back-ache, he lusted after his sleeping wife. He caressed her gently and she woke up. Keng Yi missed him terribly, and amidst their worries they indulged in their love for each other. The whole family was downstairs waiting for them. Ai Li and her family were also present. They arrived early in the morning and Jo Lin, who was not fully informed of what really happened, except that her father would like to see her, would arrive later in the evening with her family, as they had a longer drive. Now that everything was over, the three kidnapped children looked none the worse. In fact, fifteen year-old Gary could not wait to tell his story, but Malam's children were disciplined enough to learn to wait for their father. After greeting Ai Li, her husband

and his two granddaughters, Malam sat at the head of the table as usual, and while they had their breakfast, Gary finally related the story of their kidnapping, with his two siblings interrupting with parts of their version.

The children were bound hands and feet at the back of the truck. Alex and Lily cried, but they were warned by two men who sat at the back with them, that if they did not stop, they would be beaten and gagged. That kept them quiet and they lay on their side. They knew that they were being driven into the jungle as the truck bumped and scraped branches. They could not see anything as the back of the truck had some cover over it. It was an uncomfortable journey. When it finally stopped, the canvas was thrown over, and another man jumped in. They were carried by one man each from the truck to an old run-down hut. Once inside, they were surprised that the hut was a cover for some kind of bunker. A steel door was opened, and they were unbound and pushed into the cold cemented room with no window, except for some holes high in the walls. Gary could not reach the holes. Then the steel door was closed, and the interior became quite dark. But thankfully for the holes which allowed some light, their eyes got used to the darkness so they could see each other. Alex and Lily began to whimper because they were thirsty and hungry, so Gary decided to shout out to the kidnappers to bring them some water and food. The door was opened, and this time a lady, dressed as a man with the same kind of green and brown attire entered with a tray. She was quite nice for she warned the children, "Be good and you will not be hurt. Don't shout for food anymore. I shall bring you something to eat and drink two times a day." Then Gary was about to say something when she stopped him with a finger to her lips and continued, "We need money and your father is rich. If he complies with our wishes, you will be here only for seven days. You are a big boy, take care of the other two and everything will be alright." With that she left and the three children drank the pitcher of water, taking turns. Then they saw that it was only white bread with nothing on it. However, their hunger was so enormous that they finished the six pieces of stale bread without complaining. Gary was slightly relieved when Lily said that she did not feel afraid anymore. He looked at Alex who was still shaky and said, "Papa will give these people whatever they want because he loves us all." Malam looked at his third son with a great tenderness and just nodded his head as Gary continued to tell his story. True to her word, the lady came twice a day with food. Sometimes it was just water and plain bread. Other times, they had some warm porridge with very little chicken meat in it. Some nights the kind lady would bring them each a small cup of milk. They saw no one except the lady. They heard people talking, but it was a language that they did not understand. The lady always spoke to them in very good Malay. Malam drew a deep breath after the story. He was relieved that no one had laid hands on his children. At this point, he felt a tinge of respect for the communists. Then he said at all his children. "I am so proud of you all. The most important thing now is that we are one big happy family again, come what may." The last three words had a significant sadness in them. Only the adults detected the sadness.

But before the table was cleared, Malam knew that he had to speak to his children about keeping the whole situation a secret. The authorities of the schools of the children had called when the children did not show up at school for three days, and Malam had informed them that the children had come down with very bad colds. He now drew the children's attention, even the younger ones by saying, "What I am going to tell you is very important. No one must ever speak of what happened to anyone else outside this family. Bad things will happen to us if any of you do so. Gary, Alex and Lily, when your teachers or friends question you about your absence from school, you are to tell them that you were down with the cold. Your mothers will tell you more of why this has to be a family secret." The three children looked upset. To them this was an adventure and something thrilling to talk about. Malam saw the look on their faces and went on, "What happened has caused a lot of pain to me and all your mothers. If you do not promise to keep this to yourselves, worse things will happen, and we will never be a happy family again. I want all of you to say together, that you promise never to talk about this to anyone outside this house." His wives nudged the children and all except little Michael said, "We promise, Father." Malam smiled at all of them and said, "Now you all can get up."

For the rest of the day, the children went about their business and the adults theirs. It was as if nothing unusual had happened. When Jo Lin and her family arrived just before dinner, Malam greeted them, then told his other two grandchildren to play with the other children. He ushered Jo Lin and her husband into his upstairs office. Jo Lin and her police husband listened in shock as Malam related the events that led to the kidnapping and the release. He ended by pleading with his son-in-law to keep his profession out of it. His son-in-law drew a deep breath and said, "I cannot see how getting the authorities involved could help. In fact, if this came to light, you will be implicated in helping the communists. I only wish that you had more trust in me and consulted with me before taking everything into your own hands. At this point, I must honestly say, I don't know how I could have helped you then. But you are right. We have to keep this as a family secret, and we really have to make sure that all the children are aware of how dangerous it will be if the secret leaks out." Malam said that he had talked to his children and he was sure that if the mothers kept at it for a few nights, it would become clearer to them the importance of the secrecy. Then Jo Lin asked her father, "What are you going to do now without any business and income?" Her father looked sad, but said, "We will have dinner, and when all the young children are in bed, we will all meet in the ballroom and I will tell you the situation, and steps I have to take to make ends meet." With that he dismissed both of them, and when they left him, he cupped his face in his hands and sobbed quietly. He was never prepared for such a fall. He knew that businesses had their ups and downs, but to lose it all so fast was beyond him. He was a desperate man, but he would stand tall in the eyes of his family.

When all the young children and grandchildren were tucked in and fast asleep, the four wives, Ai Li and her husband, Jo Lin and her husband, David and John gathered in the huge ballroom, which had never been used again since Malam had his first attack of back ache. It was a solemn gathering, for no one spoke. All waited for Malam who after making his rounds and satisfied that all the sleeping children were safe, came slowly down the stairs. He sat on a big sofa, surrounded by the family in love-seats and bigger sofas. In the middle of the gathering were some small tea-cups and a big pot of hot Chinese tea. To celebrate the reunion of the big family, Malam's wives had baked some Nyona-cakes to accompany the tea. Malam looked at the solemn faces of his family and smiled saying, "Cheer up. Things are not as bad as they seem. I shall get to the point. I have spoken to my friend the banker, and the only way I can get any loan is by mortgaging our mansion to the bank. The market value of this big house is presently less than what I paid for it. But it is still high in value. The bank is prepared to give me half of its value, and if at any time I fail to pay them back, the whole house will be forfeited." The shocked faces of everyone present made him smile again as he went on, "I shall use the money to open the same business we had before the Japanese took it all away. Yes, I shall buy back the building and make it into a retail shop." He paused to give someone a chance to say something. After he drank from the cup of tea that Paini handed him, he continued. "We shall be starting from scratch which means many sacrifices have to be made. We won't have the resources to employ anyone. Thus, I expect my wives to take turns to help me in the enterprise. Keng Yi will have to take the full-time job of secretary, accountant and salesperson, one of you, Paini, Ah Leng or Cheng Mee will have to take turns to help everyday in walk-in sales and keeping the shop in order. I would also expect my older sons, if they have time, to chip in their part in this family business. I know that with hard work we will be able to pay the bank back and have enough for our normal needs." He stopped there and looked around with encouragement for someone to speak.

Surprisingly, it was Cheng Mee who spoke. She said, "I feel that Paini should stay home to be with the children at all times. Second Sister and I can take turns to go to the shop." Malam knew why Cheng Mee made that suggestion. She knew that some of the children did not like Ah Leng's stern ways, and especially Marlene, would suffer under her hands. Paini was loved by all the children regardless of their age. However, Malam was discreet and said, "Since Paini is the expert in the kitchen, we will all have something to look forward to after a hard day's work, I think that is a good idea. It is going to be very tough for Paini, because we will have to dismiss Mina and the gardener. We will not be able to afford them. From now on, the children who are old enough will be trained to help in house-keeping. The boys will take care of the orchard and the outside of the mansion. The girls will help indoors." Then Ah Leng said, "The only boys capable of helping are Gary and Alex. John will be having his final exams. David is at College until late evening. How much can the two boys do? Alex is only nine years old. We can still keep the gardener, and he can help pluck the fruits of our fruit trees and sell them outside the gate. Keng Yi can always take Michael with her to the shop to keep an eye on him. Mina's services are easier to terminate than that of the gardener." Malam did not want to argue with his second wife. He was glad that she did not contradict Cheng Mee's suggestion, so he simply said, "We will see about that."

Ai Li and Jo Lin knew that they could not offer their help, as they now have their own families, and they, especially Jo Lin lived quite far away. Ai Li had helped once in a while, but her journey to and from home was about an hour's bus ride. However, when situation demanded, she would still come back to help. That was her parting words to her father when they left for home the next day. Jo Lin had other things on her mind. She said, "Father, a fifth grandchild is on the way. I hope he brings you luck." Malam kissed his daughter, and congratulated her and her husband. He also said, "I sure need all the luck in the world." Keng Yi was extremely quiet when she heard Jo Lin's news. She had missed her period for three months now, and the nauseating feelings she had been getting confirmed that she was pregnant. She was not sure how the whole family would react to her news in such troubled times. She could only hope that the business would pick up fast, and that an addition in the family would not be disastrous. She intended to keep this knowledge to herself until she began to show. Right now her greatest problem was Marlene. She worried about how the girl would react to Mina's dismissal. Although Mina spent more time with Michael, Marlene was still attached to her. Marlene always claimed Mina to be her best friend. Well, Marlene too would have to make sacrifices. Hopefully, she would still be able to attend school at age six next year, instead of waiting for the official school age which was seven.

CHAPTER 24

Young Marlene experienced her first and unforgettable heartache when she was told that Mina had to leave the household. Malam was the one who broke the news to her. He had taken her to his room before bed-time to talk to her. He too could never forget how his beloved daughter looked at him. Her eyes were brimming with tears, and her voice was angry and full of hate. Hate, not towards him, but towards the unkindness of the world. Marlene was aware that the family was having some financial difficulty, because meals were getting simple, and there were no delicious ice-creams or cream cakes for dessert. Her supply of comic books was getting scarce, and she had to fight with the older boys to borrow theirs. She did not complain, but complied with the lesser luxury that everyone else was experiencing, but it never occurred to her that the person she held precious to her heart had to be taken away from her. Her father held her tightly to his chest, but she screamed and kicked until he had no choice but to let her go. She ran down and would have got out of the house to the servant's quarters if the doors were not locked. She pounded at the door in the kitchen, and shouted furiously for someone to open the door for her. Malam's back did not allow him to go after her, but her mother hearing the commotion, came running in and tried to hold her, but she pushed her away saying, "I hate you. I hate you all." Then, she just sat down and cried out Mina's name until she began to turn blue. Then there was an urgent knocking outside the door. Marlene amidst her crying heard Mina's voice. She got up quickly and shakily because she was almost out of breath. Then Keng Yi unlatched the door and Marlene fell into Mina's arms. She was completely exhausted, and Mina carried her up to her room and laid her on the bed.

Marlene recovered a little and had stopped crying. Her red eyes looked into Mina's and she said, "Please don't leave me." Mina caressed her face and said, "Hush my dearest. I am still here. It is late now. Try to get some sleep." Marlene had no strength to argue and fell fast asleep almost as soon as her eyes were closed. Marlene had her own bed in her mother's room, Anna slept with her mother on the king-size bed, and Michael slept in the cot beside his mother. Marlene got up in the middle of the night. Through the dim light on the night stand which her mother kept on every night, she could see her mother's sleeping form. For some strange reason, she needed to be with her father. She crept out of her bed, and opened the room door which was never locked. She walked on tiptoes towards her father's room, and pushed open the door which was also left ajar. It was dark in his room, but she could hear his heavy breathing. She crept onto his bed and snuggled under the sheet that covered him. Although Malam seemed fast asleep with his heavy breathing, he was awake with worry. He felt his daughter's small body beside him, and he was overcome with feelings of relief and joy that she had sought him out for comfort. He hated to admit it but he was getting a bit jealous of her attachment to the maid. Right now, she belonged entirely to him, and he was going to enjoy every moment of it. He turned towards her, kissed her forehead, put his arms around her small frame and sang one of his beautiful love songs to her. She looked at him, smiled and fell asleep in his arms. Contented that she was peacefully sleeping, Malam too fell into a deep sleep.

Mina had begged Keng Yi to let her stay on for another month without pay. Keng Yi thought that it was a good idea as it would give Marlene time to digest that her friend had to leave. Besides, setting up their new business would require a lot of time, and it would be difficult to have Michael around. However, she would not let Mina work without pay and Malam agreed that she should get her usual salary. So while Malam and Keng Yi and his wives were busy with their new business, Mina spent every spare time she had with Marlene. She gently prepared Marlene for the farewell. It was not easy, for each time she brought the subject up, Marlene began to pout. What finally made Marlene accept the fact that her friend had to leave, was that Mina's parents had found a suitor for their daughter. Knowing that for all her temperaments Marlene enjoyed romantic stories, so when Mina was told of her engagement to a man she knew and liked, she told Marlene the good news. "The first time when I held you in my arms, I felt that I would like to have a daughter like you. Now, my dream will come true. I am going to get married and have my own family. But you will always be in my heart, and when I carry my first child, it will be like holding you in my arms all over again. I have to leave soon to prepare for my big day, and I will make your father promise me that he will bring you to my wedding." Marlene was overjoyed with the news that her best friend had found her own prince, but she could not help feeling sad, so she said, "I don't want you to go away." Then Mina promised her that she would visit as often as she could. Marlene put her little hand on Mina's cheek and said in a very sad voice, "I will never be happy again, but if you promise to come back and see me often, I will try not to be sad." Then she hugged her friend and ran away. For the next few days, she kept away from Mina. It was her own way of preparing herself for the separation. When the day arrived for Mina to leave, everyone was outside to wave her goodbye except Marlene. Keng Yi was going to look for her when Malam said, "No, let her be. This is her way of telling Mina that there is no goodbye between them. She will see Mina again on her wedding day, and she is holding Mina to her promises of visiting her." Mina heard that and nodded, then entered Malam's waiting car. The gardener sent Mina to her home and her new life.

Malam and his family worked hard to establish their small business. Malam imported rice from Thailand and sold it as wholesale to the grocery shops. Sugar, flour and other food commodities were sold at retail price. Fortunately for Malam, his back seemed to have improved from the exercises the doctor instructed him to do. He was himself again. Most of his previous associates who knew him as a fair and honest men gave him a lot of business. The first month was slow, but great progress was made in the next few months and Malam was able to pay his monthly debts to the bank and to give his whole family a decent life. It was at this point that Keng Yi could not hide her pregnancy anymore. Malam was overjoyed with the news, but his other three wives were skeptical. Keng Yi's part in the business was indispensable, as she was the only one who was educated in accounting and secretarial work. However, Keng Yi promised to continue working until the very last day, and then get back to work as soon as possible. Ai Li too, hearing the news, offered to leave her family for a short time to help during Keng Yi's absence. Thus everyone was happy and the family business stabilized. However, as long as the income was substantial, Malam knowing that he was no more a young man had no intention of extending it. He knew that none of his sons had the potential of a business man. His duty towards all his children was to give them the best education that he could afford. His experience of falling down taught him not to rise too high. Also he was glad that hardship brought his family to work together. His wives were diligent in their specific duties, and if anything happened to him, they would be able to survive, like three of them did when he was lost for sometime during the Japanese Occupation.

In 1956, Mona was born. She was the first child to be delivered in a hospital. The family mid-wife had passed away. As he did for all his other children, Malam gave Mona a big welcome party, but this time only relatives were invited. Even his brothers Chin and Cheah came all the way from Malacca. They had small businesses which they both sold off when all their children were grown up and working. They came only with their wives. Chin's eyes were cloudy, for the mansion reminded him of their father's home, especially how the stairs between the kitchen and the big ballroom led to the sleeping quarters. They stayed on for three days, and on the last evening, Malam had an intimate time with his two brothers in the privacy of his office. They talked about old times, laughed at funny incidents and became sad at bad memories. When times were good, Malam had taken his family very often to visit the graves of his parents and ancestors, and spent a night either at Chin's or Cheah's home. They had promised each other that they would be buried on the same ground as their parents. That night Malam said, "I think that I would like to be buried where all my children were born, here in Klang. This is their home town." Then after a pause, he said, "Do you know that I never liked the noisy funerals that were traditional. I feel that the dead should be mourned quietly, and sent off to the next world without much fuss. I hope that my family would do that for me when I die." Chin and Cheah were quiet, but they always knew that Malam was different. They had no reason to contradict him. There was an unexplained atmosphere of sadness when goodbyes were said the next morning. All the wives of the three brothers felt that sadness too. That was the last time that the three brothers got together. Chin was then sixty five years old, Cheah was sixty four and Malam was sixty.

As Keng Yi stayed home to recover, Ai Li took leave from her family for a month, and stayed at the mansion to take over Keng Yi's duties. The small business was doing quite well, and the gardener, who was grateful that he was still in the employ of the Shih family, harvested the fruits that grew in abundance in their orchard. Instead of selling them separately, he suggested to Malam that they could be sold in the shop for daily customers. Since the fruits like rambutans, durians, mangosteens and langsats were seasonal, he also plucked fresh coconuts and cut down sugar-canes for sale. These were always fresh and they were sold out by the end of the day. Ah Leng decided to chip in her share by rearing more poultry, and took live stock to the shop for sale. All these helped to bring in revenue. Then Malam, whose back pain seemed to have disappeared, changed his mind about not extending his business. He changed it into a small supermarket. But the main part of it was still for whole-sale customers. Extending the business also meant getting more staff. He started by employing two Indian immigrants, one of them with a good sense of business. When he saw that they were good workers, he felt it was not necessary for his wives to help run the business. For now, it was enough for him and the two men to be at the shop everyday. One or two of his wives needed to come in only when the imported goods arrived, which would be the last week of the month. Thus when Ai Li went home to her family, Keng Yi continued to stay home and so did all the other wives. Then Paini and Cheng Mee decided to help with the business from home. They were both very good in making Nyona cakes which was a specialty. These too were sold in the supermarkets. Things were looking good for the Shih family, but they were aware that they could never be as rich as they were when Malam owned the big plantation. They were contented that they could still live in their beautiful mansion with enough food and clothes to wear. Whatever money Malam gave them, they saved for rainy days.

The time came to try to enroll Marlene in the same school as Lily and the other two sisters before her. She was six, and if accepted, she would be one year younger than the norm. However, Malam was confident that his beloved daughter would make the grade. Marlene had to do well in the Intelligence Tests required for under aged children. He took off from work that day to take her to the Convent School for those tests. Marlene walked into the examination room confidently and excitedly. Malam was allowed to be with her, but she let go his hand as an indication that she wanted to go in alone. His heart was full of pride as he watched his daughter close the door behind her, after giving him a smile. The tests lasted for an hour, and when Marlene came out with a teacher, there were smiles on their faces, so Malam knew that his daughter had lived up to his expectation. The teacher shook Malam's hands and said, "She could read and write better than our second graders. I would recommend her highly to be accepted into this school." Malam thanked her and as the teacher walked away, he bent down, grabbed Marlene under her armpits and was about to throw her up in the air when he cried out in pain. He managed to put his daughter back on the ground but he remained bent. Marlene, shocked at seeing her father in intense pain was about to cry, when common sense overcame her and she ran back to the room and came out with the same teacher. Malam was still in the same position when Marlene left him. Only this time, he looked pale and tears of anguish covered his eyes. The teacher knew that it was not just an ordinary sprain. She asked Malam a few questions, and then ran back to the room and came out with a chair. Slowly and carefully, she helped the big man to sit down. Then she said to Marlene, "Stay here with you father." She went to the administration office and told one of the clerks to call for an ambulance. She came back to Malam and said that the ambulance was on the way. She also informed him that she had called his home, and Marlene's mother would come for her daughter. Meanwhile, Marlene was trying to hold back her tears. She blamed herself for her father's pain. That guilt would remain with her for a long time.

The Convent School was run by nuns, and a kindly nun took care of Marlene until Keng Yi came by bus to pick her up. Paini and Ah Leng were already at the hospital, while Cheng Mee stayed home with the young children. On Marlene's insistence, Keng Yi took her to the hospital instead of going home. When they were showed to the room which Malam shared with another patient, Paini and Ah Leng were standing on each side of their husband's bed. Marlene then let out her suppressed tears and ran to her father, but was held gently back by Paini, who said that he was not to be moved. Malam's color had not returned, but he was obviously not in severe pain anymore. He smiled at his daughter and said, "The doctor has taken care of my pain. I have to stay here for a few days. Be a good girl and go back home with your mother. Don't forget that you are a big girl now and will be going to school in a few days. I promise you that I shall be home to take you to your first day of school." His voice was weak as he spoke, because the painkillers were making him very drowsy. But he managed to tell Keng Yi proudly, "Marlene did very well and has been accepted." Keng Yi knew that hospital regulations did not allow children into the hospital at odd hours, so she had no choice but to kiss her husband good-bye. Marlene stood on tip-toes and planted a kiss on her father's lips saying, "It is my fault that you are sick. I am too big now to be carried." Then before her tears began to fill up, her mother took her hand and went out of the room. Paini came running after them to say that they would take turns to be with their husband. Ah Leng wanted to stay on so she would go home with them. On the short bus journey home, Paini explained that a doctor managed to stretch Malam's back, because a nerve got caught between the ribs. But they also felt that there was something else that was not right with Malam. They would be able to determine what it was after a few days of observation and tests. Seeing how worried Keng Yi looked, she went on to say, "The doctor said that he does think it is a serious problem. We should not worry too much." She did not sound convincing enough. Thankfully, Marlene did not hear too much. She was too absorbed in her guilt to pay attention to the conversation between the two grown-ups. Even the idea of going to school soon did not overcome her depression.

Malam could not keep his promise to Marlene. He was diagnosed with skeletal tuberculosis involving the mid thoracic spine, and the adjoining vertebrae were eroding and contained some cold abscesses. It was a serious situation which could lead to lower extremity paralysis. At that time, an operation was considered risky and costly, and Malam chose not to be operated on. However, he had to be moved to a private hospital where they specialized in all kinds of tuberculosis. There he would be treated with drugs and medications. He would also learn certain exercises to help prevent paralysis as much as possible. That too was costly, but his wives insisted that he should go, and one of them could stay with him during that period. The special hospital was built on top of a hill in the capital city of Kuala Lumpur. Because there were patients with different forms of tuberculosis, some of which were infectious, children under fifteen were forbidden to visit. The doctor had informed Malam that he would have to stay there for a period of three months. Malam was devastated. He was sure that his business would not survive his absence for such a long time. It would be difficult for Keng Yi to take his part, as Mona was still an infant and Michael a toddler. There was no other choice but to trust his two employees. He also decided that none of his wives should accompany him. They were more needed at home to run the big household and help supervise the business. However, he would like them to visit him during the weekends to inform him of his children and the business. It was a very sad man who lay in the ambulance that took him to his destination for three months. He would miss his family very much, but most of his thoughts were on his daughter, Marlene. He suspected that she blamed herself for his illness. So before he left, he had asked for her, and explained to her that it was good that he was taken to the hospital that day or else, his illness would have gotten worse. He assured her that he had pains a long time ago and it was his fault not to take care of it. He also noticed that his little girl was thinner, but he thought that it was because of the change in her life. She was now a school-going kid.

Everyone was so preoccupied with Malam's health and the business that no one noticed the problems his favorite child was having. Since the day her father went to hospital in an ambulance, Marlene started to starve. She wanted to be smaller so that her father could carry her without any pain. It was easy to do that unnoticed, because there were no more family meals. Food was cooked and left in the pots, and the older children could eat whenever they were hungry. Only the younger ones like Anna, Theresa, Jan and Michael were fed at the same time. Keng Yi breast fed her three-month old baby. Marlene would go into the kitchen, take a piece of white bread and eat it. She drank a lot of water to curb her hunger. That was all she ate each day. Whenever it was her mother's turn to visit her father, she would insist on going along. Keng Yi complied for she knew that her father was always very happy to see her. Then when her first day of school arrived, and her father was still in the hospital, Marlene's disappointment became anger at her own self. However, she hid her disappointment carefully, and went quietly with Gary, Alex and Lily in their father's limousine driven by the gardener, who had collected it from the school the day that Malam went into hospital. Keng Yi wanted to accompany her on that day, but she said, "No Mama, I am a big girl now. I can manage alone. If you see Papa today, please tell him that I love him." Keng Yi looked at her daughter in the new school uniform that she sewed for her and pride swelled in her heart. Her temperamental daughter sounded so grown-up. "Malam must have had his reasons for loving her so much," she thought to herself.

Under normal circumstances, Marlene would have been the liveliest child in her class of thirty girls. Instead, she was very quiet, and did not care who sat beside her. Her class teacher had seen the results of the tests that Marlene did and was surprised to see how quiet she was. It was a short day for the first graders. There were no lessons, for that day was more of an orientation and getting to know each other. Marlene kept a lot to herself and her teacher, a young Indian lady known as Miss Rozario, came to her and started a conversation. She had heard of the incident on the day of the examinations and so she asked, "How is your father?" Without looking at her, Marlene replied, "He is still in the hospital." It was obvious that Marlene was not in the mood for any conversations, so the teacher tapped her fondly on the shoulder and went back to her desk. Keng Yi had packed a small snack box for Marlene, but when it was time for the children to have a short recess, Marlene did not even look into her box. All around her, the children were eating and chatting away, happy to make so many new friends. There were a few though, who were shy and nervous, but they managed to hold back their tears for the parents were allowed to wait in the school compound for them. Once in a while, a parent would peek into the class and catch the eye of her child to give her reassurance. Marlene noticed that, and her heart ached for her father. Thankfully, it was time to go home, and Marlene walked alone towards the waiting car. The gardener then drove the listless girl home from her first day of school.

When Marlene said goodbye to her father, she put on a brave front, but nothing her father said could convince her that it was not her fault that his condition was bad. However, she did not argue with him. Her eyes brimmed with tears when he kissed her on the forehead and said, "You will be so busy at school that the time will fly by and soon we will be together again. Even though I am away from you, I shall always keep you close to my heart. Promise me that you will be a good girl and help your mother with Michael and Mona." Marlene nodded and in a tearful voice said, "I love you Papa." She could not say more for her voice broke down in sobs. Malam's whole family, also his married daughters, their husbands and their children, were there to bid him good-bye. The nurses and doctors who witnessed the scene were touched by the love the patient had for his family, and theirs for him. One doctor commented to his nurses, "He is an exceptional man. There is an incomprehensible greatness surrounding his very being." Paini wished that Malam would change his mind about letting one of them accompany him. But, knowing her husband, she did not voice her wish. She had to accept his wishes as usual and so did her younger counterparts. She had packed some of his personal belongings and clothes into a small suitcase. She held back her tears and said, "Dearest, do not worry about anything. Together, we will take care of everything. You take care of yourself and come back to us soon. I shall be the first to visit you this weekend." Then she whispered in his ears, "I love you and have never stopped loving you." The other wives, without knowing what the other said as they whispered in his ears, said exactly the same thing; they loved him and would never stop loving him.

Malam's absence from the business was disastrous. The two employees were not as trustworthy as expected. The four wives took turns to be at the shop everyday, but they could not detect any foul play. Then one day, when Keng Yi went to the bank to withdraw money, she was told that there was not enough for the amount of withdrawal she needed to pay Malam's hospital bills. Shocked, she decided to check the ledgers and accounts of the business. She spoke to Paini about it and they both decided that Ah Leng and Cheng Mee should stay home to look after the household, while she and Paini spent everyday at the shop. They would have to take Michael and Mona along. The accounts showed that more money was going out than coming in. When questioned about it, the employees said that the wholesale buyers were unsatisfied with the products and were returning them. The commodities returned were sacks of rice, flour and white sugar. Keng Yi then made phone calls to the customers only to receive accusations of cheating them. Puzzled, she decided to check on the returned goods. The two immigrant employees showed their tempers and left saying that they quit. Both Paini and Keng Yi did not stop them, in fact they felt relieved. They would have dismissed them themselves. However a great shock awaited the two ladies as they pried open the sacks. The fifty pounds sacks of rice were supposed to contain the best grades of Jasmine rice from Thailand. However, the good rice was only at the top, and the rest was low grade broken rice. They discovered that it was the same for the ten sacks that they opened.

The other straw bags that contained the pure white sugar and high grade flour had the same problems. No wonder the buyers were angry. Normally, when the imported products arrived in bigger sacks they were divided into smaller ones. It was clear that the two men had cheated, and sold the quality products in small doses to daily customers, pocketed the money and filled up the sacks with cheap quality products. Not only that, they had not been depositing the profits into the banks.

The small Shih enterprise was at the point of bankruptcy and the big boss was in the hospital. Paini and Keng Yi knew that it was disastrous to relay to Malam the situation. Their husband was recuperating quite well and should be discharged in less than a month. They had to try to hold the fort until he was well enough to be told. They had strong faith in him. They were sure that only he alone, could save their family business. Meanwhile, they sought the help of the family lawyer, who after some investigations found out that the two perpetrators had left the country for good, and they could not be traced. He also advised the wives to keep the shop open and make whatever sales they could until Malam's return. He managed to extract more loans from the bank with the mansion as a guarantee. With the loans, the buyers could be paid off for the returned goods, as well as Malam's hospital bills. Household expenditure would depend on what the wives could make from the sales of whatever commodities were left. It was impossible to import any more new products as funds were limited. Thus Malam's four wives worked very hard to run the shop and their huge household, with only the gardener to help. They would get up early in the morning to make more cakes than before, and the gardener harvested fruits everyday for sale. Since most of the fruits were seasonal, there were not enough to bring in much revenue, but thankfully, the Nyona cakes were so delicious, that they were always sold out, and some families made a few extra orders. That meant more work for the women, but it also meant more income. There were always two of them in the shop everyday, and the other two stayed home for the children. Keng Yi had to be there every day to handle the accounts, and the other three took turns to help her. It was a very difficult time, but the four women worked without complaints and in harmony. Whenever one of them went to spend the weekend with Malam, she had to pretend that everything was normal. The good news was that when she returned home, she could tell the whole family truthfully that Malam was certainly getting better.

CHAPTER 25

Amidst the financial crisis, Keng Yi and the rest of the family were unaware that six-year old Marlene was having a life threatening problem, until one day, a week before Malam's return, Keng Yi received a call from the Convent requesting her to come to the school immediately regarding her daughter. Keng Yi, Paini and the gardener who helped during busy times were at the shop. Leaving Paini alone, the gardener drove Keng Yi to school. She was met by the Reverend Mother, a kindly looking nun, who showed her the way into a kind of parlor where she normally had conferences with parents. In answer to Keng Yi's question of whether her daughter had been in a fight, the nun shook her head and said, "No, I am afraid that the problem is more serious. Your daughter fainted during the Physical Education class." She noticed Keng Yi's worried look and continued immediately, "She is alright for the time being. She is with our school nurse and drinking a cup of hot chocolate. We made some investigations and found out that your daughter is under-nourished. It is obvious that she has been starving herself for sometime. Her classmates noticed that she always threw away the contents of her lunch box. We also feel that she is not eating properly at home." At this point, Keng Yi broke down and cried. Between sobs, she said, "How could I be so blind? I noticed that she was losing weight, but I thought that it was because of her change of life, and that she was missing her father." The nun said in very gentle tones. "From the little information I managed to get out of her, I presumed that she blamed herself for her father's illness. She has become anorexic because she thought she was too big for her father to carry her." Keng Yi nodded and wiping her eyes dry asked, "Can I see her now?" "Sure," the nun replied, "but you will have to convince her to eat again or else we will have to report her situation to the proper authorities." Keng Yi continued to nod. A shock awaited her when she saw Marlene sipping the hot chocolate as slowly as possible. Her eyes took in the frail and skinny girl, and she would have broken down again had the nun not warned her about being strong for her daughter's sake.

Keng Yi knew that they could not afford another hospital bill. She had to take care of Marlene's problems on her own. First of all, she had to erase her daughter's guilt feelings, then she had to make sure that her daughter started eating normally again. Marlene was shivering in her arms as she instructed the gardener to drive them home. No words were exchanged between mother and daughter. Once home, she asked Ah Leng if she could go with the gardener to the shop to help Paini. One look at Marlene and Ah Leng consented. Keng Yi took her daughter into the kitchen and prepared a hot chicken soup. She then tried to spoon it into her mouth but Marlene said that she was not hungry. Then Keng Yi decided to use the two most powerful weapons she could think of – Marlene's love for her father, and her desire to attend Mina's wedding in a month's time. Placing the spoon back into the bowl, she tilted her daughter's head gently and said, "Marlene, your father will be back in seven days. His shock of seeing you so skinny and sickly looking will be bad for his heart." She had to be cruel to be kind. Marlene just stared at her, so she continued, "Your father's back had been hurting him for a long time. If he had not carried you up that day, no one would have known how bad his back really was. If he had not gone to hospital that day, his back would have been so bad, that he would never be able to walk again. But because of you, the doctors were able to help him in time. Now, he will be coming back soon." She noticed a change in Marlene's face, and that encouraged her to go on. "He could not keep his promise to be with you on your first day of school, but he is going to take you to Mina's wedding. I can promise you that." Marlene's face lighted up. But she said, "Can't I take the soup later? I have just drunk some hot chocolate." Keng Yi shook her head and said, "No, you have only seven days to make up for the three months that you have not been eating. You do want to see your father smile when he looks at you, don't you?" Marlene nodded and stared at the soup. Keng Yi waited patiently, then with a shrug, Marlene opened her mouth, and Keng Yi, unable to hide her sigh of relief and happiness, fed her daughter spoon after spoon of soup.

For the next few days, Keng Yi kept Marlene home. Her daughter was still having difficulty sitting down to a normal meal, but she was progressing, and her intake of milk at breakfast and before bed was satisfactory. By the end of the week, she was almost cured, and her energy returned. She was still under weight, but she did try her best to eat as much as she could. It would take more time for her eating habits to be normal again, but the important thing was that she was not avoiding food anymore. Mina had kept her promise to visit her as often as she could, but for the last two months, she was so busy getting ready for her wedding that she had no time to call on Marlene. Keng Yi was sure that if Mina had seen Marlene earlier, she would have immediately detected that something was seriously wrong with her. Marlene on the other hand, did not miss Mina, because of her own problems. Right now, like the others, she was excited and looking forward to see her father again. On the day of his return, she put on her favorite dress which hung loosely around her body. Her mother adjusted the dress by tying a ribbon round her waist. She asked her mother, "Do I look good?" Keng Yi smiled and answered, "In your papa's eyes, you are the most beautiful girl in the world." Marlene was hesitant, and her eyes were questioning when she said in a quiet voice, "I hope he does not know any bad things about me." Keng Yi was quiet, because she had advised Paini to tell Malam about it on their way back. She felt that it was important that Malam did not make any comment of how thin his daughter was. However, she had to say something to reassure the little girl. "Your papa loves you, and he knows that you love him just the same. We should be going out to wait for him." Then with Mona in her arms, she took Marlene by the hand to join the others on the porch.

Malam, unaware of Marlene's anorexic problem and the failing business, was looking forward to seeing his family again. His tuberculosis was in remission, but the doctors warned him that he would have more and more difficulty using his legs with time. At the moment, he was able to move quite normally, but with the help of a walking stick. Paini and the gardener drove up to bring him home. Paini did not talk to him about the business, but she understood the urgency of informing him of Marlene's problem. Malam took it quite badly, and said that it was his fault to have left his little girl without making sure that she was convinced that it was not her fault. Paini saw the agony in her husband's face and quickly pacified him by saying, "Oh she is alright now. She is eating quite normally, but of course she still looks a little under nourished. She does not want you to know, so when you see her, pretend not to notice her weight. Malam kept quiet. He was quite agitated that his wife had no confidence in his discretion. He loved all his children and he would protect each and every one of them with his life, but there was an undeniable and incomprehensible bond between him and his eighth child and first-born of his last wife. He would not hide that feeling for her anymore. If any one was jealous, he or she would have to live with it.

It was Sunday, and his whole family including his married daughters, their husbands and children, were there for his home-coming. As the car drove into the driveway, the children from Gary downwards, including toddler Michael, ran with the car until it made a full stop at the porch. Malam's heart was bursting with pride and joy. Paini got out of the car, and David went immediately to help his father out. Paini had the walking stick in her hand, and as soon as Malam was completely out, she handed him the walking stick, and all his younger children crowded around him. They were warned to be careful, so they touched him gently, and he bent down to plant a kiss on each of them. Marlene stood aside quietly for she was so afraid of hurting him again. However, when he had finished kissing everyone, he extended his free hand to her. She ran to him and buried her face in his stomach. Malam could feel her shaking with emotion, so he stroked her hand and allowed her to hold on to him for sometime. Then Keng Yi gently said, "We also need a kiss." Marlene moved away, and it was the grown-ups turn to show how they welcomed him home. David then said, "I think we should all go in so that father can sit down." He held his father by the armpit, and led him into the house and onto a waiting chair. As Malam slowly sat down, David who had not said anything to him yet, whispered in his ears, "Dearest Father, it is good to have you home again. We all missed you terribly." Malam smiled at his eldest son and said, "I missed you all too. I am glad to be home, and I hope that I don't have to leave you all again." While Malam chatted with all his children, sons-in-law and grandchildren, the four wives adjourned to the kitchen to prepare a festive dinner. No matter how financially tight they were, Paini had decided that Malam's home-coming was a joyful occasion, and should be celebrated on a grand scale among the family.

While they were preparing food in the kitchen, Paini said, "Tonight is the night. Malam must know the truth. He had insisted on our way home that he would like to go back to work immediately. I could not tell him anything. Once the children are in bed, we should all gather in his room and tell him everything. Ai Li and Jo Lin have to leave, as their husbands have to go back to work, and the children have to go to school. So Ah Leng, please tell David and John to meet us in their father's room tonight." The other three agreed, except that Ah Leng had something to say. "There is some consolation in the fact that David is finished with his teaching degree, and has a job in one of the local schools. John is finally finished with school, and decided that he would work as a veterinarian assistant, and save the money he gets for further education. I know that this will not help much, but David will be bringing in some income and we have one mouth less to feed." No one understood why Ah Leng even mentioned that. But she had her private reasons which would become obvious in the near future. Keng Yi, who knew exactly how bad the business situation was, was sure that it would not survive another month. Cheng Mee who was quiet all this time, voiced her thoughts, "Malam could sell the mansion and we could find a house big enough for all of us to rent." All the three women looked at her. They were shocked at first, but realization dawned on them, and they felt that she touched a subject that no one else dared to do so.

Malam on the other hand, knew that something was wrong with his business. Whenever one of his wives visited him over a weekend, they would avoid his questions of how things were at the shop. Their answers were always very brief and short like, "Oh as usual. Things are a bit slow, but we are managing." They never mentioned the dismissal of the two immigrants and their swindle. When he asked about them, they would shrug and say, "So, so." Malam thought that without his presence and his expertise, it was acceptable that the business was not blooming. He felt that he would be able to change all that when he returned. It was a shocked Malam who listened as Keng Yi read out the accounts, and explained how the two employees fled to India with their money. They now owed the bank a tremendous amount that had to be paid soon, or Malam had to declare bankruptcy and lose everything he owned. At first Malam was furious that his wives never told him anything, but then he realized that they did so because of their love and loyalty towards him. His health was more important to them than their livelihood. He would not have recovered that fast if he was under such pressure. He did not say anything, but deep in his heart he knew that it was going to be downhill for him and his family all the way. They were close to poverty. He dismissed his wives and sons, but not before complimenting them on how well they all managed the situation. That night, Malam lay awake. His heart ached for his family. He thought that they had survived the kidnapping, but now with his failing health and the imminent paralysis that he would have, he could not see how he could continue to provide his wives and children a moderate life. He knew that there was no way to hold on to the mansion. Tears filled his eyes with that thought. Just before he fell asleep in the early hours of the morning, he had made up his mind that things had to move fast while he still had use of his legs. Come what may, his family would not face hunger as long as he lived.

None of the wives could sleep that night. Like Malam, they were aware that it would never be the same again. Their future and that of all their children were at stake. Ah Leng however did not worry as much as the others. Her daughter's husband was now a police commissioner and had a good income. Jo Lin had been giving her some money, which she had secretly saved. She was sure that David too would give her part of his salary, so would her second son, John. Gary would finish school in two years time and there was only Alex and Jan. But unlike Ah Leng, Paini thought of all the other wives and their very young children. She knew that the time would come when Malam would be bed-ridden. She thought of ways of how they, his wives and elder children could help bring in revenue to support all of them. She and Cheng Mee had the same idea. They both knew that they were good at cooking and sewing. They would continue baking the Nyona cakes and sell them in small restaurants. They could also take in clothes for alterations, and sew children's dresses for sale to their friends and relatives. Keng Yi had the most worries. She had four small children. She had the qualifications to go out and work in a firm as a secretary, but her kids needed her. Marlene could look after herself, but her temperaments would cause her to get into a lot of trouble with Ah Leng and her half brothers. However, she decided that if it had to be, she would have to leave her children under the care of Paini and Cheng Mee. After all, Malam, handicapped or not, would be there for his beloved daughter. He would still have control of everyone in his household.

It was a school day the next morning, so the women had to get up to prepare their children for school. Paini knew that her husband needed help to get dressed, so she waited outside his door to hear some stirring. She entered Malam's room as soon as she heard a slight cough. Her husband was sitting at the edge of the bed with his feet on the ground. Paini saw his hunched back and thought to herself, "How much he has aged." Malam turned round when he heard her footsteps and gave her a wan smile. Paini told him to stay in bed and she would fetch him his breakfast, but he shook his head saying, "Oh no, there are a lot of things to take care of today. Help me wash up and get into my suit, I have to go to the bank." When he finally got downstairs, his children were already having their breakfast. They were so happy to see their father again, and did not notice his special look towards his favorite child. He told them that he was going with them to school, and when he saw the questioning look on their faces, he laughed and said, "Hey, I can still drive. The walking stick is just to help me get around without putting too much strain on my legs." Then looking directly at Marlene, he continued, "I hope to be able to send my two girls to school every morning. Alex is now old enough to cycle with Gary to school." Alex looked happy. He had wanted to do that for sometime, but his mother thought that he was still too young. It was just about twenty five minutes of cycling, so Malam warned Gary to keep up with his younger brother, and that Alex should never cycle back on his own. The two boys agreed. Marlene was overjoyed that her father would be taking them to school, and what was better was that Alex would not be in the same car. Although Alex never laid hands on her again, he never stopped teasing her and trying to make her cry. Both Malam and Keng Yi were glad to see that Marlene was eating almost as though she never went through the period of anorexia.

After dropping his daughters at the school gate, Malam drove directly to the bank. It was still too early, but he wanted to be the first to see the bank manager, who was also a good friend of his. He knew what he had to do to save his family from sudden poverty. The bank was still closed when he arrived, so he sat in his car and waited. He stroked the wheel of his limousine, and a feeling of nostalgia overcame him, for he knew that he had to part with it. His next stop was the car dealer. He had not spoken to any of his wives about his plans, but the effectiveness of his plans would depend on the outcome of the meeting with the bank manager. Before he left the house, he had instructed the gardener to cycle to the shop to open it, but only to do business with the daily customers. He would get there as soon as possible. He told Keng Yi that he would come back later that day to take her to the shop.

When the bank opened, Malam remain seated in his parked car. Then when he saw his friend, the manager driving in, he came out of his car and walked regally with his walking stick towards his friend. The manager caught sight of him and walked towards him. There was a sympathetic smile on his face as he greeted Malam. "Mr. Shih," he said as he extended his hand for a handshake. "It is nice to know that you are well again." Malam took his friend's hands and said, "I hope you have some time for me, Mr. Lee." Mr. Lee said that he would always have time for a great friend and customer. Together they walked into the bank. As Mr. Lee passed his secretary, he told her that he was not to be disturbed until Malam left his office. Then he also instructed her to bring in Malam's file into his office. While waiting for the file, Mr. Lee said, "Your young wife was here, and I guess she must have told you about the bad financial situation. I know how difficult it is to leave your business in the hands of strangers, especially when they turned out to be dishonest and crooked." Malam nodded and replied, "My biggest mistake was to be so trusting. Keng Yi is the only one who could have run the business in my absence, but she just had a baby and three other young ones. Well, I am here today to see what I have left in assets. I am not asking for any more loans or help. I will appreciate your advice though." They were quiet as the secretary came in with the file, and a tray with two cups of hot coffee. As Malam sipped his coffee, he watched his friend going through the papers with a solemn face.

Finally, Mr. Lee looked up and said, "You are three months behind in your payment towards your loans. We had not sent you any warning as I knew of your hospitalization. Then again, your enterprise owes a few of your clients a great amount of money. Under normal circumstances, the bank would have taken all your assets and paid up your bills. Well, at the moment your big house is your only asset, minus what you owe the bank and your customers." He waited to see if Malam digested everything he said, and then he continued, "Thankfully, because of the rapid development of this town, your house has increased in value. However, your business would not survive the blow. You will have to sell it, or surrender it to the bank to pay up the outstanding loans and debts." Then Malam said, "I know that I have to sell my business. What I want to know is how much is the loan I have against my house." "Well, if you manage to sell the house at its present market value, one third of the money will pay up your mortgage and another few thousand would cover your debts. You will have in your pocket a little less than two thirds of the sale." Malam knew that what was left would not help him to start another business. Besides, his health would not allow him to work hard anymore. More details were discussed, and when Malam left Mr. Lee's office, he had no other alternative but to put his house and shop up for sale.

Malam then went to the car dealer and got a good deal for his limousine. He exchanged it for a smaller, and cheaper but reasonably good vehicle. By the time he drove home, he was completely exhausted, and his legs were giving way. But he had no time to rest. He had to go back to the shop, and with Keng Yi by his side, his energy returned. His wives saw the new car, but their only comments were that it looked good. On the way to the shop, he told Keng Yi everything. They would try to sell whatever was left in the shop, and then put it up for sale. If that did not work out, the bank would take over and sell it for them. Then with deep sadness in his voice, he said, "Our mansion would also go on sale. I hope that whatever money I have left, would hold on for a few years more until most of the children are out of school and working. Our next move is to look for a house big enough for all of us. We will not be able to buy one, but we can rent one." Keng Yi listened quietly, but she knew that Malam overlooked his health. He would require a lot of medical attention, and most of the money would go into his medical bills. The money that Malam talked about would not stretch too long. But the man was in pain mentally and physically, and she had no heart to tell him so. All she said was, "We will see through all this together. You have married us for good or bad, in health and sickness, and in wealth and poverty. We are behind you all the way." Malam's eyes welled with tears, but he held back. No matter how poor he became, he would always be rich in love. Keng Yi spoke for all his wives. When they arrived at the shop, it was almost time to pick up his two girls from the school. Keng Yi knew that Malam was completely exhausted, so she suggested that Malam should rest in the small office in the shop, and let the gardener do the driving.

When Marlene and Lily saw the gardener leaning on a strange car they were puzzled, and the first thought that struck their minds were that their father had an accident, but the gardener's smile was reassuring as he said in Malay, "Your father is very tired. He is at the shop, and if you want we could drive there so that you could be with him." Seeing that the girls were curious about the car, he continued, "It is a nice car, isn't it. It is easier for your father to handle a smaller car now that his legs are not so strong anymore." Both the girls accepted the reason and got into their new car. However, Marlene was quiet. This is the second time that her father could not keep his promise due to his health. She felt in her heart that nothing would ever be the same again. She knew that there would be more changes, and she would be ready for them. Nothing was going to surprise or shock her anymore. As long as her father was around, she would be contented. She also wondered if her father would take her to Mina's wedding this week-end. She missed her friend very much, but she was beginning to understand the relationship between friends and family. Friends came and went, and sometimes they stayed away forever. Family members stayed together whether they liked each other or not. If they went away, like her two married sisters, they always came back for big family occasions. Her conclusion was that family was forever. However, she would be deeply disappointed if she could not go to Mina's wedding, but she made up her mind not to make a big fuss of it. She had to be good for her father's sake. She had caused him enough pain and worry.

It was a very solemn family dinner. Malam sat at the head of the table, with Paini at the other end. On Malam's right, closest to him, was Ah Leng followed by David, Gary, Cheng Mee, Lily, Alex and Jan. Keng Yi sat on his left with Mona in her arms, and little Michael was in a high chair. John sat between Marlene and Anna, and Theresa sat closest to Paini. For some reason, the little ones felt that there was something strange in the air. They were quiet as they ate. No one talked, and when Malam was sure everyone had enough to eat, he said, "This is the first time I am addressing not only the adults but all my children, young and old. Ai Li and Jo Lin are not here because they now have their own family. I want you children to be as quiet as you can, and if there is something that you cannot understand your mothers will explain it to you later in your own room." He looked at the puzzled faces of his young children.

From the corner of his eye, he noticed that Marlene was just looking at her empty plate. She did not look up like the others, but he knew that she was listening to every word he said. Then he looked at the younger ones, and when his eyes fell on the baby Mona, his heart ached for her. She would never know what it felt like to grow up in the mansion. However, he had to subdue that ache for more pressing matters.

Malam remain seated as his legs would not allow him to stand too long. Drawing a deep breath, and with a strong voice he spoke to his family. "I have never thought that a day like this would come. As I watched my family grow in numbers, it has never occurred to me that a day will come when I will not be able to continue to offer you the good and luxurious life that I have always known. As I speak, my heart is breaking." Malam paused as he felt his eyes warming up, with tears about to break out, but he pulled himself together and continued, "We have lost everything. We have to give up our business and most terrible of all, our house. But we have each other, and no money in the world can buy that. If I was still a young and healthy man, I would continue to fight and keep what we have, but alas, I know when to quit." The four wives started to sob quietly, while their young children looked at them only half understanding of what was going on. Malam would not allow his tears to flow out, so with glassy eyes behind his spectacles, which he acquired about four years ago, he went on, "After the sale of the business and our house, there will be some money left, and if God willing, it should last us for another few years. Right now, we don't have to think of what will happen after that. It is however important, that all of us accept that we are no longer rich, and that we have to give up the luxuries that we are used to. First of all, we will have to move into a smaller rented house. Then our meals will be humble ones. My promise to you all is that as long as I live, there will be a roof over your head and you will never face hunger." No one spoke until now. But when Malam made a longer pause, David stood up and said, "I speak for all your children. You, our father have worked hard to give us all a good life. You would continue to do so if you can, but you can't. We will all do our best to help you stretch whatever funds you have until some of us start to work. The children under David's age and up to Lily nodded. Marlene just kept her head down. At that moment, her understanding of poverty meant that her father and all the adults were sad. She also understood that there will be less to eat, what she could not understand was why they had to move out of their house. Her mother would have to explain that to her.

Malam was so proud of his elder son that he thought to himself, "If it takes poverty to bring out the loyalties of your loved ones, than poverty is not that bad after all." Then before he dismissed his family, he said, "I shall spend the next few days looking for a proper house for us. But be ready to move out of this house once it is sold. I love you all, and I shall retire now to my room. If any of you need to talk to me, please do so, but not all at once." He stood up shakily, and Paini ran to his side to give him his walking stick. He had sat too long and his legs were cramping. Paini gestured to David and John to help their father up the stairs to his room. She and Cheng Mee came later to help him wash up and dress in his pajamas. They stayed on for a short time to chat with him. It was more than a chat, for Paini said, "Malam, all is not completely lost. We, your wives can bring in some revenue with our Nyona cakes. You did not mention about terminating the gardener, but he has already told me that if you did so, he would beg you to let him stay on without pay until the house is sold. He has no where to go, and a roof ever his head and some food is enough. He would be a great help to us for our little endeavor. He could take our cakes to the small coffee shops on his bike." Malam looked at both his wives and said, "At this point, I cannot discharge the gardener, as there are times when I would need someone to drive me around. We will still pay him his salary until we move. Then there won't be any more room for him. And yes, any kind of income would help. I know that I can rely on all four of you." They kissed him good-night, and before closing the room behind her Cheng Mee said, "Malam, you are still the richest man in town. No one has the amount of love that you have." Malam smiled at her and looked after the closed door, with a heart full of love for each and every member of his family.

There was one more important matter to settle. He would not disappoint his daughter Marlene again. She had looked forward to attending the wedding of her best friend. So that weekend, he woke his darling up with a kiss and said, "Hey, sleepy head, we have a date to keep." Marlene had not talked about it, but before she went to sleep, she hoped that her father had not forgotten about the wedding. She jumped out of bed and rushed to the bathroom. Her mother was already up and had her dress waiting for her. As her daughter rushed to put on the dress, Keng Yi said, "You have plenty of time. The wedding starts only in the afternoon. Put on your home dress first and go down to breakfast with the rest of the family." Marlene was too excited to eat. So when afternoon came and the gardener drove the car to the porch, she was in it even before her father came out. Malam was a little off that day, so he told his gardener to drive them and wait for them. "We will not stay long," he told his daughter, "You will see that Mina will not be able to talk too much to you. That is the custom. The bride has to be very quiet." Marlene did not believe that Mina would not have time for her, but she just nodded. This was the first time that Marlene had attended a Muslim wedding. Her father was right, for the only time that she could see Mina personally and talk to her, was in the changing room. The room was crowded with women, so Marlene had to retain her joy and emotion of seeing her friend again. However, she did enjoy the wedding ceremony, where the bride had to change clothes a few times. She also laughed a little, when the spectators were making jokes at the defenseless couple, seated on top of a covered and brightly decorated podium. Once or twice, she managed to catch Mina's eyes and she felt good. So when they left, after a sumptuous dinner of mutton curry and yellow glutinous rice followed by sweet cakes, she was a contented and happy girl. It was an hour journey home, and she cuddled in her father's arms and thought to herself, "This is where I belong." Malam kissed her forehead and contented himself that his world was complete with this bundle of love in his arms.

CHAPTER 26

In 1957, three months after the mansion was put on sale, a business man and friend of Malam bought it. He was fair and did not bargain on the market price. He also bought all the expensive furniture and the piano. Not only that, he asked Malam if he could keep the three Alsatians too. Malam knew that Marlene would be terribly broken hearted, but it was expensive to feed those three dogs, and he was not sure if they could afford a house that could cater to the freedom of those dogs. When he told his daughter about it, she surprised him by not showing much emotion. But he could see the pain in her eyes. His little girl had grown up. After all the loans and debts were paid off, what was left should last the big family to have an average standard of living for at least ten years without any income, if circumstances were normal. But Malam, his wives and older children knew that Malam was not a healthy man, and a lot of the money would go into medical and hospital bills. So the wives immediately put their plans into action. Under Paini and Cheng Mee's supervision, Ah Leng and Keng Yi too became experts at making the Nyona cakes. They would all get up about four o'clock in the morning to make them fresh for the coffee shops each day. Besides that, Paini and Cheng Mee took clothes in for alterations, and sometimes sewed a few dresses for their friend's children. The gardener on his part, took the cakes in boxes to the shops, and also plucked the seasonal fruits and sold them outside the gate of the mansion. These small enterprises did bring in enough money for daily expenditures. Meanwhile, Malam, who was still able to move around, had found a house to rent outside Klang.

So exactly a month after the mansion was sold, the Shih family took leave of their faithful gardener who would live on to work for the new owner. With heavy hearts they moved into their new rented home. The house was big enough to hold the whole family, but there were only four bedrooms. Thus the children, regardless of age, would have to sleep with their respective birth mothers. Paini would have to room in with Cheng Mee and her two daughters, while Malam occupied the smallest room in the house. That room could contain only one single bed and an armchair, which Malam definitely needed. The house was wooden, with a zinc roof which could get heated very easily. It was semi-level, with a flight of six steps leading from the living room to the sleeping quarters. The same amount of steps led the upstairs to the kitchen. The whole family had to share one bathroom and one toilet. The toilet was a bucket system about thirty feet away from the house. Though it was an old fashioned kitchen with wood burning cooking holes, it was huge, and could contain all the family at one sitting. Thankfully, for the children, especially Marlene, the compound was big and wooded. Behind the fenced area at the back of the house was a small unkempt jungle. It was government property, but not considered forbidden ground to those who dared explore that jungle, filled with creeping snakes and all kinds of jungle animals.

At this point, David was a teacher in a school nearby, and John was away during the week for his training. He came back every Friday night and left on Sunday evenings. He had saved enough money for a motor bike and as did David. Gary was in his last year of school, Alex and Lily who were eleven and ten years old were in their fourth and third year of Primary school, and Marlene was in her second year. Anna, Theresa and Jan who were about the same age, had to wait another two years before going to school. Michael was just a little more than two years old, and Mona had turned one. Since there were no more badminton courts, the children started playing hockey. David bought a few hockey sticks and they had good games in the huge compound. Marlene seemed to excel in that game, and David paid more attention to her techniques than he did to the others. When Malam watched his children enjoying themselves, he was happy that they had adjusted to their environment so fast. His wives continued to bring in income with their cake making and tailoring. Keng Yi could not go out to work yet, as both Mona and Michael needed her. The other three women had their hands full trying to make ends meet, and looking after their sickly husband, whose lower body was getting stiffer. Soon his bed would have to be taken down into the living room, as he could hardly climb up and down the stairs even with help. Financially, they were still able to cope. There was enough food to feed the family, and the children were still able to wear good clothes. There was enough for school fees, uniforms and books. Thus the necessity of Keng Yi to work did not arise. She, however, did her share in helping with the making of the cakes and delivering them to the shops by bus.

Then a year later after the big move, Malam woke up one morning, and found that he could not move his legs at all. Not only that, he was in great pain, and had to be taken to the hospital. It was also at this time that bad news came from Malacca. Chin had a stroke and died. Malam was heart-broken that he was not able to attend the funeral of his eldest brother. All that made his recovery slow, and he had to stay in the hospital for three months. When he finally came home, he was paralyzed from the waist downwards. A lot of money went out for his hospitalization and for the medications and frequent doctor's visits. The financial situation was badly affected. The wives toiled on to earn more money, and even with the older sons' help, more money went out than what came in. Jo Lin and Ai Li chipped in to help with their cake money from their husbands, but still more money was needed as Malam's situation got worse. At this point, his doctor advised him to have surgery, but Malam declined. He saw no point in a surgery that did not guarantee his life or the use of his legs. Besides, the surgery would leave his family completely penniless. So Malam was bedridden, and during his waking hours, he sat propped up in his bed. His bed was now in the living room, and a temporary curtain was installed to give him privacy. But it was only used when he needed to answer the call of nature. He wanted to show his family that he was there for them. All his school-going children kissed him goodbye before they left for school, and he was also the first person they saw when they came home.

Marlene was beginning to understand the seriousness of her father's health, and also the true meaning of poverty. The meals were very simple, with more rice to fill the stomach than meats and vegetables. It was a treat if one of her favorite dishes was on the table, which was very seldom. Like everyone else, she had to outgrow her school uniform before she had a new one, and that also goes for her sports shorts. She used to get new books every year, now she had to make use of Lily's old text books or second hand books. Even the cake money that they received to buy goodies during the breaks was reduced to half. They had to take the bus to school, now that the only car they had was also sold. No more birthdays were celebrated, except that the birthday person received a small gift. She got used to all this quite gracefully, but she missed sitting on her father's lap. Even when she was allowed to sit on his bed, she had to be careful when she got up or down. Her father's hugs for her were still warm and full of love, but they were not as strong as they used to be. She kept on hoping that he would get better soon. It never occurred to her that his situation of not being able to walk was forever. A year had passed and he never left his bed, but still she did not give up hope that her father would be well. She longed for that day when he would catch her under her armpits and throw her in the air.

An incident happened in school to bring her hope alive. She was in her third year of school and was about to lose her temper. "Marlene!" She heard a stern voice calling her name, and her swinging arm dropped as suddenly as it was raised. The voice belonged to that of her class teacher, Sister Renee. She turned and saw that the normally twinkling eyes, behind a pair of dark-rimmed glasses, now held an angry look. She was caught in the act of almost hitting one of her classmates, who with two others were jeering at her and calling her a liar. Calling her a liar implicated that her beloved father too was a liar, for all Marlene did was to tell them what her father told her the night before. Marlene would not have lost her temper if they left her father out of the argument. Seeing the angry look on her teacher's face sent a chill up her spine. The Convent School emphasized discipline. Girls should behave like little ladies, and misconducts were dealt with punishments in various forms, according to the degree of misbehavior. Marlene had a reputation of being a tom-boy and a temperamental girl. So far, she had used words to vent her anger. She had a way with the teachers, who did not have the heart to report her to the higher authorities, so most of the time she got away with a reprimand and a warning. Her tom-boyishness had met a lot of disapproval, but she too got away with that. This was the first serious offence where she saw no way of escaping. She would face the worst punishment, and that was to be sent to the office of the Reverend Mother who was also the headmistress of the whole school. She had heard that the pupil would have to kneel in front of the nun, and stretch out her hands with her fists tightly closed and facing upwards. The nun would hit her knuckles hard with a ruler. She would continue doing that until the child begged for mercy. Marlene could stand the pain, but what she could not accept was that she would have to bring a letter home to her parents, that would reveal the reason for her punishment. She was sure that it would break her father's heart. That incident took place during the break, and just as Sister Renee approached her, the bell rang to announce the end of recess. Although one of the girls said before running off for assembly, "Saved by the bell," Marlene knew that it was not so.

Malam sent all his daughters to the Convent School because of the good reputation it had. It had always topped other schools in the academic fields, and the girls that graduated from that school were more reputable than the girls from other schools. However, he had always stressed to his children that they were not to join in any of the prayers. He was not a staunch Buddhist, but he did not want any of his children to be influenced by the Christians. There were always two assemblies, one before the classes started, and the other one after Recess. During these assemblies, a hymn was sung and a prayer was said. The Shih girls were not allowed to join in either the singing or the prayer. They were also forbidden to make the sign of the cross with their hands. At this particular assembly, Marlene wished that she could disappear. Sister Renee's eyes were on her, and it was very obvious that she did not join in the prayers. The Reverend Mother stood on the podium and led the prayers. Marlene had always felt that she was a kind person, but that day, Marlene thought that she looked stern. Her heart pounded with dread as the headmistress dismissed the pupils to march back into their respective classes. Sister Renee stood at the door as usual while her students marched in and took their places. Marlene looked down and meekly went to her take her place. Satisfied that all her pupils were sitting down, Sister Renee went to the blackboard and started writing some Mathematical exercises on the board. She wrote on for fifteen minutes without a break, then turned round and said, "I want you all to do these sums in your exercise books. I have to go out for a while and I shall put Connie in charge until I come back. If you are finished before I am back, you can read a book. No one should talk or walk about." Connie was the class monitor, and well liked and respected by all her classmates. In fact, she and Marlene were good friends and if she had been around Marlene then, the fight would not have started.

Then the inevitable happened. Sister Renee stood at the door and called out to Marlene to follow her. Marlene's knees were shaking as she stood up, but she did not want to expose her fear to the three girls who had caused her to be in this mess. She walked as steadily as she could with her chin up towards the door. Sister Renee walked ahead and Marlene followed meekly at a distance. Once out of sight, the nun turned around and gestured Marlene to speed up. Surprisingly for Marlene, the stern look had disappeared. Her twinkling eyes were back. She waited until Marlene caught up with her. Then she walked slowly so that Marlene's little legs could keep up with her pace. Marlene kept her head down, and unconsciously allowed her legs to move in the direction of the private office of the Reverend Mother, when she felt the nun's hand on her shoulders drawing her into another direction. Without daring to hope for the best, Marlene allowed Sister Renee to hold her hand as they walked towards the beautiful Convent garden. This area was forbidden ground to all students and other teachers. It belonged only to the nuns. It was very well kept with the smell of blooming roses of different colors. It could only be seen from the windows of the library, and the nuns spent their free time here meditating or reading. Marlene was amazed at the beautiful plants that grew here. Beside the roses, different kinds of orchids, a few very rare ones, surrounded a statue of a lady holding an infant in her arms. There were a few trimmed shrubs scattered here and there. The grass was well cut and green. The freshness of the garden and its scent of roses and oleanders gave Marlene a feeling that she was in a story book. Her fears and worries left her as the nun gently led her to a bench and sat down beside her.

Then Sister Renee put her arms around Marlene's small shoulders and in the gentlest tone asked, "Why were you so angry with your friends?" The reality finally got to her. This wonderful person was not going to report her to the Reverend Mother. The relief brought out the held back tears of fear, frustration and anger. Sister Renee tilted the girl's head, and wiped her tears with a clean white handkerchief that she took out of the pocket of the white habit she had on. "It is okay to cry. We are alone here. Let it all out and you will feel much better." Her words made Marlene cry more, and the nun held on to her shaking body saying comforting words, "I know that inside this bad tempered girl is a wonderful and precious little being. I only wish to see more of that being. I am not angry. I want to help you. Tell me everything when you are ready." She allowed Marlene to cry a little longer, and when she began to calm down, the nun said, "Tell me everything. Maybe I can help." Encouraged by the softness of her voice, Marlene replied, "The girls called my father and me liars, because I told them what my father told me." "And what did you father tell you?" Marlene decided that she could confide in the nun so she told her everything. Yesterday, she saw her parents cooking good food like chicken, roasted pork and yellow glutinous rice. It was a long time since they had such good food. But when they were not served those delicious dishes at dinnertime, she was frustrated and puzzled, so she went to her bed-ridden father and complained. He explained to her that it was the week of the dead and their spirits were free to roam the earth. If food were not laid outside the house for them, they would enter the house and disturb the occupants. He also warned Marlene, that she should stay indoors after sunset. That was when they would come out. Marlene wanted to warn her friends, but all they did was jeer at her and called her a liar. She also added that calling her a liar alone would not have made her so angry, but they implicated that her father was a liar, and that made her furious. At the end of her story, Sister Renee said, "Furious enough to face the most serious punishment." Marlene looked down and kept quiet. Then the nun continued to say, "I know that inside this angry child is a lot of goodness. That is why we are here. Your father would be so proud to know what you will go through to defend him." She paused and tilted Marlene's head so that their eyes met. Marlene's eyes were still wet but she had stopped crying, and managed to return the sweet smile that Sister Renee gave her.

"I am going to tell you a story," Sister Renee said. "You love your father very much and I am sure he loves you just as much if not more. But there is one above us and he is looking down on us right now. He loves each and every one of us very much. Each time we do something bad we hurt him. But he still loves us no matter how much we hurt him." As the nun talked, Marlene's eyes looked at the blue sky with scattered clouds. Her ten year old mind began to form a picture. She saw the clouds gathering, and as she looked they seemed to form the face of an old man with long white hair and a long white beard. She heard Sister Renee say, "He is God, the father of all of us. He loves us so much that he sent his only son to help us. The bad people nailed him to a cross, but it was meant to be so. The blood he shed saved us all." She stopped talking and turned Marlene's face to look at the cross hanging on a cord around her neck. "This is Jesus, his son." Marlene looked at the cross and saw the agony of the man. Her heart went out to him. There were questions in her mind, but she remembered her father's warning about the sign of the cross so she kept quiet. Then Sister Renee looked at her watch and said, "It is time for us to get back to class. I shall be in the Chapel after school. If you want to hear more, come to the Chapel. I shall make sure that you catch the bus home in time." Marlene nodded. She needed to know more about the God and his son. The picture that the clouds formed would remain in her mind for a very long time. As long as she did not make the sign of the cross, she was not disobeying her father. She would never need to tell him that she went into the chapel. However, she was not sure if she should listen to more, but curiosity got the better of her. Just before they reached the door of the classroom, she took Sister Renee's big hand in her small one and said, "Thank you. I want to hear more."

The next two last periods were Geography taught by another teacher. Marlene could not wait for the bell to ring. She was very distracted and was reprimanded a few times for not paying attention. The three girls that Marlene was fighting with were wondering if Marlene was punished. She came back to class looking quite radiant. They did not have a chance to find out. Marlene was the first to leave the class as soon as she heard the school bell. She rushed to the chapel and saw the good nun kneeling on a raised plank. She had a rosary in her hand. It was the first time that Marlene had been so close to the chapel. She was afraid to go in, even when Sister Renee gestured with her hand that Marlene should come in. After a few seconds when Marlene just stood at the door, the nun got up and came to her. "Don't be afraid," she said quietly. "This is a place of peace and goodness. No one can hurt you when you are in here." In a daze, Marlene allowed the nun to guide her into the chapel. Sister Renee was right. The Chapel was so quiet, that Marlene could hear her own breathing and her heart beats. She put her hand to her heart afraid that the nun might hear the beats too. Sister Renee's whispered words seemed to echo back. Marlene had heard hymns being sung in the Chapel, but she had only seen the place from a distance. It was strange to be inside and see figure-sized statues in the corners. Her eyes fell on the huge cross behind a raised platform, holding a huge table with a form like a little house. Sister Renee whispered, "That is the altar. And the cross is similar to the one I wear around my neck, except that it is many times bigger." Then she introduced the statues to her. They were that of Joseph the earthly father of Jesus, St Christopher carrying the baby Jesus on his back, St Patrick, the patron saint of Ireland, and a few others. What awed the girl most, was the picture of the beautiful lady holding an infant in her arms. "That," Sister Renee explained, "Is the symbol of which our school is named. That is the Virgin Mary carrying her baby Jesus. Can you tell me the name of this school?" Marlene whispered in reply, "Convent of the Holy Infant Jesus." Sister Renee smiled and nodded. What Marlene did not understand was how could Jesus, who was supposed to be the son of God have a mother and a father like everyone else. Sister Renee could see that she was puzzled, but there was not much time left if Marlene were to be in time for her bus. She said, "We have to leave now." As they walked out, Marlene observed that for the second time the nun dipped her hand into the bowl hanging by the door, and then made the sign of the cross. She looked into the bowl and saw that it contained only water. As they hurried towards the gate where all buses waited, Marlene asked about the water. Sister Renee answered her questions with a short story of the miraculous water of Lourdes. She had time to explain how the water cured millions of people from all kinds of diseases.

Thankfully, they arrived just as the bus was pulling up. Marlene's elder sister, Lily, who was now in the Sixth grade and last year of Primary school, was getting worried for Marlene. The other three younger girls who were almost of the same age, Anna, Theresa and Jan were also looking hard for Marlene. They were in their first year. They shouted to Lily when they saw Marlene and Sister Renee hurrying towards them. After Sister Renee left, Lily said, "Don't tell me you got into trouble again. Papa is ill and you should not worry him too much." Marlene had other things on her mind to argue, so like the others she climbed into the bus. The bus journey was about half an hour, and it was an unusual situation to see Marlene sitting quietly and looking out of the window. Once in a while, she gazed at the clouds. They were scattered, but she could still picture the old man. However, her thoughts were filled with the story of the Holy Water. If only she could get hold of some of the water. Her father too could be cured. But he had always warned them not to be influenced by the nuns and their religion. He would be angry with her if he found out that she had gone into the chapel and listened intensely to the things Sister Renee told her. Somehow, Marlene felt convinced that whatever Sister Renee said was true, and most of all she wanted to believe in the curing power of the Holy Water. She would be the happiest girl if her father could walk and throw her up in the air. She missed the activities they did so badly. She must find a way to get that water, and then make him drink it. He need not know what water it was.

As usual, Malam was sitting propped up with pillows on his bed to greet his four girls returning from school. Each one of them would go up to kiss him on the cheeks and chat a little about their day. Marlene was no exception, except that she spent more time with him than the others. This day she looked into the cup and jug of water beside his bed with all kinds of pills. She asked, "Have you taken your medicine." Jokingly Malam said, "Not yet Doctor." Marlene's little mind began to work fast and she said, "Oh Papa, let me be your doctor. Let me give you your medicine every day when I come back from school." "Well, it is a little early. You will have to take your lunch first. Yes, I would like you to be my little doctor. You can put the pills in my mouth and then pour the water into the cup for me." Marlene kissed him and said, "OK, wait until I come back after eating. I love you." She was sitting on his bed. She jumped down with a secret glee in her heart. Marlene never left her father without the words: I love you. Her father's answer was always a flying kiss after her. Everyone in the family had accepted the special bond between Marlene and her father. He was a sick man, and they know that Marlene's presence made Malam happy. Ah Leng was still not very compromising about the biased love Malam had for Marlene, but she had stopped showing it since Malam's illness. Alex and Marlene were still at each other. There was really no love lost between the two, and that too became an acceptable fact in the family. Alex was three years older and bigger than Marlene, but he had refrained from physical abuse of his sister. So as long as only words were used, the adults said nothing. It was obvious that Marlene needed no help. She could hold her own against her half brother.

CHAPTER 27

That night was a night of beautiful dreams for Marlene. She dreamt that when she got up to go down to wash and get ready for school, her father was waiting for her at the bottom of the stairs. He was standing without a walking stick, and his arms were extended for her to jump from the top of the stairs into them. Somehow her legs were stuck and she was not able to move. Then she saw the beautiful lady from the chapel. She smiled at her and also extended her arms to Marlene. Still Marlene could not move. Then a cloud flooded the room where her father and the Virgin Mary were standing. She looked hard, and saw the clouds forming the face of the old man, who she now knew as God. He moved towards her and swept her off her feet. She was floating in the clouds with him. She looked down and saw only her father this time. His arms were still extended, and she said to God, "Please let me go to him." Just as God was putting her down into her father's arms she heard her mother's voice. "Marlene, it is time to get up." With great disappointment, she realized that all that had just happened was only a dream. She got up reluctantly, but the first thing she did was to run downstairs to where her father slept. He was still fast asleep. However, she went up to his bed and planted a kiss on his cheek. "I love you," she said quietly and walked away to get ready for school. On the way to school, she made up her mind that she would ask Sister Renee to tell her more about the story of Our Lady of Lourdes.

As soon as the bus stopped, she was the first one to get off, and she wasted no time running into the Convent grounds. She must find Sister Renee before the bell rang for morning assembly. She saw the nun walking towards the assembly ground, and she ran to her. Sister Renee saw Marlene running towards her and stopped. When Marlene caught up with her she asked, "What is it dear? You seemed to be in such a hurry. Is everything alright?" While catching her breath Marlene nodded, and then half panting she said, "Sister, can you tell me the whole story of the Holy Water?" Sister Renee looked at the watch on her wrist and said, "We have no time now, but if you can give up your break, we can meet outside the Chapel again." Marlene nodded eagerly and went off to join the gathering girls getting ready for the bell to ring.

This time Sister Renee did not invite Marlene into the Chapel for there were other nuns saying their prayers. Instead she drew the girl into one of the empty classrooms nearby, and when they were both seated, Sister Renee told the story of the significance of the Holy Water. Long ago, in a grotto near Lourdes in southern France, the Virgin Mary, mother of Jesus appeared to a young peasant girl by the name of Bernadette. She appeared to this girl several times, and revealed herself as the Immaculate Conception. She asked the girl to tell the people to build a chapel on the site where she was standing. No one believed Bernadette when she told them of the apparitions of the Holy Lady. So one day, the Holy Lady told the girl to drink from a fountain in the grotto. There was no fountain, but when Bernadette dug at a spot designated by the Holy Lady, a spring began to flow. Then when people saw the spring, they cheered and began to drink the water. Miraculously, the sick that drank from it became well, the blind began to see, the crippled began to walk, and more people with all kinds of sickness and handicaps came to Lourdes to drink that water from the Grotto.

Marlene was enraptured as she listened. At the end of the story, she asked, "Is the water in the chapel the water from the spring?" Sister Renee smiled and replied, "No, but the water is blessed by the priest, and it signifies the water from the spring. The spring still exists and has curing powers for the believers." "Can the water from the chapel cure my father who cannot walk?" Sister Renee's eyes dimmed with unshed tears for this helpless girl who truly loved her father very dearly. "God works in mysterious ways. If you believe that it can help your father, it will. But, it may not be the way you want it to. Trust in God, my child." Then she stood up and said, "Wait here for me and I will give you a bottle of water to take home." Marlene was so happy. Somehow the nun had read her thoughts. She waited impatiently, and after what seemed ages to her, the nun came back with a small bottle containing the Holy Water. Marlene took it carefully and asked if she could go to class to keep it in her school bag so that no one could see it. No pupils were allowed to be in their classes during Recess, so Sister Renee accompanied the girl to their classroom. As they walked she said, "I am here for you. If ever you feel angry and want to beat up someone, come and look for me. If there is anything you need to tell someone, I too will lend you my ear. But remember that I would be happy if you allow the good girl in you out more often. Push the naughty girl away and keep her buried somewhere deep in your body." It was hard for a ten-year old to understand exactly what the nun meant, but Marlene simply presumed that the good nun wants her to be a good girl.

Sister Renee went back to the chapel to pray for Marlene and her father. She was born in a small village in southern France, not too far away from Lourdes where the grotto and the spring water still existed. She was eighteen when she joined the order of the Sacred Heart of Jesus. After ten years of moving from different parts of France, she was surprised to be transferred to a country so far away from home. Like all nuns, she never questioned her superiors, and accepted her posting as the will of God. God had a plan for her. Now as she knelt in the chapel, she was sure that Marlene was the reason why she was sent here. She knelt before the cross and meditated on her vocation. From the very first day that she saw Marlene in her classroom, she was attracted to the girl. Marlene's liveliness, wittiness and intelligence were very appealing to many who knew her. But there were times when the nun noticed the girl sulking and brooding. There were also times when she sensed the girl's temperaments were at their worst. This part of her caused a few of her classmates to dislike and fear her. Using her discretion, she observed the girl without her knowing it, and detected that there was some kind of sadness, pain and loss that the child could not handle. In her prayers, Sister Renee thanked God for giving her the opportunity to help this girl. She would not fail him.

Marlene could not wait for school to be over. When it did, she held on to her school bag, for it carried a very precious bottle. She normally left her bag with one of her sisters, so that she could run to the play ground and play until the school bus came. That day, she just stood around with her four sisters and waited. Lily noticed that Marlene did not leave her bag on the ground. She held on to it the whole fifteen minutes. When they got into the bus, Lily, who always sat beside Marlene asked, "What do you have in your bag? I hope you did not take something that did not belong to you." Marlene shook her head and retorted, "Why do you say that? Have I ever done anything like that before?" "No, but you seem to act strangely these last two days. You used to tell me everything, but now you seem to have a secret and will not share it with me." Marlene respected and loved her older sister, but she was not prepared to tell her about the conversations she had with the nun. Her sister would not understand how Marlene could disobey her father and listen to the stories the nun told her. Seeing that Lily was expecting an answer she said, "I got into trouble yesterday, and I was afraid that I would be sent to Reverend Mother's office. But my teacher let me off and I am trying to be good." She did not want to say more, and Lily decided that as long as Marlene kept out of trouble, it should not matter if she had a secret that she did not want to share.

Marlene got off the bus and ran into the house. She was disappointed to see that her father was not awake. Paini was there to greet them and to tell that they had to be quiet. Malam had a bad spell, and had taken a lot of painkillers which made him drowsy. Marlene's quiet excitement turned to dismay. That meant that he would have taken his medicine already. Paini saw the unhappy look on the girl's face, and having heard the conversation between her and her father yesterday she said, "He still has pills to take later on in the afternoon. You can still be the doctor. Let him sleep for a while more. Get into your house clothes and go into the kitchen for lunch. Then do your homework. I am sure he will wake up by then." Marlene obeyed her. She went into her bedroom and took out the precious bottle of water. She stroked it gently and said softly to it, "Please cure my father." Then she put it back into her bag. Although she was very hungry she could not eat much. Then she went back into the living room where her father slept to check on him. He was still fast asleep, so she went back to her room and did her home-work on the floor. Just as she was finishing, she heard her father's voice. She took the bottle out of her bag and ran downstairs. Paini was helping him to sit up. He saw her and said, "So my doctor has arrived." Marlene nodded happily and climbed on the bed with the bottle. "You see," she said, "I have water ready for you to take your medicine with." He chuckled, "You really mean business don't you." Then Paini handed him the pills, and gave a mug to Marlene to pour the water into it. Marlene shook her head and said, "Papa can drink from the bottle. We don't want to waste any of this water." She almost added 'holy', but managed to swallow that word before it came out.

Marlene watched with growing excitement as her father swallowed the pills and drank the water from the bottle. He was still holding the bottle when he said, "What's next, doctor? Do you want to put your ears close to my heart to hear the beats?" Marlene nodded, and as she did so she whispered, "Do you feel better? Can you move your legs?" Her father chuckled again and said jokingly, "Oh yes, I feel well. You are a very good doctor." Marlene not knowing that her father was joking shouted gleefully, "I knew it will work." She clapped her hands and looked up and said, "Thank you God." The atmosphere changed as soon as she mentioned 'God'. Malam's voice was quite serious when he asked, "Why are you saying such things?" Marlene's joy was so great that she did not notice the tone of voice her father used, so she said happily, "You just drank the holy water and like the story Sister Renee told me, you too are cured." Malam looked at the bottle in his hand and threw it on the floor so hard, that it broke into tiny fragments. Marlene looked at the pieces on the floor, then at her father. Realization dawned on her that her father was very angry with her. By now the commotion brought all the four women from the kitchen. Keng Yi saw her daughter sitting on Malam's bed with her mouth open and her eyes brimming with tears. She was in a state of shock, and Malam was having difficulty to breathe. Just as Keng Yi was reaching out to lift her daughter off the bed, Marlene jumped down and cried hysterically as she ran up the stairs to her room. While the other three wives took care of their husband, Keng Yi ran after her daughter.

Malam was holding on to his heart, and the wives thought he was having a stroke. Gary who was now the eldest child at home, took it on himself to get the family doctor. He cycled as fast as he could since there was no telephone in the house. When the doctor arrived in a small mini-car, the wives had managed to calm Malam down, but his heart beat and pulse rate were still too fast. The doctor examined him and said, "Well, he is in no immediate danger, but another excitement of any sort could be fatal. I shall give him an injection to normalize his heart beat. Let him have some quiet and peace." After the injection, Malam began to breathe normally, and he was getting very sleepy. Keng Yi was still upstairs with Marlene, so before he went off, he gestured Paini to him. She put her ears close to his mouth and Malam whispered weakly, "Please tell Marlene that I still love her. I am not angry with her, but the ..." He did not want to finish his sentence, but Paini knew that he wanted to say either 'the Convent' or 'the nun'. She nodded and kissed his forehead. "You rest and don't worry." The doctor left with the assurance that they should not hesitate to call on him if Malam's situation got worse. He was a kindly man, and had been the family doctor for a long time. Paini asked him how much his fee would be. He just shook his head and said, "Regard me as a close friend ready to help." Then he said again, "Please make sure that there is no more excitement of any kind for him. He is very frail, and his heart is not as strong as it used to be." Paini nodded and thanked the doctor.

Marlene was sobbing her heart out, and in between sobs she told her mother everything that happened in school from when she was fighting. Keng Yi's greatest worry was that her daughter would again blame herself for her father's relapse. She could not imagine how this ten-year old would handle the blame. She must be able to persuade her that she was innocent of all that happened. "Listen Marlene, it is not your fault. Your father has been very sick for a long time. You did what you did because you love him. He is not angry with you. He is angry with himself for sending you to a Catholic school. I can hear the doctor downstairs, so everything will be alright. You know that your father loves you more than any one else. If you blame yourself you will hurt him all the more. For now, just stay in our room and read some books. I am sure that when he feels better he will want to see you. You also look very tired, so read your favorite books and try to sleep a little. When you wake up you will see that everything is alright." Marlene's sobs were subsiding as Keng Yi talked. "Papa told me that he felt better when he drank the water and I believed him," she told her mother. Keng Yi smoothed her daughter's ruffled hair and said, "Well you were both playing a game." Marlene seemed to understand, but she did not lose faith in the Holy Water. She kept it to herself. She also remembered the words of the nun 'God works in mysterious ways'. When her mother left her, she closed the door and knelt beside the bed and whispered, "Please God, don't be angry with my father for throwing down the bottle. Dear Lady of Lourdes please help my father to walk again." Malam slept long, and was still sleeping when Keng Yi brought food for her daughter. She did not want Marlene to be taunted by her half-brothers, especially Alex, who had already voiced that Marlene was bad luck for the whole family. Marlene did not have a nap, so she was quite tired after dinner. She slept almost immediately on the same bed with her sister Anna and brother Michael. Mona slept on a smaller bed with Keng Yi who was still downstairs with the other wives. They were all making cakes for sale the next day. David was sitting close to his father reading the newspaper. Gary and Alex were playing some card games in their room. All the other children went to bed early, although the next day was a Saturday. David would look up from his papers to glance at his father every few minutes. Although Malam's breathing was quite regular, his face was ghostly pale.

Marlene was awakened from her dreamless sleep by the gentle shaking of her mother. She opened the eyes, and in the darkness saw her mother's silhouette above her. She bent down and whispered, "Your father wants to see you." Marlene was wide awake and needed no persuasion to get down to her father. She went downstairs to the living room, the only lighted one. She did not know what time it was, but guessed that it must be close to midnight. Actually it was three in the morning. The other three wives and David were gathered round Malam's bed. He was sitting propped up on a few pillows. When he saw Marlene, he extended his arms towards her. She ran to him and buried her face on his chest. Everyone watched quietly as father and daughter exchanged their emotions of bond and love without words. Then Malam tilted Marlene's head and looked into her wet eyes saying, "I am not angry with you. I am also not angry with your nun anymore. I want you to tell me her name." At first Marlene was reluctant to do so, unsure of her father's intention. Malam saw her hesitance and continued, "I want to know more about her God." Marlene's face lit up. She did not voice her thoughts this time, but she believed that the Virgin Mary had answered her prayers. So she said, "It is my class teacher, Sister Renee." Then Malam directed his voice to David and instructed, "You heard it. Go and beg her to come and see me." David looked at his watch and said, "But Papa, it is three o'clock. No one is awake." Paini went to David and whispered, "Do what your father wants. I am sure the nuns will not refuse the wish of a dying man." David shrugged and said, "Alright Papa, I shall try." David went to his motor bike and rode like the wind in the darkness of the night. Then Malam said to Marlene who was still in his arms, "You better get out of your pajamas to greet our guest."

As the family waited, Malam fell asleep but woke up every few minutes to ask if David had returned with the nun. Marlene sat on her mother's lap and also went to sleep. She woke up each time she heard her father's voice. It was almost daylight when they heard the roar of David's motorbike, followed by a small black car. Three people stepped out of the car. A Chinese priest dressed in a black robe, who was also the driver. Then two nuns in their white habits walked behind the priest. Marlene ran to Sister Renee and held her hand, then recognizing the other as the Reverend Mother, she remembered her manners and said, "Good morning Reverend Mother." The regal lady smiled at her and Sister Renee winked at her. But before they entered the house, Sister Renee said to the priest, "This is Marlene, the little girl I told you about." The friendly priest took Marlene's small hand in his and said, "I am so glad to meet a brave girl like you." Marlene did not understand why he said that she was a brave girl, but she was also wondering why he and Reverend Mother came along, when her father just wanted to see Sister Renee. Once inside, David introduced them to his father who took their hands each in a strong handshake. To Sister Renee, he said, "I thank you for the Holy Water. You seemed to convince my daughter that your God is the one and only true God. Maybe you can tell me more about Him." Then the priest intervened, "I represent God and I too can help you to understand. It would be better if we are both alone." On hearing this, Paini invited the nuns to have some cakes in the kitchen. Everyone followed Paini into the kitchen, Marlene as well, for she wanted to be close to the nun, whose love she felt and reciprocated.

The nuns were well trained in the Malay language, so the four women chatted comfortably with them. The nuns already knew of this big family. It was no secret that Malam was the only man who could keep his four wives under one roof. They also knew how he fell from wealth to poverty. However, their conversations in the kitchen were trivial and light. Marlene was now sitting on Sister Renee's lap. There was no mention about the Holy Water, and Marlene was thankful for it. She did not want the outburst between her father and her to be revealed. Only God knew about it, and had forgiven her father already. Everyone was getting tired as they waited for the priest to finish his talk with Malam. Marlene was about to fall asleep again in the arms of the nun, when they heard Malam's angry voice. "Your God is a tyrant if he does not let me keep my wives. If he is full of love then he should understand what love is all about. Get out, take your God with you, and tell those nuns never to talk to my children about Him ever again. I shall have to remove them from the Convent." By now, his four women were by his side trying to pacify him. They remembered the doctor's words, and they begged the priest and nuns to leave immediately. Malam was panting hard and shaking. Keng Yi discreetly took the weeping Marlene to the bedroom. She comforted her daughter saying, "Go to sleep. You have nothing to worry about. It was your father's wish to see the nun and he allowed the priest to talk to him. So whatever happens now has nothing to do with you." Marlene did not feel comforted, and when her mother left her she sobbed until weariness overcame her, and she fell into a deep and well deserved sleep. Thankfully, Malam did not have a relapse. Paini gave him the pills the doctor had left, and he took them and went into a deep sleep. Everyone else went to sleep except Keng Yi. She had to take the cakes to the coffee shops before people start coming in for breakfast. They could not afford to have a day of no revenue coming in.

When Keng Yi came back tired after taking a few buses to deliver the cakes to some coffee shops, the younger children who had slept through the night were waking up. Gary, who got up for a short while because of the commotion and went back to sleep, was up. Seeing how tired Keng Yi was said, "Go and try to sleep. I shall take care of the little ones. Anna can play with Mona in your room. I shall take the others for a long walk and maybe spend some time in the playground." Keng Yi was happy that Gary was growing up to be a nice and sensible young man. She was glad that Marlene was still fast asleep, so that would keep her away from Alex. Thus Gary packed up the cakes that were left for breakfast, and told the children to keep as quiet as they could because their father was quite sick last night and all the adults did not go to sleep until early the next morning. Anna was contented to be in the same room with her sleeping sister Marlene and her mother, who after feeding Mona went off to sleep. She and Mona sat on the floor and played with some toys quietly. Gary was out with the other children until almost noon and when he came back almost everyone was up except for Marlene and her mother. Malam too was awake but was in great pain. Paini and Cheng Mee were massaging his legs while Ah Leng was in the kitchen cooking. As the two wives were working on his legs, Malam began to cough and had difficulty breathing. David decided to get the doctor back. The doctor examined Malam and was angry when he heard about the excitement in the early hours of the morning. He took Paini aside and said, "I have warned you about his condition. There is nothing to be done but hope for the best. Your husband's reluctance to go into the hospital has made his condition worse. The Tuberculosis is getting into his lungs. I hate to say this, but he could go anytime now." The doctor knew that he was not being kind, but at the same time, he wanted the family to be prepared. He knew that Malam's reason for not wanting to go into the hospital was finance. Malam had a big family and he did not want to leave them penniless. Paini held back her tears, but as soon as the doctor left, she broke down in Cheng Mee's arms and told her what the doctor said.

That evening when the school-going children were in bed, David and the four wives sat in the kitchen for a big discussion. John would have been there too, but he had to stay at the veterinary that weekend as there was a lot to do. Paini told everyone what the doctor had said. The other three women felt their hearts breaking, but they just kept quiet. David looked at them and his admiration for his father grew. "If I could find just one woman to love me like how these four love my father, my life will be complete." David was not too happy when his father married Cheng Mee. His resentment towards his father grew when he married Keng Yi. But he kept it all to himself, and never said a word to anyone about it. However, when he saw how his father sacrificed his business to save his children from the kidnappers, his love and admiration for the man returned. When no one said anything, David stood up and said, "Father is going into the hospital. We should not worry about the future. Right now father's health and life matter most. If we have to spend every penny that we have left, let it be so." His mother looked at him shocked, but the other three women looked up to him as the good son. They did not say anything though, so David continued, "I shall go out and find a phone to talk to Ai Li and Jo Lin. Their financial support will help. Then after school tomorrow, I shall go to the doctor to get an admittance letter from him. An ambulance will take him to the hospital." Paini finally spoke again, "I only hope that you can convince your father to go to the hospital." "Well, all of us should." Then David left the kitchen followed by the four wives.

Surprisingly, Malam seemed to be awake and alert. When he saw David he said, "Help me to sit up son." Then seeing his wives, he jokingly said, "Hey women, I am hungry." Ah Leng went back into the kitchen and heated up his food. It was a steamed chicken drumstick with ginger and green onions served on soft cooked white rice with some garden vegetables. Malam's meal was different from what everyone else had. He was not aware of it, but everyone's meal was very simple. They had a lot of rice, enough vegetables, and occasionally some meat or fish. Whenever Malam had the appetite to eat, he would get enough meat and vegetables. The wives watched as he ate hungrily. It was a long time since he had such a good appetite. Then he asked about everyone. He did not mention anything about the eventful happening early that morning. Seeing that his father was in such a good mood, David decided that it was a good time to tell him what they all thought was best for him. He listened quietly, but Paini sensed that his mind was already made up. She only hoped that he would not get angry. He did not. When David was finished with his proposal, Malam told them all to find a chair and sit down. Keng Yi sat on his bed at his foot, Paini sat on the chair beside him. David pulled two chairs from the dining table for Ah Leng and Cheng Mee, and stood behind them. Malam drew in a deep breath and said, "What I am going to say is final, and there should be no more discussions after this. I agree with you David that the hospital is where I should be. But that is not where I belong. I am here and I have you all with me. Whether my life ends tonight or tomorrow, I shall die a happy man, for I have spent my last minutes with the people I love most of all. Each day when I am awake and hear the voices and laughter of my wives and children, I am happy. I don't want this happiness to be taken away. The hospital may provide me medications to ease my pain, and maybe give me an extra few days of life, but I'd rather die today in the company of my loved ones." Malam sounded like the man they knew a few years ago, in command of everybody. No one said a word and Malam continued, "Maybe it is time for you all to prepare yourself that I may leave you in the near future. But until then, bear with me and each other." The wives knew what he meant by preparation. Black attires had to be sewn for the whole family, and a coffin had to be ordered. As Malam sank a little down on his propped pillow, David and Paini helped him to lie down comfortably. Paini whispered in his ears, "Your wish is our command." She gave him his medicine, and left to help clear the kitchen and make cakes for the next day.

When Marlene was at school the next day, she avoided eye contact with Sister Renee. She did not know what to believe any more. Her father was in a worse condition than before. She had no chance to even say goodbye to him on her way out to catch the school bus. Whether he was fast asleep or not, she had no idea. All she was told was that her father needed peace and quiet, and they should leave the house as quietly as they could. Her head was buried in her exercise books trying to solve a mathematical problem, when she felt a firm hand on her little shoulder. She knew it was the hand of her class teacher. She did not look up, and hoped that the nun would just continue her rounds. But the nun bent down and whispered in her ears, "Don't lose faith my child. God is looking after you." Marlene still did not look up, and she was relieved when Sister Renee moved away from her desk. During recess time, instead of playing with her friends as she normally did, she kept to herself. She felt lonely and lost. Although no one at home mentioned the incident with the Holy Water, she felt that everyone blamed her for upsetting her father. Her mother had made sure that she kept away from the taunting Alex, but she had to face him somehow, and this time she would not be able to defend herself when he accused her of being a trouble maker and causing their father to suffer. She wished that she could find a place to hide. She did not want to go home, neither did she want to be in school. At the same time she cannot bear to be too far away from her father. Thankfully, Sister Renee did not show up in class after the break. The rest of the day was taken over by a relief teacher. That was unusual, but Marlene was glad. The rest of the day in school was relaxing for her, and she did not think anymore about the incident with the Holy Water.

A shock awaited Marlene when she got off the bus in front of her house. There were three cars parked on the driveway. The small black one, she presumed belonged to the family doctor, and the other two belonged to her married sisters. The first thought that came into her mind was that something bad had happened to her father. She stood at the gate not daring to face the tragedy, while Lily and her three younger sisters ran towards the house. She just stood there for what seemed ages. Then she saw someone in white approaching her. It was Sister Renee, her mouth held a smile and her eyes behind her dark rimmed glasses were twinkling. Her legs relaxed and she ran towards the open arms of the nun. "Didn't I tell you that God is with you?" Marlene heard her say, but she was still puzzled. All she could ask was, "Is my father all right?" "Come in, he is waiting for you." The black car belonged to the priest after all, and he was sitting on a chair with Malam. Everyone was gathered in the living room.

310

Marlene was so happy to see her father smiling, that she did not notice that her mother, Cheng Mee, and Ah Leng weeping quietly. Marlene went directly to her father's bed and he said, "My darling, I have made up my mind to be a Catholic. I do believe in God and the Catholic Church." The priest nodded when Marlene looked at him. All her young mind could think of was that her father had been cured by the Holy Water, so she took her father's hand and said, "Get up and walk. Show me." Sister Renee then put her hand on Marlene's shoulder and said, "His soul is saved. Remember that God works in mysterious ways. Go to your mother. She needs you." For the first time, Marlene felt the sadness that hung over the rest of the family. David stood at a distance from everyone, and looked outside with his hands folded. Alex and Gary were still in school. Jo Lin had her arms round her weeping mother, and her adopted sister Jan. Lily and Theresa stood beside the tearful Cheng Mee. Ai Li stood beside Paini. There were no tears in their eyes but they both looked very sad. Keng Yi was carrying Mona in her arms and Michael and Anna were standing on both sides of her. When Marlene saw her mother in tears she went to her and asked, "Why are you all crying?" Her mother answered, "Your father had chosen your God over us." Marlene could not comprehend her words. Again it was Sister Renee who had to explain everything to her.

The Catholic Church only allows a man to have one wife. He could only marry again if his wife died. The same went for the woman. Thus, when Malam chose to be a Catholic, only his first wife could remain with him. The others would have to go away. His children were his and they could remain with him. Marlene was shocked when she heard this, but Sister Renee managed to convince her when she said, "This is only the beginning. All the women who loved him will be with him again in the next world. I am sure that they all loved him enough to follow his new Faith. You must not feel sad for your mother. You will still be able to see her whenever you want. You must support your father, and help him to remain strong and firm in what he has chosen to believe. I know you can do that." Marlene looked at her mother and then at her father, who was still talking to the priest. She loved her mother, but she felt closer to her father. Right now, he mattered more to her than anybody else. Even though her father could still not walk, she could see that his face held a radiance that had disappeared since he became ill. There was a clear sign of happiness in his eyes. She felt happy for him, but at the same time, she hurt to see her mother so sad. At the tender age of ten, Marlene learned to set her priority. Her father's well-being and happiness came first, and she expected that of every one who loved him.

Marlene had to close her eyes and ears to the scene of farewell at her father's bed. The priest and the nun waited outside to show the way to David who would use Ai Li's car to drive his mother and two stepmothers to the mission house, where they would be temporarily housed. It was a pitiful scene, as each said tender good-byes to their husband. He promised each and every one of them that he would be waiting in the next world for them. Malam's eyes were as wet as theirs, but he kept his voice steady. The children cried too when their mothers kissed them, and told them to look after their father. Marlene was shaking when her mother came to her and said, "I love you and you must believe me that you have done nothing wrong. This is destiny, and no one can change it. Try to visit me everyday after school with your brother and sister." Keng Yi took Mona with her, because Paini would have too much to manage on her own. Malam sat up on his bed and waved at the departing cars. His heart was breaking, but his mind was still set on becoming a Catholic. The priest would return in the evening with more nuns, and some people from his parish, to perform the Sacraments of Baptism, Holy Eucharist, Confirmation and lastly the Sacrament of Matrimony to Paini. It was not normal practice to perform all those sacraments on the same day, but Malam was an extraordinary man, and all those who came into his path recognized that, including the priest.

CHAPTER 28

Earlier that morning, David decided that he should inform his two sisters of his proposal to commit their father into the hospital, and hoped that they could change his mind. He called them before he went to teach, but when they arrived, Malam had asked Keng Yi to take the bus to get the priest. He needed to talk to him again. Keng Yi could not refuse him, so she did exactly as she was told. The priest then rang the Convent and the Reverend Mother sent Sister Renee with him. Ai Li and Jo Lin had no chance to talk to their father for they arrived almost at the same time as the priest, Keng Yi and the nun. Malam wanted them all to hear his decision when he told the priest that he wanted to be converted, and that he was prepared to give up his three wives for the love of God. David was still teaching, so it was only Ai Li and Jo Lin who voiced their strong opinions that their father was not thinking properly. He looked at his daughters sternly and said, "I am not able to walk, but my mind is strong. I know what I want, and as your father, I expect you to accept my decisions. Jo Lin ran out and drove her car to David's school. He managed to get permission to leave school early, but he too was reprimanded by his father, when he insisted that his father was wrong to give up the women he had loved for such a long time for a God that he did not know. When the three women left, Jo Lin took off, and David said that he would not be there that evening. He told Paini who tried to persuade him to stay back, "I cannot bear to see my father making a fool of himself." Ai Li knew that her mother would need help, so she stayed back to help with the younger children

At seven o'clock that evening, Paini had washed and dressed Malam in the same suit that he used on the day of their wedding. The top hanged loosely around his shoulders, because he had lost a lot of weight. The trousers too were loose, but it did not matter as Malam could not get up. Paini too put on her wedding dress which was a bit tight around the waist, but she managed to put it on anyway. When she looked into the mirror, her eyes watered as she thought of how happy and young she was when she first wore the sarong Kebaya. Once again, she would know how it felt like to be his one and only wife. Then she made sure that all the children were dressed in their best. While looking for a suitable dress to wear, Marlene noticed a pile of black clothes at the very top shelf of her mother's cupboard. She shuddered as she realized what the clothes were for. Then her heart lightened when she told herself, "God will make my father better. We won't need those clothes for a long time." All were dressed and ready when a few cars arrived. There was not enough space for all the cars, so some were parked on the side of the main road. The priest had a white robe over his normal habit, and a purple band with some Latin words sewed in gold thread, hanged around his neck. He led the procession with two altar boys holding white candles in their hands, as they entered the gate. Five nuns followed behind him, and close to them were five other church goers, two men and three women.

It was a simple ceremony. The priest and the two altar boys, now with lighted candles in their hands, stood close to Malam's bed. Malam sat upright propped up by pillows. One of the men, who was chosen to be Malam's godfather, stood at the head of the bed. The nuns and the other four people stood behind the priest, holding small black books with an open page. Malam's remaining family stood quietly in the background, and watched as the priest said prayers and asked questions. The priest words were loud and clear. "Do you believe in God the Father, God the Son and God the Holy Ghost?" and names of certain saints were mentioned, and the Blessed Virgin Mary was one of them. To all those questions, Malam replied "I do." Those two words were said a few times as loud as the priest, and with great conviction. The priest had suggested that Malam took the name of Moses, who had a big family too. At the end, the priest poured water on Malam's head and said, "I baptize you Moses, in the name of The Father, The Son and The Holy Ghost." Hymns were sung to conclude the baptismal ceremony. Then the Sacrament of Eucharist was performed, with the priest taking a drink of wine from the Chalice before passing it on to Malam who took it in both hands and drunk from it, as the priest said, "Drink for this in my blood." Then he took a round piece of flat baked flour and broke it into two parts. He swallowed one half, and gave the other half to Malam saying, "Body of Christ." Malam's "Amen," before he extended his tongue to receive the other half was just as clear. Then followed the Sacrament of Confirmation, which was quite similar to the Holy Eucharist, but more prayers were dedicated to The Holy Ghost. All these three Sacraments were performed in less than an hour.

Then the time came that Paini in the background was waiting for. The Reverend Mother, and Sister Renee went to her and led her to her husband's bed. Joyous hymns were sung by the holy people, and even the prayers seemed lighter than those for the other three Sacraments. Paini stood beside her husband, and both their right hands were holding on to each other. Malam's grasp was firm on her hand and Paini wished that she could close her eyes, and allow the years that had passed to disappear. The voice of the priest brought her back to reality as he asked, "Moses, will you take this woman to be your lawful wife, to hold and to cherish, in sickness or in health, till death do you part," Malam's grip on Paini's hand tightened as he said strongly, "I do". The same words were repeated to Paini, and her eyes dimmed as she looked at the man she had always loved and answered with her heart, "I do." The ceremony ended with applause and handshakes. But the priest knew that for Malam it was an exhausting period, so he bade everyone to take their leave. Before he left he told Paini, "Any time at all, I shall be at your beck or call. Don't hesitate to send for me if your husband needs me." Paini nodded and thanked everyone for coming. Sister Renee had taken Marlene aside when everyone else was saying goodbye. She said, "If only you know how great a deed you have done for God and your father. He will always be there for you. God bless you and sleep in his peace my child." Then before she left she added, "Reverend Mother has given you and your sisters, permission to stay home tomorrow." She winked and left with a flying kiss for Marlene.

Marlene woke up with a start. Michael was crying for their mother. She felt a sudden sadness when she realized that her mother was not there for them. Anna was beginning to stir, and as Marlene was trying to calm Michael down, Anna asked, "Why do they have to send Mama away? She is our mother." Marlene had no answers, but she now felt that she was responsible for her two younger siblings. Michael continued to cry for their mother, and then Ai Li entered the unlocked room and sat on the bed. Marlene was grateful to her when she took Michael in her arms and said gently to him, "Papa need to be as much alone as possible. Second Mother and Third Mother are also not here. If you are a good boy, I will take all of you after breakfast to visit them." The thrill of going in a car pacified Michael. Then Ai Li helped Marlene to dress him up and then told them all that their father was waiting to have breakfast with them." Her words took Marlene by surprise, and when she winked, Marlene thought that she was joking. But when Marlene went to the kitchen from her room, nothing was laid on the kitchen table. Paini then came in looking happy, and said that breakfast was being served in the dining room.

Marlene was overcome with joy when she saw her father's leg dangling from his bed. He was sitting by the side of his bed, and his legs were not under any blanket. Marlene dared not hope for more, but when Malam asked Paini for his walking stick, she had to pinch herself to make sure that she was not dreaming. Gary and Alex were at school, so it was only the girls, Michael, Paini and Ai Li who witnessed Malam's first walk after so many years of being bed-ridden. Ai Li and Paini helped Malam out of his bed, and with also the help of his waking stick, he managed to take at least five steps towards the table where his children were sitting and looking at him in awe. Marlene had chosen the seat closest to him, and as the ladies held on to him as he sat down slowly, he gave her a wink. Thankfully there were no cakes that day. Everyone was sick of having the same thing for breakfast everyday. Paini and Ai Li had cooked porridge, which was rice with more water than usual, to be taken with small salted fish, salted eggs and salted vegetables. It was a treat for them to have a warm breakfast. The children were about to dig in when Malam said, "Marlene, on the table beside my bed is a prayer book. There is a prayer before the meal and another one after the meal. You will read the prayer before the meal from this book, and Lily will read the one after the meal." Marlene's heart throbbed with joy as she got up, took the book, and came back to the table. Her voice was shaking as she read, "We thank thee Lord for what we are to receive." Then she and her father made the sign of the cross.

Ai Li kept her promise and took the children to see their mothers, but Marlene wanted to stay back. Although Malam went back to lie in bed as soon as breakfast was over, she wanted to be there when he got off the bed again. But Paini told her that her father would not be getting out of bed again that day. He should not do too much in one day. So, she squeezed into the small car with her other siblings. The mission home was in the compound of the church. It was a flat low building divided into three partitions, and could hold about four to five people in each one. Each partition had its own entrance. There was a big common kitchen and a bathroom in the building. The bucket system toilet was behind the building. The purpose of the mission house, was to give temporary residence to abused women and their children and sometimes to people who were kicked out of their homes because they could not afford to pay their rents. The longest stay allowed in the house was three months. After that, with the help of the priests and good Catholics, they had to find other homes. Malam's three wives could have gone back to their own relatives if one of the blocks had not been free. They were glad that they could be close to their children and their husband in case anything happened to him. Thus they were prepared to share the humble dwelling with each other. All three women were overjoyed to see their children, who blabbed about how their father sat with them at breakfast. None of them realized how glad their mothers were for the man they loved, but broken hearted that they were not there with him on that special morning. The children visited for more than two hours, and Ai Li said that since her father was out of danger, she was going home that same day. Michael wanted to stay back with his mother and refused to get back into the car. So they left Michael with Keng Yi and Mona. Marlene promised to come back with his clothes after school the next day.

When Ai Li took leave of her father she said, "I am glad to see you so well. Your wives sent their love." Malam felt an ache in his heart when she said that, but he replied without showing his emotion, "I miss them, but God is great and I have to obey him." Then he closed his eyes and pretended to sleep. He thought of each one of them, and there was no regret in his heart, that they came into his life and gave him wonderful children. He then prayed to the God that he had surrendered his soul to, "Please forgive me for still loving them. Look after them and all my children." His eyes were still closed. When the children came back, Marlene was disappointed to see him fast asleep. But she soon got over her disappointment, and went out to play with the others, until Paini called them in for lunch. Malam did not get out of his bed, and remembering what Paini had said, Marlene accepted that. But she was happy when Malam called all his children including the boys, to kiss and hug before they went to bed. He had a special word for each and every one of them, and they all looked happy when they left his bed. To Marlene he said, "My dearest child, you have shown me the way to God. No matter where I am, I shall always be with you. If I am not with you in person, my spirit will always be there. I love you and will never stop loving you." At this point all Marlene understood was that her father loved her and would never leave her. She kissed him and said, "I am so glad that you are better. I love you too."

Paini, who was not used to going early to bed any more since they started the cake making business, decided to stay close to her husband. She lit a candle and did some patching. She would have to wake him up at midnight to give him his medicine. In the dim light of the candle, between stitching, she would look up and see the serene look on her husband's face. His breathing was regular and he seemed to be sleeping quite peacefully. She felt sad that her sisters were not here to share her joy of watching him take his first steps, after almost two years of not leaving his bed. She had been heart- broken when he took Ah Leng as his second wife, but after that, it did not hurt her as much when Cheng Mee and Keng Yi came into their lives. There were times, when she felt a tinge of jealousy towards the youngest wife, but she reconciled herself to the fact that she had his love all for herself for a long period of time. Keng Yi never had that opportunity. She remembered his mother's words: Malam had a heart big enough to love many. She was right, he could love and love again without unloving the person who was already in his heart. Then she thought about his children and his special bond to Keng Yi's eldest daughter. That bond had caused him to give up Buddhism, which he had practiced all his life, for a new religion. Then glancing at him and seeing how peaceful he was, she thought to herself, "Maybe this was the right path. He seemed to be at peace with himself." Her thoughts were broken when he stirred and opened his eyes. He called her name in a whisper, and Paini laid down her sewing and went to him.

"It is not yet time for your medicine," she said gently. He tried to say something but had difficulty voicing his words. It was then that Paini realized something was wrong. Malam's chest was heaving and he was having difficulty in breathing. At the same time, Paini heard the sound of David's bike. He had a girlfriend, and would spend some evenings with her. It was his usual time to come home. Paini was thankful to see him. He saw her, and knew that something was wrong with his father. Paini turned to him and said, "Go get the doctor." Then David saw his father gesturing him to come closer. David bent down and his father managed to whisper, "The priest." David wasted no time. He took his bike out again and went first to the doctor, then drove to the church. The priest was still working in his office, and when he saw David's pale face, he said, "I shall be there in a few minutes." He was there before the doctor, and the priest knew that the end was near. He had brought with him the special oil for the last Sacrament. He whispered to Malam that he was going to perform the Sacrament of Extreme Unction on him. Malam could only nod. The priest then placed a rosary in his clasped hands. Just then the doctor came in. Without acknowledging the priest, he went to Malam, and took his pulse. Then he took out the instrument to hear his heart beat. He did not say anything but moved aside to let the priest finish his task. Paini looked at him, and her heart went cold when the doctor shook his head sadly. When the priest had finished anointing Malam's forehead with the holy oil, he turned to Paini and said, "He is still breathing. I think he is not willing to go until he sees someone. Why don't you go and wake up the children." David heard that and knew who he meant.

Marlene was struggling to get out of a beautiful and yet painful dream. She was sitting on the steps leading to the dining room, and watching her father, when she saw the Virgin Mary taking form at the open door of the house, and extending her hand to the sleeping man. Her father opened his eyes and sat up easily. The Lady approached his bed and took his hands.

He was in his white suit, and he got up from the bed and allowed her to guide him towards the door. It was a wonderful apparition. and Marlene just looked on in awe. But as her father left the door she found her voice and said, "Don't leave me here. I want to go with you too." The Lady smiled at her and said, "It is his time. Yours will come one day." Marlene began to cry, and her father was reluctant to leave her. She was still crying in her sleep when David shook her, and she woke up. "Marlene," he said gently, "It is time. Go to Father now." Marlene dried her tears with the sleeve of her pajamas, and followed David downstairs. By now, the commotion had woken up all the children, who left their room sleepily to see what was going on. When Marlene saw the priest and the doctor, she felt a chill down her spine. She ran to her father whose eyes were closed, and called, "Papa, papa, talk to me." It was then that Malam opened his eyes for the last time. He looked at the beloved face close to him and took his last breath. His eyes remained open, so Marlene thought that he was still looking at her. She kept on asking him to talk to her, but his slightly open mouth did not say a word. Then Paini threw herself on his body and started weeping. David pulled Marlene away and closed his father's eyelids. Marlene was still uncertain of what was happening, then when David too started crying, she just looked at the still body of her father and knew that he had died. Marlene went into a corner of the room and sat on the floor, bringing her knees to her chest. While every member of the family wept and cried, she just sat still, without even blinking an eye.

The doctor confirmed that Malam had died ten minutes after midnight on October 20, 1960, eight days before his sixty-fourth birthday. David left with the priest to inform his mother and stepmothers of the bad news. The priest allowed him to use the diocese phone to call Ai Li, Jo Lin and John. When the three wives arrived, they threw themselves on their husband's body and sobbed their hearts out, scolding him for leaving them without saying goodbye, and on the other hand begging him to take them along. Most of all, they voiced their undying love for him. The children continued to cry with their mothers. Then Keng Yi suddenly realized that Marlene was not among the crying children. She looked around and saw her daughter sitting quietly in a corner of the room. She rushed to her daughter, and her heart almost stopped beating, when she realized that Marlene was in shock. She shook Marlene and forced her to look at her. She was about to shout for help when her saw her daughter's eyes blinking. Then, Marlene began to cry, and relieved, Keng Yi buried her daughter's face in her bosom, and allowed the hysterical tears to flow. David, who had returned after making the calls to his siblings, drew up the sheet that his father used as blanket over his head and said, "Let us get dressed for mourning. Soon our relatives and friends will be pouring in. I will have to go with the doctor to sign some papers, and then I will have to make arrangements for the funeral. Please be strong and support me." He directed this speech to all the mothers. He knew that it would be a few hours before his married sisters and their family arrived. He hoped that John would arrive soon to help him with all the preparations. The four women knew that after they had dressed themselves and their children in black, there was a lot of cooking to be done. Sorrow must not take away their responsibility towards making sure that their late beloved husband has an honorable funeral. When David left, Paini took charge. The four women washed the body of their husband, and dressed him up in a white shirt, his favorite tie, and the cream suit that he used when they took the family picture outside their new mansion. When they were finished, they looked at his body, and saw only a man sleeping peacefully. Malam had never lost his good looks even through his illnesses and paralysis. He was ready for the whole world to look at and to admire. David returned from the doctor's office, and when he saw how stately and regal his father looked, his sadness at his loss became unbearable and he started crying without shame and remorse.

John came back early the next day, followed by his married sisters and their family. Jo Lin was beyond control with her grief. She could not forgive herself for not taking leave from her father peacefully. She had left him in anger. It was Paini who managed to calm her saying, "Your father has forgiven you even before he became a Catholic. He has loved you very dearly and his love for you has never changed. Be happy for him. See, how peaceful he looks." Jo Lin looked at her father's still form, and realized that Paini was right. She had never seen him look so well and peaceful, since he had his first back injury. She took his cold hand in hers, and with controlled sobs said, "Papa, I am so sorry for running away like I did. I love you and will never stop loving you." Ai Li too grieved for her father, but she comforted herself that he would not suffer anymore and that he had found his own peace. John cried quietly. He was sure that his father expected his sons to be brave. There was not time for him to hang around. He had to help his older brother with the funeral preparations.

David and John borrowed Ai Li's car and drove to the church, where the priest explained to them about the rites of Christian burial. "First of all," he said to the two young men. "We must consider the three stations. They are the Vigil, which usually takes place in a funeral home, but in this case it will take place in your home. The celebration of the Vigil, is the time for the Catholic community to offer both prayer and consolation to you and your family. They will read and reflect on the word of God, and call upon our God of Mercy through intercessory prayer, and to provide an opportunity for family and friends to recall the memory of their loved one. Other prayers, such as the Rosary, are also encouraged, since they help us to reflect upon the Paschal Mystery, and so lead us to a better understanding and hope at this time of grief." The priest paused, and seeing that the two brothers had no questions, he went on. "The second station is the Mass, which takes place in the church. Celebrating the Mass is the fullest expression of our faith in God's abundant mercy, our hope in the resurrection of the dead, and the love that God has for us, which is not distinguished even by death. Family members usually select the Scripture reading for the mass. In this case, I shall choose an appropriate one. After the Scripture has been read, one of you will cover the casket with the pall, and place Christian symbols on the casket. Here members of the parish community will also participate in the funeral liturgy and join with the bereaved family in the celebration of the funeral rites, by proclaiming the Word, leading the faithful in song, serving at the altar, and helping with the distribution of communion." The priest knew that the two men had no idea, but they were prepared to carry out their father's wishes until he was laid in peace beneath the earth. He knew that he had to help them through it all. Then he continued after a short pause. "The very last station is at the burial site itself. It is called the Rite of Committal. Through the committal of the Body to its place of rest, we express our hope that the deceased will experience the glory of the resurrection."

When David was sure that the priest had given them all the information, he finally spoke. "I know that we could buy a ready made-casket today, but do we have to apply for a plot in the Catholic cemetery?" The priest assured them that he will take care of that. He also told them that two nuns would stand Vigil from this afternoon until the casket is transported to the church. They would be relieved every four hours by two other nuns or volunteers from the parish. Knowing that the family was not financially able to preserve the body, he suggested that the Funeral take place late afternoon the next day. He would send an obituary to the newspapers right now, so that friends could pay their respects early the next day. Both David and John appreciated and admired the priest for his help. Without his advice, they would be totally lost. Just before they left the priest, David said, "When all this is over, you can tell me about your Christian God. I have to understand why my father made such a decision a few days before his death." The priest nodded and smiled. "I shall be over in two hours with the nuns. We shall bring the candles along. Just make sure that you get the casket, and that his body is in it before we arrive." Even though the two men knew that there was not much money left to cover the whole funeral expenses, they still bought one of the most expensive coffins. They could only pay a quarter of the price with cash. David used his monthly salary as a guarantee to pay the rest.

The family of Malam's late brother Chin, as well as Cheah, his second brother and his whole family, came all the way from Malacca to pay their last respects. Cheah was very upset about Malam's conversion, but he kept it to himself. He strongly believed that now Malam would never join his ancestors. However, he had to come to see his brother for the last time. Malam's casket was placed on a long low table covered with a black cloth. His body was preserved by huge blocks of ice, covered with coconut husks under the table. They were replaced every few hours before they completely melted. His bed had been dismantled and put away. The table in the living room also was removed. There were chairs along the wooden walls of the living room. Malam's body lay in the uncovered casket in the middle of the room with his legs facing the main door. He looked so peaceful with his hands together on his chest clasping a rosary. There were always two people sitting one on each side of the coffin, reading prayers or reciting the rosary. They never ceased praying, as friends, relatives and well-wishers, took their turns to walk around the coffin to pay their last respects. Some would bend down and plant a kiss on Malam's forehead. Malam's direct family wore black clothes, and male relatives wore white shirts with a black band on their right sleeves. Some female relatives wore black like the family; others wore clothes of subdued colors. No one, not even friends, had any red or lively colors on. The younger ones, who had not felt the impact and loss of death, played outside or in their rooms with other children of their age. They were not allowed to run or speak in the Vigil room. Thankfully, Malam's four wives were kept busy the whole afternoon of the Vigil. They stayed in the kitchen, and made sure that there was enough food and refreshments for everyone. Their eyes were red and swollen from too much crying, and each time someone approached them to give his or her condolences, the tears would just flow.

Sister Renee and another nun, an Indian lady by the name of Sister Justine, were the first to open the Vigil ceremony. As she prayed, Sister Renee was watching Marlene from the corner of her eye. The girl had been sitting at the top of the stairs, which led from the sleeping quarters to the dining room. She looked forlorn and lost, but her gaze never left the body of her father. Her eyes too were swollen and red. Once in a while she would wipe her eyes with her hand. Sister Renee had no chance to talk to her when she arrived. She sensed that Marlene was avoiding her. The girl wanted to be alone to mourn the death of her dearly beloved father. The whole four hours that the nuns sat beside the coffin, Marlene had not moved an inch, neither did she remove her gaze from the still body that lay in the coffin. When Marlene finally realized that her father was gone forever, her belief in the Holy Water dissipated. She was also angry with the Virgin Mary for taking her father away so suddenly. Most of all, she blamed herself for ever getting involved with the nun, and believing every word she said. She was sure that her father would still be lying on his bed at the corner of the living room, and that even if he could not walk, they could still talk to each other. Now, he lay still, and she was not allowed to even put her arms around him. As she watched the whole scene before her, people walking around the casket without saying a word, some of them complete strangers, she wished that this was all a dream, and that she could close her eyes, and open them again to see her father on his bed smiling at her. She remembered her dream of last night, and wished that she had shouted to the Lady to leave her father alone. Marlene continued to sit there, angry with God, the Virgin Mary, Sister Renee and herself, until exhaustion overcame her, and she fell asleep with her head on her folded arms, which were resting on the landing of the top floor. She was too tired to wake up completely, when she felt a pair of strong arms lifting her, and carrying her to lay her on the softness of a mattress.

While the Vigil continued, Marlene was in another world. They were back in the beautiful mansion, and she saw her father in his white suit dancing. Sometimes, he had one of his wives in his arms, other times he was dancing with strange beautiful women, women she had never seen before. He looked so young and happy, and as she stood in the corner watching him, she wished that she was old enough to dance with him. Her wish was granted. Her father approached her, and as she slipped into his arms, she seemed to have grown a few inches. She felt like an adult. After that he only danced with her, then suddenly he began to fade away, but before he disappeared completely, he managed to say, "I have found peace and happiness. I have to leave you now, but don't be sad, for my spirit will always be with you. It shall follow you wherever you go." He blew her a flying kiss and disappeared completely, leaving her in the darkness of the ballroom. She was alone and a child again. She sat down and started to cry, but stopped when she heard a distant voice saying, "Don't cry, my darling daughter, I am always with you." Marlene stopped crying, and all the hate, anger and anguish she felt when her father died, dissipated. She woke up on her own, and saw the sun shining through the window. No one else was in the room with her. She saw the black dress hanging on a chair. Some sorrow came back when she realized what day it was. However, she braced herself, for the words in her dreams kept echoing in her head. "Yes, Papa", she said quietly. "I believe you, and I shall try to be strong."

It was a picture-perfect day for a funeral. The church was crowded with family, relatives, friends, believers and non-believers. After the service, the six pallbearers transported the coffin into a black hearse. The pallbearers were David, John, Gary and three of Malam's nephews, sons of Chin and Cheah. There were dark clouds in the sky, and as the hearse started to move towards the cemetery, which was about two miles away, light rain began to fall. Everyone walked, some had umbrellas, others tied scarves around their heads, and most of the men wore black hats. The six pallbearers walked alongside the hearse, Malam's family were directly behind the hearse. The wives cried quietly, for they remembered what Malam said when he was very much alive. He had said, "I wish that when I die, my funeral will be a quiet one." He had criticized the loud banging of drums, and the loud screaming of mourners, and the paid screamers at the Buddhist funerals that he had seen and attended. Following the family closely were the nuns who helped to take care of Malam's younger children. Marlene had automatically given her hand to Sister Renee, who clasped it firmly, hoping to give hope and courage to the girl. Somehow, she sensed that it was not necessary. Marlene's eyes were not as red as the day before, and she held her chin up as she trudged along. Sister Renee thought that something must have happened to make this girl, whose love for her father knew no bounds, to be so brave. She was happy for Marlene and she was sure that Marlene would survive the loss. Behind the eight nuns, were the relatives, friends and the parishioners.

The final scene at the last station, which was at the cemetery, was one that would remain in the mind of all the people present for a long time. After the priest had commited the body to its resting place, the coffin was then lowered into the pit. The quiet and serene atmosphere was suddenly disrupted by a loud scream. Paini could not hold her anguish within herself any longer. She cried and screamed, "Malam! Take me with you!" Then the other three wives also lost control. All four began to cry and scream their husband's name, begging him to take them all along with him. They began rushing towards the lowered coffin, and if not for friends who held them back, they would have thrown themselves down with him. Malam's younger children, hearing the distress in their mothers' cries also began to cry. Everyone's heart was wrenched with compassion for the bereaved family. They looked at the coffin which now rested at the bottom of the hole, and thought to themselves, "A great man has just left us." One of Malam's close friends said aloud, "I would die a hundred times to have so much love surrounding me." The weeping and the screaming went on for almost half an hour. When finally, the women got back their control, Paini was handed a handful of earth. Ai Li helped her towards the hole. She threw the earth onto Malam's sealed coffin and said, "We will meet again." Her voice was weak, but there was determination in it. The other three wives did the same thing, and although they did not say out loud, everyone sensed that they too believed that they would see him again in the next world.

While all the screaming went on, Sister Renee held on to Marlene, who covered her face in the nun's habit. She sobbed silently not for her father, but for the women who loved him so much. There was a time in her young life when she thought that it would have been so nice if her mother was his only wife. Now, without realizing that, she echoed the words of her late grandmother who she never knew, she looked up at Sister Renee and said, "My father had a big heart, big enough to love so many women at one time." Sister Renee, whose eyes were wet as she watched the anguish of the women, heard what the girl said and nodded her head, "Yes, you are lucky to be one of his children, and especially one that he loved so much." In her heart, Marlene said, "Yes, and he will never stop loving me. He will always be with me." As they moved away from the cemetery towards waiting cars that were hired to take the family home, Marlene turned back to look at the site of her father's resting place. She thought she saw him waving at her with a smile. She smiled back and blew him a flying kiss. Sister Renee saw the kiss and said to herself, "Thank you God for this great miracle."

CHAPTER 29

The funeral had absorbed a large amount of what was left of the family money. Whatever was left lasted for another six months, after which, the revenue that came in with the cake making business was not enough to cover the household expenditure. David's salary helped to pay the rent. But the children were all growing up, and school fees and books had to be taken care of. Mona was almost three years old, so Keng Yi decided that she should try to get a secretarial job, and help with the situation at home. Paini and Cheng Mee would help take care of her children. But secretarial jobs did not come easily for married women with children. Most of the successful men were looking for young and unmarried secretaries. Keng Yi then was prepared to take any job as long as it could bring in some money. Her chance came when she took Mona to the family doctor for a vaccination. When asked how things were going, Keng Yi told the doctor about her desperate job search. Then the kindly doctor, who just lost his assistant pharmacist to a better paying job, offered her position to Keng Yi. "The pay is not much, but I hope it will help a little." The doctor was right about the pay, but Keng Yi knew that he would have to train her in the art of distributing medication, before she could be an independent dispenser. She accepted the job, and started working almost immediately.

All went well, until Ah Leng began to change. She acted like she was the head of the family, and made sure that everyone was aware that her sons were bringing in the most income. By then, John had finished his apprenticeship and was a full-time veterinarian. She stopped helping with the cake business, and it became too much work for both Paini and Cheng Mee. Paini was not feeling too well and when she went to see the doctor, he diagnosed her with Diabetes. On hearing this, Ai LI, knowing that the situation with Ah Leng was not good, offered her mother to move in with her and her family. At first, Paini was reluctant. She could not leave Keng Yi who needed her to help with her children. But both Keng Yi and Cheng Mee felt that Paini's health was more important. Besides, they could not bear to see her giving up her place as head of the family to Ah Leng. Between them, they managed to persuade the older lady to join her only daughter. They knew that Ai Li would take good care of their mother. At this point, the four women were attending Catechism. The priest had appointed a man from his diocese to go to the house twice a week, to teach and prepare them for Baptism. They had voiced their intentions shortly after the funeral of their beloved husband. Thus Paini said that she would stay on until then. The Baptism took place two months later, exactly a year after Malam's funeral.

The girls of the Convent school, Lily aged fourteen, Marlene eleven, and Anna, Theresa and Jan all about the same age of seven, had their Catechism in school. Alex, who was less than a year older than Lily went to the parish twice a week after school, and was privately tutored by a priest. Michael and Mona who would receive the Sacrament at the same time, were exempted from the sermons and teachings of Christ. Gary's ambition was to be a lawyer, but had to give it up when the family lost their wealth. Now at twenty, he was attending the same Teacher's College that David went to. He, David and John decided to wait a little longer with the conversion. They had attended a few sermons, but needed more time to be convinced that the Roman Catholic religion was the right one for them. However, they were inclined towards Christianity. Ai Li and Jo Lin did think about becoming Catholics, but their husbands persuaded them to take a little more time before making that commitment, as they and their children would be involved too. They agreed, but it did not stop them from going to the church in their neighborhood occasionally. They, like their mothers, believed that following their father's footsteps would mean a reunion with him one day. It was October 20, 1961, when the Catholic Church in Klang was filled with believers, to witness a mass Baptism of the bigger part of the Shih family. Paini took the name of Mary, Ah Leng chose Elizabeth, Cheng Mee was christened Rita, and Keng Yi embraced the Catholic religion with the name of Catherine. The children kept their own Christian names. The nuns and priest found appropriate godparents for all of them.

After the ceremony, everyone who attended the Baptism was invited to the Convent for a sumptuous meal, prepared by the nuns in the honor of the new Catholics. Many brought small gifts for the new converts in the forms of holy pictures, rosaries, holy books and many other things that related to the Catholic Church. When Sister Renee saw Marlene sitting with her new godmother, she had an uneasy feeling. They hardly talked to each other, and the Bible that she gave Marlene was lying on the table in front of them with all the other gifts that Marlene had received. Sister Renee was so busy with the preparations that she was unaware that a godmother had already been chosen for her Marlene. When she found out who she was, it was too late. The lady was a secondary school teacher of the Convent. She was a Eurasian and was very rich. She was chosen to be one of the many godmothers because she was a good Catholic, who never missed Sunday masses and Saturday novenas. No one, except Sister Renee, knew that inside the lady, was a cold and unfeeling person. There was no capacity in her heart to take care of Marlene's spiritual needs. Sister Renee shrugged, and in her heart she said, "Well I am here and I shall be her spiritual guide." Sister Renee had a special gift for Marlene, but she decided to hold on to it until she could get Marlene alone.

When Marlene moved on to a higher grade, she had another new class teacher. Sister Renee made an effort to talk to the girl at least once a day. Marlene was still as lively as ever, and her temperament got her into trouble once in a while but it was not serious enough to take note of. Her school work was still good, and she was still among the top ten in her class of forty children. The nun was glad that the death of her father had not affected the girl. Little did she know that Marlene was having problems at home. Alex had started his bullying again, and being much bigger than Marlene, she was no match for his physical attacks. A day did not pass without Alex striking at her. Sometimes, she would run into her room and sulk, but there were times when the slap on her face was so hard, that it brought tears to her eyes and he would jeer at her, "Cry as much as you like. Papa is not here to protect his little girl." The slap on her face did not hurt as much as the pain in her heart, when she realized the reality of his words. Then in the privacy of her room, she would talk to her dead father, and feel much better after that. She never told her mother, who always came home tired, about the bullying. Paini and Cheng Mee had scolded Alex, but Ah Leng would intervene, and said that Marlene was naughty, and all Alex did was to put her in her place. There was nothing much the two women could do but make sure that Marlene kept as far away from Alex, but that was futile, for Alex would seek her out.

The day of the mass Baptism was also the anniversary of her father's death, and Marlene, began to hurt at the memory of her father. The day before the last day of mourning, the black clothes were washed and stored away. Normally, the annual Requiem High Mass for Malam should have been celebrated that day, but it was postponed until two days from now. The priest thought that it would be best if his family attended it as Catholics. Marlene missed her father terribly, and wanted to find a spot where she could bury herself in her thoughts of him. It had been her way of feeling him close to her. Sister Renee found her sitting in her white dress on the bottom of the stairs that led to the chapel. The nuns had sewn and donated the white dresses to all the girls. They even bought them white shoes and socks to go with the dresses. Marlene's dress had frills that covered the top part of her arms, and the layered skirt was trimmed with the same frills, and reached a little below her knees. The white velvet two-inch band around her small waist emphasized her petite figure. To Sister Renee, she looked like a little angel. Marlene sat with her knees curled up to her chest. A chill ran through the spine of the nun, for she remembered seeing Marlene in that same position a year ago.

When Marlene saw the nun approaching her, she unfolded her legs and smiled. That smile was strangely sweet, with a tinge of sadness. Sister Renee put her arms around the girl and said, "Finally, we are alone." She dug in her deep pocket and brought out a small wooden box. "This is my gift to you." Marlene opened the lid of the box and saw a wooden crucifix in it. It was so beautifully carved, that every feature of the anguished Jesus could be seen on his face. It was about the size of her palm. She looked at it in wonder as Sister Renee said, "My brother is a sculptor. He gave this to me when I left our home to join the order of The Sacred Heart. I have written to him, and told him that I have to give this crucifix, which had helped me through the trials of my vocation, to someone special. I told him about you, and he said that I should give it to you with his blessings." Marlene kissed the crucifix and said, "Thank you Sister. Please tell your brother that I shall treasure this cross, and hope that it will help me as it has helped you." Sister Renee wished that Marlene would talk more to her. There is something that the girl is holding back. But she knew from her own experiences that Marlene was not ready to tell her yet. She would be patient and wait for the right time. She stood up, pulling the girl with her saying, "The party is almost over now. Your mother will be looking for you. Don't worry about your godmother. Between you and me, I shall take her place." To that Marlene replied, "I would love that." She stood on her toes, and the tall nun bent slightly to receive Marlene's kiss on her cheeks. Three weeks after the Baptism, except for Michael and Mona who were still too young, the rest of them received the Sacrament of The Holy Eucharist. The third Sacrament of Confirmation would be administered to them the next year.

The family that Malam had tried to hold together started to break up. Paini left immediately after receiving the second Sacrament of the Holy Eucharist, to live with her daughter in another town, about a hundred miles from Klang. That was the end of their little business. Cheng Mee held on for a while to help Keng Yi, until Michael was ready to attend school. With Paini gone, Ah Leng decided that the income that her two sons brought in should pay for the rent and utilities, and food just for her and her own children. Keng Yi's salary should support Cheng Mee and their children. Realizing that was not possible, Cheng Mee had no choice but to accept the offer of her two unmarried brothers. Their father had died a few years ago, and seeing the financial difficulty their sister was going through, suggested that she and her children move in to live with them. They would welcome her help in cooking, and keeping the house clean while they went to work. One was a taxi driver and the other worked as a packer in the paper mill. Their house was a humble home, but there was a room for Cheng Mee and her two daughters. Keng Yi was glad for both Paini and Cheng Mee, but she could see a very dim and sad future for her and her children. Ah Leng's grudge for Malam's favoritism towards Marlene became obvious in time, and she also suspected that Alex was bullying her daughter. The meager salary that she earned as a dispenser was hardly enough to feed her four growing children, let alone the school fees, books and uniforms. Unlike the other two women, she had no choice but to stay on and try to make ends meet. Michael was old enough to attend Kindergarten, so she could appeal to the church to let him attend the pre-school that belonged to the parish, without a fee. Hopefully, her doctor would allow her to bring Mona with her to work. The three year old child was quite good, and could play on her own in a corner, where Keng Yi could keep an eye on her. Michael was accepted, and the doctor agreed to let her bring Mona to work, as long as she did not disturb her mother.

When Keng Yi found out that she could not make ends meet after a month, she had to cancel the children's school bus rides. That meant an hour's walk each way for the girls and Michael. That began their real hardship. They had to wake up an hour earlier to get to school on time. Keng Yi's clinic was about half way, and although she started work only at eight while the school began at seven, she would walk the half way with her children, carrying Mona on and off, thus being about an hour early for work. Marlene's class teacher began to notice Marlene's lack of attention to her school work, and her lack of energy during Sports practice. The change was so obvious, that she, knowing the bond between the girl and Sister Renee, confided in the nun about the obvious changes she noticed. Sister Renee wasted no time in seeking out her young friend. She had not seen Marlene for almost a week as she was down with the Flu. When she looked the girl up and down, she was shocked to see that Marlene had lost a lot of weight. The first thing she did was to invite Marlene into the kitchen, where two nuns were preparing lunch. There was a small table with two chairs in one corner. She told Marlene to sit on one of the chairs while she made a hot cup of chocolate, and filled a bowl with some cookies. She gave them to Marlene, and parts of her unasked questions were answered as she saw how hungrily, the girl ate the cookies and drank the hot chocolate. Sister Renee heard the bell that announced the end of Recess. She got up and Marlene followed suit, but she said, "No, no. You sit here with these good Sisters and finish your cookies. I will come back in about five minutes."

Sister Renee needed more than five minutes to do what she planned. First of all, she had to tell Marlene's class teacher that Marlene might miss the next lesson completely, secondly, she had to look for a relief teacher to take over her class until she came back and finally, she had to tell the Reverend Mother that she suspected that Marlene was in great trouble. It was sometime before Sister Renee came back, but Marlene was being well entertained by the two nuns. They joked with her as they cooked, and made her the tester of the foods. It was a long time since Marlene had tasted such good food, and she enjoyed herself tremendously. Sister Renee saw her giggling away with the two nuns, and smiled to herself thinking, "I have not seen Marlene so happy since her father died." Then she took Marlene back to the Convent garden, and sat on the same bench they shared more than a year ago. "My dearest child, please trust me and tell me everything. I know that something is wrong at home. I need to know to be able to help." Marlene hesitated for sometime. She wanted to gather her strength so that she would not break down in the midst of her sad story. Then she sat up straight and poured out her grievances to the kindly nun. "We are no more one family. My First and Third Mothers have left us. My Second Mother has never liked me, and she will not feed us anymore saying that my mother, who is working for our family doctor earns enough money to feed her own children. That is not true. We have been living on white bread and margarine, and rice with eggs and some vegetables. We have not tasted any meat or fish since my two mothers left us. Then to be able to continue to feed and clothe us, my mother had to cancel our transportation to school. I feel so tired that I cannot concentrate on my school work. Then it is so hot to walk back in the late afternoons." She did not mention the bullying from Alex. The nun was quiet as she listened. Her heart was filled with compassion for Marlene's mother. Tears were gathering in her eyes, but she felt ashamed when she realized how brave Marlene had been as she told her sad story.

Gathering herself, Sister Renee said, "Marlene, you have a very important Government Examination coming up next year. I want you to concentrate on your school work. If you do well, we will be able to recommend a Government fund for your studies. That would cover your school fees, your school uniforms, your school books and your transportation to school. Besides all these, you will get a monthly sum of money to spend at will. It is not much, but you will see that it will go a long way. This fund will continue throughout your school career, and if you excelled in your Final year of school, it will also fund your studies in the University." Marlene listened, and understood every word the nun said. She could not imagine how that was possible. She had already thought of leaving school, and helping her mother earn some money. Somehow the nun read her thoughts and said, "As long as I am alive, you will not leave school before your time. I have spoken to Reverend Mother, and suspecting that your problems are financial, we will help with the bus fares, and my colleagues will sew the school uniforms for you and your sister. This is what we can afford to do. The other thing is that your mother will have to go the priest and apply for charity. The mission provides flour, rice, milk powder and margarine for the needy. The amount of supply depends on the number of people in the family. It will be handed out every month. Your mother should not even think about pride. The lives of her children are at stake." Marlene could not thank the nun enough. The best part of it was to be able to ride the bus again. Before she left, she said, "I am now very sure that my father is looking after me." She wanted to add, "Through you," but she did not. She was so thankful to the nun, that she could not hold back her tears. The nun allowed her to cry, for she knew those tears was happy tears, and then she offered Marlene her handkerchief to dry her tears. "Just like the first time," Marlene said, and smiled as she dried her tears. Sister Renee smiled back and said, "Go back to class and work hard." She kissed Marlene on the forehead, and went back to her class with a lighter heart. That same day, during the last period in school, Marlene got a note from Sister Renee to go with her sister Anna to the sewing room, which was in the same block as the kitchen. The two happy girls were measured for new school uniforms, and a pair of shorts each for sports.

Keng Yi's application for charity was approved, and for sometime everything seemed to go well for her and her children. Now, children who became six years old before January could attend school and Michael belonged to that category. So when Marlene went into her Final and important year of Primary School, Michael started his first year at a Catholic school for boys, which was run by Jesuit Brothers. Anna was now in her third grade, and four-year old Mona was accepted by the church kindergarten, also as a non-paying preschooler. It was also around this time that the newly converts received the Sacraments of Confirmation. Paini received hers in the diocese whose church she attended. Here again, Mona and Michael were excluded. They would receive the two Sacraments with other children their age. Everything seemed to be working out well, except for the abuses that Marlene had to endure almost everyday. She kept in her room as much as possible, but she had to keep an eye on her younger sister, Mona, who liked to play with the chickens that Ah Leng reared. Whenever Alex saw her he would first torment her with words and when Marlene ignored him, he would rush to her and smack the back of her head or push her roughly challenging her, "Hey tomboy, want a fight?" Marlene would glare at him, but common sense would overcome her, and she would just walk away towards her room, closing her ears to his jeers and unkind teasing.

One day, something awful happened to change the lives of Keng Yi and her children again. Marlene was in need of a new box of color pencils, so Keng Yi gave her the money to buy one at the school book shop. She was in her room, finishing a drawing for her art class, when Jan burst into the room with Alex close to her heels, "There," screamed Ah Leng's adopted daughter. "I know that she took my color pencils." Marlene surprised by the intruders, was unprepared for what happened next. She was lying on her stomach and doing her homework on the floor. Alex came into the room, called her a thief, and grabbed the box and the rest of the color pencils that were lying on the floor. Marlene had one in her hand, and when Alex tried to grab it from her, she shouted, "Leave my things alone!" She got to her feet and tried to snatch back all the pencils from Alex, when his free hand punched her so hard that she fell. His fist hit the area around her eye. He saw the blood flowing and panicked. Anna, Michael and Mona who were in the room began to cry as they saw their sister lying on the floor quite still, with blood covering her face. Ah Leng heard the commotion and came running to see what was wrong. She saw her son standing in shock, and following his gaze noticed the still form of Marlene on the floor, her head covered with blood. A shiver ran through her, and she quickly went on her knees and called Marlene's name, but the girl remained still. Ah Leng had the common sense to feel the pulse. She sighed in relief when she realized that Marlene was just temporary knocked out. However, she slapped her son's face hard to arouse him from his trance and said, "Cycle as fast as you can to the doctor. Tell Fourth Mother that there was an accident involving Marlene. Don't say anything else. She will know what to do."

Keng Yi and the doctor wasted no time. They were in time to see Marlene stirring as Ah Leng cleaned the blood from her face. There was big bruise above her eyebrow, and the blood that flowed were broken blood vessels in her eye. The impact of the punch had caused the vessels to break. Nothing Ah Leng said could convince Keng Yi that Alex did not attack her daughter. While the doctor tended to Marlene, she screamed at Ah Leng and Alex, "Why can't both of you bury your hatred with the dead? Why did you even become Catholics when so much hatred is in your souls?" Ah Leng said nothing, and just shoved Alex and Jan out of the room. After the doctor was sure that all Marlene suffered was a slight concussion, and that her eye was in no danger, except that the white would remain red for a few days, he said, "This is a case for the police. I leave it up to you. Here are some painkillers, to ease the pain and swelling. Stay home for the day. I will have to get back to my patients. Keep Marlene under observation, and if you see any negative changes, bring her to me immediately." He left, and Keng Yi sat with her children in the room watching Marlene as she lay in bed with her eyes closed but not asleep. She was tempted to file a complaint with the police, but the memory of her husband stopped her. However, she needed someone to talk to, and to advise her of the next steps. This incident was serious and should not be ignored. She could not leave Marlene alone, so she gave Anna a coin, and wrote a number on a piece of paper. "Go to the shop opposite and give the coin and number to the owner. Tell him to call the number, and I want you to speak to Father Lee. Tell him that there was an accident, and beg him to come to see me." Father Lee was the priest who had baptized Malam and the whole family.

On hearing the voice of little Anna, Father Lee knew that Keng Yi would not have sent a little girl to make a phone call if it was not serious. He was at the house in less than an hour after he spoke to Anna. He was shocked when he saw Marlene's bruised face and red eyes. It was hard for him to understand that a family that was raised in an environment of love, could brew so much hate in some of the members. He took it upon himself to talk to Ah Leng and her son. By now, David too had come back from school. He wondered what the priest was doing when he saw the car. He was angry when his mother told him what Alex did. He was entering Keng Yi's room to check on Marlene just as the priest was leaving to talk to his mother and Alex. His anger turned to shock when he saw Marlene's face. Seeing the set look on the priest's face, he knew that the priest would say what he should have said to his mother and brother long ago, then this would not have happened. Father Lee could see that

Keng Yi's words had affected Ah Leng. The lady looked like she had been crying so he only spoke to Alex, "You have done a very bad thing. If it was not for the memory of your father, we would take this case to the police and they would keep you in prison for sometime. However, since that is not going to happen, I am giving you a warning. Do not touch Marlene ever again. Don't go near her and don't say anything at all to her. Is that understood? Serious steps would be taken if you do not heed my warnings." Alex nodded and bowed his head. The priest left mother and son and went back into Keng Yi's room. "I think it is best that you all leave this house which is no longer a home. The mission house is full at the moment, but I shall look around for something else. Meanwhile, there is nothing more to worry about. Let me assure you that both mother and son have learnt a lesson. I am sure that the doctor must have advised you to keep Marlene home for a few days. Well, I will have to tell Sister Renee about the incident. She loves the child very much, and she has the right to know." He then blessed the room and its inhabitants with the sign of the cross, and said, "God be with you." Then he left without saying goodbye to Ah Leng, David and Alex.

Marlene insisted on going to school the next day, even though she had a bad headache and a dull pain around her eye. She could not bear to be alone in the house with her Second Mother. Keng Yi understood her, but at the same time, Marlene was still too weak to be able to concentrate on her studies. However, she gave in to her daughter's persistence and allowed her to go to school. Without Marlene's knowledge, she rang the school to speak to Sister Renee, to whom the priest had already spoken to. Sister Renee assured Keng Yi that as soon as Marlene arrived, she would take the girl, and tell her to spend the day at the school clinic. There she would have her rest, and at the same time have the service of a qualified nurse if needed. The bus ride was already causing Marlene to feel more pain, so it was without any resistance that Marlene spent the whole day at school, sleeping on and off on the soft bed in the clinic. She would have continued sleeping the whole day if the nurse had not woken her up in time to catch the bus home with her sister. Marlene felt much better but she still shuddered at the thought of going back to the house, which for her was no longer a home. Sister Renee caught up with her as she was leaving the clinic. She touched the bruise on Marlene's head gently and said, "Promise me that you will not hide anything from me again. If only you had told me about the problems you were having with your half-brother, we could have done something about it. But never mind my child, I am glad to see that you are quite yourself again." Marlene never again had

335

to fear Alex or his mother. Ah Leng did not speak to her, and Alex kept out of her way. Nevertheless, Marlene could not wait to leave that house forever, which she now named in her heart as 'the house of pain'.

CHAPTER 30

Father Lee wasted no time in spreading the word around that he was looking for a temporary accommodation for a widow and her four children. It reached the ears of another widow, who just lost her husband, but had three grown-up sons living with her. They had a small hut on their property that was used as a servant's quarter. The sudden death of her husband in an accident affected her financial situation, so she had to dismiss the servant. Her youngest son, also called Michael was in High School, and Thomas, the second boy just went into the University. Lawrence, her first son had another two more years of internship. He was studying to be a doctor of internal medicine. When the city council inspected the hut, they ordered it to be torn down as it did not meet the requirements to house human beings. The widow, Mrs. Lazarus of Indian origin, begged for time to do some renovations. She hoped to be able to rent that property out to get some needed income. Time went by, and she was still not able to finance the renovations and with time the city council too lost interest in that property. On hearing about the widow and her children, she checked the little hut again. The first thing she did was to check on the electricity in the hut. It was in working order, and then she went through the whole structure. Its roof was made of attap, the dried leaves of tropical palm trees and the hut had wooden sidings. The whole floor was earthen. She noticed that the sunlight seemed to be creeping through the roof in the living room and that meant that rain could also come through. Her sons could easily fix that by applying more attap on the exposed area. Some of the wood was rotting, which meant that it was infected with termites and rodents. Adjoining the dining room were two bedrooms, one beside the other with a narrow passageway that also led to the kitchen. One of the rooms was intact. There were no signs of leakage, and the raised wooden platform used as a big bed was still solid. The other room, which was never used by the servant, was beyond repair. Left alone, the rats had enjoyed themselves making holes into the wooden walls, and using this part of the hut as their play room. Broken attap seemed to be falling off the roof. Mrs. Lazarus decided to seal off this room with a wooden barricade. The kitchen was not in very good condition. The wood burning stoves were cracked, and above them were also some cracks. However, the kitchen was quite big, and there was a huge area that could be used for cooking and dining. The new inhabitants could buy a small gas stove and set it on an old table that she had stored in her garage. The bathroom was outside the house. It was open, with no roof, but had a partition to provide privacy. There was a pipe hanging over a huge earthen barrel. She turned on the water and was satisfied with the clean flow that came out. The toilet was beside the bathroom. It was another bucket system and needed some cleaning. She would take care of all that needed to be taken care of before she made an offer to the priest.

A month after the attack on Marlene, Keng Yi moved with her children to this humble home, taking with them the mattresses of the big and small bed, the pillows they slept on, the sheets they used as blankets, the dressing table and her big closet from her bedroom, and all their personal items like books and clothes. Before the move, the priest had driven only Keng Yi to check on the hut. He explained to her that the lady did not expect any rent, but Keng Yi would have to pay for the electricity. When she went through the hut, she felt a sharp stab in her heart thinking of how fast their lives changed. They came from a big mansion, almost like a castle, to a smaller house, and then to this hovel. However, it was better to live in a hole than in a house full of painful memories and hate. She also saw the advantages of living close to the church, and to both the schools that her children were attending. It was only fifteen minutes walk each way to those destinations. They could save money on the bus fares to church twice a week, on Saturdays for the Novenas, and for the Sunday masses. That extra money could be used for better nourishment for her growing children. The children, however, did not see the hut as a hovel. To them it was a new adventure. The attap roof and earthen floor gave them a feeling that they were in a strange and foreign place. Even the expensive houses around them did not dampen their spirits. They felt they were finally free. They ran through the house, and were convinced that they were going to have more fun than they had since their father died. Marlene felt the same way, even though she could see that it was a home for the very poor. But like her mother, she would rather live in a hole than continue staying with her Second Mother and her children. The priest managed to get some old furniture, namely two dining tables and ten chairs. One of the tables was put into the living room together with five chairs for the children to do their homework. That filled up the small room. The other table and the five chairs went into the kitchen. Keng Yi had already bought a gas stove which sat on the table that the landlady put in. The two mattresses fitted snugly on the platform in the bedroom. The children were warned about the hazards of the barricaded room.

Marlene, happy and contented with her new environment, studied and worked hard for the coming Government examination. The Government offered only one study scholarship per school annually, for the best and most deserving pupil, based on their financial status and results of the Standard Six Examination. Sister Renee and her class teacher had confidence that Marlene could win the scholarship. Then just three months before the big examination, Sister Renee came into Marlene's class and asked the teacher's permission to take Marlene out. Marlene was quite surprised. She had not seen Sister Renee around for about a week. When she asked another nun about it, she was told that Sister Renee was not feeling well, and was advised to stay in bed for sometime. Marlene thought it was again the Flu. She was happy to see her, although she noticed that the nun had lost some weight. Once again they went into the garden, this time Marlene had a strange foreboding. She detected some sadness in the nun as they sat down together on the familiar bench. She tensed up as she waited for the nun to start the conversation. "Remember the very first day when we sat here?" She asked after sometime. Marlene nodded, afraid of what may come next. Then the nun continued, "God above is watching us at this moment. I can feel his love and I know that you too can feel it." Marlene remained quiet, for what she was feeling was an uncanny dread that something bad was going to happen, and the next words of the nun confirmed her fears. "My work here is finished. God has another job for me and I have to obey his orders. I have to go back to my country." Sister Renee said all that in one tone. She could not bear to prolong the pain of beating about the bush. She saw the look of anguish on Marlene's face, and noticed the sudden gush of tears in her eyes. There was no stopping, the nun had to continue, "I once told you that God works in mysterious ways. He puts a lot of obstacles, some of them very difficult ones in our paths. Each time we get over an obstacle, we become stronger, and our path towards God becomes shorter and easier. He has brought us together and it is his wish for us to part. The pain of parting is the obstacle. We shall both cross it, and it will bring us nearer to God." Marlene was still too sad to say anything but her tears had stopped. The nun pointed to the sky, and as Marlene looked up, the nun said, "There is a place beside God that is reserved for you. No matter what path you choose as you grow up, God will lead you back to the right way toward that reserved seat. Your father is there with him, and he is always watching over you. I will be far away from you, but I am leaving my heart with you. I love you and I want you to be brave. Will you do that for me?" Looking at the pleading eyes of the nun, Marlene nodded. Her heart was broken, but because of her love for the nun, she put up a brave front, and in as steady a voice as she could muster, she spoke for the first time, "When are you leaving?" The nun replied, "In two days time. I promise that I will write to you as often as I can." Marlene, afraid that she was going to break down again, pulled the nun's face to her and kissed her on her cheeks saying, "I too love you and I will never stop loving you." Then she got up and ran as fast as her legs could carry her. The nun stood up looked at the back of the running girl. "God be with you my child. We will be watching over you," she said as the tears filled her eyes.

Two days later, the whole school gathered outside the Convent building to wave goodbye to the nun who was loved by all that knew her. Marlene was among them. Her heart was heavy, but she kept her promise to be brave, so she held back her tears as others around her cried quietly. Sister Renee also tried to be brave, and though she sensed Marlene's presence in the crowd, their eyes did not meet. It was only as the car that was taking her to the airport drove off, that Sister Renee looked back and for a moment their eyes met. She waved frantically and Marlene blew a kiss. When the car disappeared in a cloud of dust, pupils and teachers began to disperse to go back to their classes. Marlene did not move, than she felt a hand lightly touching her shoulder. It belonged to that of the Reverend Mother, who knew of the bond between the departing nun and the girl. "You have been very brave. She will be so proud of you. I want you to know that I am here if you need someone to talk to." Marlene was touched and said, "Thank you, Reverend Mother." She went back to class like the others. For the next few days, Marlene did not give herself time to be sad. She buried herself in her books to get ready for the coming Examination. It would mean so much to her mother if she won the Scholarship, and no matter what happened after that, her studies would be guaranteed. Her father would be so proud of her, and she would not let down the nun who loved her, and had so much confidence in her.

Eight days after Sister Renee left the country, the school bell rang at an odd time. For the pupils and teachers, the sound of the bell meant an assembly at the big open space of the Canteen. Puzzled, everyone marched out of their class in line and walked towards the canteen. All eight nuns of the Convent, except for the Reverend Mother were standing around the podium. When everyone took their place, the headmistress walked to the podium, stood on it, and prepared herself to make an announcement. She braced herself and when she spoke her voice was shaky and filled with pain. "My dear teachers and pupils of this school, I have very sad news to impart. Our dear Sister Renee passed away last night." Marlene did not hear the rest of her words. Her knees gave way and she fainted. She recovered in the same clinic that she was in, not so long ago. Only this time, a doctor was hovering over her and calling her name. There was another person in the room. At first, Marlene thought it was Sister Renee, but as the nun spoke, she was jolted back to realization. She began to sob, and the Reverend Mother held her tightly saying consolingly, "She is with God, whom she loved and served till her last breath. Be happy for her because she is happy." Marlene continued to sob and the doctor, sure that the girl was alright, left the room. The nun held the shaking girl and said, "Let it all out now, I understand." When Marlene finally stopped crying, the Reverend Mother said, "Sister Renee had Leukemia and suffered a lot. She was supposed to have gone back to France earlier, but she held on. She begged me to let her stay on until the end, because she felt that you needed her. Then she saw that you had survived your father's death and the hardships that came with it. She felt that you will also survive this, and knowing that her time was running out, she agreed to leave. Now you have to be strong for her. She had one worry before she left, and that was that her death may affect your studies. I promised her that I will do my best to help you. Now listen to me. Mourn for her if you must, but reward her memory with your success." "Why does God take away the people I love?" Marlene asked sadly. "This is another obstacle that you have to get over. Sister Renee and I know that you will overcome this obstacle as you did the others." Marlene remembered the last conversation she had with the dearly departed nun, and looked into the eyes of her new friend. "She will always be with me." The nun smiled and nodded, then when she saw that Marlene was getting off the bed, she said, "Oh no, you will have to lie for a few more hours. I have dismissed the whole school after the assembly. You are going to rest a little more. I shall send someone to bring you food, and then I shall come back to check if you are strong enough to go home." She tucked Marlene back into bed and left the girl with her thoughts. "Oh Sister, please keep your promise and be with me forever." Marlene closed her eyes and remembered the wooden cross the nun gave to her on the day of her Baptism.

Despite the aching pain for the death of her beloved nun, Marlene continued to work hard at her school work. Then two days before the Examination, she was called to see the Reverend Mother at her private office. The nun had a broad smile as the girl entered the room. "I have a surprise for you," she said, as she got up and handed Marlene an envelope. "It is from France." The first thought in Marlene's head was that Sister Renee kept her promise of writing to her. But a second glance on the envelope which was addressed to her, care of the Convent, told her that it was not the handwriting of her nun. Seeing her disappointment, the Reverend Mother said, "Open it and read. I shall leave you alone for a while." Left alone, Marlene tore open the envelope and read. "Dear Marlene," the letter began, "You don't know us but we know you very well. We were very close to Sister Renee. We were with her during her last days in the hospital. We were once her students, and it broke our hearts when she left us. She made us see the reason for her leaving, and before she died, she made us promise to write to you. First of all, she wants us to tell you that although she has left the earth, she has not left you. She wants you to be brave, and feel her presence in the Holy Cross that she gave you." Marlene's hand went into her pocket and felt the cross that she carried with her since the day she heard of Sister Renee's death. Then she continued reading. The rest of the letter was about the three writers. They were all seventeen years old, and would like her to keep in touch with them. They ended by wishing her all the best in the coming Examination. They said that they would pray for her. They signed off with love from Bernadette, Nichole and Michele. Marlene left the office of Reverend Mother with the letter close to her chest. She promised herself that as soon as the Examination was over, she would reply to the letter. She felt comforted to know that she had found friends from the same town where her beloved Sister Renee was born and then went back to die.

The Government Examination lasted two days, and Marlene had to compete with one hundred and twenty students for the scholarship. When it was over, she felt that she did well, and so did a few others. Now, she could only pray and wait. The school's year ended with the Examination, and the results would be announced two weeks later, a week before the new school season. With three weeks of school vacation, Marlene wrote vigorously to her new pen-pals. She knew that it would take two weeks for her mail to arrive and another two weeks for theirs to reach her. Nevertheless, she sent out one every week. She saved her small amount of pocket money for the stamps. The days went by fast, and the results were in. The school sent all the students notifications of their grade in the post. The grades came in A, B, C and D. A, meant that the students had passed with distinctions, B, signified that they did fairly well, Students who scored C grades meant that they just managed to qualify to attend the next level of school which was the Secondary School. D gave the students a second chance to stay back one year and repeat the Examination. After that, if they still did not succeed in getting a C or better, they would have to leave the school. Marlene got an A, but she did not know if she had won the scholarship. The only way to find out was to go to school. Marlene was getting ready to leave the house when her mother came back. She had received a phone call from the Reverend Mother and her boss had given her permission to leave early to convey the wonderful news to her daughter. Keng Yi came running into the house, shouting excitedly, "Marlene, you did it! You got the scholarship!"

When the new school term started, Marlene was disappointed to find that the Reverend Mother who had befriended her was replaced by another one. However, when she saw the new Reverend Mother, she took an immediate liking to the kindly face. She was a much smaller lady than the last one, and smaller than Sister Renee. But the twinkling eyes behind her frameless spectacles reminded her so much of Sister Renee. She was a Malaysian with a mixture of Chinese and European blood. She was known as Reverend Mother Irene. Without Marlene's knowledge, this nun had heard a lot about her, and in a way felt that she too was sent to guide the girl, and to help her. At the moment, Marlene seemed to be doing well. The new head of the Convent noticed that the girl could be temperamental, but was very likeable. Her athletic skills were showing, and she was one of the youngest to represent her school in district sports. She excelled in her school work, and the nun began to doubt that the girl needed help. Occasionally, when she passed Marlene, she would smile at her. Marlene detected that there was more than just a friendly smile and she warmed to it. But when Marlene smiled back, the nun felt that the girl was trying to forget her unhappy past by putting her mind in her school work and sports. Her doubts about the girl needing her came and went.

Then just when Keng Yi thought that their financial situation was improving, her boss fell seriously ill and had to retire. That left Keng Yi in a tight spot. Without an income, there was no way they could survive. Marlene was then fourteen years old, and had two more years of schooling left in the Convent. After which, if she did well in the Final School Examination, she would attend two years of High School in Kuala Lumpur to qualify her for the University. Keng Yi was desperate, and started applying for jobs. But it was not easy. She was jobless for three months and was about to work as a maid for some rich family, when the son of her old boss wrote her a letter, offering her a job in his clinic in Kuala Lumpur. He mentioned that due to her experience working for his father, her pay would be substantial, enough to rent a small apartment in the big city. Keng Yi could not believe her luck, but then she thought of Marlene. She could transfer her other three children to new schools, but she was afraid to take Marlene away from the Klang Convent, where she was now doing well both in her studies and Sports. At this time, Marlene was not only representing her school in athletics, she had been selected to represent the district of Klang in the Track and Field events. She decided to talk to Marlene before making any decisions.

She was right about Marlene not wanting to leave Klang at this point. It was on Marlene's suggestion that she asked Cheng Mee if Marlene could stay with them for another two years. Cheng Mee and Keng Yi had never lost contact with one another, and Marlene was still very close to Lily. Lily was in the phase of the Final School Examination, and quite often, she would seek Marlene out during Recess to find out how her sister was doing. Cheng Mee was happy to take care of Marlene. So everything was settled. Keng Yi moved to her new life in Kuala Lumpur with her three younger children, and left Marlene in Cheng Mee's care. However, Marlene should visit them as often as possible. She was big enough to take the bus to Kuala Lumpur on her own. For sometime the arrangements seemed to work out well, until the District Sports Council hired a professional trainer to coach their junior athletes. The coaching was three times a week, from three in the afternoon until six in the evening. It was held in the newly built sports stadium. It was compulsory to attend all coaching sessions to remain on the team. It also involved taking part in competitions every second week. At first, Marlene attended all the coaching sessions, but she could never get home before eight in the evenings. Then she was too tired to do any homework or study. The reason was that not too many buses operated on the route from the stadium to Cheng Mee's brothers' house. Marlene had to change two buses and then walk for another fifteen minutes. There was always a school bus in the mornings and afternoons after school.

Marlene knew that if her school work kept going down, she would lose the scholarship, so she set her priority and told the coach, a Malay man by the name of Malik, that she had to quit. Malik had seen that Marlene was a very talented girl in the field of Sports, and losing her would weaken the girls' team. Malik was a Muslim, married, with two beautiful girls. He was a very strict coach, but he had a kind heart and a great sense of humor. All the young athletes liked him, and Marlene was no exception. So it was easy for Marlene to give in, when he suggested that he would drive her home after every coaching session. It was out of his way, but he could not afford to let Marlene go. The girl had talents, and Malik could see a future star athlete in her. Thus, with Malik driving her home, she was not tired to spend time on her school work, and Cheng Mee felt more at ease, that the young girl was no longer exposed to the danger of walking alone in the dark from the bus stop to the house. Thus, Marlene continued to take part in the district and inter-district games, and going to Kuala Lumpur to visit her mother and siblings every second week. Her school work was not affected. She continued writing to her French pen-pals. Whenever the Reverend Mother saw her, Marlene seemed to be laughing or chatting happily with her friends. She had occasions to see Marlene, one of which was to express her pride that one of her girls had been selected to represent the district of Klang in Athletics. The other times were when Marlene and her sisters received new uniforms, and they would all go personally to the Reverend Mother to thank her. Each time they met, the Reverend Mother would spend some extra time for a friendly chat. Marlene liked her very much, but was careful about getting too involved. She did not want to have to go through the pain again of getting attached to someone, and then losing her. She knew that these holy people did not stay long in one place. Father Lee, the priest who converted all of them had also been transferred to another parish just before her mother lost her job in Klang.

Marlene was now in the third year of the Secondary School, when there was another Government Examination. It was just as important as the last one. But Marlene was doing well, and confident that she would be able to maintain her scholarship, and stay on in the science stream. Even though representing the District in Sports required a lot of her time, Marlene still found enough time to study. She sailed through the Examination, and was promoted to Form Four A, securing her scholarship. There was another hurdle to overcome the following year, before she would have to leave the good old Convent to pursue her higher studies in another bigger Convent in the same town where her mother worked. By now, Marlene's skills in other Sports were becoming obvious. There were talent scouts in all competitive games between schools in the district. Marlene represented her school in field Hockey and Badminton. The scouts picked her for both these events, but Marlene could only choose one. It was a hard decision, for she was fond of both the games. Her athletic coach Malik helped her with her choice. "Badminton is an individual Sport, and so is Track and Field. You are now in Track and Field, so choose Hockey, because that is team work. One day, when you grow up, you will have to work with other people, and this team work will help you to develop that sense of working with other people."

The relationship between them had blossomed from coach and trainee to great friends. There were times, when on the way to her home, Malik would stop by an ice-cream store to get some ice-cream for both of them. Malik was in his early forties and almost old enough to be her father. Marlene wished that she had known her father when he was Malik's age.

She had heard stories of his acting days, and his achievements in Sports. She could not act, but she had his talents in the field of Sports. She found Malik to be a good listener, and she began confiding in him. He listened with great sympathy when she told him that even after all these years, she still pined for her father and Sister Renee. Sometimes talking about them would bring tears into her eyes, and Malik would put his arms around her shoulder, stemming from a natural instinct of pure friendship. She in return felt comforted, and was glad that she had found another good friend. The other athletes, especially the girls, were envious of the friendship between the two. They started a rumor that implicated that there was something deeper than just friendship between the older man and the young girl. Some of Marlene's close friends warned her about the rumors, but because of her innocence and naivety, Marlene did not take them seriously.

Due to the seasonal monsoon at the end of the year, Malik told all his athletes that if it should rain heavily on the day of practice, the practice session would be cancelled. However, if the rain was not heavy and was over before noon, they should be at the Stadium at the usual time. Unlike the others, Marlene too had to train for Hockey. But luckily for her, the Convent field was used. So the chosen girls from other schools had to go to the Convent twice a week for practice. It was a co-incidence that the practice days for hockey did not coincide with athletics. It was on Tuesdays and Thursdays between four and six in the late afternoon. Going back from the Convent was much easier. It only took Marlene an extra half an hour to get home, compared to the normal time when school was over. She was also able to finish her homework and put in some study while waiting for the practice time. Thus with the extra sport, Marlene still had time for her school work. Looking at her, everyone thought that she had no care in the world. But no one, not even the Reverend Mother, who discreetly watched Marlene closely suspected that it was Marlene's way of hiding her deepest feelings. She had never got over the pain of losing both her father and Sister Renee. The only way, she could bring back them back into her life, was when she had time to think of them. Then when they went away, the aches returned. Keeping herself busy kept the painful memories at bay.

CHAPTER 31

It took Marlene three months to recover physically, but longer emotionally. The nuns took great care of her, and when her nightmares returned, she would wake up in the arms of one of the novices or nuns. Reverend Mother Irene visited her almost every week. She had delegated a nun, who studied Psychology, to win Marlene's confidence, and help her gain back her emotional balance. The screams from her nightmares occurred almost every night. Then after six months, Marlene began to have fewer nightmares, and gradually, she left her traumatic and dreadful experience behind her. It was the Reverend Mother herself who came to take Marlene back to stay in the Convent. Sometimes, from their rooms in another block, the nuns could hear Marlene screaming, but whenever one of them reached her, Marlene was sleeping peacefully. Then one day, the screaming stopped completely. Marlene was once more in control of herself. She still had nightmares of the abduction, but she was no longer afraid. Marlene attended classes, and as expected, she was at the same level with her studies as the rest of her classmates. She did not have to deal with questions of her long absence. Reverend Mother Irene had told all those concerned that Marlene had a very serious injury and had to undergo surgery, which needed a long time to heal. It was easy for everyone to believe what the nun told them, especially when Marlene was not allowed to participate in any strenuous activity.

The Reverend Mother had a very intensive conversation with Malik, when she found out that he could be the cause of Marlene's abduction. She advised him to find a job in another town and take his jealous wife with him. If he did that, this matter would be closed. Malik was shocked and furious with his wife. There was nothing he could do. He was forbidden to visit Marlene. Thus, he left Klang to start a new life with his repentant wife, together with their children. They moved to a coastal town on the east of Malaysia. Peninsular Malaya had changed its name since the Nation got its Independence from the British Empire. Malik's sudden departure, and Marlene's absence from the district team created some talk, but the gossip did not last long, and when Marlene came back to Klang there was no trace of any doubts that she had had an accident and was hospitalized in the big city for a long time. There was something that Reverend Mother Irene kept from her ward. Before Malik left, he asked to see the nun. He handed her a letter, and begged her to give it to Marlene. The nun took the letter without promising that Marlene would get it. As soon as Malik left, she tore the envelope carefully and read the contents. In it, Malik apologized for his wife's insane jealousy and said that he wished that he could undo what was done to her. He also wished her every success, and encouraged her to never to give up what she was very good at. He was sure that one day, Marlene would be representing the Nation in field hockey. His letter was very sincere. But as the nun folded it and put it back into the envelope, she decided that Marlene would only get this letter on the day that she would leave the Convent forever.

Marlene's life as the first and only boarder in the Convent was peaceful, and gave her a great sense of security and nearness to God, and with the two people who left her to join him. She attended masses with the nuns every morning before school started. Reverend Mother Irene had suggested that Marlene should not travel for sometime, so her mother and her siblings came down to see her on Saturdays. In time, Marlene got stronger, and as she entered the last year of Secondary school, she wanted to get back into the hockey team. She had no problem being accepted again, and Reverend Mother Irene approved of it as the practices and coaching location was still within the Convent grounds. Sometimes, she would watch some of the matches and think of the letter that Malik had written. The girl showed great potential of being a National player. She was smaller and younger than most of her team-mates, but she was faster and more skillful than most of them. At the same time, she felt sure that for Marlene, her academic qualifications were her priorities. Marlene had already voiced her ambition to study abroad. To get that scholarship for overseas studies, Marlene had to A's all her subjects in High School. That required a lot of effort and self-discipline. Playing Hockey in the professional level might jeopardize her chances for the scholarship.

The Reverend Mother wanted Marlene to have the normal life of a sixteen year old, so she encouraged the girl to attend birthday parties of her classmates. The nuns had their own car now, with the night watchman as the driver. Whenever Marlene attended any of these functions, she would be driven to and from the location of the party. The only restriction that the nuns had, was that Marlene should be in the Convent by eleven o'clock in the night. Marlene was quite popular and was invited to many parties. It was at one of those parties that Marlene saw Michael, who was the youngest son of the widow, who had let Marlene and her family live in her hut a few years ago. At first Michael did not see her. Then he heard one of the boys saying, "Look at her. She thinks we are not good enough for her." It was not Marlene's nature to be proud. Her traumatic experience made her afraid of the opposite sex. She always moved away when a boy approached her and never accepted their requests for dances. She would dance in groups, but not in the arms of a boy. That frustrated the boys and they began to call her names, like 'ice cube', 'miss high nose' and many other unpleasant names. If Marlene had any inkling of what they were talking about behind her back, she would have stopped going to her friends' parties. Michael, who was the oldest of the boys, heard those comments and turned to look at the subject. He could not believe his eyes when he saw Marlene. No wonder the boys were talking about her. To him, she was very beautiful. She was petite and held her athletic body very well. He decided to approach her, and Marlene was about to move away when she realized that the person approaching her looked familiar. As he came nearer, she smiled for she recognized him. She called his name, and that jolted him, for he too recognized her. He could not help saying, "My God, you have grown up to be a beauty." Jealous eyes looked at them as they were lost in their own world, chatting about old times and finding out more about each other.

Michael had a degree in accountancy and worked in one of the new banks in Klang. His brothers were married, so he decided to stay on with his mother, who refused to sell their house and land. As they were talking, slow tempo music started and automatically, Michael drew Marlene into his arms and they danced. Michael was invited to the party because the older sister of the birthday girl was interested in him. Jealously, she stopped the music and said aloud, "Michael, everyone is waiting for you to play your guitar." The sound of clapping forced Michael to let go of Marlene. Not only was Michael a good guitarist, he was also a good singer. He sang a beautiful love song, and it was obvious that he dedicated the lyrics to Marlene. His eyes never left her face. She too was enraptured, and she realized that she had heard his voice many times in church. He was the soloist in the church choir. The choir had their own partition above the rest of the congregation, thus although Marlene admired the voice of the singer, she never saw who it belonged to. Her heart thudded as she realized that she was falling in love for the first time. Then her heart sank when her friend's sister took Michael's hand for the next dance. She could not know that Michael protested and looked for her. She had walked out of the house to await the driver. She was early, but she hoped that he too would be early. Just as Michael found out where she was, the car was pulling up the driveway. Michael stood outside the house and watched Marlene hurriedly enter the car. He called after her, but the drone of the engine overpowered his voice. Disappointed, Michael watched the car drive away with the girl who had stolen his heart.

It took Marlene sometime to fall asleep. She thought of Michael, and her heart ached for him. Then she reprimanded herself for being such a silly teenager, but that did not heal her broken heart. Her very first love had to end even before it started. He belonged to someone else. She tried to put him off her mind but that was impossible. She lay awake for a long time and fell asleep dreaming of him. The next day was Sunday. She got up and changed to get ready for mass. Then she realized that Michael might be singing. "Well," she said to her self, "At least I can hear his voice." Just before she left the room, she looked at herself in the mirror and decided to apply some lipstick. Then immediately she rubbed it off. She had never applied lipstick unless she went to a party. She did not want the nuns to see any tell-tale signs of her short encounter with love. She joined the nuns as they were walking towards the church. Reverend Mother Irene looked at her and asked, "Did you have a nice evening?" Marlene nodded but avoided eye contact with the nun. Reverend Mother Irene saw some traces of smudged lipstick on her lips and took out her handkerchief, "You should have left the lipstick on," she said teasingly to the blushing Marlene, who took the handkerchief from her and wiped her mouth vigorously.

When Michael's rich voice filled the church, Marlene thought she was going to faint. She could hear the throbbing of her heart and hoped that no one else could hear it. Then she forgot that the people in the choir would come down towards the altar to receive Communion. She kept her eyes shut after she saw the first member of the choir passing her. She was too afraid of the consequences that might follow if she saw Michael. On the other hand, Michael was looking for her. His eyes were searching the benches near the nuns, instead of looking at the floor like everyone else. His heart too began to beat fast, when he saw Marlene kneeling down with her eyes closed. He made up his mind that he was not going to let her get away. When he had finished his prayers of thanks, he told the choir leader that he could not join them for the last hymn. He had urgent business to attend to. It was a surprised Marlene, who heard the voice of her dreams calling her name as she was coming out of the church. She looked at Michael and was about to go to him when she realized that the nuns were behind her. Michael saw the hesitation and moved towards her. He took her hand, "We have to talk," he said. Just as Marlene was pulling her hands away, Reverend Mother Irene came to them. She extended her hand to Michael and said, "You have a wonderful voice." It was obvious that she knew who the soloist was. Michael thanked her for the compliment. Then the nun put her hand on Marlene's shoulder and said, "I am sure you two young people would like to spend some time without this old lady hanging around. Go on Marlene, you just need to be back in time for lunch."

Left alone, Michael said, "Why did you leave without saying goodbye, last night?" "You were dancing with your girlfriend," Marlene replied with a pout. Then Michael smiled and took her hand again. This time he held it tighter so that she could not pull it away. "I have no girlfriend. I thought I was finding one when she ran off and left me broken hearted." He looked at his watch, and taking her by the hand said, "We have two hours before your lunch time. Let us go for a drive." Marlene felt that she was moving with the clouds as Michael guided her to his car. He opened the door and in a happy daze she got in. They drove towards a small quiet park, where he parked, and turned to look at her. "Marlene," he did not want to beat about the bush, "I never believed in love at first sight. But it happened to me last night. Tell me that you feel the same way." Marlene's eyes were bright with happiness as she looked at him and said, "It is the same with me. Oh Michael, I never knew that falling in love could be so wonderful." Marlene felt elated as she received her very first kiss. Michael started gently and then when he felt her innocent response, his kiss became more passionate. After that, they spent more time kissing than talking. They never left the car. Michael took Marlene back to the Convent with the promise that he would take her to visit her mother the next week.

Between her studies and hockey practices, Marlene thought of Michael, and buried herself in the wonder of her first love. When Marlene approached Reverend Mother Irene to ask her permission to let Michael drive her to Kuala Lumpur the next week, the nun knew that cupid's arrow had found its way into her ward's heart. She knew Michael's family and was glad for Marlene. He came from a respectable Catholic home and she always admired his singing and liked him. However, it was her duty to advise Marlene about the facts of life. So when the girl came to ask her permission she said, "That is nice of Michael. Of course, he can drive you." Then before she continued, she took in a deep breath, took the girl's hand in hers and said, "Marlene, you are still a virgin, and I am sure you and Michael will not abuse my trust. It is God's design that men and women should be joined in matrimony before they indulge in the art of sex." She saw Marlene's shocked face, but she knew what it was about, so her next words put the girl at ease again. "It is alright to show your love for each other with kisses and holding hands. Do not go beyond that." When Marlene nodded eagerly, she felt uneasy for the girl's naivety. However, she did not know what else to say. She did not want to dampen the happiness of the girl. Marlene had gone through a lot and she deserved to be happy again. She was glad that it was Michael, and not someone else who was the reason for the radiance in the girl's face. She had confidence that Michael, who was a good Catholic, would respect Marlene's innocence and dignity.

As the relationship between Marlene and Michael blossomed, so did Marlene. At sixteen, her femininity began to show. All traces of her terrible experience disappeared. Knowing that Marlene had a busy schedule, Michael was patient and dated her only once a week. He had driven her to visit her mother and siblings a few times, but never spent the night with her. He always went back on Sunday afternoon to bring her back to the Convent. As the date of the final school examination drew near, Marlene stopped going to Kuala Lumpur. She still attended some parties, but only if Michael too was invited. If she went out with Michael on a Saturday, they would meet briefly after mass for a short conversation, or else they would spend the whole Sunday going for picnics or a show. Marlene was often invited to have Sunday lunch with him and his mother. Marlene's former landlady liked her very much, but had her misgivings about the age difference. Michael was twenty two years old, and Marlene, who seemed mature for her age was still biologically a teenager. It was obvious to her that her son was Marlene's first love, and she hoped that he would not be too broken hearted when Marlene entered the world of opportunities.

There was one more week left before the examination, and Marlene and Michael met only for a short time after the Sunday mass. When Michael dropped her off at the Convent gate, the Reverend Mother happened to see Marlene get out of the car from her study window. She noticed that Marlene just shut the car door after her, without even glancing back or waving goodbye to her boyfriend. Michael sat in the car looking at her back for sometime. Then he drove off. The nun thought to herself, "Something is wrong. This is not how two sweethearts part." Then she realized that Marlene's examination was around the corner, and emotional turbulences at this point could affect her concentration. She did not like to interfere in their quarrels, but she had to make sure that what she saw was not serious. When she finished her lunch with the other nuns, instead of joining them for a short stroll, she went into Marlene's separate little dining room. She noticed that the girl had hardly eaten anything. She was just sitting there and toying with her fork and spoon. She said, "My, my, we are not hungry today, are we?" Marlene looked up from her table and gave the nun a wan smile. "I am sorry, I shall finish the food this evening." She got up to take the dishes into the kitchen when the older lady said, "Don't worry about clearing up. Take a walk with me." They moved away from the Convent garden for the other nuns were gathered there admiring the flowers. They walked towards the personal office of the Reverend Mother. She sat on one of the sofas and gestured Marlene to sit on the other one beside it.

"Something is troubling you, and I want you to tell me about it." Marlene knew that the nun could see through her by now so without hesitating she said, "Michael and I had a big argument." "What was the argument about?" Then Marlene poured out her heart to the sympathetic nun. "We were talking about my future. Michael wanted to know what I would do when I have graduated from this school. He was happy when I told him about high school and university. It was when I mentioned that I planned to apply for a scholarship to study abroad that started our quarrel. He tried to convince me that getting a degree from our local university is just as good. He could not understand that I longed to see more of the world." She paused as the last part of the conversation was hurtful. "He said that if I loved him, I would not go so far away from him. I could not explain to him or to myself why I had this longing to go abroad. Then he gave me an ultimatum when he said that if I truly love him, I will not even think about that any more. I felt that was very selfish of him and I told him so. He turned back and said that I was the one who was selfish, because I was only thinking of myself and disregarding his feelings." Then her eyes started to become wet, but she continued, "I shouldn't have said what I said after that. I still love him, but now it is over between us." The nun asked, "What shouldn't you have said?" "I told him to take me back and that I don't ever want to see him again." "That is typical of my Marlene," the nun thought to herself. Then she felt it was time to give her advice. "Love does not disappear just like that. Michael still loves you and in time he will understand your need to see another part of the world. Right now, you must not be upset. Your first priority is the examination. Believe and trust me that your relationship with Michael has not ended."

Marlene put her whole heart into her studies, and when the first day of the examination came, she took her assigned seat in the examination hall with confidence. The examination lasted five days and the fifth day was also the end of the school term. The results of the school examination would be announced in the National newspapers a month later. It involved the fifth formers of the secondary schools in the whole country. The headquarters of this examination was still in Cambridge, England, although Malaysia was now an independent country. Marlene knew that she did well and there was no question about her entrance into the two years of High School. The Klang Convent did not offer that level of study, thus Marlene would be doing those two years in the big Convent in Kuala Lumpur. She opted to be a day student as she wanted to be reunited with her direct family again. She had two more days left before she left the Convent and the loving care of the nuns forever. The Convent car would be taking her to her next destination on Sunday after mass. She had hoped that Michael would call on her on Friday evening, and celebrate the last day of the examination with her. She was disappointed that he did not show up, then when he still did not call on her on the last evening, she was sad. Reverend Mother Irene too can make a mistake, she thought. That relationship ended when she walked away from him a week ago.

Marlene was packing her last belonging into two suitcases that the nuns had given her, when she heard a knock on the door of her room. It was the Reverend Mother. Marlene's wan smile always had sadness behind it, and she could guess the reason. She told Marlene not to stop packing as she sat on the bed. "I feel sad to see you go, but on the other hand, I know that you are waiting to go out into the world and conquer it," She began with a sad note but chuckled at the last part. Marlene looked up from her packing and said, "Not yet, there is still a lot to learn and I intend being a good student." She closed her suitcase and went on her knees in front of the nun. "Reverend Mother," she started, and her voice quivered as she continued. "When Sister Renee left me, I thought that I will never be able to love anyone again. The pain of loving and losing was unbearable. But you opened my heart again. You brought back the magic that love can bring. I love you and I beg you not to die on me." She giggled at the last sentence, and they both started laughing. Then the nun became serious and said, "I wanted to be with you alone. All the others are waiting downstairs to say goodbye to you. They too love you, and if you have a chance, do come back and visit them. Well, my job here is finished. I will be going to another Convent up north. I have your mother's address and as soon as I get there, I shall write to you. I am confident that you will achieve whatever your heart desires. Just promise me that you will not stop writing to me." Then the nun took an envelope out of the pocket of her habit and said, "I have kept this letter for a long time. But I know that you are now ready to read it." Marlene took the envelope and saw that it had been opened. A nod from the nun acknowledged that she had opened it. Marlene took out the letter and read. There was no trace of emotion in her face and the nun felt happy. Marlene could never forget the brutalities of the abduction, but she had completely recovered from them.

There was more to be said, but they were interrupted by another nun, who put her head through the open door to say, "Reverend Mother, can I talk to you?" Marlene heard them whispering, and thought that the nun came to say that the driver was ready and waiting. Reverend Mother Irene came back with a broad smile on her face and said, "Marlene, you have a visitor. He is waiting in the parlor for you." Marlene blushed and her heart beats began to speed up. "Leave your bags. Go to him now." Marlene ran down the stairs, but held herself back at the bottom. She walked slowly towards the parlor where the nuns entertained their visitor privately. As she opened the door, Michael stood up. They just looked at each other, both unsure of what to say. Then Michael moved towards her with extended arms and she fell into it. No words were necessary. Then Marlene pulled herself away and pouted. "Why didn't you come earlier? I am leaving today." "I know," said Michael pulling her back into his arms. "My elder brother had a slight accident of Friday and I had to take my mother to see him. She is still with him, but I rushed down to catch you before you go." Earlier, Marlene had hoped that even if he did not want to see her, she could still hear his voice for the last time at mass. When she did not hear him, she resigned herself to the fact that it was really over between them. Now, her heart was filled with joy. He loved her enough to leave his sick brother to be with her. "My darling, I am so sorry for being so thoughtless about your needs," Michael continue to say. " I am just afraid of losing you." Marlene put her fingers on his lips and said, "Hush. Let us just enjoy whatever time we have. I still have two more years to go and Kuala Lumpur is just an hour away with your car."

It was not the Convent car that drove away with Marlene. The Reverend Mother granted Michael permission to drive Marlene to her next destination. Marlene cried as she hugged and kissed each and every one of the nuns who had looked after her in different ways for the last one and a half years. The hardest was to wrench herself away from the arms of Reverend Mother Irene. She wetted her habit with her tears as she buried her face in her chest. "My dearest one, I will always have you in my prayers. You once showed me the wooden cross that Sister Renee gave you. I have made this rosary myself out of wooden beads. See, the cross is missing. Now you can attach the cross to it. Then you will always remember the two nuns who loved you with all their hearts." Marlene looked at the beads that Reverend Mother pushed into her hands. When she was packing, she had put the cross carefully into a compartment of her suitcase. "Oh yes, as soon as I unpack my things, this is the first thing I shall do." Her eyes were still wet when she entered the car. As the car left, Marlene looked back and waved until they were out of sight. Reverend Mother Irene and the nuns looked at the departing car. The Reverend Mother was sad that her work with Marlene was over. But she had confidence that the girl was strong enough to overcome all obstacles that lay in her way. She was a survivor. As she and the nuns dispersed for their normal routine, her heart said a prayer, "Please be with her O Lord and guide her away from harm."

As the Convent disappeared from her sight, Marlene knew that, that was also the end of a sheltered and protected life. She looked at the string of beads in her hand and clasped it tightly. Then she saw the veins that showed at the back of her clutched hand. She stroked the veins with her other hand and said in her heart, "My father's blood flows in my veins. Like him, I too have a big heart. Sister Renee, you and Reverend Mother Irene have found your places within my heart and you will remain there forever." Then she looked at the driver, who did not say anything because he did not want to interrupt her thoughts. She put a hand on Michael's arm which was on the wheel and said aloud, "You too have found a place in my heart." To herself she added, "No matter what happens, you will also stay there forever." Michael smiled at her and releasing that arm from the wheel, he put it around her shoulder and pulled her closer to him. Marlene snuggled to him, happy and confident that whatever the world had in store for her, she was ready for it. She was sixteen going on seventeen, with enough experience to value love and to avoid hate. She foresaw that there would be many obstacles to cross, but with the help and guidance of loved ones old and new, she would overcome them all.

THE END

About the Author

Helen Weyand is a Malaysian born Chinese, now residing in the United States of America. She was a Physical Education instructor in a Teacher Training College in Malaysia, before she came to the United States to do her Masters. After that, she never went back to Malaysia. Instead, she married a German, and lived in Germany for sixteen years. While in Germany, she did some free-lancing for newspapers and magazines. She is currently living in Webster, New York, and has given up her teaching career to be a full-time novelist. "The Big Heart" is her very first novel. "Marlene", her second book, will be ready for publications in the near future.

Printed in the United States
55914LVS00003B/55-63